A Corner in E

CONTEMPORARY CANADIAN STORIES

I(T)P™

International Thomson Publishing
The trademark ITP is used under licence

Published in Canada by
Nelson Canada,
A Division of Thomson Canada Limited
1120 Birchmount Road
Scarborough, Ontario
M1K 5G4

ISBN 0-17-603978-3
Teacher's Guide 0-17-603987-2

Managing Editor: Jean Stinson
Project Manager: Tara Shields
Senior Production Editor: Sandra Manley
Art Director: Bruce Bond
Series Design: Tracy Walker
Cover Design: Julia Hall
Cover Illustration: Simon Ng
Typesetting: Zenaida Merjudio

Printed and bound in Canada

4567890 / TCP / 21

Canadian Cataloguing in Publication Data

Main entry under title:

A Corner in each life: contemporary Canadian stories

ISBN 0-17-603978-3

1. Short stories, Canadian (English)*. 2. Canadian fiction (English) - 20th century.* I. Armstrong, Sean. II. Corbeil, Carole (Carole Cecile).

PS8321.C67 1993 C813'.0108054 C93-094477-1
PR9197.32.C67 1993

Reviewers

The publishers thank the following people who contributed their valuable expertise during the development of this book:

James Barry, Toronto, Ont.
Terry Benbow, Collingwood, Ont.
Patti Buchanan, Vancouver, B.C.
Robert Bullen, Toronto, Ont.
Susan Church, Halifax, N.S.
Regi Maher, Regina, Sask.
Carmen Marshall, Toronto, Ont.
Nazira Mawji, Whitby, Ont.
Greg Ponsart, Vancouver, B.C.
Alex White, Calgary, Alta.

This book is printed on acid-free paper. Nelson Canada is committed to using, within the publishing process, the available resources, technology, and suppliers that are as environmentally friendly as possible

As requested by individual copyright holders, some selections may retain original spellings, punctuation, usage, and style of measurement.

A Corner in Each Life

CONTEMPORARY CANADIAN STORIES

REFLECTIONS IN FICTION

EDITED BY SEAN ARMSTRONG
AND CAROLE CORBEIL

Nelson Canada

CONTENTS

FOREWORD

These stories were chosen to reflect the diversity of contemporary Canada. Each region of the country is represented, along with many viewpoints and life experiences. The theme of communication comes up again and again—the difficulties of hearing others, and the need to listen to what they are saying. Through the stories, the point emerges that we need to pay attention, to live together in this land we all share.

Stories are told in different ways. *Burn Sugar* by Marlene Nourbese Philip is almost a performance monologue—it begs to be read aloud, so you can hear the individual speaking voice. Diane Schoemperlen's *Red Plaid Shirt* tells the story of a young woman's emotional life through the clothes hanging in her closet. Margaret Atwood's *My Life as a Bat* and Brian Fawcett's *My Career with the Leafs* are imaginative flights of fancy—"what if." Most of the stories are conventional strong narratives: for example, Mary Burns' *Suburbs of the Arctic Circle* is long and complex, as it lays bare the patterns behind events in a Yukon village.

We wanted before all else to find good stories, and we have been especially diligent in trying to create a book where young women as well as young men can identify with characters and situations; more than half the stories are by women. We hope you find something of yourself described here.

The Editors

LANGUAGES

This is a country where you have to know more than one language to survive; knowing only one language will do you no good at all. Once they found a woman babbling in some crazy unknown tongue so they put her in a madhouse for years and years where she kept on babbling. Then someone understood her language and found out that her husband and child had been killed, and she had been trying to tell people ever since. But by now she really was crazy; her mind was a pattern in plaid. They put her in an old folks' home where she babbled less and less until she stopped it altogether and said nothing, and finally died. The language she had spoken was Ukrainian, which is not one of the official languages, so it will definitely do you no good at all. But knowing only one language of any kind in this country will do you no good; you simply have to know more than one to survive.

BY GWENDOLYN MACEWEN

Why My Mother Can't Speak English

BY GARRY ENGKENT

"'Your mother has been living in Canada for the past thirty years and she still can't speak English?'"

My mother is seventy years old. Widowed for five years now, she lives alone in her own house except for the occasions when I come home to tidy her household affairs. She has been in *gum san*, the golden mountain, for the past thirty years. She clings to the old-country ways so much so that today she astonishes me with this announcement:

"I want to get my citizenship," she says as she slaps down the *Dai Pao*, "before they come and take away my house."

"Nobody's going to do that. This is Canada."

"So everyone says," she retorts, "but did you read what the *Dai Pao* said? Ah, you can't read Chinese. The government is cutting back on old-age pensions. Anybody who hasn't got citizenship will lose everything. Or worse."

"The *Dai Pao* can't even typeset accurately," I tell her. Sometimes I worry about the information Mother receives from that biweekly community newspaper. "Don't worry—the Ministry of Immigration won't send you back to China."

"Little you know," she snaps back. "I am old, helpless, and without citizenship. Reasons enough. Now, get me citizenship. Hurry!"

"Mother, getting citizenship papers is not like going to the bank to cash in your pension cheque. First, you have to—"

"Excuses, my son, excuses. When your father was alive—"

"Oh, Mother, not again! You throw that at me every—"

"—made excuses, too." Her jaw tightens. "If you can't do this little thing for your own mother, well, I will just have to go and beg your cousin to..."

Every time I try to explain about the ways of the *fan gwei*, she thinks I do not want to help her.

"I'll do it, I'll do it, okay? Just give me some time."

"That's easy for you," Mother snorts. "You're not seventy years old. You're not going to lose your pension. You're not going to lose your house. Now, how much *lai-shi* will this take?"

After all these years in *gum san* she cannot understand that you don't give government officials *lai-shi*, the traditional Chinese money gift to persons who do things for you.

"That won't be necessary," I tell her. "And you needn't go to my cousin."

Mother picks up the *Dai Pao* again and says: "Why should I beg at the door of a village cousin when I have a son who is a university graduate?"

I wish my father were alive. Then he would be doing this. But he is not here, and as a dutiful son, I am responsible for the welfare of my widowed mother. So I take her to Citizenship Court.

There are several people from the Chinese community waiting there. Mother knows a few of the Chinese women and she chats with them. My cousin is there, too.

"I thought your mother already got her citizenship," he says to me. "Didn't your father—"

"No, he didn't."

He shakes his head sadly. "Still, better now than never. That's why I'm getting these people through."

"So they've been reading the *Dai Pao*."

He gives me a quizzical look, so I explain to him, and he laughs.

"You are the new generation," he says. "You didn't live long enough in *hon san*, the sweet land, to understand the fears of the old. You can't expect the elderly to renounce all attachments to China for the ways of the *fan gwei*, white devils. How old is she, seventy now? Much harder."

"She woke me up this morning at six, and Citizenship Court doesn't open until ten."

The doors of the court finally open, and Mother motions me to hurry.

We wait in line for a while.

The clerk distributes applications and tells me the requirements. Mother wants to know what the clerk is saying, so half the time I translate for her.

The clerk suggests that we see one of the liaison officers.

"Your mother has been living in Canada for the past thirty years and she still can't speak English?"

"It happens," I tell the liaison officer.

"I find it hard to believe that—not one word?"

"Well, she understands some restaurant English," I tell her. "You know, French fries, pork chops, soup, and so on. And she can say a few words."

"But will she be able to understand the judge's questions? The interview with the judge, as you know, is an important part of the citizenship procedure. Can she read the booklet? What does she know about Canada?"

"So you don't think my mother has a chance?"

"The requirements are that the candidate must be able to speak either French or English, the two official languages of Canada. The candidate must be able to pass an oral interview with the citizenship judge, and then he or she must be able to recite the oath of allegiance—"

"My mother needs to speak English," I conclude for her.

"Look, I don't mean to be rude, but why didn't your mother learn English when she first came over?"

I have not been translating this conversation, and Mother, annoyed and agitated, asks me what is going on. I tell her there is a slight problem.

"What problem?" Mother opens her purse, and when I see her taking a small red envelope—*lai-shi*—I quickly cover her hand.

"What's going on?" the liaison officer demands.

"Nothing," I say hurriedly. "Just a cultural misunderstanding, I assure you."

My mother rattles off some indignant words, and I snap back in Chinese: "Put that away! The woman won't understand, and we'll be in a lot of trouble."

The officer looks confused, and I realize that an explanation is needed.

"My mother was about to give you a money gift as a token of appreciation for what you are doing for us. I was afraid you might misconstrue it as a bribe. We have no intention of doing that."

"I'm relieved to hear it."

We conclude the interview, and I take Mother home. Still clutching the application, Mother scowls at me.

"I didn't get my citizenship papers. Now I will lose my old-age pension. The government will ship me back to China. My old bones will lie there while your father's will be here. What will happen to me?"

How can I teach her to speak the language when she is too old to learn, too old to want to learn? She resists anything that is *fan gwei*. She does everything the Chinese way. Mother spends much time staring blankly at the four walls of her house. She does not cry. She sighs and shakes her head. Sometimes she goes about the house touching her favourite things.

"This is all your dead father's fault," she says quietly. She turns to the photograph of my father on the mantel. Daily, she burns incense, pours fresh cups of fragrant tea, and spreads dishes of his favourite fruits in front of the framed picture as is the custom. In memory of his passing, she treks over three kilometres to the cemetery to place flowers by his headstone, to burn ceremonial paper money, and to talk to him. Regularly, rain or shine, or even snow, she does these things. Such love, such devotion, now such vehemence. Mother curses my father, her husband, in his grave.

When my mother and I emigrated from China, she was forty years old, and I, five. My father was already a well-established restaurant owner. He put me in school and Mother in the restaurant kitchen, washing dishes and cooking strange foods like hot dogs, hamburgers, and French fries. She worked seven days a week from six in the morning until eleven at night. This lasted for twenty-five years, almost to the day of my father's death.

The years were hard on her. The black-and-white photographs show a robust woman; now I see a withered, frail, white-haired old woman, angry, frustrated with the years, and scared of losing what little material wealth she has to show for the toil in *gum san*.

"I begged him," Mother says. "But he would either ignore my pleas or say: 'What do you need to know English for? You're better off here in the kitchen. Here you can talk to the others in our own tongue. English is far too complicated for you. How old are you now? Too old to learn a new language. Let the young speak *fan gwei*. All you need is to understand the orders from the waitresses. Anyway, if you need to know something, the men will translate for you. I am here; I can do your talking for you.' "

As a conscientious boss of the young male immigrants, my father would force them out of the kitchen and into the dining room. "The kitchen is no place for you to learn English. All you do is speak Chinese in here. To survive in *gum san*, you have to speak English, and the only way you can do that is to wait on tables and force yourselves to speak English with the customers. How can you get your families over here if you can't talk to the immigration officers in English?"

A few of the husbands who had the good fortune to bring their wives over to Canada hired a retired school teacher to teach a bit of English to their wives. Father discouraged Mother from going to those once-a-week sessions.

"That old woman will get rich doing nothing. What have these women learned? *Fan gwei* ways—make-up, lipstick, smelly perfumes, fancy clothes—like whores. Once she gets through with them, they won't be Chinese women any more—and they certainly won't be white either."

Some of the husbands heeded the words of the boss, for he was older than they, and he had been in the white devils' land longer. These wives stayed home and tended the children, or they worked in the restaurant kitchen, washing dishes and cooking *fan gwei* foods, and talking in Chinese about the land and the life they had been forced to leave behind.

"He was afraid that I would leave him. I depended on him for everything. I could not go anywhere by myself. He drove me to work and he drove me home. He only taught me how to print my name so that I could sign anything he wanted me to, bank cheques, legal documents..."

Perhaps I am not Chinese enough any more to understand why my mother would want to take in the sorrow, the pain, and the anguish, and then to recount them every so often.

Once, I was presumptuous enough to ask her why she would want to remember in such detail. She said that the memories didn't hurt any more. I did not tell her that her reminiscences cut me to the quick. Her only solace now is to be listened to.

My father wanted more sons, but she was too old to give him more. One son was not enough security he needed for old age. "You smell of stale perfume," she would say to him after he had driven the waitresses home. Or, to me, she would say: "A second mother will not treat you so well, you know," and, "Would you like another mother at home?" Even at that tender age, I knew that in China a husband could take a second wife. I told her that I didn't need another mother, and she would nod her head.

When my father died five years ago, she cried and cried. "Don't leave me in this world. Let me die with you."

Grief-stricken, she would not eat for days. She was so weak from hunger that I feared she wouldn't be able to attend the funeral. At his grave side, she chanted over and over a dirge, commending his spirit to the next world and begging the goddess of mercy to be kind to him. By custom, she set his picture on the mantel and burned incense in front of it daily. And we would go to the cemetery often. There she would arrange fresh flowers and talk to him in the gentlest way.

Often she would warn me: "The world of the golden mountain is so strange, *fan gwei* improprieties, and customs. The white devils will have you abandon your own aged mother to some old-age home to rot away and die unmourned. If you are here long enough, they will turn your head until you don't know who you are—Chinese."

My mother would convert the months and the days into the Chinese lunar calendar. She would tell me about the seasons and the harvests and festivals in China. We did not celebrate any *fan gwei* holidays.

My mother sits here at the table, fingering the booklet from the Citizenship Court. For thirty-some years, my mother did not learn the English language, not because she was not smart enough, not because she was too old to learn, and not because my father forbade her, but because she feared that learning English would change her Chinese soul. She only learned enough English to survive in the restaurant kitchen.

Now, Mother wants *gum san* citizenship.

"Is there no hope that I will be given it?" she asks.

"There's always a chance," I tell her. "I'll hand in the application."

"I should have given that person the *lai-shi*," Mother says obstinately.

"Maybe I should teach you some English," I retort. "You have about six months before the oral interview."

"I am seventy years old," she says. "*Lai-shi* is definitely much easier."

My brief glimpse into Mother's heart is over, and it has taken so long to come about. I do not know whether I understand my aged mother any better now. Despite my mother's constant instruction, there is too much *fan gwei* in me.

The booklet from the Citizenship Court lies, unmoved, on the table, gathering dust for weeks. She has not mentioned citizenship again with the urgency of that particular time. Once in a while, she would say: "They have forgotten me. I told you they don't want old Chinese women as citizens."

Finally, her interview date is set. I try to teach her some ready-made phrases, but she forgets them.

"You should not sigh so much. It is bad for your health," Mother observes.

On the day of her examination, I accompany her into the judge's chamber. I am more nervous than my mother.

Staring at the judge, my mother remarks: "*Noi yren.*" The judge shows interest in what my mother says, and I translate it: "She says you're a woman."

The judge smiles. "Yes. Is that strange?"

"If she is going to examine me," Mother tells me, "I might as well start packing for China. Sell my house. Dig up your father's bones, and I'll take them back with me."

Without knowing what my mother said, the judge reassures her. "This is just a formality. Really. We know that you obviously want to be part of our Canadian society. Why else would you go through all this trouble? We want to welcome you as a new citizen, no matter what race, nationality, religion, or age. And we want you to be proud—as a new Canadian."

Six weeks have passed since the interview with the judge. Mother receives a registered letter telling her to come in three weeks' time to take part in the oath of allegiance ceremony.

With patient help from the same judge, my mother recites the oath and becomes a Canadian citizen after thirty years in *gum san*.

"How does it feel to be a Canadian?" I ask.

"In China, this is the eighth month, the season of harvest." Then she adds: "The *Dai Pao* says that the old-age pension cheques will be increased by nine dollars next month."

As we walk home on this bright autumn morning, my mother clutches her piece of paper. Citizenship. She says she will go up to the cemetery and talk to my father this afternoon. She has something to tell him.

The Leaving

BY BUDGE WILSON

"She moved to the centre of the room and faced him. 'My name,' she began, and faltered. She cleared her throat and ran her tongue over her lower lip. 'My name,' she repeated, this time more steadily, 'is Elizabeth.' "

She took me with her the day she left. "Where y' goin', Ma?" I asked. She was standing beside my bed with her coat on.

"Away," said Ma. "And yer comin', too."

I didn't want to go anywhere. It was three o'clock in the morning, and I was warm in my bed.

"Why me?" I complained.

I was too sleepy to think of any more complicated questions. In any case, there were no choices and very few questions back then when we were kids. You went to school and you came home on the school bus. If your father wanted you to shovel snow or fetch eggs, he told you, and you did it. He didn't ask. He told. Same with Ma. I did the dishes and brought in the firewood when it was required. She just pointed to the sink or to the woodbox, and I would leave whatever I was doing and start work. But at 3:00 a.m., the situation seemed unusual enough to permit a question. Therefore I asked again, "Why me?"

"Because yer the smartest," she said. "And because yer a woman."

I was twelve years old that spring.

Ma was a tall, rangy woman. She had a strong handsome face, with high cheekbones and a good firm chin line. Her lips were full. Her teeth were her own, although she smiled so rarely that you seldom saw them; her mouth tended to be held in a set straight line. She did not exactly frown; it was more as though she were loosely clenching her teeth. Her eyes were veiled, as if she had shut herself off from her surroundings and was thinking either private thoughts or nothing at all. Oh, she was kind enough and gentle enough when we needed it, though perhaps we needed it more often than she knew. But when we had cut knees or tonsillectomies, or when friends broke our hearts, she would hold us and hug us. Her mouth would lose its hard tight shape, and her eyes would come alive with concern and love.

Her lovely crisp auburn hair was short and unshaped making her face look uncompromising and austere. She wore baggy slacks over her excellent legs, and she owned two shabby grey sweaters and two faded graceless blouses. I did not ask myself why my mother looked this way, or why she had retreated behind her frozen face. One accepts one's parents for a long time, without theory or question. Speculation comes later, with adolescence and all the uncertainty and confusion it brings.

But when she woke me that chilly May morning, I was still a child. I rose and dressed quickly, packing my school bag with my pyjamas and toothbrush, the book I was reading, a package of gum, the string of Woolworth pearls that my grandmother had given me on my tenth birthday, and some paper to write and draw on. I wore jeans, my favourite blue sweater, my winter jacket, and rubber boots. I forgot my hat.

My mother had told me to be quiet, so I slithered down the stairs without a single board creaking. She was waiting at the door, holding a black cardboard suitcase with a strap around it. A shopping bag held sandwiches and some of last fall's bruised apples. She wore a brown car coat over her black slacks, and her hair was hidden under a grey wool kerchief. Her mouth had its tense fixed look, but her eyes were alive. Even at my age and at that hour, I could see that.

We stopped briefly before walking out into the cold night air. The stove in the kitchen was making chugging noises, and from different parts of the small house could be heard a variety of snores and heavy breathing. My four brothers and my father were not going to notice our departure.

For a moment, my mother seemed to hesitate. Her mouth softened, and a line deepened between her eyebrows. Then she straightened her shoulders and opened the door. "Move!" she whispered.

We stepped into the night and started walking down the mountain in the direction of town, ten kilometres away. I did not quarrel with the need for this strange nocturnal journey, but I did question the reason.

"Ma," I said.

She turned and looked at me.

"Ma. Why are we leavin'?"

She didn't answer right away. It crossed my mind that she might not be sure of the reason herself. This was a frightening thought. But apparently she knew.

"I plans t' do some thinkin'," she said.

We walked quickly through the night. North and South Mountains closed off the sky behind us and far ahead, but a full moon made it easy to see our way on the frosty road. The hill country was full of scrub growth, stubby spruce, and sprawling alders, unlike the tidy fields and orchards of the Valley. But the frost lent a silver magic to the bushes and the rough ground, and the moonlight gave a still dignity to the shabby houses. It was cold, and I shivered. "Fergot yer hat," said Ma. "Here." She took the warm wool kerchief from her head and gave it to me. I took it. Parents were invincible, and presumably would not feel the cold. My mother was not a complainer. She was an endurer. It was 1969, and she was forty-five years old.

When we reached Annapolis, we stopped at a small house on the edge of town, and Ma put down her suitcase and dug around in her purse. She took out a key and opened the door. Even my silent mother seemed to think that an explanation was required. "Lida Johnson's in Glace Bay, visitin' her daughter. Said I could use the house while she's gone. Normie's at a 4-H meetin' in Bridgetown. Joseph's truckin'. We'll wait here till th' train goes."

"Ma," I asked, "how long we gonna be gone?"

She bent her head down from its rigid position and looked at the floorboards of the front hall. She touched her mouth briefly with her fist. She closed her eyes for a second and took a deep breath.

"Dunno," she replied. "Till it's time."

We slept in the parlour until we left for the station.

I guess that ten-kilometre walk had shunted me straight from childhood into adolescence, because I did an awful lot of thinking between Annapolis and Halifax. But at first I was too busy to think. I was on a train, and I had never been inside one before. There were things to investigate—the tiny washroom with its little sink, and the funny way to flush the toilet.

In the main part of the Dayliner, the seats slid up and down so that people could sleep if they wanted to. I watched the world speed by the windows—men working on the roads; kids playing in schoolyards; cows standing dumbly outside barns in the chilly air, all facing in the same direction; places and towns I had never seen till then. My ma looked over at me and placed a comic book and a bag of peanuts on my lap. "Fer th' trip," she said, and smiled, patting my knee in an unfamiliar gesture. "Mind missin' school?" she added.

"No," I said. But I did. I had a part in the class play, and there was a practice that afternoon. I was the chief fairy, and I had twenty-five lines, all of which I knew by heart already. But this trip was also a pretty special, if alarming, adventure. It had a beginning but no definite end, and we were still speeding toward the middle. What would Halifax be like? We never had enough money to have more than one ride on the Exhibition ferris wheel at Lawrencetown; but here we were buying train tickets and reading comics and eating peanuts and travelling to heaven knows what expensive thrills.

"Maw," I asked, "where'd the money come from?"

She looked at me, troubled.

"Don't ask," she said. "I'll tell you when you're eighteen."

Eighteen! I might as well relax and enjoy myself. But I wondered.

Before long, she fell asleep, and I felt free to think. Until then, it was almost as though I were afraid she would read my thoughts.

Why had we left? How long would we be gone? How would Pa and my brothers cook their dinner? How would they make their beds? Who would they complain to after a hard day? Who would fetch the eggs, the mail, the water, the wood, the groceries? Who would wash their overalls, mend their socks, put bandages on their cuts? It was inconceivable to me that they could survive for long without us.

When we reached Halifax, we went to what I now realize was a cheap and shabby hotel in the South End of the city. But to me it seemed the height of luxury. The bed was made of some kind of shiny yellow wood. The bedspread was an intense pink, with raised nubbles all over it. A stained spittoon sat in the corner. There was actually a sink in the room, with taps that offered both cold and hot water. A toilet that flushed was down the hall. I checked under the bed; there was no chamber pot. But who needed it? There were two pictures on the walls—one of a curly-headed blonde, displaying a lot of bare flesh, and another of three dead ducks hanging upside down from a nail. I spent a lot of time inspecting both of these pictures.

Halifax was a shock to me. How could the buildings be so huge and the stores so grand? Here I was in the province's capital city before I really understood what a capital city could be. I admired the old stone buildings with their carvings around the doors and windows. I stretched my neck to see the tops of the modern apartments, with their glass and concrete reaching up into the clouds. The buses and cars alarmed me as they rushed up and down the long streets, but they excited me, too. The weather changed; it was warm and comforting, and the wind was gentle and caressing. We went down the hill to the harbour and saw the bridge; rooted in the ground and in the sea bottom, it lifted its enormous metal wings into the sky. I marvelled that a thing so strong could be so graceful, so beautiful. What a lovely way, I thought, to get from one place to another. We walked across the bridge to Dartmouth and watched the ships, far below, headed for Europe, for Africa, for the distant North. My mother, who had started to talk, told me about all these things. It was as though she were trying to tell me something important, but didn't want to say things right out. "They're goin' somewheres," she said. Later on, she took me out to Dalhousie University, and we walked among the granite buildings and beside the playing fields. "If yer as smart as the teacher claims," she said, "maybe you'll come here some day t' learn." I thought this highly unlikely. If we couldn't afford running water, how could we afford such a thing as that? I said so.

"They's ways," she said.

We walked up and down Spring Garden Road and gazed in the big windows. I looked at a candy store with at least five million kinds of candy, shops with dresses so fancy that I could scarcely believe it, shelves full of diamonds and gold and sparkling crystal. "Is there ways for all this, too?" I asked my mother. She hesitated.

"Don't need all that stuff," she concluded.

The weather was dazzling—a sunny Nova Scotia May day. We walked through the huge iron gates into the Public Gardens and ate our sandwiches and apples beside the duck pond. I kicked off my rubber boots and wiggled my toes in the sun as I watched the swans and the yellow ducklings. The Gardens were immense, full of massive and intricate flowerbeds, winding paths, and strange exotic trees. There were statues, a splashing fountain, an elaborate round bandstand, and a little river with a curved bridge over it.

Lovers strolled arm in arm, and children shrieked with laughter as they chased the pigeons. I asked Ma why everyone seemed so happy. "Dunno," she said. "Weather does things t' people." She looked around. "And maybe some of them's free," she added.

On the second day, we watched women racing to work in the morning, mini-skirts flipping, heels clicking, faces eager, faces tense. We looked on as shopping women pulled twenty-dollar bills out of their purses as though they were nickels. We saw the drunks sleeping on the pavement outside the mission. We visited the courthouse and looked at the pictures of the stern-faced judges as they watched us from the walls. "They fixes things what aren't right," said Ma. I wondered how. "But not always," she added.

We spent an hour in the public library, looking at the shelves and shelves of books, smelling their wonderful book smells, idly turning the pages. On a book dolly, she picked up a copy of *The Feminine Mystique*. She, who had not to my knowledge read a single book since I was born, said shyly, "I read this book." I was astonished.

"You!" I exclaimed. "How come? When?"

"I kin read!" she retorted, miffed. "Even if y' leaves school in grade five, y' kin read. Y' reads slow, but y' knows how."

"But where'd you get it?" I demanded, amazed.

"Y' remember that day the Salvation Army lady brought us that big box o' clothes?" she asked. "Yer pa was mad and said we didn't need no charity. But I hid the box, and after a time he forgot about it. Well, there was other things in there, too—an eggbeater, some toys what I gave to Lizzie's kids, even a string o' yellow beads and a bracelet that I bin savin' fer you. And some books. There was comic books and that big colourin' book y' got fer Christmas, and them *Popular Mechanics* magazines the boys read, and a coupla others. And this." She placed the palm of her hand on the book. "Seemed like it was for me, special. So I read it. She was real tough goin', but I read every word. Took me near a year. Finished it last Thursday."

I could hardly believe it. My ma didn't even read recipes. She kept them all in her head. I asked, "Was it good?"

She thought for a moment before answering. "She was a real troublin' book. But she was good."

I couldn't understand that. "If it was so troublin', why was it so good?"

She answered that one without hesitation. "Found I weren't alone," she said. She stroked its cover tenderly before putting it back on the dolly. I liked the library, with all the silent people bent over their books, and the librarians moving soundlessly to and fro. I wasn't used to quiet places.

In the afternoon, we climbed the Citadel and went into its museum, walking up and down among the sea things, old things, rich things. Later on, we went to what I thought was a very fancy restaurant. There were bright, shiny chrome tables with place mats of paper lace and green glass ashtrays. I ordered a hot dog and chips, because that was my favourite meal. My mother, her mouth now soft and cheerful, ordered something with a strange name.

"Ain't gonna come all this way and spend all th' hen money jest t' eat what I kin eat at home," she said.

The egg money! So that was it. I let on I didn't notice. But a thrill of fear ran through me. I wondered what Pa would do.

In the evening we returned early to the hotel, and I slept deeply, but with strange and troubled dreams.

On the third day, Ma said, "It's time. T'day we go home." I asked why.

"Because," she said.

"Because why?" I insisted.

She was silent for a moment, and then said again, "It's time." I was pleased. It had been an interesting trip, but it frightened me a little because there were no explanations, no answers to my unspoken questions. Besides, I was afraid that someone else would get to be chief fairy in the school play. "Have you done yer thinkin'?" I asked. She looked at me strangely. There was hope in her look and an odd fierce dignity.

"I has," she said.

We took the bus home instead of the train, and it was late afternoon when we arrived in Annapolis to start the ten-kilometre climb to our farm. The day was damp and cold, and I wore my mother's wool kerchief again. We were very quiet, and I knew she was nervous. Her mouth was back in its taut line, and her eyes were troubled. But even in the wind, her shoulders were straight and firm, and I could feel a difference in her. Fearful though her eyes were, she was fully alert, and you could sense a new dogged strength in the set of her face.

There was no such strength in me, except such as I derived from her. Home is home when you are twelve, and I did not want to live a tourist's life in Halifax forever. But I worried every step of the long journey.

As we turned the bend at Harrison's Corner, we could see the farm in the distance. It was as though I were seeing it for the first time. The house had been white once, but it had needed paint for almost nineteen years. Around the yard was a confusion of junk of all kinds: two discarded cars—lopsided and without wheels—an unpiled jumble of firewood, buckets, a broken hoe, rusty tools, an old oil drum for burning garbage. To the left were the few acres of untidy fields, dotted with spruce trees and the grey skeletons of trees long dead of Dutch elm disease. To the right, close to the henhouse, was the barn—small and unpainted, grey and shabby in the dim afternoon light. We could hear the two cows complaining, waiting for milking time.

When we opened the kitchen door, they were all there. My four big brothers were playing cards at the table, and my father was sitting by the kitchen stove, smoking a cigarette and drinking from a bottle of beer. I had forgotten how darkly handsome he was. But because it was not Sunday, he was unshaven, and his eyes glared at us from beneath heavy black eyebrows.

Pa rose from his chair and faced us. He was very tall, and his head almost reached the low ceiling. He seemed to fill the entire room. He crushed out his cigarette on the top of the stove.

His voice was low and threatening. "Where you bin, woman?" he said.

She spoke, and I was amazed that she had the courage. Then I realized with a jolt that his words were little different in tone and substance from hundreds I had heard before: "How come my supper's not ready, woman?" "Move smart, woman! I'm pressed fer time!" "Shut up them damn kids, woman!" "Move them buckets, woman! They're in my way!" "This food ain't fit t' eat, woman. Take it away!"

She spoke quietly and with dignity. "You is right to be angry, Lester," she said. "I left a note fer y', but I shoulda tole y' before I left."

"Shut yer mouth, woman, and git my supper!" he shouted, slamming the beer bottle down on the table.

She moved to the centre of the room and faced him. "My name," she began, and faltered. She cleared her throat and ran her tongue over her lower lip. "My name," she repeated, this time more steadily, "is Elizabeth."

He was dumbfounded. My brothers raised their heads from their card game and waited, cards poised in midair.

Pa looked at her. He looked at me. Then he looked at Jem and Daniel and Ira and Bernard, sitting there silent and still like four statues, waiting for his reaction.

Suddenly my father threw back his head and laughed. His ugly laughter filled the little kitchen, and we all listened, frozen, wishing for it to stop.

"'My name is Elizabeth!'" he mocked, between choking guffaws, slapping his thighs and holding his stomach, and then he repeated himself and her, mincingly, "'My… name… is… Elizabeth!'" Then his face changed, and there was silence. "Git over here 'n' make my supper, woman! I'm gonna milk them cows. But my belly is right empty, and y' better be ready when I gits back from th' chores!"

I watched my mother. During the laughter, I could see her retreat for a minute behind her eyes, expressionless, lifeless, beaten. Then she took a deep breath and looked at him directly, squarely, with no fear in her face. Pain, yes, but no fear. My brothers looked down and continued their card game.

"Act smart there, Sylvie," she said to me, as soon as he had left. "I need yer help bad. You clean up, 'n' I'll fix supper." She was already moving swiftly about the kitchen, fetching food, chopping onions, peeling potatoes.

In the sink was a mountainous pile of dirty dishes. Open cans, crusted with stale food, cluttered the counter. I surveyed the scene with distaste.

"Ma," I asked, complaining like the true adolescent that I had now become, "how come they couldna washed the dishes themselves? They goes huntin' and fishin' and has lotsa little vacations in th' winter. We always do their work for them when they're gone. How come we gotta clean up their mess?"

"Listen," she said, cutting the potatoes and dropping them into the hot fat, "the way I sees it is y' kin ask fer kindness or politeness from time t' time. But y' can't expect no miracles. It's my own fault fer raisin' four boys like they was little men. I shoulda put them in front of a dishpan fifteen years ago. Now it's too late. Yer pa's ma did the same thing. She aimed t' raise a boy who was strong and brave, with no soft edges." She wiped her forehead with the back of her hand. "All along I bin blamin' men fer bein' men. But now I see that oftentimes it's the women that makes them that way." It was a long, long speech for my ma. But she went on. "The boys is seventeen, eighteen, nineteen, and twenty years old. Y' can't start makin' 'em over now. They's set." Then she smiled wryly, with a rare show of humour. She bowed formally in the direction of the card game. "I apologizes," she said, "to your future wives."

Then she stopped, and looked from one son's face to the next, and so on, around the table. "I loves you all, regardless," she said softly, "and it's worth a try. Jem"—she spoke to the youngest—"I'd be right grateful if you'd fetch some water for Sylvie. She's real tired after the long walk."

Jem looked at his brothers, and then he looked at her. Water carrying was woman's work, and she knew she was asking a lot of him. He rose silently, took the bucket from her, and went outside to the well.

"And you," she said, addressing Daniel and Ira and Bernard, "One snigger out of you, and yer in bad trouble." I'm sure she knew she was taking an awful chance. You can say a thing like that to little boys, but these were grown men. But no one moved or so much as smiled when Jem returned. "I thank you right kindly," said Ma, thereby delivering a speech as unusual as her other one.

You could say, I suppose, that our leaving made no large difference in my mother's life. She still worked without pay or praise, and was often spoken to as though she were without worth or attraction. Her days were long and thankless. She emptied chamber pots and spittoons, scrubbed overalls and sheets on her own mother's scrub board, and peeled the frozen clothes from the line in winter with aching fingers. But not all things remained the same. She now stood up to my father. Her old paralytic fear was gone, and she was able to speak with remarkable force and dignity. She did not nag. Nagging is like a constant blow with a small blunt instrument. It annoys, but it seldom makes more than a small dent. When she chose to object to Pa's cruel or unfair behaviour, her instrument was a shining steel knife with a polished cutting edge. A weapon like that seemed to make my father realize that if he went too far—if he beat her, or if he scolded too often or too unjustly—she would leave. After all, she had done it once before. And this time, she might not return.

So there were changes. One day, for no apparent reason, he started to call her Elizabeth. She did not let on that this was remarkable, but the tight line of her mouth relaxed, and she made him a lemon pie for supper. She fixed up the attic storeroom as a workroom for herself. The boys lugged up her treadle sewing machine, and she brought in an old wicker chair and a table from the barn. It was a hot room in summer and cold in winter, but it was her own place—her escape. She made curtains from material bought at Frenchy's, and hooked a little rug for the floor. No one was allowed to go there except her. She always emerged from this room softer, gentler, more still.

I never did hear a single word about the missing egg money. Maybe Pa didn't notice, or perhaps Ma attacked the subject with her sharp-edged knife. Possibly it was the egg money that sent me to Dalhousie—that and my scholarship and my summer jobs. I never asked. I didn't really want to know.

When I was home last February during the term break, I stole a look into Ma's attic room. There were library books on the table, material on the sewing machine, paper piled on the floor for her letters to me and to the boys. I respected her privacy and did not go in. But the room, even in that chilly winter attic, looked like an inviting place.

My ma is now fifty-five, and has a lot of life still to live. My pa is fifty-eight. He still shaves once a week, and he has not yet cleared up the yard. But he often speaks to my mother as though she were more of a person and less of a thing. Sometimes he says thank you. He still has a raging temper, but he is an old dog, and new tricks come hard. He loves my mother and she him, with a kind of love that is difficult for my generation to understand or define. In another time and in another place, the changes could have been more marked. But my mother is a tough and patient woman, and these differences seem to be enough for her. Her hair is worn less severely. Her mouth is not set so straight and cold and firm. She talks more. She has made a pretty yellow blouse to wear with her baggy slacks. She smiles often, and she is teaching her two grandsons how to wash dishes and make cookies.

I often wonder about these things: but when my mind approaches the reasons for all that has happened, my thinking slides away and my vision blurs. Certainly the book and the leaving do not explain everything. Maybe my mother was ready to move into and out of herself anyway; and no one can know exactly what went on in her thoughts before and after she left. Perhaps she was as surprised as I was by the amount of light and warmth she let in when she opened the door to step into the dark and frosty morning. But of that strange three-day departure, I can say, as Ma did of her book, "She was a real troublin' trip. But she was good."

Saturday Climbing

BY W.D. VALGARDSON

" 'You all right?' his daughter called. 'Yeah,' he lied. 'Just resting.' "

Twenty metres up the cliff, the toe of his climbing boot resting on a ledge no wider than a dime, two fingers curled around a nubbin of rock, Barry was suddenly afraid that he would fall. "Rope," he called.

At the foot of the cliff, his daughter let out the golden line of rope that joined them. As Barry felt the rope go slack, he raised his right knee and pressed his toe into a shallow depression. Grunting with the strain, he stood up on his right leg, then paused, uncertain of his next move.

The cliff had proven to be deceptive. The conglomerate, with its rough, gravel-like surface, had looked easy. Close to the base, there were large handholds, so that at first the climbing was little more difficult than walking up stairs. Then, unexpectedly, the surfaces smoothed; the places where he could get a secure hold were spread farther and farther apart. At the same time, the numerous cracks dwindled until there was no place to set any protection. Unable to go back because of his pride, he had continued on until he now found himself dangerously far above his last piton. If he fell, he would drop eight metres to the piton, then eight metres past it before his rope came taut and held him. There was, because of the elasticity of the rope, a chance that he would ground out.

The thought flitted through his mind that it would be like falling from the top of a six-storey building. Tensing his fingers, he straightened his elbow and leaned back from the rock so that he could search for his next

hold. Above him, there was a one centimetre ledge. He reached up, got a good grip, then lifted his left leg higher than he had ever imagined he could and set his foot on a rough patch that would provide the necessary friction to hold his weight.

He had been scared many times but never like this. Never before had he been this close to paralysis, to a sensation of letting go so that the tension and the fear would be over. The way he felt, he imagined, was the way a wounded animal felt when it finally gave up fleeing and allowed itself to be killed.

Fifteen centimetres from his left hand there was a vertical crack that seemed hardly wider than a fingernail. Cautiously, he explored it with his fingers. Just within his reach it widened slightly. He ran his hand over his rack and unsnapped the smallest chock nut. He forced the aluminum wedge deep into the crack. From the wedge there hung a wire loop and from that a carabiner. Catching hold of the rope tied to his harness, he lifted it up, forced open the spring-loaded gate of the carabiner and fitted the rope into the aluminum oval.

Once the gate snapped shut, he sighed with relief. The chock nut, the wire loop, the carabiner, the rope, fragile as they looked, would hold ten times his weight. If he wanted to, he could let go and simply hang in space.

"You all right?" his daughter called. "Yeah," he lied. "Just resting."

His voice sounded faint and breathy. He was glad she could not see his momentary weakness. He could not control the trembling of his legs. The muscle of his right arm jerked spasmodically. Ever since his wife had left him, he had tried to compensate by providing unhesitating leadership for his daughter. He did his best to keep life simple and uncomplicated. It was, he thought, the way to provide security.

He glanced down. Among the scattered grey boulders, Moira's red hair gleamed like a burnished cap.

"You're doing fine," she hollered. The crosscurrents of air that played over the cliff face blurred her voice, making it seem farther away than it really was. To hear what she said, he had to strain toward the sound. "You've got another six metres to a big ledge. You can do it easy."

He was grateful for her confidence. Before they had started climbing, there had crept into his daughter's voice a constant note of disparagement and disappointment. The times he had managed to overcome his own insecurity and had asked her what was the matter, she had turned her back on him, answering, "Nothing," with a tightly controlled voice.

Bewildered, he had sought the advice of women at work who had teenage daughters. They had been no help. Behind their competent, efficient professional selves, they too, he realized, were just as confused as he was. In desperation, he had gone so far as to pose the question of the relationship of fathers and daughters to his class. He had not been prepared for the reaction he got. From every corner of the room came cries of bitter disappointment and resentment.

As he had left the classroom, one student had called to him. He had stopped to wait for her. She had frizzy dark hair, wore long dresses that might have come from a western movie set, a rainbow assortment of beads, and a nose ring. She always talked as if she was thinking in some exotic language and was translating it badly. She was the only student he'd ever had who insisted on analyzing *War and Peace* by consulting the *I Ching*.

"The caged bird proves nothing but the power of the captor," she had intoned.

For a moment, he suffered vertigo, and the cliff seemed to sway as if in an earthquake. He pressed his forehead to the cool stone and shut his eyes. Inside his flesh, his bones trembled.

Taking up rock-climbing had been an act of desperation. All the past activities Moira and he had done together—going to foreign films, visiting Seattle, beachcombing—she dismissed with a contemptuous shrug of her shoulders. At one time, they had played chess nearly every day. Lately, she pretended she had never seen the game. When he had noticed an advertisement for rock-climbing, he remembered that she had spoken admiringly of classmates who had hiked the West Coast Trail. He had registered them and paid their fees. Then he informed her.

He hoped she would be pleased. Instead, she was incensed that he had committed her to something without her consent. He knew she was right to be angry but he was too frantic to care. Over the previous month, she had come home late a number of times. Each time, the sweet-sour smell of marijuana clung to her, and her pupils seemed unnaturally large. He had not dared to accuse her of smoking dope. If he was wrong, she would never forgive him for being unjust. Being right frightened him even more. If she said, "That's right, I'm smoking dope, six joints a day, and sniffing coke and participating in orgies," he didn't know what he would do. Ranting and raving had ceased to work. Reasoning with her had no effect. He felt utterly helpless.

By emphasizing that the money was spent and there was no refund, he won the argument over rock-climbing. However, he took the car to the first class while she took her bike. She went prepared to sneer at everything, but once she saw her classmates, her attitude changed. Instead of Moira being isolated by her youth, Barry was isolated because of his age. Of the fifteen members, eleven were under twenty. The instructor still didn't need to shave more than once a week.

By the time the three hours were over and he realized that rock-climbing wasn't going to be rough hiking, it was too late to back out. There were only three girls in the class. In return for the attention of one-third of the young men, Moira was prepared to scale the Himalayas.

Barry began with an attitude that was typical of someone raised on the Prairies. Anything over a metre was a substantial elevation. During the second class, he was expected to climb vertical cliffs. He gave some thought to dropping out of the class but realized that, after the fuss he had made about the fees, he would look like a dreadful hypocrite.

Gradually, as a dozen Saturdays passed, what had seemed impossible was reduced to the merely difficult. Cliffs that had looked flat and smooth as polished marble became a series of problems and solutions. The names of the unfamiliar equipment became a part of his vocabulary. Young men in climbing boots frequented his backyard and kitchen. To his relief, Moira accepted him enough to spend an occasional hour practising knot-tying with him.

This weekend there had been no class. In an attempt to heal a rift caused by an argument over her going away to college—she was two years ahead of herself in school and, therefore, in spite of being in grade twelve was only sixteen—he had offered to go climbing with her. To his surprise, she'd accepted.

"Climbing," he called.

"Climb on," Moira answered.

He stepped up, away from the safety of his perch. His life, he realized, was in her hands. If he fell, she was his protection.

The thought of giving her so much responsibility was like the prick of a thorn. In all other things, he had been trying to keep her from rushing headlong into taking on too much responsibility at once. The result had been a long series of disagreements. She did not have the decency to let one dispute finish before she began another. Sometimes three or four overlapped.

On Fridays, when he went to the faculty club, he ordered double brandies and brooded over whether he shouldn't have insisted on Sunday school in a good fundamentalist church all the past years. His colleagues, the majority of whom were the epitome of liberal tolerance about most things, when they talked about their teenage children reverted to wistful fantasies about convents and boarding schools in inaccessible locations.

The weekend past, Moira had wanted to go to an all-night party with a boy he just vaguely recognized as having drifted through the house two or three times. Barry was dumbfounded. At the same age, he'd had to have his girlfriends in before midnight. If he had kept a girl out all night, her father would have met them with a shotgun.

"Good girls," he said, quoting something he'd heard in adolescence, "don't stay out all night."

"Good fathers," she shot back, "don't think the worst of their daughters."

That afternoon was filled with slamming doors, weeping, and raised voices. He found himself fighting so hard against her staying out all night that he compromised on three o'clock and afterward, when he had calmed down, wondered how it had happened. He had been determined to start with a deadline of midnight and let himself be persuaded to accept one o'clock. Although Moira claimed not to remember the chess moves, he had the distinct feeling that he'd been checkmated.

The final blow had been her insistence on going away to college. They had the money, he admitted. It just wasn't sensible, at sixteen, to travel over three thousand kilometres to attend a school when the local university was every bit as good, even if it did have him on the faculty. He suspected the choice had more to do with her all-night-party boy than with academic excellence.

Now, as he worked his way up toward the large ledge where he was to set up a belay station, it was as if Barry were in danger of being pulled backward by the sheer weight of his memories. It was with a sense of relief that he heaved himself onto the ledge. He paused to catch his breath, then anchored himself to a boulder.

"On belay," he shouted down, giving Moira the signal that he was ready.

His daughter, twenty-five metres below, seemed so small that Barry felt he could lift her into his arms. She looked no larger than she had been when, at three, she had eaten a bottle of aspirin. He had scooped her up and run with her four blocks to the hospital. After that desperate race and the struggle to hold her down—it had taken both him and a nurse to control her flailing limbs while the doctor had pumped her stomach—he was acutely aware of how tenuous her life was, of how much he would suffer if he lost her. For a long time afterward, he thought of her as being intricately constructed of fragile paper.

"Climbing," Moira answered.

"Climb on," he shouted.

From time to time, she paused to pull loose the chock nuts and pitons her father had left behind. These, since they would be needed later, she clipped to a sling that hung over her shoulder. Once, when she deviated from the route her father had taken, she became stuck at an overhang. Not having dealt with the obstacle himself, Barry could not help and had to leave her to find her own solution.

The climb seemed agonizingly slow, as if it would never be completed. Then, when it was over, and his daughter, grinning, breathless, was climbing over the edge, it was as if hardly any time had passed.

They sat side by side, sipping orange juice, their feet dangling in space.

"I thought you were in trouble," Moira said.

"I thought you were, too," he replied, matching his weakness with hers. Then, ashamed, he admitted, "I gripped."

Moira twisted about. Her red hair was snugged at the back with a rubber band. Being outside had sprinkled her nose with light freckles.

She studied the cliff face. It rose another thirty metres. There was a crack that ran more than halfway, then a small series of outcrops. He tried to see the route they should take, but the last four or five metres seemed impossible.

"I'd come home for Christmas," she said in a rush, "and classes are out in April. It's not as if it was such a long time to be away."

She had caught him unawares, and none of his carefully prepared arguments were at hand.

"It's just so unexpected," was all that he could manage.

"I've got to leave sometime."

The house will be so empty, he wanted to say. How will I get used to being alone? It is as if you lost your first tooth only last year. As if I took you to kindergarten six months ago. You're barely rid of your braces.

She lifted her index finger and rubbed the side of her nose. She had done it as long as he could remember. It was her signal that she was going to impart a confidence or confess a wrongdoing—that she liked some boy in her class, that she had got a detention or spent all her allowance before the end of the week and needed more money.

"I'm not innocent, you know."

He wondered what she meant by that but was afraid to ask.

"I mean," she continued, "Vic Hi's a big school. You hear a lot. Everybody's on the Pill. The dope's there if you want it. There's lots of opportunity."

He was tempted to let loose his anxiety in a lecture, but the memory of the frizzy-haired student in his class stopped him. She had stood on one foot all the time they were talking, the sole of her left sandal pressed to her right knee. She had passed her hand before his face in an affected arc. He'd heard her father was a prominent lawyer in the East but found it hard to believe.

She talked in aphorisms and riddles, then a silence had fallen between them. He'd wondered why she had bothered to call after him, what she had really wanted to say. He had left her but, after a few steps, glanced back. She had given up her storklike stance and was standing with feet together, shoulders slumped, her face slack beneath her gaudy makeup. For the first time, he had seen how much younger she was than he had thought. If he had not known better, he'd have said she was a lost child.

Just then, she had seen him watching her. Immediately, she had drawn up her shoulders, flung back her head, given an exaggerated sway of her hips and pranced away. That had been the last time he'd seen her. She had never come back to his class, and one day a yellow drop-slip with her name on it had appeared in his mailbox.

"I want to lead this pitch," Moira said.

Barry was startled. She had never led. Always before she'd been second or third on a rope.

"I was thinking of rappeling down," he answered. "I can't see a clear route up."

"There," she said. "There and there and there." She jabbed her fingertip at a series of holds.

"But where would you set your protection?"

Her hand wove a series of stitches in the air. "There. Up there. To the side. Back across. Up about two metres."

His fear for her was not without reason. The climbing, after seeming so dangerous at first, had begun to lose its aura of hazard. They all fell from time to time, but their ropes kept them from suffering more than bruised knees and elbows. Then, one of the climbers who was leading had ignored instructions and, overconfident, had put in only one piece of protection. He placed it improperly, and when he slipped and fell, his weight jerked it loose. For a moment, no one had been able to move, then those who were not belaying or climbing had run toward the boy who lay sprawled on his back. Bright red blood seeped from his nose and ear.

"Jackets," Barry had demanded. Red Cross training that he'd not thought about in years came back with an intense clarity. "Every piece of clothing you can spare. We mustn't let him get cold."

They all had moved automatically, clumsily, unable to think. Having done as he instructed, they all stood stupefied. Their faces were shocked white beneath their tans.

He sent two of the students racing down the hill for help.

For an hour, they huddled in a ragged circle around the boy whose hair was paler than the sun-drenched grass and whose skin might have been molded from wax. He slipped in and out of consciousness. Each time his eyes shut, they all tensed, afraid he had died. But then, he would groan or let out his breath harshly, and the moment would pass. Someone, Barry had not noticed who, had started collecting gear. One, and then another, began to pack. They moved slowly, silently, as if any noise would disturb the delicate balance between life and death.

Grounded out. That was what they called it. Because his safety had not been properly set, he had grounded out. Barry remembered that the air force had been like that too. Pilots never failed. They washed out. They never died. They bought it. *Grounded out.* The semantics covered up the fear.

Now, for a moment, it was as if, once again, he could hear the sharp startled cry; see the backward arc, the body, falling without grace or beauty, the rope writhing and twisting, the red-shirted boy settling in a cloud of unexpected dust.

"Ron," Barry protested, surprising himself at remembering the boy's name.

"Do you think I'd be so careless?"

It was asked in a tone that allowed no argument.

Stiffly, he stood up and tested his belay.

Don't climb, he thought, *it's too dangerous. Let us go back the way we came and find somewhere that'll always be safe*. But even as he thought it, he knew that it was impossible.

Once again, it was as if he were standing before the frizzy-haired girl, watching her long green nails sweep slowly before his face. At the time, he had not wanted to understand. "The world seeks balance," she'd said. "Extremism begets extremism."

"On belay," he said.

"Climbing," Moira replied.

His daughter, easily, with the supreme confidence of youth, grasped a handhold and pulled herself onto a flake. Smoothly, she worked her way up one side of the crack, straddled it, and crossed over.

Below her, her father, ever watchful, full of fear, smoothly payed out the rope, determined to give her all the slack she needed while, at the same time, keeping his hands tensed, ready to lock shut, ready to absorb the shock of any fall.

My Career with the Leafs

BY BRIAN FAWCETT

What if our favourite athletes were also poets? Brian Fawcett imagines what it would be like to be a poet who played pro hockey.

I'll explain how I came to play hockey for the Toronto Maple Leafs. It was surprisingly easy, and other people with similar ambitions to play in the Big Leagues might be able to pick up some valuable tips. I'm a poet, you see, and one of the things we do as part of our job is an occasional public reading. I had a reading to do in Toronto, and one of the first things I did when I got there was to drop down to Maple Leaf Gardens. The day I went, the Leafs happened to be practising.

As I sat in the stands watching the Leafs skate around the rink I got an idea. I walked down to the equipment room, and politely asked a man who turned out to be a trainer if it would be okay if I joined the practice.

"Sure thing," he told me, just like that.

I asked if I could have a uniform to wear.

"Sure," he said. "What number would you like?"

"How about number 15?" I said innocently.

The number belonged to Pat Boutette at the time, but he was injured and I knew he wouldn't be around. I felt a surge of ambition—maybe I could beat him out of a job! Minutes later I was out on the ice with the Toronto Maple Leafs.

I skated around for a while, carefully declining any involvement in the passing and shooting drills while I tried to get my floppy ankles to co-operate. Instead of co-operating they were beginning to hurt so I drifted in the direction of the coach, Red Kelly, who was yelling instructions at the players. I leaned casually on my stick the way I'd seen Ken Dryden do on television, and looked down at my skates. I watched the drills for two or three minutes until the ache in my ankles started to fade, then edged closer to Kelly.

"Mind if I take a turn?" I asked as evenly as I could.

"Not at all," he replied. "Let's see what you can do."

Somebody pushed a puck in front of me and as I reached for it I tripped on the tip of my left skate and fell flat on my face. What to that point had almost been a dream turned abruptly into a nightmare. I lay on the ice for a second, peering at the puck as if it had tripped me, and wondered why I couldn't wake up. I thought about quitting then and there.

I had nothing to lose, so I didn't quit. I got up, picked up my stick, and looked Red Kelly in the eye. He didn't move a muscle—didn't laugh or anything. I pushed the puck forward and skated after it in the direction of the goalie—it was Gord McRae I think—slowly gathering speed. About five metres from the net I deked to my left without the customary deke to the right. The deke took MacRae with it, and I cut to the right. The net was wide open and I shovelled the puck into it on my backhand.

All of this is incredibly difficult for a left-shooting skater to do. In fact, the whole manoeuvre is an impossible one, and everyone who saw it knew, including Kelly, who was staring at me with his mouth open. For my part, I had no idea how I'd done it, except that it had been awful easy.

"Not bad," Kelly shouted. "Not bad at all."

If scoring that first goal had been easy, the rest of the practice wasn't. I'm not a great skater at the best of times, and I wasn't in shape. I seemed able to score goals almost at will, but I had difficulty with the defensive drills, particularly the ones that involved things like skating backward. I fell several times, and one time I went into the boards so hard that Kelly skated over and told me to take it easy.

As the practice ended, he asked me if I could drop by his office after I showered. I told him I'd be pleased to, and after a shower I can't remember at all, I was sitting in a stuffed red Naugahyde chair staring across a big desk at Red Kelly and Jim Gregory, the General Manager of the Leafs.

Kelly was writing something on a pad of yellow foolscap. Gregory did the talking.

"You've got some interesting moves out there," he said. "I caught the whole thing from up in the box. Where'd you learn your hockey?"

I decided to tell them the truth.

"Well," I replied, "I really haven't played organized hockey since I was about twelve. I watch *Hockey Night in Canada*, of course, and I guess I've learned a lot from that."

"Where do you come from?" he asked.

"That's kind of a hard question," I replied, trying to figure out what the truth was. "I'm from the West Coast. Well, not the coast, actually. I'm from up north."

"What brings you to Toronto?"

"I'm a poet," I said, "here on business, doing a public reading."

"No kidding," he said, looking reasonably satisfied with my answer.

"I guess you know Rota. He's from up there."

I was stumped. I didn't know any writer from up north named Rota. Kelly saw my confusion.

"New kid," he said. "Plays for Chicago."

"I've heard of him," I shrugged. "But I never played with him. He's a bit younger than I am."

There was a silence, as if the two of them were trying to decide which of them should speak. Finally, Gregory stood up and cleared his throat.

"How would you like to play hockey for the Toronto Maple Leafs?" he said.

"I'd really like that," I said quickly. "I'd prefer to play just the home games, though. I hate travelling."

Gregory seemed puzzled by my request, but he agreed to it, probably because I didn't ask for anything else.

"We play Boston Monday night," he said. "We'll see you at the rink at 6 p.m." He paused. "Make that 5:30, and you can get in an extra half hour of skating."

I stood up. "I can probably use it," I smiled.

Kelly grunted, and then grinned, and I followed him out of the office and down the long concrete corridors of Maple Leaf Gardens to the players' entrance. He shook my hand.

"Good to have you with us," he said, with a lot of sincerity.

"It's good to be part of an organization that takes chances," I said, with even more sincerity. "Toronto treats its visitors well."

Kelly smiled and waved goodbye as I stepped through the open door into a fine early winter blizzard.

The next thing I knew I was sitting in the Leafs' dressing room beside George Ferguson, suiting up for the game. Kelly came in and announced the player assignments.

"Fawcett here is going to be playing home games for us," he shouted, pointing vaguely in my direction. "He'll play on the wing with Ferguson and Hammerstrom for a while, and we'll see how things go. Any questions?"

To my surprise, a fair number of the players knew who I was, and it turned out that some of them had even read my work. Out of the corner of my eye I saw the two Swedes, Hammerstrom and Salming, exchange glances. Maybe they thought having a poet on the team might take some of the heat off them. They were still relatively new in the league, and they were taking a lot of physical and verbal abuse from the rednecks and goons who were worried about foreigners changing the game and taking their jobs. The rap on the Swedes was that they were chicken, particularly Hammerstrom, who the papers were saying was allergic to the boards. Personally I thought his skating more than made up for those faults.

I wondered a little at Kelly putting me on a line with him, but decided that he was trying to compensate for my poor skating. Every team in the league would stick their goons on our line, that was certain. Kelly probably figured Hammerstrom would skate his way out of trouble, and I would talk my way out.

We'd see soon enough. It was nice to be able to play with Ferguson, who I thought was one of the smarter centres to come into the league in a while. I planned to do what any rookie should—keep my head up and my mouth shut. It would be a new way of working, that was for sure.

The first period of that game was nothing to remember. My check, predictably, was Wayne Cashman, probably the dirtiest player in the league. I went up and down my wing without incident, partly because Cashman wasn't much of a skater either. He cut me with his stick several times, but I didn't bleed much, and I ignored it when he got me with the butt end just as the period ended. I waited until I could breathe again and skated off to the dressing room with the rest of the team.

Early in the second period Lanny McDonald and Don Marcotte were sent off for trying to remove one another's vital organs, and Kelly sent me out with Hammerstrom on a five on five. The Bruins sent out Greg Sheppard and Cashman. The face-off was in our end, and Hammerstrom won it, got the puck back to Ian Turnbull, and he banked it around on the boards to where I was waiting. I circled once, almost lost my balance, and headed up the ice. As I crossed the red line, I saw Cashman skating toward me with a gleam in his eye. I kept going toward Orr at the blue line, did the deke to my left as if to move between Orr and the boards, and then cut sharply right. Orr went for the first deke and so did Cashman, who by this time was right behind me prodding at my liver with his stick. When I deked to the right, Cashman ran into Orr and both of them went heavily to the ice. I had a two on one with Hammerstrom, and I slid the puck over to him. He drew Al Simms over, passed back, and I had only Cheevers to beat. I did it again; deked left, cut right, and plunked the puck over the bewildered netminder into the upper right corner of the net.

I stuck my stick up in the air the way I'd seen it done on television, and was trying to honk my leg when I ran into Hammerstrom and we both fell down. Turnbull came over to congratulate me and Salming skated over to dig the puck out of the net. He handed it to me, grinned, and said something in Swedish I didn't understand. Hammerstrom grinned at me the same way and pointed to Cashman, who was skating in small circles at centre ice with his head down.

It was a tight-checking game, and the score was still 1-0 halfway through the third period. That was as far as I got that night. I skated into the corner for a Ferguson pass, Cashman went in behind me, and only Cashman came out.

Eventually I came *to*, but that was well after the game was over. The Leafs had won it 2-0. Cashman got a penalty for hammering me, and Sittler scored on the ensuing power play. That's what they told me, anyway.

I made it to the practice the next afternoon, none the worse for having spent the night in the hospital to make sure I didn't have concussion. I didn't get much sleep because the interns kept coming in every half hour to see if I was going to go into a coma.

"Are you there?" they asked, and lifted my eyelids with one finger to flash their penlights at my pupils. About 4 a.m. a very young intern came in. He was a hockey fan.

"You're the new guy with the Leafs, eh?" he asked.

"Yeah," I croaked.

"Nice move you made on that goal you scored," he said. "Where'd you learn that?"

"Watching television," I answered, telling the truth.

"I hear you write poetry too," he said.

My head hurt, so I just grimaced.

"Pretty strange," he said. "Watch out for Cashman."

He checked my eyes so carefully I thought he was looking for poems, but he said I'd probably be able to leave in the morning.

At the practice the next day, Ferguson told me to watch out for Cashman too.

"You were lucky," he said. "Cashman spent two periods setting you up. We all knew it was coming, but I guess you had to pass the test like anyone else."

"Some test," I complained. "All I can remember about it is my bell ringing when it was over."

I played the three games in that home stand, scoring again in the last one against the Rangers, and setting up a goal by Ferguson. The team was away for the next three games, and then back for three more. While they were away I worked on my skating, circling the rink again and again until my ankles were too sore for me to move anymore. I tried skating without a stick, but found, as I had when I was a kid, that skating that way was beyond me. I needed the stick for balance and without it I could barely stand.

When the team came back, I confided to Ferguson that I couldn't skate without a stick.

"You're kidding," he said.

"No," I told him. "It's true. I only got skates every three years, and the first year they were too big and the third year they were too small."

Ferguson had a good eye for details. "What about the second year?" he asked.

"I had weak ankles back then."

"You still have weak ankles," he said.

"I use the stick for balance," I said, as we went on circling the rink.

Ferguson was skating backward to tease me. "Skating is easy," he laughed. "For me it's like breathing."

"I feel that way about some other things," I replied, "but not about skating."

"You don't look as if breathing is very easy right now," he pointed out.

While we unlaced our skates after practice, he asked me cautiously what it was like to be a writer.

"It's my way of breathing," I said.

"How'd you get into it?" he asked with genuine curiosity.

"I guess I was about thirteen," I said. "Right after I quit playing minor league hockey."

Ferguson and I became friends. He taught me a lot of the basics of pro hockey and I gave him books to read in return. I was interested in Rilke and an American poet named Jack Spicer at the time, and he pored through everything I lent him. I always had books in my equipment bag, and he dug through it regularly to see what was there. He asked me if Canadian writers were as good as Americans.

"The old guys are pretty tame," I said, "But there's a few writers under forty who might turn out to be interesting."

"Jeez," he said, "how long does it take to get good at it?"

"Usually about fifteen years of hard work," I said. "A few get good earlier than that because they have special attentions or come from environments that encourage them," I went on. "But that's rare. Most of us have to learn pretty well everything about the culture twice, and that takes time. After that, there's the job of keeping on top of it as it changes. A lot of writers get one good review of their work and they have to please their public, or, worse, they decide that they're geniuses, and don't have to listen to anything. So they imitate themselves until they lose their ability to learn. After that they just get drunk, or academic, or spend all their time trying to please the reviewers and filling out grant applications."

He wanted to know about the grants, so I explained to him the economics of trying to be a serious artist in a country that wants to have serious art without having to put up with the inconvenience and cost of paying the artists.

He looked skeptical. "Except for that, hockey is pretty much the same," he said after a moment's thought. "Only hockey players get screwed up more easily and a lot faster."

"That's because there's more people paying attention," I said, "and there's more money involved."

That home stand was a good one. I scored my third goal, drew assists on one of Ferguson's and another on the power play, passing from behind the net to Sittler in the slot. Only four goals had been scored while I was on the ice, and after seven games I was plus five. Then the Leafs were off again on a five-game road trip and I went back to my solitary skating, circling the ice over and over again until slowly, very slowly, my skating began to improve. I skated clockwise first, and then counterclockwise. Going counterclockwise was easier, maybe because on the corners my stick was closer to the ice. But I couldn't quite master skating backward, and stopping remained a problem unless I was close to the boards. But I developed reasonable speed skating straight ahead, and during games I combined my lack of stopping skill with my speed to provide the team with some excellent bodychecking.

Ferguson and I went out on the town the night after the team flew in from Los Angeles. He showed me the important sights of Toronto, like Rochdale and Don Mills, and later that night we walked down to Lake Ontario and threw rocks at all the empty milk cartons floating in the water. There had been a thaw, and it was like spring—dirty snow was piled up everywhere, abandoned cars were being towed off the streets, and the curious sensation I'd had of being in Middle Earth began to dissipate. There were lovers everywhere, discussing Parliament, and kissing and fist-fighting as the fog rolled in from the lake to meld with the darkness coming up from the East.

We played our only other home date of the season with the Bruins several weeks later. As the game approached, I got a lot of good-natured ribbing from the guys about what to do with Cashman.

"Check him into the boards with a powerful metaphor," advised Sittler.

"And then slash him with an internal rhyme," someone else chimed in.

I laughed at the gags, but deeper down I was worried. The press had picked it up and were amusing themselves, mostly at my expense. Alan Abel in *The Globe & Mail* wrote something about it being a test of whether the stick is mighter than the pen, and in an interview, Cashman noised it around that he not only disliked my style, he detested poetry. Anybody who wrote poetry, he said, had to have something wrong with their hormones. That wasn't all he said, either. He told the interviewer he was going to show the fans that there was something fishy about me, promising to make fillets out of me *and* my poetry.

As I skated out for the pre-game warm-up, Cashman gave me the evil eye, so I gave the fans a demonstration of how fast I could skate through the centre-ice zone. Kelly, out of kindness I guess, kept our line away from Cashman's as the game began, but on the second shift I saw the Bruin right-winger head for the bench right after the face-off, and Cashman came over the boards. Somebody froze the puck, and as we lined up for the face-off deep in Bruin territory, Cashman skated up to the circle, and around me once with his stick about a centimetre from my nose.

"I hope you got a nice burial poem written for yourself," he sneered. "You skinned my behind and I'm gonna carve yours off and throw it to the crowd."

I looked him right in the eye and mustered up all my powers of language.

"Suck eggs," I said.

On the face-off Ferguson drew the puck back to Salming, and I skated to the corner to wait for a pass. Cashman ignored the puck and followed me. I ducked an elbow. It missed me, but the Ref didn't miss it, because I slid down the boards as if I'd been pole-axed. Cashman got whistled for an elbowing penalty, and then got a misconduct penalty when he tried to chase me into the stands. I skated away from him, and three of my teammates stayed between us to make sure I stayed alive. Kelly kept me on for the power play and I banged Sittler's rebound past Gilles Gilbert to make it 1-0.

When I got to the bench, Kelly told me Howie Meeker wanted to interview me after the first period. It was Saturday, and the game was being televised nationally.

I'd forgotten it was *Hockey Night in Canada*. You get like that in the pros—you forget everything that makes the world tick for real people. You also pay a price. The price I was going to have to pay for my forgetfulness was an awful one. I hadn't brought any poems in my equipment bag. I was being handed the largest audience any poet in this country ever dreamed of and I wouldn't have a thing to read.

A few minutes later I was sitting in front of several television cameras with the customary towel over my shoulder, watching Howie Meeker introduce me to the nation and thinking that the dream was going to turn into a nightmare if I couldn't think of something quickly. My mind was a blank.

"We've got Toronto left-winger Brian Fawcett here in the *Hockey Night in Canada* studios at Maple Leaf Gardens," Meeker announced in a voice that sounded more nasal in real life than on television.

He was hunched toward the cameras and I noticed he sat closer to them than I did. I hadn't seen a brushcut for years or, for that matter, as much make-up as he had on his face, and I was sorting through all that novelty without listening to what he was saying. Luckily, he was babbling as inanely as usual at the camera and ignoring me completely:

"... nice to see a young player come up to the NHL with a good grasp of hockey fundamentals and play sound, heads-up positional hockey the way you've been doing. Gee whiz, but I just get thrilled when I see a young kid with his mind on the game skate away from a player like Wayne Cashman. And it pays off, don't you see? It must have been less than a minute before you scored that beautiful goal like you were born with a stick in your hand and skates on your feet."

He hadn't actually asked me a question, but he seemed to have finished.

"Actually, Howie," I said, too nervous to do anything but tell the truth, "I haven't played much hockey since I was twelve or thirteen years old, and I'm thirty, so I'm not much of a kid any more. I've been mainly concerned with language, and more specifically with disjunction in poetry, for the last few years. You might say I've been learning the tools of an extremely complex trade."

Meeker appeared not to have understood. Maybe he thought I was speaking French. He ignored everything I said, and went off on another rant.

"Well, Brian, how do you like being with a team like the Leafs, eh, with their tradition of ruggedness and hard work?"

"Well, Howie," I said, still not sure if he realized that I understood English, and pretty sure he didn't know I was a poet, "I find the ruggedness something of a problem. Northrop Frye and Margaret Atwood created a problem a few years ago by writing some books about the importance of Nature and the frontier, and a lot of similarly empty glamour nonsense about rugged Canadian pioneers, and as a result a lot of the writers in this country now go around wearing logging boots and punching people for no reason. I used to do it myself, actually."

Meeker was staring at me, his jaw somewhere down around his navel. I took this as a signal to continue.

"I mean, violence may be natural, but Nature isn't a very good model for behaviour. It's been really overestimated."

I knew I was gesticulating too much, and starting to yap. I'd forgotten about the cameras—it was Howie Meeker I wanted to convince. I couldn't stop.

"Art is really about civilization," I said, "not about Nature. All Nature does is overproduce, then waste most of it, and then resort to violence when the garbage starts to stink. When human beings follow Nature, you get guys like Hitler."

I was really flying, so I went to Meeker's question about hard work next.

"Hard work, like you say, is really important, Howie. The more I know about this game, the more I begin to realize that the real secret is hard work. I guess that goes for hockey as well."

Meeker, for some reason, seemed to have lost his voice, so I went right on.

"If you'd given me a little more notice, I could have brought some work here to read, but I guess these interviews are a bit too short to give the folks at home any real idea of what's going on, let alone a sense of the breadth and skill and variety of good writing going on in this country today."

Meeker stuttered back to life.

"Ah, ahhh.... Yes, well.... Well, Brian, I wish you and the Leafs the best of luck in the upcoming second period," he said, regaining a measure of control that didn't show in his face.

"Back to you, Dave Hodge!" he said hoarsely.

I smiled politely at the camera until fade-out. I'd seen a few guys start to pick their noses when they thought they were off-camera, and I wanted people to remember what I'd said.

Meeker turned on me. "What was that all about, you crazy sonofabitch?"

I began to explain, but he walked out of the studio without listening to my answer.

The dressing room was oddly silent when I returned. I sat down next to Ferguson and pulled the towel from around my neck. He was sitting with his head between his knees, as if he were airsick.

"Didn't you know about Meeker?" he asked incredulously.

"Know what?" I said, stuffing the towel into my equipment bag as a souvenir. "He seemed kind of ticked off when I talked about writing, but then he did ask those dumb questions, and he didn't stop me from answering them the way I wanted to."

"Geez, man, that's the unwritten law of hockey," Ferguson said. "You're supposed to pretend you're really dumb."

It was my turn to be incredulous.

"Darryl thinks there's some kind of agreement between the owners about it," he said. "When you get out of Junior Hockey, you're given a sheet of things you can say to the press. You talk dumb, talk about teamwork, and all that crap."

My head was reeling. When I was a kid I believed that the world was full of secret rules and conspiracies, but this was real life—the Big Leagues. I couldn't believe what I was hearing.

"I mean, a few years ago," he continued, "when Kenny Dryden started getting interviewed, he used all kinds of literate words like 'tempo' and so on, pronounced all the words properly, and there was a terrific uproar. But he was in law school and they had to accept it. I dunno. They may get him yet—force him to retire."

Ferguson shrugged, and a note of hopelessness entered his voice. "Rumour is," he said, "that this whole business about us being stupid and inarticulate is an explicit policy of the Feds—right from the top."

I looked around me to see if he was kidding. A couple of guys just nodded and looked the other way, but most of them were glaring at me. Kelly looked really angry.

"Aw, come on, you guys," I said to no one in particular. "Why put up with this? I've seen what's really true. Look at the books lying around the dressing room."

Several players slipped large hardbound books into their equipment bags. Sittler, everyone knew, was a big Henry James fan—said it helped his passing game. And Tiger Williams had come up from Junior already heavily into Artaud. The league had its share of jerks, it was true, but unless you noised it around, you were left alone if you had intellectual interests. I guessed they were mad at me because they thought I might have let the cat out of the bag. Hockey, Kelly told me later, was in enough trouble.

There was a TV set in the dressing room, and we watched as Meeker came on the screen to do the highlights of the period. My goal wasn't one of them. A few of the guys exchanged significant looks, but everybody remained seated, as if they were watching something very sad.

When a commercial came on, I asked Ferguson who'd died.

"You did, dummy," he said.

"Aw, come on," I said. "Why? Is it that bad? All I did was to get Howie Meeker mad at me."

"It's a lot worse than you think. You'll be blacked out," he said, grimly. "No radio perks, no television interviews, and as little newspaper coverage as they can give you. What you *will* see will be bad."

"That's okay," I said, philosophically. "I'm pretty used to that."

I scored the winning goal in the third period by going around the defence in the usual way, and I didn't even get third star. I went up and down my wing against Cashman, took his checks, many of which were flagrantly vicious and should have drawn penalties, and I threw a couple of my own in his direction. Cashman was given third star, actually, and Meeker said he was the one Bruin on the ice who had dominated his opponent.

Ferguson and I had a few beers after the game. I invited the rest of the guys, but nobody seemed interested.

"You're really a goof," Ferguson said cheerfully. "Do you know that?"

"How was I supposed to know?" I said, irritably. It seemed like everybody knew the rules but me.

"Look," I said, " I didn't go through the system like you guys did. For me it was all watching the tube, and thinking about it. How was I supposed to know—I mean, I've never believed much of what I've seen on television, but I did think *Hockey Night in Canada* at least was for real."

Ferguson grunted. "Rules are rules," he said. "Nobody but you believes they're supposed to be just."

"I'd settle for knowing what they are," I said bitterly.

"Would you really?"

"I'm not sure," I admitted. "I guess I really want to know who the big shots are who make them."

I didn't find out who the big shots were, that night or on any of the ensuing nights that season. I played my hockey as well as I could, and I played it in more or less the kind of obscurity I had been warned to expect. I scored nine goals and built twelve assists in twenty-seven games, and I was invited back for training camp the following season even though I played increasingly less often toward the close of the season.

As I was packing up to go home, the two Swedes came over and mentioned how much they'd enjoyed my presence during the home games, and asked if I'd be able to visit them in Sweden during the summer.

"I've got a lot of writing to catch up on," I told them. "My season's really just starting now."

Salming grinned that same grin I'd seen in my first game.

"I understand this," he said. "No fun to go to Sweden if you're interested in the Pros in English language."

"Something close to that," I admitted.

He and Hammerstrom left the dressing room laughing. They sure weren't like the Scandinavians I knew from watching Ingmar Bergman movies. I wandered over to where Ferguson was packing his equipment, and said goodbye. His bag was full of books, and he was having a hard time getting them all in. Finally, he had to give up, and he left with a pile of them under one arm. He turned at the door.

"I'm going to try to write some stuff myself this summer," he said. "Mind if I send you some of it?"

"Do," I replied. "You've got my address?"

"Sure have," he smiled. "Well, see you. Stay in shape."

"You too," I said. But I was talking to his shadow. He'd disappeared.

That summer passed in a flash, and by mid-September I was back skating and shooting again with the Leafs. The season started, and by December I had four goals and as many assists and, I thought, I was doing okay.

But the team wasn't doing well at all. We were fourth in our division, and Ballard could be heard snorting and snuffling all the way to Buffalo.

Then, before a practice right after a road trip that had gone badly, King Clancy walked into the dressing room, announced that Kelly had been fired, and that John McLellan was the new coach. Two days later Ferguson was traded to Pittsburgh. The day after that McLellan called me into his office.

"Brian," he said, "I talked things over with Jim, and we, uhh...."

He seemed to be stumbling for the right words.

"We don't think your heart is really in this game. You're not skating...."

"I can't skate," I cut in, but he ignored that and went on.

"We want you to retire."

"I'm practically a rookie!" I sputtered.

"You're thirty-one," he said, "and you're not going to get any better. Meeker is still after your behind, and you're a target for every goon in the league. Both Jim and I spent some time over the summer reading your work. You're a better poet than a hockey player. You've got to go for that."

I fussed and fumed, but I ended up agreeing with him. I had two, maybe three years of good hockey in me. With poetry I had maybe forty years, and I would only get better. I'd miss the crowds and the attentiveness of the critics, even though they'd done a good job of ignoring me. But I wouldn't miss Toronto and its bars, and I wouldn't miss the poetics, which, try as I did to ignore them, are as venal and profit-oriented at Maple Leaf Gardens as they are in the English departments of the nation's universities. If more poets were to play hockey instead of pretending flowers or vacant lots are really interesting, things might get better. But I wasn't going to hold my breath.

"You're right," I told McLellan. "I'll retire right now."

And I did. I walked out the way I had come in, gave back the blue on white and the number 15, and stepped out into the dull Toronto streets as if it were the next morning and not the next year I'd awakened to.

Three weeks later I got a letter from Ferguson, postmarked Atlanta. In it was this poem:

It's cold in Pittsburgh, colder still
in Philly. The north wind blows all night
from Canada, and these raucous crowds
that hoot and holler for our blood, Hey!
They're the coldest thing of all.
Skate and shoot, the coaches tell us
Skate and shoot. But masked men block the goals
and I am checked at every turn.

Each year more miles to go
More senseless contests of the will.
My heart is like the puck; often frozen
too often out of play, too often

stolen by the strangers
in the crowd.

My Life as a Bat

BY MARGARET ATWOOD

What is life like for other species?

1. REINCARNATION

In my previous life I was a bat.

If you find previous lives amusing or unlikely, you are not a serious person. Consider: a great many people believe in them, and if sanity is a general consensus about the content of reality, who are you to disagree?

Consider also: previous lives have entered the world of commerce. Money can be made from them. *You were Cleopatra, you were a Flemish Duke, you were a Druid priestess*, and money changes hands. If the stock market exists, so must previous lives.

In the previous-life market, there is not such a great demand for Peruvian ditch-diggers as there is for Cleopatra; or for Indian latrine-cleaners, or for 1952 housewives living in California split-levels. Similarly, not many of us choose to remember our lives as vultures, spiders, or rodents, but some of us do. The fortunate few. Conventional wisdom has it that reincarnation as an animal is a punishment for past sins, but perhaps it is a reward instead. At least a resting place. An interlude of grace.

Bats have a few things to put up with, but they do not inflict. When they kill, they kill without mercy, but without hate. They are immune from the curse of pity. They never gloat.

2. NIGHTMARES

I have recurring nightmares.

In one of them, I am clinging to the ceiling of a summer cottage while a red-faced man in white shorts and a white V-necked T-shirt jumps up and down, hitting at me with a tennis racquet. There are cedar rafters up here, and sticky flypapers attached with tacks, dangling like toxic seaweeds. I look down at the man's face, foreshortened and sweating, the eyes bulging and blue, the mouth emitting furious noise, rising up like a marine float, sinking again, rising as if on a swell of air.

The air itself is muggy, the sun is sinking; there will be a thunderstorm. A woman is shrieking, "My hair! My hair!" and someone else is calling, "Anthea! Bring the stepladder!" All I want is to get out through the hole in the screen, but that will take some concentration and it's hard in this din of voices, they interfere with my sonar. There is a smell of dirty bathmats—it's his breath, the breath that comes out from every pore, the breath of the monster. I will be lucky to get out of this alive.

In another nightmare I am winging my way—flittering, I suppose you'd call it—through the clean-washed demi-light before dawn. This is a desert. The yuccas are in bloom, and I have been gorging myself on their juices and pollen. I'm heading to my home, to my home cave, where it will be cool during the burnout of day and there will be the sound of water trickling through limestone, coating the rock with a glistening hush, with the moistness of new mushrooms, and the other bats will chirp and rustle and doze until night unfurls again and makes the hot sky tender for us.

But when I reach the entrance to the cave, it is sealed over. It's blocked in. Who can have done this?

I vibrate my wings, sniffing blind as a dazzled moth over the hard surface. In a short time the sun will rise like a balloon on fire and I will be blasted with its glare, shrivelled to a few small bones.

Whoever said that light was life and darkness nothing?

For some of us, the mythologies are different.

3. VAMPIRE FILMS

I became aware of the nature of my previous life gradually, not only through dreams but through scraps of memory, through hints, through odd moments of recognition.

There was my preference for the subtleties of dawn and dusk, as opposed to the vulgar blaring hour of high noon. There was my déjà vu experience in the Carlsbad Caverns—surely I had been there before, long before, before they put in the pastel spotlights and the cute names for stalactites and the underground restaurant where you can combine claustrophobia and indigestion and then take the elevator to get back out.

There was also my dislike for headfuls of human hair, so like nets or the tendrils of poisonous jellyfish: I feared entanglements. No real bat would ever suck the blood of necks. The neck is too near the hair. Even the vampire bat will target a hairless extremity: by choice a toe, resembling as it does the teat of a cow.

Vampire films have always seemed ludicrous to me, for this reason but also for the idiocy of their bats—huge rubbery bats, with red Christmas-light eyes and fangs like a sabre-toothed tiger's, flown in on strings, their puppet wings flapped sluggishly like those of an overweight and degenerate bird. I screamed at these filmic moments, but not with fear; rather with outraged laughter, at the insult to bats.

O Dracula, unlikely hero! O flying leukemia, in your cloak like a living umbrella, a membrane of black leather which you unwind from within yourself and lift like a stripteaser's fan as you bend with emaciated lust over the neck, flawless and bland, of whatever woman is longing for obliteration, here and now in her best negligee. Why was it given to you by whoever stole your soul to transform yourself into bat and wolf, and only those? Why not a vampire chipmunk, a duck, a gerbil? Why not a vampire turtle? Now that would be a plot.

4. THE BAT AS A DEADLY WEAPON

During the Second World War they did experiments with bats. Thousands of bats were to be released over German cities, at the hour of noon. Each was to have a small incendiary device strapped onto it, with a timer. The bats would have headed for darkness, as is their habit. They would have crawled into holes in walls, or secreted themselves under the eaves of houses, relieved to have found safety. At a preordained moment they would have exploded, and the cities would have gone up in flames.

That was the plan. Death by flaming bat. The bats too would have died, of course. Acceptable megadeaths.

The cities went up in flames anyway, but not with the aid of bats. The atom bomb had been invented, and the fiery bat was no longer thought necessary.

If the bats had been used after all, would there have been a war memorial to them? It isn't likely.

If you ask a human being what makes his flesh creep more, a bat or a bomb, he will say the bat. It is difficult to experience loathing for something merely metal, however ominous. We save these sensations for those with skin and flesh: a skin, a flesh, unlike our own.

5. BEAUTY

Perhaps it isn't my life as a bat that was the interlude. Perhaps it is this life. Perhaps I have been sent into human form as if on a dangerous mission, to save and redeem my own folk. When I have gained a small success, or died in the attempt—for failure, in such a task and against such odds, is more likely—I will be born again, back into that other form, that other world where I truly belong.

More and more, I think of this event with longing. The quickness of heartbeat, the vivid plunge into the nectars of crepuscular flowers, hovering in the infra-red of night; the dank lazy half-sleep of daytime, with bodies rounded and soft as furred plums clustering around me, the mothers licking the tiny amazed faces of the newborn; the swift love of what will come next, the anticipations of the tongue and of the infurled, corrugated and scrolled nose, nose like a dead leaf, nose like a radiator grill, nose of a denizen of Pluto.

And in the evening, the supersonic hymn of praise to our Creator, the Creator of bats, who appears to us in the form of a bat and who gave us all things: water and the liquid stone of caves, the woody refuge of attics, petals and fruit and juicy insects, and the beauty of slippery wings and sharp white canines and shining eyes.

What do we pray for? We pray for food as all do, and for health and for the increase of our kind; and for deliverance from evil, which cannot be explained by us, which is hair-headed and walks in the night with a single white unseeing eye, and stinks of half-digested meat, and has two legs.

Goddess of caves and grottoes: bless your children.

The Man Who Stopped Trains

BY FRANÇOIS BARCELO

TRANSLATED FROM THE FRENCH BY MATT COHEN

The fable has a long history in Québec. This story is a fable that could be about several things: about boredom? about the collision between traditional men and non-traditional women? about... what?

Like most amateur runners Gonzague Gagnon feared and detested the stretch between the first third and the halfway mark.

Along the small dirt road where he ran ten kilometres every day before turning around and walking back, he had planted stakes to mark the main stages of his course: a tenth of the way, a fifth, a quarter, a third, half-way, two-thirds, etc.

The first third went by most easily because Gonzague Gagnon did not yet feel tired and because this third was divided into numerous fractions, which gave the impression of rapid progress.

But as soon as he had passed the stake signalling the one-third mark, Gonzague Gagnon moved into a no-man's-land: one and two-thirds kilometres without any stake, only the temptation to give up because his legs were beginning to hurt.

As he was not very well educated Gonzague Gagnon didn't realize that, due to a bizarre mathematical caprice, the gap between a third and a half is actually twice as large as that between a quarter and a third. He thought it was only an illusion. And so it amounted to the same thing.

Even worse, about a third of the way along, the winding road that was so pleasantly shaded where it followed a small stream turned into the open countryside and straightened out as it travelled between two flat and treeless fields. To the right was a little-used railway track. To the left, in the distance, flowed a river which at this point was very wide and not the least bit interesting or attractive.

The stake signalling the halfway mark was just on the other side of the narrow wooden bridge that crossed the St Nicol River. After that the road became shaded again, and full of those thousand and one distractions that transform the most monotonous course into a constantly changing experience. It made you think you were going a lot faster than in the open field.

So once the halfway mark was passed, everything went more easily and Gonzague Gagnon knew that the hard part was over. There was no point in giving up then. Soon he would reach the two-thirds stake, soon after that the three-quarters, the four-fifths, and finally the stake marking the end.

Had it not been for that diabolic stretch from the third to the half, he would have found the run very easy—too easy perhaps. And on the rare occasion when he had to give up and walk back, it happened somewhere between these two stakes.

Gonzague Gagnon manned a gas pump at the Gagnon garage, the only service station in St Nicol. There was a small apartment above the garage which he shared with Gaston Gagnon, garage mechanic and vague relation—everyone in St Nicol being more or less related and called Gagnon. But Gonzague and Gaston had nothing more in common than their employer and their apartment. They hardly ever talked to each other because they had nothing to say. Gaston found Gonzague's passion for running ridiculous. And Gonzague found it ridiculous not to have such a passion.

He'd never seen statistics on the subject but Gonzague Gagnon knew that most men die at about seventy years of age. He told himself that his running habit would help him live a little longer than the old men of St Nicol. Maybe until he was seventy-five.

When Gonzague Gagnon turned twenty-five, he calculated that he had arrived at the one-third mark of his life. He resigned himself to facing the most difficult part of his existence, between twenty-five and thirty-seven-and-a-half: that flat and lengthy stretch between the third and the half.

Not that the first third of his life had been particularly eventful. His birth, six years at school, the death of his mother, the hundreds of thousands of litres he had poured into the same cars and trucks week after week had been the only milestones in his life so far. But he had not found the time long, because this first third of his existence was only the first, and what he experienced during it was for the first time.

The beginning of the second third seemed excessively repetitive and monotonous—all the more so since he had twelve years and six months to go before reaching another important fraction of his life.

He began to seek out distractions.

Television put him to sleep as did drinking more than one bottle of beer. So the two principal amusements of the Nicolois didn't help him at all.

During his first twenty-five years Gonzague Gagnon had been content to daydream in his rocking chair which he didn't even rock—during the summer, on the balcony behind the Gagnon garage, looking out on the fields where the cows grazed nearly motionless; during the winter, in his room with the door shut to block out the sound of Gaston Gagnon's television.

But when he became aware that he was in the long, boring stretch between the third and halfway points of his life, the time seemed even more boring and endless than before.

It was then that a public library opened in St Nicol. The mayor had decided to take advantage of a grant that had been set up for this purpose because the firetruck needed repairs. He requested the necessary amount from the Department for the Propagation of Culture in Deprived Regions. Since about a hundred dollars remained after the repairs, the mayor, being a man of conscience, designated this money for the establishment of a public library. He had a shelf put up at the fire station. And he had the town of St Nicol subscribe to a series entitled *Great Mysteries of the Universe.*

According to an advertisement in the TV guide this series was made up of marvellous books, elegantly bound and embellished with numerous photographs and illustrations—many in colour. It seemed to the mayor of St Nicol that the series would please people who liked reading, people who liked leather-bound books, and people who liked photographs and illustrations in black and white or colour. When the funds for the library were exhausted he had the subscription cancelled. And he looked with satisfaction at the first nine volumes of *Great Mysteries of the Universe* that were carefully lined up on their shelf in the fire station.

Gonzague Gagnon was a volunteer firefighter. But this was only a very occasional distraction, since fires were infrequent in St Nicol. And anyway, whenever there was a fire, the firemen always came too late. Gonzague Gagnon had applied to be a volunteer out of a sense of duty, because he was the fastest runner in the village and was always the first to arrive at the scene.

One day Gonzague Gagnon discovered the dust-covered volumes. He had never read a book, had never even held one in his hands—except for some greasy, well-thumbed schoolbooks with many of their pages pulled out.

The first book in the series was called *And If You Could....* Gonzague Gagnon read it in two nights, sitting in the driver's seat of the firetruck. Then he went to the other books, even though he read slowly and could not grasp the meaning of words without saying them out loud. But his favourite by far was *And If You Could....* He reread it a dozen times. The author claimed that each and every human being has special powers but that most people live in ignorance of their gift. But with a bit of systematic research, everyone could discover their own extraordinary powers.

The last chapter of *And If You Could...* was made up of a list of nine hundred and one parapsychological powers. Each was preceded by two boxes, "yes" and "no," in which the reader could make a mark depending on whether or not he was gifted with this faculty. Here are some examples from the list.

Yes	No	
☐	☐	Bend forks at a distance
☐	☐	Levitate small animals (birds, cats, rabbits, etc.)
☐	☐	Levitate furniture (chairs, pianos, television sets)
☐	☐	Change the colour of objects without painting them
☐	☐	Make rain
☐	☐	Stop snowstorms

This list took up twenty pages and opened up some fascinating possibilities to Gonzague Gagnon.

He tried every experiment. Hunting with his eyes, for example, which would have allowed him to bring down partridges or rabbits with a simple wink. Heating water by plunging his hands into it. Instantly giving the answer to any complicated arithmetic calculation.

But nothing worked for him. The partridges continued their flight without even slowing down. The rabbits took off at full speed. The water stayed cold in the pot. And Gonzague Gagnon gave the most absurd replies to the simplest problems.

The author of *And If You Could...* specified that these powers weren't necessarily permanent, that one could acquire or lose them during the aging process, that for certain people certain powers only worked on Mondays, that the inexplicable powers had by definition the tendency to inexplicably appear or disappear.

That is why Gonzague Gagnon reread the list several times a week, although he knew it almost by heart. And this activity helped him pass the time between the third and the halfway points of his life.

Although the author of *And If You Could...* asserted that he had undertaken in-depth research in order to draw up the most complete list possible, he encouraged his readers to carry out their own experiments.

So Gonzague Gagnon gave free reign to his imagination. His daily run gave him numerous opportunities. Transform the waters of the St Nicol River into milk... make buckwheat grow through snow... move houses closer together... shape clouds in his own image... make cows sing the "Kyrie"... turn fenceposts into Easter candles... Why not? All he had to do was to keep trying. One day something would work.

Telepathy held his attention for a long time. It seemed more "normal" than making cows fly or snakes sing. Had it not often happened, without planning, that he and his employer would broach the same subject?

"It must be about time to change the oil in the Ford," they would both say at once.

When, at the age of thirteen, Gonzague Gagnon had entered into his vocation, he had invented a game: to guess if the driver of the car approaching the service station was going to ask for regular or super. But he had to give up the game when he knew which cars took regular and which took super. Anyway this game didn't really help pass the time since it could only be played when a car was approaching—the very moment when Gonzague Gagnon would have something to do.

So several years later Gonzague Gagnon returned to telepathy, telling himself that perhaps he had a gift for it.

He began by trying to transmit thoughts. For example, he would stare at his employer's neck when he turned his back and try to give him commands: "Lean over. Take out your wallet. Scratch your left buttock."

But his employer never responded. Except once, when he turned towards Gonzague Gagnon—who was ordering him to turn towards him—and said, “Why are you looking at me like that? What’s wrong with you?”

The gas station attendant mumbled: “A dog does well to watch his master.” To which his employer had shrugged his shoulders and gone back to dismantling the transmission of Nésime Gagnon’s Chevrolet.

Forced to concede that he didn’t have the power of mental projection, Gonzague Gagnon concluded that he must, on the contrary, excel at thought reception.

Fortunately he lived with an ideal subject: Gaston Gagnon, who spent hours in front of his television, watching programs that didn’t seem to interest him—and therefore spent hours thinking.

For several evenings Gonzague sat in the armchair next to Gaston’s. He closed his eyes, emptied his mind and concentrated, ready to seize the least reflection, the smallest image, the tiniest scrap of words or ideas emanating from his colleague.

But, perhaps because Gaston never thought about anything, Gonzague never perceived anything.

He had more success with Groaner, his boss’s dog, a bastard albino who loved to pretend to be vicious but was actually afraid of field mice. During the summer, Gonzague Gagnon would sit on a chair in front of the service station, a few steps from Groaner’s kennel. And Groaner would sit on his hind legs and watch him. Gonzague Gagnon would tell him what to do: “Bend your head, fold back your left ear, blink your eyes.” And Groaner would obey. But Gonzague found little to be proud of in this because the dog did not respond to more complex instructions: “Bark five times, do a somersault, say hello.”

There was no glory in making a stupid dog do stupid things.

By the time he had reached his thirty-fifth birthday, Gonzague Gagnon had given up trying to discover paranormal powers within himself.

Of the first half of his life, only two years and six months remained. Surely then the months and the years would begin to whizz by as quickly as the kilometres after he was halfway through his run.

The morning of his birthday, Gonzague Gagnon laced on his running shoes, determined to make an assault on a goal he had set long ago: to run ten kilometres in thirty-five minutes on his thirty-fifth birthday. For many years he had made similar goals: thirty-two minutes at thirty-two, thirty-three minutes at thirty-three years, and so on. He'd never succeeded. But as the years went by, the goal became easier. And last week he had managed to run the distance in thirty-six minutes.

It was six o'clock in the morning, which meant that he had two hours in which to run his ten kilometres, walk back, take a shower and go down to work.

It was a beautiful morning and Gonzague Gagnon congratulated himself once more on being born in May, rather than having been conceived in the spring and then born in November or December, like most of the villagers. He ran the first two kilometres at an easy pace, to make sure his legs were warmed up. Then he lengthened his stride and began to speed up. He reached the one-third stake three minutes later. As always, he began to feel a bit out of breath. But if he wanted to get in under thirty-five minutes, he couldn't slow down, even though every step seemed to drag.

From a distance, Gonzague Gagnon saw the St Nicol River. Just on the other side he would find the five-kilometre marker. But his legs were growing heavy. Should he slow down and risk not doing his ten kilometres in thirty-five minutes? Or maintain or even accelerate his pace, and risk not finishing?

A far-away rumbling attracted his attention. It was the passenger train. It gave a long whistle and Gonzague Gagnon couldn't resist the temptation to turn his head, even though he knew he would lose a fraction of a second.

The train was quickly catching up to him, along the railway track that ran parallel to the road.

It was always the same train, no doubt always with the same passengers and the same conductor.

Once more Gonzague Gagnon looked ahead. The wooden bridge that straddled the St Nicol River was now at most thirty metres away.

At that moment Gonzague Gagnon realized that he had not tried to exercise his powers on anything mechanical. Why had he always tried to move tables, chairs, and other immobile objects? Was it not mobile things like cars, trucks or trains that he—Gonzague Gagnon, apprentice mechanic—would be the most likely to affect?

He glanced to the right. The train was about to draw up level with him and would soon begin to cross the metal railway bridge upstream from the wooden one.

"Stop," said Gonzague Gagnon.

He had spoken in an undertone, for fear of appearing ridiculous. But even if the train had had ears and hadn't been making so much noise, it could hardly have heard him from such a distance.

Nevertheless the train braked. Its wheels locked and screeched, sending up great showers of sparks. Then the engine stopped, just a few turns of the wheel from the metal bridge.

Gonzague Gagnon also came to a halt, a few steps from the wooden bridge.

Out came the engineer and the brakeman, gesturing wildly, the former shouting abuse apparently directed at the latter. They leaned over the track, inspected the wheels, then climbed back up. The train started up again, advancing slowly and with caution. Gonzague Gagnon watched as it gathered speed and pulled away.

He forgot his running. "I can stop trains," he said to himself over and over again as he walked back home. But upon due reflection, he had to conclude that the experiment was not conclusive.

He waited impatiently for the train to appear again the following week. Just as it was on the point of crossing the St Nicol River, he said, as he had the last time, "Stop." And the train stopped.

For several weeks that summer, Gonzague Gagnon took great pleasure in commanding the train to stop and watching the engineers leap frantically onto the track. Each time, the locomotive carried more inspectors, more mechanics, more people whom Gonzague Gagnon guessed to be specialists of all kinds, from places farther and farther away, from positions which were more and more exalted.

The authorities had a length of the track replaced. Nothing changed. In the village people began to talk about a curse, about a haunted railway track. When they brought the subject up with Gonzague Gagnon he smiled but said nothing.

Finally, when a team came to demolish the old metal bridge in order to replace it with a new one, Gonzague Gagnon told himself that he had gone too far. The authorities were delighted that the new bridge had solved the problem of the inexplicable stoppages of the train, even if the stoppages themselves remained unexplained.

"Today my life is half over," Gonzague Gagnon realized one fine December morning.

He brushed his teeth and put on his tights and his tracksuit, taking special care to slide into place a little handkerchief folded in four. It kept the cold from a particularly sensitive part of his anatomy.

His usual road was well ploughed, but with a base of slippery ice that encouraged caution. For this reason, Gonzague Gagnon was unable to achieve his goal of thirty-seven-and-one-half minutes at thirty-seven-and-one-half years of age. "That pleasure will be for my thirty-eighth birthday." He came to this conclusion philosophically, though his recent failures might have led him into bitterness. For a long time he had been convinced that eventually it would be easy to run the ten kilometres in the number of minutes equal to his age. But age was weakening him, and each year he needed more than an extra minute to run his distance.

On this particular morning he ran without any precise goal, without pushing himself, with no purpose other than enjoying the outdoors and feeling the harmonious working of his thirty-seven-and-a-half-year-old body.

He was even taking pleasure in musing that since he had now reached the middle of his life, the rest would be easy and full of excitement. Soon he would be two-thirds of the way through, then three-quarters. Never again would he be as bored as he had been between the third and the halfway mark.

Approaching the halfway point, the St Nicol River, he ran easily though without great speed. He was getting ready to cross the wooden bridge when he noticed a black silhouette against the frozen white bank of the river.

He slowed down. Sitting on a log, waving a short rod above a hole in the ice, someone was fishing in the river.

The fisherman suddenly raised his eyes towards him, as though he had sensed his presence.

Gonzague Gagnon stopped short. The fisherman was a woman. He had seen women fish before, but a woman fisherman alone, on the river—he had never seen that.

He decided to go closer and crossed the ditch at the edge of the road, aware of the snow working its way into his shoes. He advanced with difficulty, sinking to mid-thigh with each step.

Soon he was on the river. The wind had swept it clean of snow. The woman watched as he came near. He saw that she was beautiful. That frightened Gonzague Gagnon. He wanted to turn back. But what would she think after having seen him come towards her? That he was afraid?

Of course he was afraid. More and more afraid as the woman became more and more beautiful. What was he going to say to her?

He stopped a few steps away from her.

"Hello," he said.

"Hello."

"Are they biting?"

She didn't reply. Gonzague Gagnon only needed to look at the fish that surrounded her on the ice—ten perch and two pike. The most recently caught still flopped about before freezing and dying—or dying and freezing.

For a few moments he stood still, watching her. Suddenly the woman jerked her rod. Then she stood up and pulled out a beautiful perch, wriggling through the hole. Gonzague Gagnon moved forward to take the fish off the hook.

"I can do it," said the woman, removing her gloves.

Gonzague Gagnon stepped back. He would have liked to spend the day there, not speaking, just watching her. But he felt he should speak. He searched for a subject of conversation that would be interesting or, better still, would make him interesting.

"I'm a runner," he finally said.

"So it seems."

He ought to have added that he was an apprentice mechanic. But for the first time in his life, he was ashamed of his trade. Not that it suddenly seemed too humble. But too ordinary. Doubtless every village in the world had at least one apprentice mechanic, and maybe there were hundreds in the city that this woman came from—it seemed certain that she came from a city.

Again Gonzague Gagnon made his silent search for something to say. Then there was a faint trembling in the air, hardly noticeable.

"It's the train," thought Gonzague Gagnon, pricking up his ears.

In fact the trembling had become a deep and far-away rumbling.

"It's the passenger train," said Gonzague Gagnon.

The woman nodded her head distractedly. All of her attention was on the tip of her fishing rod, which she was shaking in brief staccato bursts.

Gonzague Gagnon turned to watch the train. It was now visible, and rapidly growing larger.

"I can stop trains," he said.

Immediately he regretted having spoken. The woman had given him a look that was both incredulous and indifferent, as if he were insane.

"I'm going to show her," he said to himself. And then, aloud: "You'll see."

But suddenly he feared that his power might have weakened with the passage of time. He ran towards the railway track, to be closer to the train.

A second doubt seized him: what if the young woman found his ability to stop trains absolutely useless? Would he not be more sure of impressing her if at the same time he demonstrated his courage?

He climbed the embankment and positioned himself on a railway tie, facing the train. The train was only about a hundred metres away. Gonzague Gagnon could feel the track vibrating beneath his feet. He waited a few seconds. Then he crossed his arms and closed his eyes.

"Stop," he said in a firm voice, loud enough for the young woman to hear.

The screeching of the wheels was enough to shatter his eardrums—but the noise reassured him of his power. The train came to a stop so close that he felt the heat of the engine on his cheeks.

He opened his eyes and looked towards the woman. She was still there, standing up, a black silhouette in the middle of her circle of fish. She was too far away for him to be able to see if she was watching him. But how could she not?

Voices drew his attention.

"This hasn't happened for years," Gonzague Gagnon heard one rough voice say.

A moment later he was facing two men in overalls.

"What are you doing?" the larger of the two asked him.

"I just wanted to stop the train," stammered Gonzague Gagnon.

"You think you're funny?" the big man asked.

The smaller of the two said nothing, but threw a punch at Gonzague Gagnon's nose.

This tiny fellow was a former boxing champion, which explains how Gonzague Gagnon was literally lifted from the earth. He flapped his arms in the air, expecting to land on the railway track or roll down the embankment.

But he was so close to the bridge that he fell into the river, in a place where the ice was thin.

He was immediately snatched up by the current. He tried to use his nails to grasp the rough surface of the ice above him: but the current was too strong. Then he said to himself that it would be better to let go and hold his breath: the open river wasn't far away and a fit man like himself had only to let himself be carried along under the ice until he was in the clear.

He stayed on his back in the water, pushing with his palms against the ice to make himself go more quickly.

He saw a long shadow across the ice and at the end of this shadow two darker patches. This must be the woman, he thought. Now he should tell her not to worry, that he would be back soon. But he reminded himself that he was under water. So he kept his mouth closed tight even though his lungs were beginning to burn. A few seconds later he decided to swallow just a little water, because that would be less painful than continuing to hold his breath.

Through the ice he saw the shadows of the great willow trees that flanked the river. He thought that he would soon be safe.

After that he saw nothing more.

"Impossible," he thought. "I am only halfway through my life."

When spring came Gaston Gagnon, who was religious, nailed a crossbar onto the stake which, on the other side of the river, had marked the halfway point of Gonzague Gagnon.

Charlie

BY LEE MARACLE

"No one but his wife knew how his thoughts ran. How he wondered with a gnawing tightness why it was he had to send his little ones, one after the other, far away to school."

Charlie was a quiet boy. This was not unusual. His silence was interpreted by the priests and Catholic lay teachers as stoic reserve—a quality inherited from his pagan ancestors. It was regarded in the same way the religious viewed the children's tearless response to punishment: a quaint combination of primitive courage and lack of emotion. All the children were like this and so Charlie could not be otherwise.

Had the intuitive sense of the priesthood been sharper they might have noticed the bitter look lurking in the shadows of the children's bland faces. The priests were not deliberately insensitive. All of their schooling had taught them that even the most heathen savage was born in the image of their own sweet lord. Thus, they held to the firm conviction that the sons and daughters of the people they were convinced were God's lowliest children were eternally good. Blinded by their own teaching they could not possibly be called upon to detect ill in the warm broad faces of their little charges.

Charlie did not do much schoolwork. He daydreamed. Much standing in the corner, repeated thrashings and the like had convinced him that staring out the window at the trees beyond the schoolyard was not the way to escape the sterile monotony of school. While the window afforded him the luxury of sighting a deer or watching the machinations of a bluejay trying to win the heart of his lady-bird fair, the thrashing he knew could be counted on for committing the crime of daydreaming was not worth the reward. So, like the other children, he would stare hard at his work, the same practised look of bewilderment used by his peers on his face, while his thoughts danced around the forest close to home—far away from the arithmetic sums he was sure had nothing to do with him.

He learned to listen for the questions put to him by the brother over the happy daydream. He was not expected to know the answer; repeating the question sufficed. Knowing the question meant that, like the others, he was slow to learn but very attentive. No punishment was meted out for thick-headedness.

"What is three multiplied by five, Charlie?" The brother's brisk, clipped English accent echoed hollowly in the silence.

Charlie's eyes fixed on the empty page. His thoughts followed the manoeuvres of a snowshoe hare scampering ahead of himself and his half-wild dog. The first snow had fallen. It was that time of the year. The question reached out to him over the shrieks of joy and the excited yelping of his dog, but it did not completely pluck him from the scene of his snow-capped, wooded homeland.

"Three... times... five?" muttered Charlie, the sounds coming out as though his voice were filled with air. A tense look from the brother. A quizzically dull look on Charlie's face. All the children stared harder at their pages—blank from want of work. He was still staring at the teacher but his mind was already following the rabbit. Did the brother's shoulders heave a sigh of disappointment?

"Thomas," the boredom of the teacher's voice thinly disguised.

"Fifteen," clearly and with volume. Poor Thomas, he always listened.

The bell rang. The class dutifully waited for dismissal. The brother sighed. The sound of scholarly confidence carefully practised by all pedagogues left his voice at each bell. Exasperation permeated his dismissal command. It was the only emotion he allowed himself to express.

As he stood by the doorway watching the bowed heads slink by, his thoughts wandered about somewhat. *Such is my lot, to teach a flock of numbskulls... Ah, had I only finished and gotten a degree. Then, I could teach in a real school with eager students.* Each day his thoughts read thus and every time he laid out plans to return to university, but he never carried them out. At home every night a waiting bottle of Seagram's drowned out his self-pity and steadied him for the morrow.

Charlie was bothered at meal times. The food was plain and monotonously familiar: beef stew on Monday, chicken stew on Tuesday—the days with their meal plan never varied. Unvarying menus did not bother Charlie though. Nor was it the plain taste of domestic meat as opposed to the sharp taste of wild meat that bothered him. He was bothered by something unidentifiable, tangible but invisible. He couldn't figure it out and that, too, bothered him.

From the line-up, he carried his plate to the section of the eating hall reserved for sixth grade boys. He looked up to watch the teenage boys exchanging flirtatious glances with the young girls in a line opposite them. In the segregated classes of the school, boys and girls weren't permitted to mingle with, talk to, or touch one another. They sat in the same eating hall, but ate on separate sides. Charlie bored quickly of watching the frustrated efforts of youth struggling to reach each other through the invisible walls of rigid moral discipline erected by the priesthood.

His eyes began wandering about the eating room of his own home. The pot of stew was on the stove. It always had something warm and satisfying to the taste in it. He scarcely acknowledged its existence before he came to residential school. Now he saw it each day at meal time.

At home no one served you or stopped you from ladling out some of the pot's precious contents. Here at school, they lined you up to eat. Each boy at each age level got exactly the same portion. A second plate was out of the question. He felt ashamed to eat.

A stiff-backed white man appeared in the room and the low murmuring of voices stopped.

"EAT EVER-Y-THING ON YOUR PLATE!" he bellowed, clicking out the last *t* on the word plate. His entrance never varied. He said the same thing every day, careful to enunciate each word perfectly and loudly, in the manner he was sure best befitted the station of principal of a school. He marched up and down the aisles between tables in a precise pattern that was designed to impress on the boys that he was, indeed, the principal of the school. Finished with the last aisle, he marched stiff-legged out the door.

The boys were more than impressed. They were terrified. They likened the stiff-legged walk to the walk of an angry wolf. They had come to believe that whites were not quite human, so often did they walk in this wolf-like way. They knew the man who had just pranced about the eating hall to be the principal, not by the superiority of his intellect as compared to the other instructors, but by virtue of his having the stiffest walk and, hence, the fiercest temperament of the pack.

Night came and Charlie prepared for the best part of his incarceration. Between prayers and lights out, the children were left alone for fifteen minutes. Quickly into pyjamas and to the window.

The moon and the stars spread a thin blue light over the whitening ground below. Crystal flake after crystal flake draped the earth in a frock of glittering snow. As always, a tightness arose in his small boy-chest. He swallowed hard.

"LIGHTS OUT!"

Darkness swallowed the room and his little body leapt for the bunk with a willingness that always amazed him. He did not sleep right away.

"Hay, Chimmy, you got your clothes on?"

"Yeh."

"Ah-got the rope."

"Keh."

Runaway talk! Charlie hurriedly grabbed some clothes from the cupboard beneath the top of the night-table he shared with another boy.

"Ah'm comin' too," he hissed, struggling to snap up his jeans and shirt.

"Hurry, we're not waitin'."

He rushed breathless to the closet and grabbed a jacket. The older boys had already tied the rope to the metal latticing that closed the window. Each boy squeezed through the square created by one missing strip of metal lattice, and hanging on to the rope, swung out from the window, then dropped to the ground below.

Safe in the bosom of the forest, after a tense but joyous run across the yard, the boys let go the cramped spirit that the priesthood so painstakingly tried to destroy in them. They whooped, they hollered, bayed at the moon, and romped about chucking snow in loose, small balls at each other.

Jimmy cautioned them that that was enough. The faster they moved the greater the head start. They had to get through the forest to the railroad tracks by night cover.

The trek was uneventful. The older boys had run away before and knew exactly where they were going and how to get there. Stars and a full moon reflected against white snow provided them with enough light to pick their way along. As time wore by, the excited walk became dull plodding. They reached the tracks of the railroad sometime near daylight. All were serious now. They cast furtive glances up and down the track. The shelter of darkness was gone. Discovery became real in the bright light of day. Surely the priest had sent the police in search of them by now.

The boys trod light-footed and quickly along the trackline, fear spurring them on. A thin wisp of smoke curling upward from the creaking pines on their right brought them to a halt.

"It's mah uncle's house," Jimmy purred with contentment. The empty forest carries sound a long way in winter, so the boys spoke in whispers. It never occurred to the other boys to ask Jimmy what his uncle's reaction to their visit would be. They assumed it would be the same as their own folks' response.

A short trek through the woods brought them to the cabin's door. Uncle and aunt were already there to greet them. They were now used to the frequent runaway boys that always stopped for a day or two, then not knowing how to get home, trudged the fifteen or so kilometres back to school. The holiday, uncle mused to aunt, would do them no harm. Besides which, they enjoyed the company of happy children.

A good meal... a day's play... nightfall... heavenly sleep in this cabin full of the same sweet smells of his own cabin brought sentimental dreams to Charlie.

Charlie's dreams followed the familiar lines of his home. In the centre stood his mama quietly stirring the stew. Above her head, hanging from the rafters, were strips of dried meat. Hundreds of them, dangling in mute testimony to his father's skill as hunter and provider. A little ways from the stove hung mama's cooking tools. Shelving and boxes made of wood housed such foodstuffs as flour, sugar, oatmeal, salt, and the like. All here was hewn from the forest's bounty by Charlie's aging grandfather.

Crawling and toddling about were his younger brother and sister, unaware of Charlie's world or his dream of them. Completing the picture was his dad. He stood in the corner, one leg perched on a log stump used as a kindling split. He had a smoke in his hand.

No one but his wife knew how his thoughts ran. How he wondered with a gnawing tightness why it was he had to send his little ones, one after the other, far away to school.

Daily, he heard of young ones who had been to school and not returned. More often, he would come across the boys who had recently finished school, hanging about the centre of the village, unwilling and poorly equipped to take care of themselves. Without hunting or trapping skills, the boys wasted away, living from hand-to-mouth, a burden on their aging parents. One by one they drifted away, driven by the shame of their uselessness.

It was not that they could not learn to hunt or trap. But it takes years of boyhood to grow accustomed to the ways of the forest, to overcome the lonely and neurotic fear it can sometimes create in a man. A boy who suddenly becomes a man does not want to learn what he is already supposed to know well. No man wants to admit his personal fear of his home.

The pull of years of priestly schooling towards the modern cities of a Canada that hardly touched their wilderness village grew stronger. For a while, family and city pulled with equal strength, gripping the youth in a listless state of paralysis. For some, the city won out and they drifted away. Charlie's father worried about the fate of his young ones.

His private agony was his own lack of resistance. He sent his son to school. It was the law. A law that he neither understood nor agreed to, but he sent them. His willingness to reduce his son to a useless waster stunned him. He confided none of his self-disgust to his wife. It made him surly but he said nothing.

In his dream, Charlie did not know his father's thoughts. He saw his father standing, leg-on-log, as he usually stood while he awaited breakfast, and he awoke contented.

Jimmy's uncle had given up wondering about the things that plagued Charlie's father. His children had grown up and left, never to return. He did not even know if there were grandchildren.

He lived his life without reflection now. Jimmy was the eldest son of his youngest brother. It was enough for his life's labours that this boy called him grandfather out of respect for the man's age.

"I'm going to check the short lines," he said, biting into his bannock and not looking at the boys.

"Can we help?" The older boys looked at their plates, studiously masking their anxiety.

"Sure." Staring at them carefully, he added, "but the small one must stay." The old man was unwilling to risk taking the coatless boy with him.

Charlie followed them to the edge of the woods. He knew that no amount of pleading would change the old man's mind and crying would only bring him shame. He watched them leave, and determined to go home where his own grandfather would take him to check his short lines.

The old aunt tried to get him to stay. She promised him a fine time. It was a wasted effort. He wanted the comfort and dignity of his own cabin, not a fine time.

Charlie knew the way home. It had not taken him long to travel the distance from the tracks near his home to the school. He had marked the trail in the way that so many of his ancestors might have: a rocky crag here, a distorted, lone pine there. He gave no thought to the fact that the eight-hour trip had been made by rail and not on foot.

The creaking pines, straining under the heavy snowfall of the night before, brought Charlie the peace of mind that school had denied him. A snow-bird feeding through the snow curled Charlie's mouth into a delighted smile. A rabbit scampered across the tracks and disappeared into the forest. He had half a mind to chase it.

"Naw, better just go home." His voice seemed to come from deep within him, spreading itself out in a wide half-circle and meeting the broad expanse of hill and wood only to be swallowed by nature's huge majesty somewhere beyond his eyes. The thinness of his voice against the forest made him feel small.

The day wore by tediously slow. Charlie began to worry. He had not seen his first landmark.

"Am I going the right way?" What a terrible trick of fate to trek so very far only to arrive back at school. The terror of it made him want to cry.

Around the bend, he recognized a bare stone cliff. Assured, he ran a little. He coughed and slowed down again. He tired a little. He felt sleepy. He touched his bare hands. Numb.

"Frostbite," he whispered.

In his rush to leave the dormitory he had grabbed his fall jacket. The cold now pierced his chest. Breathing was difficult. His legs cried out for rest. Charlie fought the growing desire to sleep.

The biscuits aunt had given him were gone. Hunger beset him. He trudged on, squinting at the sprays of sunlight that cast a reddish hue on the snow-clad pines in final farewell to daylight.

Darkness folded itself over the land with a cruel swiftness. It fell upon the landscape, swallowing Charlie and the thread of track connecting civilization to nature's vastness, closing with maddening speed the last wisps of light from Charlie's eyes.

Stars, one by one, woke from their dreamy sleep and filled the heavens. Charlie stumbled. He rose reluctantly. His legs wobbled forward a few more steps, then gave in to his defeated consciousness that surrendered to the sparkling whiteness surrounding him. He rolled over and lay face up, scanning the star-lit sky.

Logic forsook him. His heart beat slower. A smile nestled on his full purple lips. He opened his eyes. His body betrayed him. He felt warm again. Smiling he welcomed the Orion queen—not a star constellation but the great Wendigo—dressed in midnight blue, her dress alive with the glitter of a thousand stars. Arms outstretched, he greeted the lady that came to lift his spirit and close his eyes forever to sleep the gentle sleep of white death.

On the Eve of Uncertain Tomorrows

BY NEIL BISSOONDATH

This story gives insight into how people wait on the doorstep of Canada. A man who has been persecuted and tortured in some unnamed country in Latin America waits to see if he will be accepted into Canada as a refugee. This is a disturbing story. It describes terrible violence. Yet many families from other countries can tell similar stories.

"Miguel says, 'If Canada will not give Flavio a visa, then God will.'"

It is the violence of beating wings that attracts Joaquin's attention.

Two pigeons, colour only hinted at in the half-light, press in fluttering desperation against the chickenwire enclosing the little wooden balcony. They are too engrossed in battle to notice him at the open door. The air—though soft with the underlying warmth of the spring Jeremy Windhook, the lawyer, says is coming—feels cold, and he folds his arms against its subtle bite.

The wings of the birds flare like pouncing condors, the male—Joaquin now understands—pinning the female beneath him. He sinks his beak into her neck feathers, inflicting submission; steadies himself and, avoiding the ineffectual battering of her wings, awkwardly mounts her.

In the distance, past the complex geometry of withered buildings—garages, storerooms, walls of tin and brick—pressing in on the rear of the rooming-house, the colourless towers of a few tall buildings of the city sit one-dimensional against the sky. They suggest an unknown life, a world of blood and flesh and everyday ambition, a life within his sight but not, still, yet, within his grasp.

The wings scratch and scrape at the wire, batter at it. Create, in their terrified clamour, a raucous plea for escape.

His heart races, temples engorge with blood. Lucidity slips, his mind an ungraspable swirl, as he steps out onto the balcony, knowing for the moment nothing but the noise of the birds.

Slaps at the wire with the back of his open hand.

To no sound, no effect.

They cannot—will not—take note of his protest.

He stands back. Horrified. Witness, in the quiet of the morning, to unwilling coupling, an avian rape. It is the way of nature, he tries telling himself. But they are unattractive birds, with panicky, red-rimmed eyes, and this lack of beauty denies them his sympathy: they call to mind infection, physical corruption.

It is all over in seconds. The male has answered the call of nature, the female has been violated. Then, unconcerned, their congress concluded, they wing away in separate directions, are quickly swallowed by the dark grey sky.

Only then does it occur to Joaquin that the wire netting wrapped around the balcony is there not to keep the pigeons in but to keep them out, its function reversed. And he is the one confined, by the chicken wire and by so much more.

"They say that the waiting is the worst thing." Amin, who says he will one day take the name Thomson, carefully pours the boiled coffee into their cups. "But it is not so, I believe." Joaquin silently admires Amin's delicacy, the economy with which he speaks, moves, handles objects, as if he has an abhorrence of excess.

Amin, usually not an early riser, has been up for a while, fussing and puttering in the bathroom. His curly black hair glistens with a shampooed freshness. His every movement tosses off a perfume that conjures for Joaquin a sweet but sweaty armpit. Amin is wearing the outfit that Jeremy Windhook brought him last week: a simple white shirt, pleated trousers, dark socks. It is a specific look that Jeremy Windhook seeks, that of a genteel poverty, an effect he must labour over for people like Amin, who, in their hunger, can so easily look brigand-like. Amin has taken special care this morning. He has showered, he has shaved, he has even clipped his nose hairs—for today, Joaquin knows, is his tomorrow; today is the day that will determine whether tonight he celebrates, or whether tonight he cries.

"The waiting is simple, after what we have been through." The words swish easily from between his barely parted lips, as if he speaks only with his tongue. "The hard part is not knowing what tomorrow will bring for me. Where will I be? What will I do? Will I be happy, or will I be sad?" He lets the condensed milk flow long and thick into his coffee, stirs it without letting the spoon clink against the side of the cup. "These are sad questions, my friend, to ask about tomorrow. No man should have to ask them, I believe."

Joaquin takes his coffee cup in both hands, blinks rapidly at the steam as he raises it to his lips.

"You did not sleep last night," Amin says.

Joaquin smiles minutely at him. The coffee is bitter, the boiled grounds gritty between his teeth.

"I see it in your eyes, my friend. It is not good, I believe." He sips from his cup, adds, "Eh?" Amin has an ear for language. The exclamation is one of his new acquisitions. Joaquin thinks he is having an affair with one of the secretaries in Jeremy Windhook's office, although Amin says she is only helping him with his English.

Joaquin gives him a thin smile, an acknowledgement of his concern. But he is not sure how he really feels about Amin; he's too self-confident, in the sly way of the street-survivor. Joaquin worries when Amin claims a communality of experience with him. He has never spoken to Amin of his life, has listened with silent skepticism to Amin's eagerly offered autobiography of civil war, starvation, forced conscription. Joaquin wonders whether Jeremy Windhook has told Amin his story; but Jeremy Windhook has never mentioned any of his other clients to Joaquin, so he has no reason to believe this. He thinks instead that Amin is simply assuming the comradeship of those involved in the same enterprise. It is, he thinks, a sign of Amin's struggle with his isolation, the isolation they all share.

Amin reaches into the cupboard for a box of crackers, stuffs two into his mouth with one hand as the other digs into the box for more. He no longer bothers to offer them to Joaquin, knows he does not like their salty dryness.

In the silence disturbed only by Amin's crunching, Joaquin wonders whether he should tell him about the pigeons—it seems somehow important—but Amin's camouflaged nervousness reveals itself in the desperation of his jaw. Joaquin knows that his tale of the pigeons will force Amin's natural melancholia to the surface, will smother his summoned ebullience. So he says nothing.

This day has no dawn.

It is the sun, in any case, and not mechanical precision that marks Joaquin's sense of time. Midday or midnight on his illuminated alarm clock is meaningless. So it is only with the lightening of the sky, its dimming of the lights in the distant buildings, that the day after tomorrow truly becomes tomorrow.

Tomorrow: it is like a forbidden woman, enticing, creeping into his daydreams, invading his fantasies. It robs him of sleep, grates his nerves into a fearful impotence.

It was earlier, when he couldn't stir except with the greatest of effort, when the stillness that gripped his body threatened to harden into a conscious permanence, that he struggled from the clasp of the blankets and trudged the cool confines of his room. He was thankful, in those moments of struggle, for the nightlight—the glowing Mickey Mouse face Jeremy Windhook's little daughter no longer needs—that held the darkness at bay. Joaquin cannot abide darkness. He has had too much of it, has experienced too intimately the concrete and imagined terrors of it. So he stalked his room in the thin glow, three paces one way, three paces the other, the scuffed boards squeaking like mice underfoot.

Stalked through the figures and effigies of nighttime evocations: the slow tearing of nails from fingers, the cracking of bone, the bite of saw-toothed metal into nipple. Liquid coursed thick and warm across his stomach. The gurgle of strangulated breath caught his throat, a blindfolded darkness pressed in on his eyes. Pain came in vivid memory, flushing hot and cold through his belly and into his chest. His hands throbbed, nipples burned—

Space: he let himself quietly out of the room, padded through the darkened corridor to the kitchen. To the tyranny of shadowed things: the fridge, the stove, the sharp angles of cupboards. The tap dripped rhythmically, maddeningly, into the aluminum sink. He tried the light, but it wouldn't work—the bulb had blown the day before and no one had bothered to change it—and so he opened the door to the little balcony, for space, for air, for escape from the demons of his mind.

Amin, satisfied, belches contentedly into his cupped palm. In the webby light, the hairs on the back of his hands and fingers stand out like stiff, black bristles. He offers more coffee and Joaquin accepts with a nod of his head. Amin refills the cup, careful not to pour in too much of the sediment. He empties the grounds into the sink, rinses the pot, places it on the counter; turns on the stove and, hands clenching and unclenching in his pant-pockets, waits for the burner to redden.

From within the house float the distant stirrings of the awakening others: doors and floorboards creaking, the splash of water and the tremble of old pipes, throats discreetly cleared. They are seven in all, the Magnificent Seven, as Jeremy Windhook mumbles in moments of exasperation: Joaquin, Amin, a Vietnamese couple, a Haitian, a Sikh, a Sri Lankan. Except for the Vietnamese couple—the man restless, the woman watchful, the two hard-eyed in the way of the ravenous—who spend much time walking the streets of the city, the others keep to themselves, frittering time away in newspapers, television, comic books, or the solitary flipping of cards. Joaquin prefers it this way—life has taught him that the friendliest smile may conceal the sharpest teeth—but he is secretly grateful, too, for Amin's extroversion, the ease of his conversation, the way he will begin talking as if he has been asked a question when he has not been—or as if he is anticipating the questions he may be asked and is eager to provide the answers. Amin fills empty time, provides distraction, but not in the impersonal way of the television; this is what Joaquin appreciates about him, why Joaquin will sit and listen to him, watch the graceful and communicative gestures of his hands, watch his smoke turn the air a soft blue-grey.

Amin takes a cigarette from his shirt pocket, holds the unfiltered end to the glowing element until a thin curl of smoke rises from it. Flicking off the stove, he pulls carefully at the cigarette, encouraging the fire, sucking until the end glows healthily and smoke billows from his nostrils. Sitting on the chair with an uncommon energy, he crosses his legs, looks intently at Joaquin through narrowed eyes, says, "I will tell you why Thomson."

Joaquin already knows why Amin says he will one day change his name to Thomson, but he does not interrupt, for to do so would be to disrupt Amin's optimism, his insistent planning for tomorrow; and thus to disrupt his own. And what else do they have, people like him and Amin and the Vietnamese and the Haitian, but fantasies of tomorrow, how it will be, how they will be? Besides, he likes the deliberation Amin has brought to the enterprise. It shows an initiative he wishes he himself had.

"Because no other name will do, I believe." He sucks at the cigarette held between thumb and index finger. "Canadian people respect certain names, but sometimes they fear them, too. Names of men who are rich and who are bright—maybe too bright, eh? Rich, bright men must not expect popularity in this world."

Joaquin nods in agreement. Amin speaks like a man of the world, a man who understands much beyond his circumscribed experience—and who is he, this Joaquin, electrician by profession, union organizer by necessity, to contradict him? So he listens to Amin, believes he is learning something useful.

"So Thomson it will be. Rich, and bright, no doubt. But not a name that makes simple people—what is the word?—thrimble?"

Joaquin nods again. He thinks of the word *temblar*, raises a quivering hand before him.

"Yes, it is thrimble, I believe. This, the name Thomson does not do to simple people. Respect, yes, and admiration. But thrimble, no. So this is who I will be, eh? Amin Thomson, Canadian."

Joaquin smiles thinly at Amin, envies him his certainties.

Amin goes to his room to finish getting dressed. The Vietnamese couple—eyes of a hounded intelligence—come quietly in. With a challenging glare at Joaquin, they slam the balcony door shut and—an eye always on Joaquin—wolf down a couple of peanut-butter sandwiches. They are gone after only a few minutes.

The Sikh, his hair twisted into a knot on top of his head, comes in, makes coffee, and drinks it sitting across the table from Joaquin. They nod at each other, but neither speaks.

Outside, the day proceeds through heavy cloud. Pigeons, soaring in the distance, present swift silhouettes.

To Joaquin, the day already feels old.

He looks at his hands, as he does at least once every day. They continue to heal. Slowly. Very slowly. They will never be as they were before, although the doctors tell him greater flexibility will return in time. He will never again hold a screwdriver or a pen—it is how they put it, confirming the expertise of those responsible—but he may, with patience, be able to type.

Jeremy Windhook, a solemn young man intent on evidence, proof, *the full story,* tells him with no hint of irony to look on the bright side. Show them your hands at the hearing, he says, keep them in plain sight, *front and centre*. They have never seen hands like yours. Let them see the fleshy cavities where once there were fingernails, let them see the knotty lumps of crushed knuckles left untended, show them the scars on the back where once flesh was sliced through to the whiteness of bone. Throw the scars at them, he says, bring home to them the enthusiasm with which your hands have been redesigned. Evidence, yes. Dramatic and irrefutable. Jeremy Windhook cannot see his hands without blanching, but it is as if he is in love with them, he speaks of them like a teenager ruminating on imminent coitus: with fascination, with fear.

And what more do you want, Mr. Lawyer? Joaquin thinks. Maybe that I sit there naked so they see the greater mutilation? The hardened welts on back, chest, buttocks?

Tell them about the whip of steel cable, he urges.

The tattoo of cigarette burns on my stomach?

Marlboros, weren't they?

The circle of ragged flesh that has replaced my left nipple?

Make them feel the bite of the sharpened pliers.

All the practised disfigurement to which I have been subjected, Jeremy Windhook?

But no, Jeremy Windhook has had pictures taken, from every angle. His briefcase is stuffed with medical reports—the language cool and factual, menus of distress that Joaquin has seen—detailing anal violation, organ disruption, bodily dysfunction. It is amazing, Jeremy Windhook says—with fear, with fascination—that he survived.

Joaquin is relieved when, as the Sikh leaves, Amin returns. He is wearing the sombre grey jacket that is the final touch to the outfit Jeremy Windhook has provided. He sits and laces up his shoes. They are of brown leather, do not match the rest of his clothes, but they are freshly shined. He has decided not to wear the tie. Ties, like nooses, make him nervous. "Do you know, Hakim—" It is Amin's name for Joaquin, his closest approximation. "—that it takes thirty-five gallons of sap to make one gallon of maple syrup?"

"Sap" is not a word Joaquin knows.

"It is juice from a tree," Amin explains. "They take it the way doctors take blood. Then they boil it to make a sweet syrup. It is a Canadian delicacy, I believe."

Joaquin knows where Amin gets all this information, from his friend the secretary and from the newspapers he is always reading. He hopes that one day he, too, will acquire such knowledge.

Amin suddenly stares at him. His eyes, of a glittery and undiluted black, are steady and imploring. "You know, Hakim," he says, his voice breaking, "you know."

Joaquin nods: he knows.

"It is not too much to ask, I believe. A simple life. Khappiness. We forget to enjoy it when we have it, we let it wash over us like water—and then it is gone. If only we knew how to record it, like a film, so that we can recall it and comfort ourselves with the memory. But our brain—it is not strong enough. Khorror will come back with all its power. Khorror will frighten us many months later. But khappiness? Khappiness many months later will make us sad. This is the thing, Hakim. We, you and me, have too many prisons—" He taps at his temple with a finger. "—here." His breathing goes raucous. "We must learn how to make the keys, Hakim, for when our tomorrow comes."

If our tomorrow comes, Joaquin thinks but does not say, for he wants to believe Amin is right yet fears, too, to believe it.

The front door bell buzzes twice. Amin glances at his watch. "Jeremy Windhook," he says.

They hear the door being opened, the Haitian's gravelly voice greeting the lawyer.

Amin stands up tucking his shirt more neatly into his pants. He buttons the jacket, runs his hands through his hair. "Well?" he says.

Joaquin examines him, finds him stiff-looking. He reaches out and undoes the jacket button.

Just before Amin leaves, he glances through the window at the sky. The clouds are thinning, beginning to break up. "Look, Hakim," he says, "the sun! It is a good sign, I believe, eh?"

Joaquin stands up. He cannot speak. Instead, he offers his damaged hand and, for long seconds, they share a firm handshake.

The day advances steadily into the forecaster's prediction of bulky cloud rifting into periods of delicate sunlight. The streets are dry. Cars rumble by spouting music, tires gritty on the asphalt. A sheet of errant paper, whipped along in the wake of the traffic, rasps on the sidewalk. The air teems with sharp, clean sounds unfamiliar from his months of winter waiting.

Joaquin removes his mittens, unzips his parka, the perspiration that is like that of fever drying instantaneously under his clothes. His senses awaken then, nudged through the heaviness of his fatigue into a heightened mindfulness.

There are people all around, people hungry for the sun like prisoners emerging into a prison yard after a too-long, too-dark night. They lounge smoking on benches in snowbound parks, they haul chairs onto their tiny balconies to read or to daydream. Coats are bundled, convertibles converted, sunglasses unfolded. A man and a woman walk by, arms around each other. The woman says, "Spring's around the corner." The man, with a laugh, replies, "Yeah, but it's a big corner."

Joaquin smiles at the little joke. He is enjoying the growing lightness in his legs. He has always been sensitive to weather and is pleased—it is like a sign of a returning normalcy—to find his body reacting with such vigour. For the first time, he feels the city to be a friendly place, an entity apart—so different from the sterile and hermetic offices of officialdom that he cannot imagine the immigration officers he has encountered leading normal lives, relaxing in sidewalk cafés or hugging loved ones. He knows that they must: knows that they watch television, read newspapers, make love. But the implications of their professional functions are, to him, too enormous. Surely they must be immigration officers all the time, as doctors must be doctors all the time, or policemen policemen all the time. So it is, he thinks, so it must be with all people who wield the powers of life and death.

Soon he has left behind the snappier streets, the expensive boutiques and neon-signed cafés and renovated condominiums giving way, as he approaches St-Laurent, to stretches of run-down housing, Korean supermarkets, Portuguese restaurants. The laneways, bordered by crumbling garages, are still dense with snow and dirty ice. Two men in bloodstained lab coats—like morgue attendants, he thinks, clearing the site of a vigorous massacre—unload slabs of fresh-cut meat from a delivery van, while a young boy, attention wandering, sprays a jet of water at the sidewalk.

He turns right at St-Laurent—which Jeremy Windhook calls Saint Lawrence—and walks hurriedly up its length, the crowds here denser, more intent on their business; past the cut-rate stores and dark restaurants, the specialty-food shops and the sex cinema, turning off at last into a quieter street of curtained windows and peeling doors and, quickly, in a movement that feels furtive, into the shadowed cocoon of *La Barricada*.

Miguel, ever watchful, spots him the moment he enters, nods to him, his eyes only slowly losing their suspicion. Satisfied, he puts the beer flute down on the counter and turns away, to prepare, Joaquin knows, two glasses of his spiced coffee.

Miguel keeps his eyes open; is owner, bartender, cook, and watchman all rolled into one. He has installed a bell that warns him when the door is opening; looks for grim men in jackets and ties with badges to flash. They have never come, but all the regulars know that, should Miguel break the beer flute, those who must are to use the door to the second floor in the common washroom while the others, feigning fear, create diversion by heading for the rear exit. It is not a perfect system, but it is a system; it offers a fighting chance—and that, Joaquin appreciates, is all that anyone truly wants.

It is a curious place, small, with whitewashed walls and fake beams overhead, bits and pieces of his country, his continent, scattered around. Baskets hang from the ceiling, shawls cling to the walls, drums and Pan flutes dangle from crooked nails. Travel posters show Andean heights, Machu Picchu, the modernistic sterility of Brasilia. Quietly, as if wafting in from a great distance, the sad music of the mountains lingers just out of reach, a fading memory even before you can seize it.

On one wall, someone has painted lace curtains framing an open window. Through it stretches a field of trimmed grass, trees, flowers, and, in the distance, stark against a perfect and unreal sky, a line of women colourfully dressed but strangely lifeless. Joaquin finds it a profoundly unsettling work, a vision of a rural paradise in which humans are trespassers. A beautiful and angry work, a work of despair. He sits always with his back to it.

Miguel brings the coffees over, the empty beer flute balanced between them; sits in front of Joaquin with elbows on the table, chin resting on his interlaced fingers. He is a handsome man, his curly black hair, infrequently cut, generously sprinkled with silver. He sleeps little, always looks tired; tends *La Barricada* until late at night, then works into the early hours of morning at the jewellery he fashions as a lucrative hobby. It is these bracelets and earrings and intricate necklaces of silver that keep *La Barricada* afloat; he wholesales them to jewellery shops on St-Denis, enters the profits into the café's books as dinners served and coffees consumed. He sips at the coffee, licks his lips. "You heard about Flavio?" he says in a flat voice.

Joaquin thinks of the sad-eyed young man he's often seen sitting by himself in a corner of the café. Remembers his discomfort at Flavio's hermetic absorption.

The truth is that Joaquin would not come here if he felt he had a choice. The furniture, of worn wood, is too decrepit, lends the place a dismal air, emphasizes somehow its sense of spirit broken into timidity. It is like a closet for the soul, built for containing dusty memories of lives long lost, for perpetuating the resentments of politics long past. Here, he thinks, there is no tomorrow; here, yesterday becomes forever.

"They're sending him back."

Back—a fearful word.

Yet where else is he to go? A chic café on St-Denis? A glitzy bar on Ste-Catherine? He's tried doing both, but in each everyone—or, at least, so it seemed—noticed his hands. Here, too, they are taken note of, but the response is not of questions or queasiness. No, here his hands are accepted as simply part of the universal damage; they evoke no shy curiosity, no willed sympathy, no embarrassed revulsion. Everyone either has endured more or knows of someone who has. And everyone has loved ones who have been, as Miguel says, "thrown through the Devil's Doorway." It is why he is drawn to *La Barricada*, why he feels safer here than anywhere else.

"They say he wasn't involved in enough union activity."

Enough—what is enough?

"Not enough to endanger his life."

Joaquin shivers, twice.

More reason for discomfort: in the corner where Flavio sat, a young woman, Teresa, whom everyone calls Tere, sits biting her nails, or rather not her nails—they are too eaten down for that—but the flesh around them. Joaquin has seen the blood on her fingertips. Miguel has told him Tere's story. They had their Canadian papers, Tere, her husband, and their two children; but on the night before their departure, with their farewell party in full swing, the door burst open. There were scuffles and screams, a brief burst of machine-gun fire; and her husband was gone. Embassy officials reacted quickly; saw Tere and the children safely onto the plane north, lodged a protest with the government, and demanded that a search be launched for her husband. But they knew—Tere knew—that all the official steps were just a cruel bureaucratic joke.

So Tere arrived, distraught, with the bewildered children; was met by a social worker who took her to a furnished apartment, left her there with mimed instructions—Tere spoke no English, the social worker no Spanish—that she was to prepare dinner for the children. The social worker returned an hour later, to find the apartment thick with smoke and the legs from two of the dining-room chairs smouldering in a cooking fire in the middle of the living room. Someone thought of calling Miguel, and it was up to him to tell Tere, two days later, that her husband had been found thrown through the Devil's Doorway. They had identified him by his ring and clothes; it was all they had to go on, considering the condition of his head and fingers.

Miguel made arrangements. A woman he knew in the community looks after the children while Tere attends English classes or, as she has taken more and more to doing, while she comes here to *La Barricada*. It has been six months, and Miguel doesn't have the heart to force her to do what he knows she should be doing. She is torn, Miguel has told him, between returning to her country, where she still has family, and staying here, where her children have a future. She is, Miguel feels, herself seeing the outlines of the Devil's Doorway through the writhing of her demons.

Miguel says, "If Canada will not give Flavio a visa, then God will." Miguel is, in a curious and personal way, a religious man. He can, for hours and with feeling, quote the poetry of the Nicaraguan Cardenal.

Three men huddle in another corner. Two of them are crouched over the hand of the third who sits bolt upright in the chair, eyes shut, lips grimly set. On the table beside them are a box of bandages, a roll of cotton wadding, a bottle of rubbing alcohol, a pair of scissors, and an open package of razor blades.

With a twist of his eyebrows, Joaquin asks Miguel what they are up to.

"Medical care." Francisco, he explains, cut his hand badly at work a couple of weeks before. He was washing dishes, a glass broke. He had no choice but to go to the Emergency. When they asked him for his medical insurance card, he said he'd forgotten it at home. They sewed up the cut, and warned him to bring the card the next time, when he went to have the stitches removed. Francisco was already paying fifty dollars a week to use someone else's social insurance number, and the man wanted two hundred for use of the medical card. Francisco couldn't afford it, so his friends—one a hospital orderly—were removing the stitches for him. The nightmare, Miguel adds, is if an appendix bursts....

In the corner, Francisco draws a sharp and lengthy breath.

Joaquin thinks: just another day at *La Barricada*. He knows, and appreciates, that he is among the least damaged, least desperate of Miguel's clients. It is maybe, in the end, why he continues to come here, not just for himself but for Miguel, too.

Miguel prepares lunch for everyone, cheese sandwiches with sticks of carrot. Tere remains at her table, nibbles at the food. Francisco's friends have to leave and Francisco, his right hand roughly bandaged, joins Joaquin and Miguel.

As they eat, Francisco complains about the man whose social insurance number he is using. He is a blackmailer, he says, this man who seemed so sympathetic at the beginning. Even though Francisco has not been able to work for two weeks, the man continues to demand his weekly money, is threatening to tip off Immigration if he is not paid in full.

"Who is this man?" Miguel asks.

"Just a man," Francisco replies.

Joaquin, eating, listening, appreciates Francisco's reticence, understands it. He knows—from the moment his mother's phone call reached him too late at work; through the hours? days? of darkness to the unexplained release, followed by the harrowing weeks of movement and concealment during the transit north—what it is to be an illegal, understands the fears that lead to continuous vagueness and, eventually, to an invented self. He wonders what Francisco's real name is and for several minutes, as Francisco and Miguel dissect the situation, he tries different names, looking for the one that best matches Francisco's face. It is a haggard face, older than its years, severely scarred by acne; a face that Joaquin could only learn to trust in time. He is neither a Juan nor an Antonio, Joaquin decides, nor a Raul nor an Andres. Luis is too soft, Carlos too round. Alberto, Federico, Mario, Manuel—none quite fits. And then, as he finishes the first half of his sandwich, it comes to him: Francisco has the face of a Jorge.

Jorge. The name echoes in his head, the consonants a harsh whisper. His hands begin to throb and he is forced to drop the carrot stick he has picked up. Francisco and Miguel glance quizzically at him, but return to their conversation after he forces a smile. He tries clenching his hands in his lap—their stiffness prevents the forming of a fist, he can squeeze only so far—but the pain he feels is not a physical one, will not go away so easily.

The pliers, Jorge. No, not those. The smaller ones.

It was his mother who came to him in those moments of searing pain, her teary face alternating with a darkness deeper than that of the blindfold.

You see how he clenches his fist, Jorge. He knows what we want to do, don't you, friend?

A face ageing instantaneously at the news of a daughter's dismemberment. A darkness sparkling with comets and exploding stars.

Any sharp knife will do. You just pull it down, from the wrist towards the fingers. See? Everything opens up. Including the fist.

Dark hairs greying before his eyes. The darkness growing brittle.

You put the pliers just so, getting a tight grip. If he's a nailbiter you have to push it into the flesh, but we're lucky with this one, he's not the nervous type, are you my friend? So you work it as you wish, a quick tug—

Face dissolving. Darkness shattering.

—or a slow twist, ripping it away—

Colours, and a roaring in the head.

—either way is effective.

Then only the face, smiling a soothing smile.

Jorge.

A long silence. Then—

Miguel: "Ten minutes?"

Francisco: "At least."

"Maybe a problem with the stomach—"

"Fifteen, even."

"That long?"

"Maybe longer—"

"Joaquin?"

"Yes—"

"Well? Ten, fifteen, longer?"

"Yes, possibly."

Miguel's eyes flicker at him—an annoyed, inquisitive look, a look that in an instant realizes, absorbs, questions Joaquin's distance—then focus on a point past him.

Joaquin turns: a plate with an untouched sandwich, an empty chair pushed back from its table. He realizes how distant he has been, he never noticed Tere leaving.

Miguel considers the chair, the nail of his little finger working at a piece of food stuck between his front teeth.

Francisco drains his beer, draws the back of his hand across his lips. He, too, but with less intensity, considers the empty chair. "So," he says.

"So," Miguel echoes.

Joaquin looks from one to the other. His hands, forgotten, relax in his lap, the pain ebbing.

Miguel dislodges the piece of food, flicks it to the floor. Abruptly pushes himself from the table. The beer flute tips, teeters, crashes onto the table top. He frowns at the pieces of broken glass. And then he is running, knocking chairs out of his way.

Blows of his fist on echoing wood.

Joaquin turns, to look.

Miguel is kicking in the bathroom door.

The stickiness that will not wash away from his hands dries quickly in the cold air.

The sidewalks are less crowded now, the streets busy with home-bound traffic. The sky, in the glow of the setting sun, is a brittle, icy blue.

Joaquin walks slowly along with his hands secure in his coat pockets, the air washing cool and fresh through his lungs. He feels good, strong; enjoys a physical self-possession too long absent.

On impulse, he stops in at a fruit and vegetable store, buys a couple of oranges. The woman smiles as she hands him his change, and he realizes with a gentle jolt that he feels less distant from these people now, strangers become a little less strange not through any act of their own but—in a twist he cannot understand—through an act of *his* own: in this city, he has helped save a life.

It was his fingers, useless for so much, that Miguel pressed to the cuts on Tere's wrists, his parka snatched from the back of his chair that Francisco threw around her shoulders. Miguel and Francisco, faces glistening with sweat, fingers nimble and efficient, worked quickly with the cotton wadding and bandages.

Tere didn't fight, sat flaccid on the toilet cover, glazed eyes passively watching them. She had rested her hands on the edge of the sink but, growing weaker, hadn't been able to hold them there. The tiled floor was slick with blood.

Francisco's bandage came loose. Joaquin saw the fragile bleeding of the wound, pinpricks of blood forming on the pulpy skin. Francisco ignored it in the greater urgency, and Joaquin thought with a prickling shame of his judgement of him. This intensity, this urge to heal: he was wrong: Francisco was not a Jorge, he just had a misleading face.

Afterwards, Tere begged them in a voice weakened and fearful not to abandon her to the hospital. Her verb struck them all, prompted among them glances of uncertainty. They had stanched the blood flow and Miguel, soothing, reassuring, murmured his assent. While Francisco disinfected and rebandaged his own wound, Joaquin and Miguel helped her upstairs, to the bare room in which those who had to could take refuge. She curled up on a mattress on the floor, one hand resting lightly in the other. Miguel gently checked her bandages and, glancing backwards at her, led Joaquin from the room back down the narrow stairs. He would keep her there, he said, would make the necessary arrangements for the children.

Miguel cleared away the broken glass, poured them each a beer. They drank in silence, absorbed. *La Barricada* seemed to have gone inert. The music was off, there was nothing to say.

Eventually, with nothing more than a nod, Francisco left. Joaquin put aside his unfinished glass of beer, offered to help Miguel clean up the bathroom. Miguel refused with a shake of his head; he seemed, in the aftermath, to have no defence against his fatigue; said he would close the place for a few hours, work at his jewellery.

Joaquin walks along, the oranges tucked into the belly of his half-zipped parka. He is not unhappy that Miguel refused his offer. He did not, in truth, relish the thought of returning to the washroom. Much prefers being out here on the sidewalk, in the grip of his sense of having taken a vital step, looking in on the bars and cafés and little restaurants moodily lit behind glass, at the warmth and suggested security of their growing animation.

He lengthens the way back to the house, following streets never before followed, turning left or right or retracing his steps on pure impulse. As the sky darkens into night, windows frame lamplit scenes of comfort and domesticity: a couple preparing salad; two children tugging at a toy; a man absent-mindedly twirling a glass of red wine by candlelight; a woman shuffling through papers in her briefcase. Joaquin drinks them in, these little domestic spectacles; they are so trivial, so inconsequential, so attractive in their banality. And as he watches a cat prancing in pleasure at the opening of a food can, Amin's words come forcefully back to him: *A simple life. Khappiness.*

A faint throb in his hands: is it too much to ask?

In the sitting room, the radio is on low in the background. The Haitian and the Sri Lankan, both slight, shy men, are hunched over the coffee table playing cards. They glance up without interest as Joaquin comes in, watch without acknowledgement as he removes his parka.

He wonders whether Amin has returned yet, but thinks it best not to ask. It would be like prying, would be frowned upon.

In the kitchen, the Vietnamese couple stands guard over a vigorously bubbling pot. They do not take kindly to his looking in so he goes to his room, puts on the overhead light, and sits on the edge of the bed. His mood, seized in the peculiar tensions of the house, robbed of air by the confines of the room, begins to evaporate. A familiar unease reasserts itself, a vice tightening in his intestines. He takes an orange, nips off chunks of the rind, chews them, the tanginess puckering the fleshy insides of his mouth, invading his nasal passages. It is not a pleasant taste, but is one he has grown to appreciate: for a week during his journey north, fresh oranges were his only sustenance; there was no part he could afford not to consume. The flavour calms him and he closes his eyes, returning in imagination to the scenes witnessed long minutes before. The salad, the toy, the wine glass. The cat circling in hungry anticipation—

The buzz of the doorbell jars him back to his room. He listens: the front door is opened, voices murmur.

Careful footsteps approach his door. He thinks: Amin. Drops the orange onto the bed, stands up, opens the door at the first knock.

No, not Amin. Jeremy Windhook. A jacket is draped over his arm. "For tomorrow," Jeremy Windhook says, holding the jacket out to him. "Eight a.m. sharp. Be ready."

Joaquin takes the jacket, recognizes it. "And Amin?" he says.

Jeremy Windhook hesitates. Then: "Amin was refused."

"Refused?"

"They've classified him an economic refugee."

"*No entiendo.*" Joaquin thinks: Are you less a refugee, Jeremy Windhook, if you are in danger of dying from hunger rather than a bullet?

"He doesn't qualify under the UN definition. He'll be deported tomorrow."

"To his country?"

"To Germany."

"Germany? Why Germany?"

"Because he made his way here from there."

"But if they say he is in no danger in his own country, why do they not send him back there?"

"Because—" He shakes his head. "Because it's the rule."

"Why, Jeremy Windhook? Tell me why."

"I don't know why."

"Is it so that another country will do the dirty work for them? The Germans will send him back to his own country, I believe." As he says the last words, Joaquin hears Amin's voice. "And he will die."

Jeremy Windhook says nothing in reply, silently eyes Joaquin.

"You can do nothing?"

"Nothing."

The word hangs hollow in the room.

Jeremy Windhook turns, leaves.

Joaquin tosses the jacket onto the bed. He sees Amin in a room he cannot imagine. He is sitting, his face in his hands, in despair: "Amin Thomson," he whispers. "My name is Amin Thomson." Joaquin swallows hard, wipes his eyes on his sleeve. Picks up the orange and makes his way to the kitchen.

The light is off. All that remains of the Vietnamese is the lingering odour of their dinner. He goes to the door, stands, looks out. His hands throb, and he watches for the pigeons, waits for the dawn, here on the eve of his uncertain tomorrows.

Night Flight to Attiwapiskat

BY PAULETTE JILES

"Marya wondered if there was an emergency-locator transmitter in the nose and then started thinking about survival gear. The pilots were all supposed to travel with gear, like those clever little folding saws, and an axe, and sleeping bags, snowshoes and so on. If this guy hadn't raised Attiwapiskat and hadn't filed a flight plan, God knows what he had in his emergency kit. Cookies, maybe."

Their plane was a white-and-maroon twin-engine Navajo; Marya had never heard of the airline before. She was nervous about getting on it. When they were loading up there was a mechanic with his head stuck in the starboard engine. He was being handed tools by another mechanic.

They had a flight of about six hundred miles ahead of them from Thunder Bay to Moosonee and then to the Cree village of Attiwapiskat on the James Bay coast. There was going to be a celebration. Marya was going to cover it for the *Northern Observer*. She was a photographer. It was the middle of January.

Marya flew on small planes a lot. It was the only way to get around and cover events in the thirty-five Cree villages of remote northern Ontario. Marya travelled on bush planes loaded to the roof with rolls of plastic pipe, quarters of caribou, travelling Pentecostal preachers, very pregnant women being flown out to hospital to have their babies, cartons of Beef-a-Roni for the Hudson's Bay stores, people flying out to political meetings in Thunder Bay or Toronto, and Boy Scouts. She had flown on

DC-3s, Twin Otters, all kinds of Beechcrafts, and once an aristocratic old Norseman.

The *Northern Observer* covered anything. They needed the readers. That was why Marya was going to Attiwapiskat on the Navajo, which was chartered by the telephone company. Direct dialling was going into the village of 200 people for the first time and there was to be a community celebration. They had some kind of new liquid batteries she would be expected to take pictures of, and there would be cake and Jell-O for everyone. The kids would be given that soapy goo you blow bubbles with; it would be forty below in Attiwapiskat and the bubbles would snap-freeze and drift onto buildings and shatter. The chief would make a speech. Then the elders would close the ceremonies with prayers. They would pray for the new liquid batteries and the direct-dialling system. She would get some elder shots and a chief shot and maybe the bubbles.

"Nah," said the pilot to the mechanic, casually. "They're all right." He slapped the cowling as you would slap a horse.

They were loading on the gear. Marya kept her camera bag to herself. There was the public-relations guy for the telephone company; his name was Tom but she could never remember his last name so she called him Tom Telephone. There was someone named John, catching a ride home to Attiwapiskat, and another white guy. The two white guys had on Eddie Bauer down things—parkas, vests—new Grebs and heavy hand-knit sweaters. They were wearing exactly what Marya expected them to wear. So were she and John; layers of things that could be unzipped in front and taken off one at a time. She wondered if people called her Marya Motor-drive.

The engines sounded normal when they took off from Thunder Bay. The runway unreeled beneath them, the tire-marks came racing at them in dark blips. They swept into the air and you could see Lake Superior in its dangerous cold blue, and the shattered ice.

"Hi, I'm Paul. Paul Kirk."

He had sat down in the seat directly in front of her. There were only four of them aboard an eleven-seater plane. The telephone company did things in style.

"I'm Marya LaFollette," she said. "I'm with the *Northern Observer*. I don't speak French." They were still climbing. She didn't like to talk when they were climbing, as she always felt she had to personally keep the plane in the air. When they levelled off it was always better.

"Yes, that's an Indian newspaper, isn't it?"

"It's for anybody that can read anything more complicated than *cat* and *dog*," she said. "In two languages."

"Oh yes, of course," he said. "You know." He rustled in all his ripstop nylon.

It was about four in the afternoon. They had taken off late because the mechanics had been poking around in the engines. Darkness would be on them not long out of Moosonee. It was already late-looking, with that orange light you had to use a blue filter for if you were shooting colour. Which she was not. Colour was for arty types. She was just your average working photographer. She had lately been waking up to the feeling that nothing important was going to happen to her except dying. But maybe that's what being mature meant. You just hung on and acted normal until you died naturally. People tended to think of the north as exotic and full of startling images, that one was edging into danger even to come up, but her stuff was always the expected things; head shots, kids, dog-team races; once she was with a trapper who'd picked up a beaver and an otter out of the ice, and, his hands being full of ice-chisels and traps, had put the otter on top of his head and the beaver around his neck. It was a bizarre shot; it looked as if he were being attacked by Fur-Bearers From Outer Space. The newspaper hadn't used it. She had a secret, hush-hush never-mentioned project, but the thing was, there was this famous photographer in a black suit and hat who nested and waxed fat in her imagination and was always saying, *this isn't good enough*. It was Cartier-Bresson, probably.

"I'm a radiologist," said Paul Kirk. He obviously didn't know she was having a raging argument in her head with Cartier-Bresson. "I'm going up for a month on a special program. It's a joint project with a native health-advocacy group."

"I see," said Marya.

"You must have worked around native people quite a lot."

He was now going to ask her what Indians were really like. And there was one sitting across the aisle from them, forward, playing cribbage with Tom Telephone.

"Right, yes," said Marya. Marya was a tall and knobby woman with sandy-red hair that was fuzzy and stuck out in all directions. Men didn't usually strike up conversations with her unless they wanted something. Like information.

"Yes, I work with Indian people."

Kirk had an expensive parka, but his toque and mitts had been picked up at a dimestore. Marya didn't know why they did that, but they did. Invariably.

Skimped on the hat and mitts. His hair was thinning, light brown, and he had some rather endearing freckles on his nose and the backs of his hands.

"Want to see some X rays?" he asked. "I'm taking them up for training with the professionals." He took a big manila envelope from a briefcase and started pulling out X rays. It reminded Marya of something. "These are some compounds." Shadowy white bones in a grey fog.

"Oh yeah," said Marya. "Interesting."

He had hard, shiny nails. He ran his forefinger over a femur.

"What a break. I mean, that's unusual."

"Is it ever."

"Yes, well, they're excellent for teaching purposes." He lifted out another one and held it to the window to get the light through it. Marya could see the landscape through the film; there were white sheets of lake. They were into the bush country. "People up north have a great many hairlines and go around without knowing it. I mean, there's a lot of drinking and quite a bit of violence, I hear."

"Yeah," said Marya.

"People wake up hungover and don't know their collarbone's broken." He put the X rays back into the envelope. "Do you find them difficult to work with?"

"Nope. I do my picture-taking and that's it."

"I see. I suppose one doesn't get mixed up in village life or whatever."

"Whatever."

"I never met Indians until this health-project thing was proposed." Then he said, rather breathlessly, leaning toward her, as if he had been waiting months to say it, "The thing is they came across very strong, I mean, we all went out for a drink together and to get acquainted in an informal way, and, well, everybody started drinking a lot, and," suddenly he was cool and remote, "they seemed to feel that white people will never understand the culture and so on."

Right, thought Marya, they came on heavy and said, you white people, look what you've done to the Indians; the bottomless wells of bitterness. Enough to freak anybody out.

"Maybe you'll like the villages," said Marya. But she knew he wouldn't, he was terrified of Indians now, angry. She could tell; foretell, anticipate, predict.

"Well, this is really quite technical," he said. The envelope went back into the briefcase. "There's no need to go around glad-handing everybody, is there?"

"Not really," said Marya.

"I hear the doctor's residence is quite comfortable. I don't see any need to meet anyone except the nurses."

"No," said Marya. "A lot of people don't."

He nodded.

"Well, that's all right." He looked out the window at the great sub-arctic, the world's biggest untouched wilderness, the terrible white refrigerator of Canada, the adventure place, the mad unknown. "Lucky I got a ride up on this charter with Tom. You've been to the villages a lot, I gather."

"Yeah, since I started working with the newspaper."

He didn't asked her how long she'd been working with the newspaper. Now he was going to fish around and try to find out if she was married or not.

"It's going to be hard to be away from my family for a month," he sighed. "How about you?"

"I'm not married," said Marya. The divorce had been absolutely poisonous. She'd taken the first job that made her feel useful and good, and fled to the north. Even her mother called her up and said, *What are you doing up there in the north by yourself Marya? Ask yourself that seriously.* Maybe she should get out her cameras and start fooling with them. People always wanted to know about them. Sometimes in the villages people offered to buy them from her. The Contax MA 137 was a good conversation piece. It had a built-in motor drive. *Thwack, thwack, thwack,* people just loved it when you started banging away. She'd have to think about selling it and the other Nikon if she wanted to buy time to finance her project. Then she'd only have one camera.

"Maybe I shouldn't ask, but what are Indians really like?"

"All different," said Marya. The afternoon was deepening into volcanic red sunset tones and indigo. She really liked lying in bed at home with a brandy and a cigarette, going through her photography books. She had collections of W. Eugene Smith and Bourke-White and Cartier-Bresson and Diane Arbus. The women photographers seemed to lead horrible lives, on the average. Bourke-White was supposed to have been this disagreeable maniac and Arbus had killed herself. Dorothea Lange had survived all right.

She was married and normal and everything. Like this guy. He was normal. He led a normal life down in Mississauga or somewhere. He asks (or will ask) how did you start working up *here*? Did people say things like that to Bourke-White? And she didn't even have a husband to wave at them. But she was good. Her work was unimpeachable. Maybe it was Bourke-White she imagined looking over her shoulder.

She looked up at Kirk. She was expecting the question with such certainty that now she couldn't even remember whether he had asked her or not. He was staring out the window so maybe he hadn't.

Well, she had brought her cameras and started work here, and it was exciting. But after five years it had all started to repeat itself. Nurses held hostage by knife-wielding youths in northern villages, and here's a shot of the nurse, looking as if she'd spent the night in a duck press. Babies born on airplanes, northern carnivals, the inevitable tug-o-war pictures, political scandals and canoe races, the repetitious mayhem, murders, drunks swinging chairs, hockey tournaments, fur auctions.

She took all the expected pictures. When the unexpected happened, it was always against the rules, and she hesitated two seconds and lost the shot. For instance, there were those skeletons at Sand Cliff. An Indian graveyard being washed out by a dam, your regulation northern scandal, bits of human remains and coffins all over a beach not one hundred yards from the Hudson's Bay post. The chief took her and a couple of officials over to see it. While they were walking around surveying the scandal, the chief bent down to pick up a thigh-bone, delicately, between two fingers. He glanced up at her. *Take it;* it was crazy, this man sort of crouched over and looking up at the camera with a human thigh-bone in his hand. Then, *no, that's not...* whatever. Right. Or: They won't like it. No meaning. Words failed her. And the moment and the vision evaporated.

They were plunging toward Moosonee and darkness at 230 knots, eight thousand feet altitude.

"Well," said Kirk, "I guess a month won't be bad."

Marya lit up again.

"If you don't, like, relate to the health-group people, why go up?"

But she knew that already. This, too, was predictable. It would go into his professional record as this wonderful charitable thing he'd done and it would make him look good. A radiologist with a heart. And afterwards he would sit around his normal house in Hamilton or somewhere with his normal wife and kids and show dinner guests pictures of when he was up in the north. Here's the cute shot of this kid I got up in Attiwapiskat with his little beaded mitts and moccasins.

"Well, it's interesting, technically. I mean, I could tell you but it's fairly technical. And professionally it can't do me any harm."

"Yes, that's true," she said. The Cree guy, John, and Tom Telephone were into their fourth or fifth game and not listening. Maybe. "Excuse me," she said, and went up to visit the pilot.

"Yeah, we just left Thunder Bay radio and picked up Moosonee," he said, over the headset. He was your predictable northern pilot, a bomber jacket trimmed in wolverine and Cougar hikers, surrounded by manifests and maps and binders full of light regs. "We'll refuel at Moosonee."

They landed in Moosonee in the intense blue of a northern evening. Maybe it's because the deep colour of the evening sky is reflected from the fields of snow. The trees were much smaller. The harsh blue-white glare of the runway lights cut through everything. Marya didn't like flying at night up the coast, but then, people did it all the time. She went over to the Austin Airways office and checked their wall map. It was a straight shot of about two hundred miles over muskeg and salt water ice-pack to Attiwapiskat, their pinpoint in the dark.

"Is the runway lighted in Attiwapiskat?" she asked the guy at the desk. He had on a down vest with feathers spilling out of tiny rips, a mack shirt and hardened, dense fingertips.

"Oh hell yes," he said. "Lit up like a damn Christmas tree."

They sped down the runway and arrowed off into the indigo black night and stars coming from the south and west like a state of mind, unhindered by clouds. There was the bare edge of a neon moon and the aurora. The Navajo was speedy and slim as a jet fighter.

They settled down again. Tom Telephone and John Attiwapiskat had cans of pop. The cabin lights were on now, they were encapsulated.

"So how do you like the north?" he asked.

"I like it all right," she said. "It's hard." She paused, waiting. If he said how hard, she'd probably tell him. It was because she was approaching this crisis in her life or career or something. She'd probably tell him about the small house she'd rented, and had filled with expensive objects ordered from the back of the *New Yorker*, crazy stuff like crystal ashtrays with a crystal frog perched on the rim, exclusive replicas of classical sculpture from major European museums ("head of ZEUS, an excellent and striking example of the 'Supreme God' of Hellenistic period") and Jack Daniels stoneware jugs. When the marriage collapsed she'd thought, *I don't need security from men, I'll make my own*, which meant spending most of her salary on furnishings. Weird. Then when she came back to an empty house from shooting some logging truck that had gone over an embankment, she could feel safe.

"You don't talk a lot, do you?" said Paul Kirk, smiling at her.

"I guess not," she said, embarrassed. When they got to Attiwapiskat he'd probably say, *Where are you staying?* and *I brought some, ahem, fairly good scotch with me* and he would hope they could find a private bedroom to drink it in, and then they'd go to bed, etc. So many of these chartered flights into northern villages with all kinds of white officials and doctors and anthropologists.

Then there was a small explosion and the Navajo slewed, the port wing came forward a bit, like someone throwing a left-handed punch.

Then the engines sounded odd. They were off-beat, somehow.

Kirk didn't notice. He was still smiling at her. In a state of terror, she smiled back. It was about seven o'clock, they were about thirty minutes out of Moosonee, over heavy, unpopulated bush.

"Where are you staying tonight?" he asked.

"Just a minute," she said. "I want to go and ask the pilot how far it is."

She got out of her seat and went forward. She looked over and saw John Attiwapiskat looking at her. He had a question in his face. She raised her eyebrows briefly. In the cockpit the radar lights shone on the pilot's face, ice green.

She sat down in the co-pilot's seat and put on the headset.

"What's happening?" she said.

"Oh nothing," he said casually. "Blew a jug."

That meant a valve. She looked out. The starboard prop was spinning in slow, coarse revolutions. The engine was dead. They were sinking, as a matter of fact. They were no longer at eight thousand feet. It looked like maybe five.

"Ah, think we'll make Attiwapiskat?"

"Of *course*," he said. "What do you mean? Blowing a jug is nothing."

"Have they got the lights on at the airstrip?"

"Oh yeah, sure," he said, cheerfully. He was calm, chewing gum and watching the radar, the altimeter. He had long, delicate fingers. His hair was short and neat. He looked very straight-arrow. "I'm radioing ahead for them to turn them on."

But Marya was scared. Sometimes on those northern strips, all kinds of things went wrong, the wiring snapped, bulbs blew and there were no replacements.

"You mean you haven't raised them yet."

"Oh, not yet, but that's usual. The guy doesn't usually get down there until just before."

Marya swallowed.

"Do they know we're coming?" Didn't this asshole file a flight plan?

"Sure, sure," he said. "No problem."

She put the headset back on its hook and crawled out of the cockpit. "It's an hour yet," she said, cheerfully. They smiled and nodded. John from Attiwapiskat looked at her a couple of beats before he smiled.

She sat down and took a deep breath. She looked out into the night. The polestar rode on their starboard wing and Orion with his great jewels flamed in the south-west. They were tracking northwestward down the Milky Way, footloose in the aurora and sinking slowly toward the revolving earth. Down in the forest she saw a tiny orange light. It would be the kerosene lamp in a trapping-cabin, a family out from Kasechewan.

Kirk looked out too, putting his hands around his face and pressing to the plexiglass.

"Aren't we kind of low?"

"Not at all," said Marya. "I think this is pretty well normal altitude."

Then the other two guys looked out.

"Hey, we *are* low."

"I think he just wants to be sure we don't miss Attiwapiskat," said Marya. "It's a real tiny village." She had to comfort Kirk, she felt.

The Cree guy leaned back in his seat and stuck some chewing-gum in his mouth, staring at the seat in front of him. Tom Telephone started to light up.

"It's better if people don't smoke, maybe," said John.

Marya wondered if there was an emergency-locator transmitter in the nose and then started thinking about survival gear. The pilots were all supposed to travel with gear, like those clever little folding saws, and an axe, and sleeping bags, snowshoes and so on. If this guy hadn't raised Attiwapiskat and hadn't filed a flight plan, God knows what he had in his emergency kit. Cookies, maybe.

She looked out of the window again. She could see individual trees, in the light of the thin moon and stars. That meant maybe four thousand feet.

Or less.

She had covered at least three fatal crashes. Fatal; like *dead*. Sometimes they hit the trees, and if they weren't too close together it sheared the wings off and there might be survivors. But if you hit the dense stuff you just blew up. They were flying over subarctic spruce forest, thick as a hairbrush. Not many lakes in muskeg country.

She was sweating. There was no sign ahead of Attiwapiskat. They were grinding, agonizingly slowly, through the pure darkness of outer space.

She got out her camera bag, and her hands shook as she took the Contax and unscrewed the .28-mm lens and started cleaning it. Paul Kirk gave her a nervous, darting look.

"This plane's in trouble, man."

He didn't know you weren't supposed to say things like that when a plane was in trouble. You were supposed to shut up. Marya didn't know whether it mattered now or not.

She suddenly endowed the pilot with superhuman qualities. *Oh keep the plane in the air*, she sort of prayed to him, *keep us in the air.*

"The engines sound really bad," said Kirk. The windows were rattling.

"Looks like we lost one of them," said Marya.

"What?"

John looked over at them.

"Yeah," he said. "About fifteen minutes back. And the other one sounds pretty bad."

Kirk looked around, outraged.

"Hey, this isn't fun," he said. "I don't want to cash it in up *here*."

The rest of them said nothing. They didn't want to cash it in anywhere. And then Marya saw Kirk's wedding ring on his freckled finger and knew he had kids and was thinking about them.

I never did my secret project, she thought. *I screwed off. I took up with too many and bought too many things out of the back of the* New Yorker. *I kept trying to think like Cartier-Bresson.*

She got out of her seat and went back up to the cockpit again. The pilot was calm. Icarus, our pilot and our downfall.

"Turn back to Moosonee," she said.

"Too late for that." He was leaning back in the seat watching the instruments. "We're past the turn-back point." He was chewing gum, sort of crushing it between his molars in fierce bites. "It's all right, really. We're going to get there." He smiled at her.

She went back. Nobody looked at her.

The windows were about to shake out of their frames. There was a bad vibration in the remaining engine, the left one. She looked out again. Each individual tree was distinguishable against the snow beneath it.

It's like a binary system, she realized. Either you're here or you're dead. There are no half-lives. Even if you tried. The long stream of her life was suddenly billowing out behind her like a long banner. They were flying into darkness at the rim of the world. She could take any photograph she wanted. Cartier-Bresson and Bourke-White flashed at her.

If I go down, you go down too, she thought, vengefully.

"What a *bitch*," said Kirk, to a silent audience. He seemed to have shrunk into his down packaging, turtle-wise.

"Talk about something else, maybe," said Marya.

He rubbed his hands on his twill pants and thought for a minute.

"Well, uh, what are you going to do when you get back to Thunder Bay?"

"I'm going to sell my Contax and one of my Nikons and take a year off and photograph the faces on war memorials," she said. "In colour."

"War memorials?"

"Yes, you know. The statues with the guys in tin hats, and they say, 'To Our Glorious Dead' and like that. Just the faces on the statues." Oh God, why did she have to talk about that now?

"Hm. Yes. I see."

"I figure the sculptors used their friends to model them. And some of them are weird, all worn down and everything. There's one in Thornbury, Ontario." She stopped. That looks like a skull, but she thought better of it.

"How interesting," he said.

"It's something I want to do," she said, anxiously, but he had turned to look out the window again.

She put the Contax on the seat beside her and began cleaning the Nikon. The cabin of the Navajo looked solid and comforting with its blue plastic interior and plaid seat covers, but it could turn into shredded trash in seconds, she knew, she'd photographed them, the frozen remnants of bushplanes scattered like metal confetti in the trees and usually the wolves got the bodies. The Navajo plunged on, trembling. The aurora leapt like green gas jets in the north. She could see that their running lights were

illuminating the tops of the spruce below them. Something was looking at them out of the void.

"Belt up!" shouted the pilot, leaning out of the cockpit. His face was now drawn and eggshell-coloured. "Belt up, you guys."

They belted up.

Since the divorce she'd been mostly celibate and her body had turned smooth and pale and ceramic, she'd felt like a set of dentures, but now as she realized it might be torn apart or burnt she flushed bright as a candle, wildly aware of the intensity of her physical self in the universe, the hot spot of being burning against the cold matrix. She felt as if she were being passed through some flame and all the sorry pinfeathers of her soul burnt away. She knew the solution was not approval or even loving any one person, it was fearlessness.

"*Eh!*" called out John. "*Weteh Attiwapiskat-ing!*"

There it was, a tiny cluster of lights. They shone out of the limitless subarctic like the lights of a great ship in mid-Atlantic, an aircraft carrier. It was maybe fifteen miles ahead. They were just above stalling speed. It was a matter of sitting and watching them become real, shining there out of their forest on James Bay. Become real and separate and run toward them, glad little shouts of light, so merry and so clean, the orange of kerosene lamps, the blues of Colemans, and then as they ground toward the village, the runway lights all flashed on, heavy blue beams slashing through the dark.

They crossed the river and sank horribly toward the strip and its gleaming powder snow. Three hundred feet above the strip they lost the other engine, dying in a silence as startling as an explosion. Everything flew out of her head, her ex-husband and the crystal ashtrays and the head of ZEUS and Cartier-Bresson and the R-Kive negative files, wives, kitchens, normality, cameras, projects. The Navajo plunged to the strip in a sharp glide. They hit very hard, throwing Marya against Kirk's seatback, and the Contax rocketed end-over-end down the the centre aisle like a square cannon ball, flying into the cockpit. They dug an enormous hole in the airstrip and the plane shot into the air again. Someone shouted, a hoarse, urgent shout. They came down again at an angle and skidded sideways down the strip, like a runaway snowplough, spouting fans of snow up over the windows. Briefly the port engine started up. They came to a stop. The port engine died again.

Marya sat, waiting for the explosion.

From the airstrip shack came ambling a tall man. He wore the James Bay coat, a long down garment in blue twill. His skidoo boots slopped off his heels as he strolled, smiling, toward them. It was Gabriel Winnepetonga. He had been told to wait for all the guests by the elders, and welcome them and take them to their billets, and this is just what he was doing. He had not noticed the landing at all.

He came smiling and rehearsing his welcome speech, which was brief.

The pilot bolted out of the cockpit and ran down the aisle. He unclamped the door handle and dropped the steps.

"Let's get out," he said. "We'd better get out."

Paul Kirk jumped out of his seat and ran down the steps two at a time. He reached the ground. He looked up and saw Gabriel smiling with his hand out.

"Welcome to Attiwapiskat," said Gabriel.

Kirk looked at the Navajo. It was not going to blow up after all. He looked at Marya walking slowly down the steps.

Suddenly he took Gabriel's hand and began to pump it. He shook the large beaded moosehide mitt. He shook it and shook it.

"Ah, welcome to Attiwapiskat," said Gabriel again, and then looked nervously over at the rest, emerging. He laughed uncomfortably. The cold was intense.

"Yes," said Gabriel. "Welcome to Attiwapiskat." Then he saw John and said, in Cree, *This man is making me uncomfortable.*

They walked off, and Kirk was holding Gabriel's elbow as if he were escorting him somewhere. Behind them came Tom Telephone and John from Attiwapiskat; they were saying something to each other, low exclamations.

Marya stood back against the plane's fuselage, holding the battered Contax. It was badly dented but the lens was intact and inside it was a picture of Kirk gripping Gabriel's mitt with the look of a man who had just been brought up from a deep mine by the appearance of a mysterious hand.

She watched the pilot taking bags out of the rear baggage compartment. The engines stank. Overhead the major stars seemed to hiss and expand. Her legs felt like they might not hold her. In the rear baggage compartment she could see no emergency equipment whatever.

"What happened to the other engine?" she asked. Their steps squeaked on the dry, acidic snow. "You told the mechanics they were all right."

"I don't know," he said. "I'll look at them tomorrow." He wouldn't face her. "Later."

His lips were pressed together even though he was chewing gum and it looked funny. His bomber jacket hung open and inside it he was stringy, as if he were made of wires, and there were dark sweat patches at the armpits of his woollen shirt. He took a deep breath and suddenly looked over at her, determined to say something even though she would not (he knew) approve.

"I've accepted Jesus Christ as my personal saviour," he said. "If He wants us to get through, then we get through. The engines were in *His* hands, not the mechanics." He turned and started to poke through the compartment to see if he had missed any bags.

Marya stared at him. He wouldn't look at her.

"I was in a crash five years ago and I was the only one to come out of it alive. It changed my whole life. That's when I knew Jesus wanted me to wake up to His grace and stop boozing."

There was a long silence. Marya felt she was being robbed of something. She was suddenly determined to get it back. He hadn't filed a flight plan, he had no co-pilot, there was no emergency gear.

"I was starting to lose my faith," he said. "I spoke to Jesus and said 'Lord, if you want this flight to be all right, it's *Your* will, not mine.' "

A man came toward them from the airstrip shack on a snowmobile, trailing a sled. He pulled up beside them and stopped. They all smiled and said *bojo* to each other. The pilot started throwing the bags on.

"Don't report this," he said. "I mean, I'll do my report in the morning myself. No need for you to." A small wind started blowing snow-crystals in whirls.

"Sure," said Marya. As a matter of fact she was going to get up at 8:30 in the morning and report it to everybody she could think of, including Thunder Bay Psychiatric and the Ontario Provincial Police.

He looked at her Contax.

"It's kind of bashed up, you know," he said. "I'll buy it from you. I need a camera." He was bribing her.

Marya looked down at it. Then she said,

"Get me eight hundred cash by tomorrow morning and you can have it. And two other lenses with it, a fifty and a seventy-two hundred zoom. Zeiss planar lenses. The best." Maybe she would wait till noon to call everybody. "Get the money sent up through Hudson's Bay. Have it by one in the afternoon and the whole outfit's yours." By three in the afternoon there would be a plane for him. The nurse would have shot him full of Valium and there would be a couple of Northern Patrol officers. Maybe. Maybe not. Suddenly she really didn't know.

"Okay, I'll have it by one," he said, and smiled a quick, mechanical smile.

"Yes, all right," she said.

Would she get up tomorrow and go and do her shooting and then get the money and betray him? If she made it back to Thunder Bay alive she might do any number of unforeseeable things. Take a lot of pictures of Our Glorious Dead, the ones that didn't make it, it couldn't have been glorious at all. Or how do we know? We haven't died yet, not like that. Actually, she didn't know anything. She felt like an astronaut. Her head was empty. The salt fogs of Hudson Bay slipped out of the atmosphere like airborne bedsheets. She took up her camera bag and walked after the sled full of baggage, alive again, walking into the unpredictable universe as if it were her native land.

Traplines

BY THOMAS KING

Has communication between fathers and sons ever been easy?

When I was twelve, thirteen at the most, and we were still living on the reserve, I asked my grandmother and she told me my father sat in the bathroom in the dark because it was the only place he could go to get away from us kids. What does he do in the bathroom, I wanted to know. Sits, said my grandmother. That's it? Thinks, she said, he thinks. I asked her if he went to the bathroom, too, and she said that was adult conversation, and I would have to ask him. It seemed strange at the time, my father sitting in the dark, thinking, but rather than run the risk of asking him, I was willing to believe my grandmother's explanation.

At forty-six, I am sure it was true, though I have had some trouble convincing my son that sitting in the bathroom with the lights out is normal. He has, at eighteen, come upon language, much as a puppy comes upon a slipper. Unlike other teenagers his age who slouch in closets and basements, mute and desolate, Christopher likes to chew on conversation, toss it in the air, bang it off the walls. I was always shy around language. Christopher is fearless.

"Why do you sit in the bathroom, Dad?"

"My father used to sit in the bathroom."

"How many bathrooms did you have in the olden days?"

"We lived on the reserve then. We only had the one."

"I thought you guys lived in a teepee or something. Where was the bathroom?"

"That was your great-grandfather. We lived in a house."

"It's a good thing we got two bathrooms," he told me.

The house on the reserve had been a government house, small and poorly made. When we left and came to the city, my father took a picture of it with me and my sister standing in front. I have the picture in a box somewhere. I want to show it to Christopher, so he can see just how small the house was.

"You're always bragging about that shack."

"It wasn't a shack."

"The one with all the broken windows?"

"Some of them had cracks."

"And it was cold, right?"

"In the winter it was cold."

"And you didn't have television."

"That's right."

"Jerry says that every house built has cable built in. It's a law or something."

"We didn't have cable or television."

"Is that why you left?"

"My father got a job here. I've got a picture of the house. You want to see it?"

"No big deal."

"I can probably find it."

"No big deal."

Some of these conversations were easy. Others were hard. My conversations with my father were generally about the weather or trapping or about fishing. That was it.

"Jerry says his father has to sit in the bathroom, too."

"Shower curtain was bundled up again. You have to spread it out so it can dry."

"You want to know why?"

"Be nice if you cleaned up the water you leave on the floor."

"Jerry says it's because his father's constipated."

"Lawn has to be mowed. It's getting high."

"He says it's because his father eats too much junk food."

"Be nice if you cleaned the bottom of the mower this time. It's packed with grass."

"But that doesn't make any sense, does it? Jerry and I eat junk food all the time, and we're not constipated."

"Your mother wants me to fix the railing on the porch. I'm going to need your help with that."

"Are you constipated?"

Alberta wasn't much help. I could see her smiling to herself whenever Christopher started chewing. "It's because we're in the city," she said. "If we had stayed on the reserve, Christopher would be out on a trapline with his mouth shut and you wouldn't be constipated."

"Nobody runs a trapline anymore."

"My grandfather said the outdoors was good for you."

"We could have lived on the reserve, but you didn't want to."

"And he was never constipated."

"My father ran a trapline. We didn't leave the reserve until I was sixteen. Your folks have always lived in the city."

"Your father was a mechanic."

"He ran a trapline, just like his father."

"Not in the winter."

My father never remarried. After my mother died, he just looked after the four of us. He seldom talked about himself, and slowly, as my sisters and I got older, he became a mystery. He remained a mystery until his death.

"You hardly ever knew my father," I said. "He died two years after we were married."

Alberta nodded her head and stroked her hair behind her ears. "Your grandmother told me."

"She died before he did."

"My mother told me. She knew your grandmother."

"So, what did your mother tell you?"

"She told me not to marry you."

"She told me I was a damn good catch. Those were her exact words, 'damn good.' "

"She said that just to please you. She said you had a smart mouth. She wanted me to marry Sid."

"So, why didn't you marry Sid?"

"I didn't love Sid."

"What else did she say?"

"She said that constipation ran in your family."

After Christopher graduated from high school, he pulled up in front of the television and sat there for almost a month.

"You planning on going to university?" I asked him.

"I guess."

"You going to do it right away or you going to get a job?"

"I'm going to rest first."

"Seems to me, you got to make some decisions."

"Maybe I'll go in the bathroom later on and think about it."

"You can't just watch television."

"I know."

"You're an adult now."

Alberta called these conversations father and son talks, and you could tell the way she sharpened her tongue on "father and son" that she didn't think much of them.

"You ever talk to him about important things?"

"Like what?"

"You know."

"Sure."

"Okay, what do you tell him?"

"I tell him what he needs to know."

"My mother talked to my sisters and me all the time. About everything."

"We have good conversations."

"Did he tell you he isn't going to college."

"He just wants some time to think."

"Not what he told me."

I was in a book store looking for the new Audrey Thomas novel. The T's were on the third shelf and I had to bend over and cock my head to one side in order to read the titles. As I stood there, bent over and twisted, I felt my face start to slide. It was a strange sensation. Everything that wasn't anchored to bone just slipped off the top half of my head, slopped into the lower half and just hung there like a bag of Jello-O. When I arrived home, I got myself into the same position in front of the bathroom mirror. That evening, I went downstairs and sat on the couch with Christopher and waited for a commercial.

"How about turning off the sound?"

"We going to have another talk?"

"I thought we could talk about the things that you're good at doing."

"I'm not good at anything."

"That's not true. You're good at computers."

"I like the games."

"You're good at talking to people. You could be a teacher."

"Teaching looks boring. Most of my teachers were boring."

"Times are tougher now," I said. "When your grandfather was a boy, he worked on a trapline up north. It was hard work, but you didn't need a university degree. Now you have to have one. Times are tougher."

"Mr. Johnson was the boringest of all."

"University is the key. Lot of kids go there not knowing what they want to do, and after two or three years, they figure it out. Have you applied to any universities yet?"

"Commercial's over."

"No money in watching television."

"Commercial's over."

Alberta caught me bent over in front of the mirror. "You lose something?"

"Mirror's got a defect in it. You can see it just there."

"At least you're not going bald."

"I talked to Christopher about university."

"My father never looked a day over forty." Alberta grinned at herself in the mirror so she could see her teeth. "You know," she said, "when you stand like that, your face hangs funny."

I don't remember my father growing old. He was fifty-six when he died. We never had long talks about life or careers. When I was a kid—I forget how old—we drove into Medicine River to watch the astronauts land on the moon. We sat in the American Hotel and watched it on the old black-and-white that Morris Rough Dog kept in the lobby. Morris told my father that they were checking the moon to see if it had any timber, water, valuable minerals or game, and, if it didn't, they planned to turn it into a reserve and move all the Cree up there. Hey, he said to my father, what's that boy of yours going to be when he grows up? Beats me, said my father. Well, said Morris, there's damn little money in the hotel business and sure as hell nothing but scratch and splinters in being an Indian.

For weeks after, my father told Morris's story about the moon and the astronauts. My father laughed when he told the story. Morris had told it straight-faced.

"What do you really do in the bathroom, Dad?"

"I think."

"That all?"

"Just thinking."

"Didn't know thinking smelled so bad."

I was in the downstairs bathroom. Christopher and Jerry were in Christopher's room. I could hear them playing video games and talking.

"My father wants me to go into business with him," said Jerry.

"Yeah."

"Can you see it? Me, selling cars the rest of my life?"

"Good money?"

"Sure, but what a toady job. I'd rather go to university and see what comes up."

"I'm thinking about that, too."

"What's your dad want you to do?" said Jerry.

It was dark in the bathroom and cool, and I sat there trying not to breathe.

"Take a guess."

"Doctor?" said Jerry. "Lawyer?"

"Nope."

"An accountant? My dad almost became an accountant."

"You'll never guess. You could live to be a million years old and you'd never guess."

"Sounds stupid."

"A trapper. He wants me to work a trapline."

"You got to be kidding."

"God's truth. Just like my grandfather."

"Your dad is really weird."

"You ought to live with him."

We only went fishing once. It was just before my mother died. We all got in the car and drove up to a lake just off the reserve. My dad rented a boat and took us kids out in pairs. My mother stayed on the docks and lay in the sun.

Toward the end of the day, my sisters stayed on the dock with my mother, and my father and I went out in the boat alone. He had a new green tackle box he had bought at the hardware store on Saturday. Inside was an assortment of hooks and spinners and lures and a couple of red things with long trailing red-and-white skirts. He snorted and showed me a clipping that had come with a lure that could actually call the fish.

Used to be beaver all around here, he told me, but they've been trapped out. Do you know why the beavers were so easy to catch, he asked me. It's because they always set the trap in the same place and you always use the same bait, and pretty soon, they're gone.

Trapping was good money when your grandfather was here, but not now. No money in being a mechanic either. Better think of something else to do. Maybe I'll be an astronaut, I said. Have more luck trying to get pregnant, he said. Maybe I'll be a fisherman. No sir, he said. All the money's in making junk like this, and he squeezed the advertisement into a ball and set it afloat on the lake.

Christopher was in front of the television when I got home from work on Friday. There was a dirty plate under the coffee table and a box of crackers sitting on the cushions.

"What do you say we get out of the house this weekend and do something?"

"Like what?"

"I don't know. What would you like to do?"

"We could go to that new movie."

"I meant outdoors."

"What's to do outdoors besides work?"

"We could go fishing."

"Fishing?"

"Sure, I used to go fishing with my father all the time."

"This one of those father, son things?"

"We could go to the lake and rent a boat."

"I may have a job."

"Great. Where?"

"Let you know later."

"What's the secret?"

"No secret. I'll just tell you later."

"What about the fishing trip?"

"Better stick around the house in case someone calls."

Christopher slumped back into the cushions and turned up the sound on the television.

"What about the dirty plate?"

"It's not going anywhere."

"That box is going to spill if you leave it like that."

"It's empty."

My father caught four fish that day. I caught two. He sat in the stern with the motor. I sat in the bow with the anchor. When the sun dropped into the trees, he closed his tackle box and gave the starter rope a hard yank. It broke in his hand and he tumbled over backwards, the boat tipping and slopping back and forth. Damn, he said, and he pulled himself back up on the seat. Well, son, he said, I've got a job for you, and he set the oars in the locks and leaned against the motor. He looked around the lake at the trees and the mountains and the sky. And he looked at me. Try not to get me wet, he said.

Alberta was in the kitchen peeling a piece of pizza away from the box. "Christopher got a job at that new fast-food place. Did he tell you?"

"No. He doesn't tell me those things."

"You should talk with him more."

"I talk with him all the time."

"He needs to know you love him."

"He knows that."

"He just wants to be like you."

Once my sister and I were fighting, my father broke us up and sent us out in the woods to get four sticks apiece about as round as a finger. So we did. And when we brought them back, he took each one and broke it over his knee. Then he sent us out to get some more.

"Why don't you take him fishing?"

"I tried. He didn't want to go."

"What did you and your father do?"

"We didn't do much of anything."

"Okay, start there."

When we came home with the sticks, my father wrapped them all together with some cord. Try to break these, he said. We jumped on the sticks and we kicked them. We put the bundle between two rocks and hit it with a board. But the sticks didn't break. Finally, my father took the sticks and tried to break them across his knee. You kids get the idea, he said. After my father went back into the house, my younger sister kicked the sticks around the yard some more and said it was okay but she'd rather have a ball.

Christopher's job at the fast-food place lasted three weeks. After that he resumed his place in front of the television.

"What happened with the job?"

"It was boring."

"Lots of jobs are boring."

"Don't worry, I'll get another."

"I'm not worried," I said, and I told him about the sticks. "A stick by itself is easy to break, but it's impossible to break them when they stand together. You see what I mean?"

"Chainsaw," said my son.

"What?"

"Use a chainsaw."

I began rowing for the docks, and my father began to sing. Then he stopped and leaned forward as if he wanted to tell me something. Son, he said, I've been thinking.... And just then a gust of wind blew his hat off, and I had to swing the boat around so we could get it before it sank. The hat was waterlogged. My father wrung it out as best he could, and then he settled in against the motor again and started singing.

My best memory of my father was that day on the lake. He lived alone, and after his funeral, my sisters and I went back to his apartment and began packing and dividing the things as we went. I found his tackle box in the closet at the back.

"Christopher got accepted to university."

"When did that happen?"

"Last week. He said he was going to tell you."

"Good."

"He and Jerry both got accepted. Jerry's father gave Jerry a car and they're going to drive over to Vancouver and see about getting jobs before school starts."

"Vancouver, huh?"

"Not many more chances."

"What?"

"For talking to your son."

Jerry came by on a Saturday, and Alberta and I helped Christopher pack his things in the station wagon.

"Nice car," said Alberta.

"It's a pig," said Jerry. "My father couldn't sell it because of the colour. But it'll get us there."

"Bet your father and mother are going to miss you."

"My father wanted me to stick around and help with the business. Gave me this big speech about traditions."

"Nothing wrong with traditions," Alberta said.

"Yeah, I guess. Look at this." Jerry held up a red metal tool box. "It's my grandfather's first tool box. My father gave it to me. You know, father to son and all that."

"That's nice," said Alberta.

"I guess."

"Come on," said Christopher. "Couple more things and we can get going."

Alberta put her arm around my waist and she began to poke me. Not so you could see. Just a sharp, annoying poke. "For Christ's sake," she whispered, "say something."

Christopher came out of the house carrying his boots and a green metal box. "All set," he said.

"Where'd you get the box?" I asked.

"It's an old fishing-tackle box."

"I know."

"It's been sitting in the closet for years. Nobody uses it."

"It was my father's box."

"Yeah. It's got some really weird stuff in it. Jerry says that there's good fishing in B.C."

"That's right," said Jerry. "You should see some of those salmon."

"You don't fish."

"You never took me."

"My father gave me that box. It was his father's."

"You never use it."

"No, it's okay. I was going to give it to you anyway."

"No big deal, I can leave it here."

"No, it's yours."

"I'll take care of it."

"Maybe after you get settled out there, we can come out. Maybe you and I can do some fishing."

"Sure."

"Love you, honey," said Alberta and she put her arms around Christopher and held him. "I'm going to miss you. Call us if you need anything. And watch what you eat so you don't wind up like your father."

"Sure."

Alberta and I stood in the yard for a while after the boys drove off. "You could have told him you loved him," she said.

"I did. In my own way."

"Oh, he's supposed to figure that out because you gave him that old fishing box."

"That's the way my father did it."

"I thought you told me you found the box when you and your sisters were cleaning out his place."

After supper, Alberta went grocery shopping. I sat in the bathroom and imagined what my father had been going to say just before the wind took his hat, something important I guessed, something I could have shared with my son.

Summer Wages

BY CAROLINE WOODWARD

"Josie and I would hitch the one hundred miles down to Fort St. John every Friday afternoon at four o'clock and on Sunday afternoons we'd hitch back up to work in less than two hours usually. We got rides fast. Two blondes with our thumbs out with no idea we were two blondes standing with our thumbs out on the highway! I can't believe it but no kid of mine would stand out there, male or female, not in these times. Only so many angels on duty per innocent kid."

First off, let's put it into perspective, as Josie used to say. I, Geraldine, have worked nine waitressing jobs and have taken the vow never to do it again. Sure, I make those tired old jokes about support hose and roller skates supplied by management but I've got other things I can do for less work and more money. No more shift work either.

I do the books for five businesses right out of my own home. Claim office expenses for one-third of this double-wide trailer under the self-employed category on income tax and I sign off with a nice flourish, let me tell you. It's better that the money comes back to me, hard-working mother of three, than to the lousy government just lusting to squander it on their corrupt friends or some U.S. kick-ass submarine thing.

But here's the kicker. My oldest, Carrie-Lynn, wants to get a job. Fine. Grade ten, smart as a whip, takes after Ab for brains and Josie for looks, like she used to look before she got into the booze. But the job she wants is waitressing up the highway this coming summer. "Just like you and Aunt Josie did."

I'm building up to spilling the beans on her, sitting her down in the next hour when she gets home and telling it like it is. Was, anyway. She's too innocent and the world is meaner and trickier than it was 1969. I'm going to let loose with the scuzzy side of me and Josie's adventures in Service With A Smileville so she'll clue in and get a decent job. Like being a lifeguard. That's classy and the money is two and a half times minimum wage. She's still got time to get the swim ticket she needs. I'd pay for it, no ifs or buts.

She wouldn't get tips unless she served booze and she's still underage so that's that. The kid's only fifteen now, sixteen in June, runs like a deer, swims like a guppy, brings home ribbons every sports day and swim meet. Lifeguard badge be a cinch for an athletic kid like her.

Getting the damn pool job is another story though. I got to be realistic on that score. Carrie-Lynn doesn't have a high-up Daddy, or Mommy, to pull strings at City Hall. Ab is the *janitor* at City Hall for crying out loud. Plus he invents things like the automated scarecrow. But until he makes some indecent amount of money, people will just laugh at him. "How's it goin', Ab?" "Built a better mousetrap yet, Ab?" And Ab will just miss how entirely mean they are and smile and say he's not that interested in mousetraps, his current project is this or that, keeps me busy, keeps me busy, he says, nodding and smiling at the snickering sons of bees. They don't know who they're talking to. Ab's halfways a genius and he's got the kindest heart in the West, not a mean bone in his body. Me, I'm mean, let me tell you.

Me, I should join the Business and Professional Women's Club, get on the power lunch and business card swapmeet circuit but I'm afraid they'd turn me down. I couldn't take that. It kills me because I'm so proud to finally get to be a bookkeeper but that might not be enough for them. A chartered accountant and on up is what to be for them. Carrie-Lynn, Carrie-Lynn, that's where you come in.

I started by default, waitressing, because they hired me to chambermaid. It was new then, it's closed now, a gas station and about ten cabins plus a café with a good reputation. Exactly halfways between Fort St. John and Fort Nelson with Pink Mountain looming up out of the muskeg some miles away. The Beatton River began a hundred yards from the café, just a little brown stream coiling around the willows and stunted spruce trees.

Josie was actually thrilled to be a waitress even when she found out there was no uniform, just a long green apron to tie on over her blouse and jeans. Still, she fixed up her hair and did her nails and worked a full shift an hour after we got there. Petticoat Junction is what the truckers called our place on account of the five young women between sixteen and eighteen that worked there. But by the first of August, Josie and I were the only employees left. The Mister had picked a fight with Henry, the gas jockey whose girlfriend was the head waitress and whose sister was the second cook. The second cook's best friend was the main cook, a farm kid from Tom's Lake who had cooked for her family since she was eleven and that Esther could cook, let me tell you.

All four of them left in a huff because of Henry being fired. They headed back to Dawson Creek and big summer dances with Bim and The Crystal Ship and maybe even Anthony and The Romans. Lucky bums. We didn't realize how much fun July had been until we watched them leave in Henry's souped-up car and the café was suddenly dull. No more Social Centre. Josie and I were on our own with the Mister and the Wife.

The Mister drank at least once every two weeks and was out of commission for three or four days at a time. The Wife was a bible-thumper and an excellent cook but she holed up in one of the motel units whenever he hit the bottle so he wouldn't hit her. Josie and I had orders to leave him be and to bring her meals three times a day. No problem. We avoided him like the plague, sober or drunk.

We never told our parents. We needed the dollar ten an hour and all this booze and sex and violence, just like the TV, only made us feel more grown-up and on our own. We didn't want to worry the folks. Hear what I'm saying? You got that little smile on.

So. After the big You're Fired! Like Hell I Am, I Quit! We All Quit! episode, Josie and I pretty well ran the place. We'd get up at 5:30 a.m., dash from our unheated shack to the café, get the grill and the coffee on, eat a stack of toast, and go our separate ways. If a tour bus to Fairbanks pulled in, Josie would holler from the back door of the kitchen. I'd set down my toilet scrubber or whatever and run over to ladle out soup and make a bunch more pots of coffee. Josie kept a clean green apron by the door for me so I'd look more or less like a waitress. We'd go flat out getting upward of fifty people fed and watered, answering their dumb questions about where we went to school and how come we didn't have pecan pie and was the soup in the crockpot homemade like the sign hanging over it said?

In July when all five of us had worked, a couple of us could have a break, walk up to the Sikanni Chief airstrip, climb up the old forestry lookout until we lost our nerve around thirty feet up. Henry made it to the top once and so did Josie. It took them forever to get down and I had to run back to cover her shift which pissed me off. It was a whole day off for me and something didn't sit right with me, down on the ground, looking up this ancient creaking tower, and them up there laughing.

Josie and I would hitch the one hundred miles down to Fort St. John every Friday afternoon at four o'clock and on Sunday afternoons we'd hitch back up to work in less than two hours usually. We got rides fast. Two blondes with our thumbs out with no *idea* we were two blondes standing with our thumbs out on the highway! I can't believe it but no kid of mine would stand out there, male or female, not in these times. Only so many angels on duty per innocent kid.

By mid-August we figured out we were putting in close to eighteen-hour days and then it dawned on us we'd just worked seven days a week for two weeks straight. We were missing the really huge parties at the Old Fort and had romances to tend to. Or we liked to think we did. Pink Mountain-view Motel or Pink Elephant Lookout as we called it behind the Mister's back was seriously interfering with our futures, and we each had two hundred dollars clear, a small fortune.

Now listen up. Our Dad phoned us right at a busy lunch spell and told us to quit if we'd had enough, give them a week's notice, come home and have a week off before school started. The Wife came in and gave me a dirty look for being on the phone, my only phone call all bloody summer. So I looked at her, said "Uh huh," when Dad said goodbye, and then I said, "Dead?! Where?" Beat. "Mile 109? Mile 136? Omigosh!" Beat. "Hitch-hikers? Have they got the murderer yet?" Beat. "Okay. Yes. Okay. Yes, we will. Bye, Dad."

The Wife pretended she wasn't eavesdropping and scuttled out the door again. Something fell in the garage (closed again) and the sliding door came up and banged down. No Mister though. We waited a couple minutes, cleaning up the last of the lunch specials for a bunch of campers from Idaho and then it was just the two of us.

We got spinny, plunking quarters in the box and dancing to Little Green Bag three times in a row. Dancing like a pair of banshees until another camper pulled in. I settled down and marched out to where the Wife was holed up in Cabin Three and told her through the door that Josie and I had to quit.

I heard the toilet flush. Quit! Flush! Like an exclamation mark. Spent half her life on the can I swear. She opened the door and glared at me.

"There's two weeks left in the season," she says in her snappy boss voice. Her breath reeked of American cigarettes. Took me hours to air out a cabin after she'd holed up in it.

"Our Dad says you owe us four percent holiday pay," I say in my most polite and careful voice.

"But you girls didn't give us two weeks' notice," she says, folding her big huge arms over her big huge bazooms.

"Our Dad says it's the law and you didn't give us notice to work fifteen days straight either." Her mouth makes an O.

I take the plunge and make a decision for Josie and me. "If you give us our pay with the four percent, we won't charge overtime. Our Dad," I say, watching her squinty little eyes, using my most extremely polite voice now that I'm lying like a sidewalk, "Our Dad will come up tomorrow morning for us and I guess he'll talk to you about it if Mister isn't, ahh, around." I raise my eyebrows at her with this last bit.

That did it. She gave me a long, hard look and slammed the door in my face. I started running up to the kitchen, leaping from plank to wooden plank so I wouldn't sink into the mud lake between the cabins and the café.

There were some customers, the geologist guys from the Pink Mountain site, so I held it in until Josie took out their order and came back into the kitchen. I retell the whole exchange with the Wife and we both get so excited our whispers shot up to squeaks and we tried to jump up and down without making noise, her in her wooden clogs and me in my gumboots.

Josie had big dark circles under her eyes and she'd lost fifteen pounds in a month and a half. She was more burnt out than me because short-order cooking and waitressing and night clean-up was all inside work, breathing a steady diet of grill grease and Pine-Sol. At least I could cart towels and linen in the fresh air between cabins. For the first few weeks there was a truck, the Alaska Highway Laundry Express, but then it folded and yours truly used an industrial washer and an outside clothes line about fifty yards long because their dryer had broken down. I liked doing laundry better than making beds and scrubbing toilets.

Outside the air smelled like spruce tea with the late summer mists hanging low and the roots dangling into the little river, steeping it a coppery brown colour. I could hear trucks downshifting miles and miles away, that throaty roar with a silent breath between gears. I stood up on the laundry line perch, singing my head off, pulling wet sheets, towels, pillow slips and kitchen cloths out of my basket and onto the line, or vice-versa.

Back inside I tried to keep my mood light and summery, battling relief and giddiness and drawing a blank when it came to what to do next. I put the apron on to help Josie with night clean-up, strolling over to the jukebox to punch in some Creedence and Three Dog Night and Greenbaum's Little Green Bag, our theme song. The geologists chitchatted about rocks and bone hunters, one of them insisting that this place was smack in the middle of an ice-free corridor during the last glacier age. I poured their refills and kept my ears open because these guys always had the most interesting arguments. Then I heard the Wife giving Josie hell in the kitchen and so did the customers. I set the coffee pot down none too gently and marched back there, do or die.

Josie was looking white and shaky, holding a piece of order pad with some figuring on it.

"You got your hopes up, girlie," says the Wife, standing with her feet splayed apart and her arms hoisted over her bazooms. She launched into a major bullying session with a tired little grade ten waitress. Honestly!

"And what's the problem here?" I snap out in a loud voice that shocks even me. Josie looks at me like we've got one last chance to live and hands over the slip of paper.

"I figured out what I've got coming to me and they won't give it," she says, close to crying.

Josie is very smart with math and so I (no genius) quickly check the end result. I pause just a few seconds. Not for nothing was Drama my best subject.

"Looks right to me," I say in my new loud way, and stare the skinflint down. By this point I am amazing myself!

"I'm paying her for nine hours a day and that includes breaks and meals," she says, looking past me at the heads of the geologists who are lining up at the till. She starts to move but I jump in front of her, wanting witnesses in case Mister crawls out of his cubbyhole in the garage and things get really weird. The Wife is scary enough but I got to her earlier with the yak about our Dad and the law and I know it.

"This poor kid works more hours than the fourteen a day she's claiming," I say. "She's opened up and closed down this joint for half the summer and she better be paid for it." Then I step aside so she can face the geologists over the cash register. Let the old bag simper and coo about how they like her homemade soup now, the frigging hypocrite!

To make a long story shorter, we got our cheques that night without one word of thanks. By 7 a.m. the next morning we were facing a chilly north wind blowing gravel grit in our faces but in no time flat we were climbing into a big fuel tanker truck. Listening to Buck Owens and Merle Haggart on eight-track stereo. Homeward bound!

It was a deluxe truck with a cabover for sleeping, tons of seat space, tinted windshield, little orange balls across the top that some truckers call Calgary willnots, don't ask me why, and swinging dice cubes in oversized green and white foam stuff. And then there were the naked ladies.

Once I saw them I couldn't stop staring at them out the corners of my eyes because they were cut up into parts and glued onto the dash and the middle of the horn and the ashtray. Mostly breasts, no heads or arms. I was glad the trucker, Al, he said he was, didn't want to talk much because I was sitting next to him. Josie always pulled the shy act when a ride slowed down for us and started whining for the outside seat. The music blared out of four speakers and Al tapped one finger on the wheel but he didn't keep time with the music, just kept the same beat. I had to make myself stop staring at that finger too.

I made myself look out at the scenery rolling by, the miles of stunted muskeg spruce and swamp tamarack giving way to taller spruce and pines and poplars. We passed a jack-knifed rig and a squashed station wagon, burnt to a grey crisp. Ugh. And there was a bunch of wild-looking horses in the ditch, at least twenty of them escaped from who knows where, up to their bellies in good grass, sly and happy-looking the way horses are when they're on the lam.

The sun was pouring into the cab even with the tinted windshield. Al put on sunglasses which made him look even more sinister with his pock-marked jowls and hooked nose, an overweight parrot in a Hawaiian shirt and dirty jeans. He asked Josie to reach into the glove compartment for his pills.

"Gotta speed up my eyeballs," he said. "Hyuh, hyuh. Don't know your ass-pirin from your elbow, do ya, girlie?" Josie's giving him a confused, rabbity look because she can't get the lid of the flat black pillbox open. He asks her to fish two pills out for him. She still can't get the bloody little box open. I could scream.

The inside of the glove compartment is completely papered over with cut up women's crotch shots from magazines. You've got to understand that I'd never seen anything like this filth in my entire seventeen years. This was beyond the regular girlie magazines in the drugstore in 1969 is what I'm saying. I know, it's everywhere today, the TV, everywhere. Makes me puke.

Josie broke a precious fingernail and finally opened the pillbox. Al gulped down two and sucked on an orange he kept up on the dash within reach.

He was really booting it, pedal to the metal, wanting to get to Edmonton by midnight. We roared through the village of Wonowon at eighty miles an hour. That's way over a hundred and twenty kliks to you. Too damn fast. Dogs and gas stations and trailer courts and little Indian kids on trikes blurred by us until a siren drowned out the Buckaroos.

Josie dug into my ribs. When Al cursed and started pumping the air-brakes and downshifting, she mouthed, "Out, out, out." Her face had gone white and every zit she'd ever had sprouted in purplish scar galaxies across her forehead and chin.

When the rig ground to a halt, we jumped out with the big brown suitcase we shared and yelled our thanks. The young constable waved us on and motioned Al down from the truck for their little talk. Josie yanked at the suitcase and my arm at the same time and broke into a run.

"Do you hafta pee or what's the panic?" I yelled. A red stock truck slowed down before I could even catch up to Josie and in it were two young guys with cowboy hats on. When I got closer I could see it was the Wayling brothers, rancher types from near the Blueberry Reserve. I didn't know them except to look at them and that was fine by me. Dark curly hair, cut short except for sideburns, grey eyes, gorgeous noses. They were, I told Josie later, like Zane Grey heroes minus their buckskin stallions.

We hopped in the truck and tried our damndest to get them to talk in full sentences for the fifty miles into town. Josie loosened them up with jokes about jogging on the highway to keep the pounds off and I, usually the yappier of us two, sat back and laughed and laughed. Josie was never funnier except they didn't get the one about hippies being living proof that cowboys screwed goats, which was just as well considering their occupation. I don't think they liked girls to swear or talk dirty and Josie figured that out in seconds. She hammed it up about disasters in the café kitchen when the only thing left to cook was freezer-burned hamburger and stale white bread. I bragged about her and Esther turning out fifteen pies at a time, cherry, apple, blueberry, and lemon meringue. Josie flirted with them way worse than I ever did with the geologists. I had the outside seat too, did I mention that? Anyway, it was amazing what a summer of waitressing did for her confidence!

But once we got to Fort St. John, the brothers asked us to go cabareting and that's when they found out we weren't old enough to get into the bar and that was the end of that but it was fun while it lasted. They dropped us off at the end of our block like we asked because we didn't want our folks to see the truck and get ideas and besides, we had to talk.

She told me there was a convex mirror on her side of the window and she'd looked into it and seen a pair of eyes between the curtains of the cabover, staring at her. That was just as we started to barrel through Wonowon. She stared back at the eyes, paralyzed with fright, and then the police siren saved the day. When I asked if it was men's eyes or women's eyes, she said she couldn't tell because of the warping of the mirror. Holy doodle. And here I was freaked out by the dirty magazine scissor work!

We tried not to dwell on it and we didn't tell our folks because the chances of us going further north to, say, Muncho Lake the next summer and earning really decent money would be shot down for sure. See? Not a brain in our heads—or more guts than brains is a better way of putting it.

Look, Carrie-Lynn, I'll spare you my grown-up jobs, nineteen years and up, the classy night spots like the Oil King Cabaret where I pranced around in red polyester hotpants. Sure, laugh. Where I got bonked on the head by a flying beer glass for stepping between my friend Ella and a very hefty, very drunk woman who'd already yanked off Ella's frosted blonde short'n'curly wig. Poor Ella, standing there in her red hotpants suit with bobby pins holding down her greasy brown hair. Don't laugh. A little giggle is all you're allowed. Now that's enough.

You could be a lifeguard. Or go down to the Tourist Information booth. You're smart, you're pretty, you've got a nice personality. Don't leave this godforsaken town until you're eighteen. Promise me that. You got the rest of your life.

Please?

Chaddeleys and Flemings: Connection

BY ALICE MUNRO

Family connections make us what we are. Her mother's people were Chaddeleys, her father's people Flemings, and the girl in this story is fascinated by her mother's cousins when they come for a visit. They're women full of the world outside her small town, and full, too, of stories about the family history.

Much later, when she is grown up, one of the cousins visits again, again making her think about her family history. By this time she is married, to a husband who doesn't think her family is good enough.

Cousin Iris from Philadelphia. She was a nurse. Cousin Isabel from Des Moines. She owned a florist shop. Cousin Flora from Winnipeg, a teacher; Cousin Winifred from Edmonton, a lady accountant. Maiden ladies, they were called. Old maids was too thin a term, it would not cover them. Their bosoms were heavy and intimidating—a single, armoured bundle—and their stomachs and behinds full and corseted as those of any married woman. In those days it seemed to be the thing for women's bodies to swell and ripen to a good size twenty, if they were getting anything out of life at all; then, according to class and aspirations, they would either sag and loosen, go wobbly as custard under pale print dresses and damp aprons, or be girded into shapes whose firm curves and proud slopes had nothing to do with sex, everything to do with rights and power.

My mother and her cousins were the second sort of women. They wore corsets that did up the side with dozens of hooks and eyes, stockings that hissed and rasped when they crossed their legs, silk jersey dresses for the afternoon (my mother's being a cousin's hand-me-down), face powder (rachel), dry rouge, eau de cologne, tortoise-shell, or imitation tortoise-shell, combs in their hair. They were not imaginable without such getups, unless bundled to the chin in quilted satin dressing gowns. For my mother this style was hard to keep up; it required ingenuity, dedication, fierce effort. And who appreciated it? She did.

They all came to stay with us one summer. They came to our house because my mother was the only married one, with a house big enough to accommodate everybody, and because she was too poor to go to see them. We lived in Dalgleish in Huron County in Western Ontario. The population, 2000, was announced on a sign at the town limits. "Now there's two thousand and four," cried Cousin Iris, heaving herself out of the driver's seat. She drove a 1939 Oldsmobile. She had driven to Winnipeg to collect Flora, and Winifred, who had come down from Edmonton by train. Then they all drove to Toronto and picked up Isabel.

"And the four of us are bound to be more trouble than the whole two thousand put together," said Isabel. "Where was it—Orangeville—we laughed so hard Iris had to stop the car? She was afraid she'd drive into the ditch!"

The steps creaked under their feet.

"Breathe that air! Oh, you can't beat the country air. Is that the pump where you get your drinking water? Wouldn't that be lovely right now? A drink of well water!"

My mother told me to get a glass, but they insisted on drinking out of the tin mug.

They told how Iris had gone into a field to answer nature's call and had looked up to find herself surrounded by a ring of interested cows.

"Cows baloney!" said Iris. "They were steers."

"Bulls for all you'd know," said Winifred, letting herself down on a wicker chair. She was the fattest.

"Bulls! I'd know!" said Iris. "I hope their furniture can stand the strain, Winifred. I tell you it was a drag on the rear end of my poor car. Bulls! What a shock, it's a wonder I got my pants up!"

They told about the wild-looking town in Northern Ontario where Iris wouldn't stop the car even to let them buy a Coke. She took one look at the lumberjacks and cried, "We'd all be raped!"

"What is raped?" said my little sister.

"Oh-oh," said Iris. "It means you get your pocketbook stolen."

Pocketbook: an American word. My sister and I didn't know what that meant either but we were not equal to two questions in a row. And I knew that wasn't what rape meant anyway; it meant something dirty.

"Purse. Purse stolen," said my mother in a festive but cautioning tone. Talk in our house was genteel.

Now came the unpacking of presents. Tins of coffee, nuts and date pudding, oysters, olives, ready-made cigarettes for my father. They all smoked, too, except for Flora, the Winnipeg schoolteacher. A sign of worldliness then; in Dalgleish, a sign of possible loose morals. They made it a respectable luxury.

Stockings, scarves emerged as well, a voile blouse for my mother, a pair of stiff white organdy pinafores for me and my sister (the latest thing, maybe, in Des Moines or Philadelphia, but a mistake in Dalgleish, where people asked us why we hadn't taken our aprons off). And finally, a five-pound box of chocolates. Long after all the chocolates were eaten, and the cousins had gone, we kept the chocolate box in the linen drawer in the dining-room sideboard, waiting for some ceremonial use that never presented itself. It was still full of the empty chocolate cups of dark, fluted paper. In the wintertime I would sometimes go into the cold dining room and sniff at the cups, inhaling their smell of artifice and luxury; I would read again the descriptions on the map provided on the inside of the box-top: hazelnut, creamy nougat, Turkish delight, golden toffee, peppermint cream.

The cousins slept in the downstairs bedroom and on the pulled-out daybed in the front room. If the night was hot they thought nothing of dragging a mattress on to the verandah, or even into the yard. They drew lots for the hammock. Winifred was not allowed to draw. Far into the night you could hear them giggling, shushing each other, crying, "What was that?" We were beyond the streetlights of Dalgleish, and they were amazed at the darkness, the large number of stars.

Once they decided to sing a round.

Row, row, row your boat
Gently down the stream,
Merrily, merrily, merrily, merrily,
Life is but a dream.

They didn't think Dalgleish was real. They drove uptown and reported on the oddity of the shopkeepers; they imitated things they had overheard on the street. Every morning the coffee they had brought filled the house with its unfamiliar, American fragrance, and they sat around asking who had an inspiration for the day. One inspiration was to drive out into the country and pick berries. They got scratched and overheated and at one point Winifred was completely penned in, immobilized, by thorny branches, bellowing for a rescue party; nevertheless they said they had mightily enjoyed themselves. Another inspiration was to take my father's fishing rods and go down to the river. They came home with a catch of rock bass, a fish we generally threw back. They organized picnics. They dressed up in old clothes, in old straw hats and my father's overalls, and took pictures of each other. They made layer cakes, and marvelous molded salads which were shaped like temples and coloured like jewels.

One afternoon they put on a concert. Iris was an opera singer. She took the cloth off the dining-room table to drape herself in, and sent me out to collect hen feathers to put in her hair. She sang "The Indian Love Call," and "Women Are Fickle." Winifred was a bank robber, with a water pistol she had bought at the five-and-ten. Everybody had to do something. My sister and I sang, two songs: "Yellow Rose of Texas," and the Doxology. My mother, most amazingly, put on a pair of my father's trousers and stood on her head.

Audience and performers, the cousins were for each other, every waking moment. And sometimes asleep. Flora was the one who talked in her sleep. Since she was also the most ladylike and careful, the others stayed awake to ask her questions, trying to make her say something that would embarrass her. They told her she swore. They said she sat bolt upright and demanded, "Why is there no damned chalk?"

She was the one I liked least because she attempted to sharpen our minds—my sister's and mine—by throwing out mental-arithmetic questions. "If it took seven minutes to walk seven blocks, and five blocks were the same length but the other two blocks were double the length—"

"Oh, go soak your head, Flora!" said Iris, who was the rudest.

If they didn't get any inspiration, or it was too hot to do anything, they sat on the verandah drinking lemonade, fruit punch, ginger ale, iced tea, with maraschino cherries and chunks of ice chipped from the big chunk in the icebox. Sometimes my mother prettied up the glasses by dipping the rims in beaten egg whites, then in sugar. The cousins would say they were

prostrated, they were good for nothing; but their complaints had a gratified sound, as if the heat of summer itself had been created to add drama to their lives.

Drama enough already.

In the larger world, things had happened to them. Accidents, proposals, encounters with lunatics and enemies. Iris could have been rich. A millionaire's widow, a crazy old woman with a wig like a haystack, had been wheeled into the hospital one day, clutching a carpetbag. And what was in the carpetbag but jewels, real jewels, emeralds and diamonds and pearls as big as pullet eggs. Nobody but Iris could do a thing with her. It was Iris who persuaded her at last to throw the wig into the garbage (it was crawling with fleas), and let the jewels go into the bank vault. So attached did this old woman become to Iris that she wanted to remake her will, she wanted to leave Iris the jewels and the stocks and the money and the apartment houses. Iris would not allow it. Professional ethics ruled it out.

"You are in a position of trust. A nurse is in a position of trust."

Then she told how she had been proposed to by an actor, dying from a life of dissipation. She allowed him to swig from a Listerine bottle because she didn't see what difference it would make. He was a stage actor, so we wouldn't recognize the name even if she told us, which she wouldn't.

She had seen other big names, too, celebrities, the top society of Philadelphia. Not at their best.

Winifred said that she had seen things too. The real truth, the real horrible truth about some of those big wheels and socialites came out when you got a look at their finances.

We lived at the end of a road running west from Dalgleish over some scrubby land where there were small wooden houses and flocks of chickens and children. The land rose to a decent height where we were and then sloped in wide fields and pastures, decorated with elm trees, down to the curve of the river. Our house was decent too, an old brick house of a fair size, but it was drafty and laid out in an inconvenient way and the trim needed paint. My mother planned to fix it up and change it all around, a soon as we got some money.

My mother did not think much of the town of Dalgleish. She was often harking back, to the town of Fork Mills, in the Ottawa Valley, where she and the cousins had gone to high school, the town their grandfather had come to from England; and to England itself, which of course she had never seen. She praised Fork Mills for its stone houses, its handsome and restrained public buildings (quite different, she said, from Huron County's, where the idea had been to throw up some brick monstrosity and stick a tower on it), for its paved streets, the service in its stores, the better quality of things for sale and the better class of people. The people who thought so highly of themselves in Dalgleish would be laughable to the leading families of Fork Mills. But then, the leading families of Fork Mills would themselves be humbled if they came into contact with certain families of England, to whom my mother was connected.

Connection. That was what it was all about. The cousins were a show in themselves, but they also provided a connection. A connection with the real, and prodigal, and dangerous, world. They knew how to get on in it, they had made it take notice. They could command a classroom, a maternity ward, the public; they knew how to deal with taxi drivers and train conductors.

The other connection they provided, and my mother provided as well, was to England and history. It is a fact that Canadians of Scottish—which in Huron County we called Scotch—and Irish descent will tell you quite freely that their ancestors came out during the potato famine, with only the rags on their backs, or that they were shepherds, agricultural labourers, poor landless people. But anyone whose ancestors came from England will have some story of black sheep or younger sons, financial reverses, lost inheritances, elopements with unsuitable partners. There may be some amount of truth in this; conditions in Scotland and Ireland were such as to force wholesale emigration, while Englishmen may have chosen to leave home for more colourful, personal reasons.

This was the case with the Chaddeley family, my mother's family. Isabel and Iris were not Chaddeleys by name, but their mother had been a Chaddeley; my mother had been a Chaddeley, though she was now a Fleming; Flora and Winifred were Chaddeleys still. All were descended from a grandfather who left England as a young man for reasons they did not quite agree on. My mother believed that he had been a student at Oxford, but had lost all the money his family sent him, and had been ashamed to go home. He lost it by gambling. No, said Isabel, that was just the story; what really happened was that he got a servant girl in trouble and was compelled to marry her, and take her to Canada. The family estates were near Canterbury, said my mother. (Canterbury pilgrims, Canterbury bells.) The others were not sure of that. Flora said that they were in the west of England, and that the name Chaddeley was said to be related to Cholmondeley; there was a Lord Cholmondeley, the Chaddeleys could be a branch of that family. But there was also the possibility, she said, that it was French, it was originally *Champ de laiche*, which means field of sedge. In that case the family had probably come to England with William the Conqueror.

Isabel said she was not an intellectual and the only person she knew from English history was Mary Queen of Scots. She wanted somebody to tell her if William the Conqueror came before Mary Queen of Scots, or after?

"Sedge fields," said my father agreeably. "That wouldn't exactly make them a fortune."

"Well, I wouldn't know sedge from oats," said Iris. "But they were prosperous enough in England, according to Grandpa, they were gentry there."

"Before," said Flora, "and Mary Queen of Scots wasn't even English."

"I knew that from the name," said Isabel. "So ha-ha."

Every one of them believed, whatever the details, that there had been a great comedown, a dim catastrophe, and that beyond them, behind them, in England, lay lands and houses and ease and honour. How could they think otherwise, remembering their grandfather?

He had worked as a postal clerk, in Fork Mills. His wife, whether she was a seduced servant or not, bore him eight children, then died. As soon as the older children were out to work and contributing money to the household—there was no nonsense about educating them—the father quit work. A fight with the Postmaster was the immediate reason, but he really had no intention of working any longer; he had made up his mind to stay at home, supported by his children. He had the air of a gentleman, was widely read, and full of rhetoric and self-esteem. His children did not balk at supporting him; they sank into their commonplace jobs, but pushed their own children—they limited themselves to one or two apiece, mostly daughters—out to Business School, to Normal School, to Nurses Training. My mother and her cousins, who were these children, talked often about their selfish and willful grandfather, hardly ever about their decent, hard-working parents. What an old snob he was, they said, but how handsome, even as an old man, what a carriage. What ready and appropriate insults he had for people, what scathing judgments he could make. Once, in faraway Toronto, on the main floor of Eaton's as a matter of fact, he was accosted by the harnessmaker's wife from Fork Mills, a harmless, brainless woman who cried, "Well, ain't it nice to meet a friend so far from home?"

"Madam," said Grandfather Chaddeley, "you are no friend of mine."

Wasn't he the limit, they said. *Madam, you are no friend of mine!* The old snob. He paraded around with his head in the air like a prize gander. Another lower-class lady—lower-class according to him—was kind enough to bring him some soup, when he had caught cold. Sitting in his daughter's kitchen, not even his own roof over his head, soaking his feet, an ailing and in fact a dying man, he still had the gall to turn his back, let his daughter do the thanking. He despised the woman, whose grammar was terrible, and who had no teeth.

"But he didn't either! By that time he had no teeth whatever!"

"Pretentious old coot."

"And a leech on his children."

"Just pride and vanity. That's the sum total of him."

But telling these stories, laughing, they were billowing with pride themselves, they were crowing. They were proud of having such a grandfather. They believed that refusing to speak to inferior people was outrageous and mean, that preserving a sense of distinction was ridiculous, particularly when your teeth were gone, but in a way they still admired him. They did. They admired his invective, which was lost on his boss, the plodding Postmaster, and his prideful behaviour, which was lost on his neighbours, the democratic citizens of Canada. (Oh what a shame, said the toothless neighbour, the poor old fellow, he don't even reckinize me.) They might even have admired his decision to let others do the work. A gentleman, they called him. They spoke ironically, but the possession of such a grandfather continued to delight them.

I couldn't understand this, at the time or later. I had too much Scottish blood in me, too much of my father. My father would never have admitted there were inferior people, or superior people either. He was scrupulously egalitarian, making it a point not to "snivel," as he said, to anybody, not to kowtow, and not to high-hat anybody, either, to behave as if there were no differences. I took the same tack. There were times, later, when I wondered if it was a paralyzing prudence that urged this stand, as much as any finer sentiment, when I wondered if my father and I didn't harbour, in our hearts, intact and unassailable notions of superiority, which my mother and her cousins with their innocent snobbishness could never match.

It was not of much importance to me, years later, to receive a letter from the Chaddeley family, in England. It was from an elderly lady who was working on a family tree. The family did exist, in England, after all, and they did not spurn their overseas branches, they were seeking us out. My great-grandfather was known to them. There was his name on the family tree: Joseph Ellington Chaddeley. The marriage register gave his occupation as butcher's apprentice. He had married Helena Rose Armour, a servant, in 1859. So it was true that he had married a servant. But probably not true about the gaming debts in Oxford. Did gentlemen who were embarrassed at Oxford go and apprentice themselves to butchers?

It occurred to me that if he had stayed with butchering, his children might have gone to high school. He might have been a prosperous man in Fork Mills. The letter-writer did not mention the Cholmondeley connection, or the fields of sedge, or William the Conqueror. It was a decent family we belonged to, of servants and artisans, the occasional tradesman or farmer. At one time I would have been shocked to discover this, and would hardly have believed it. At another, later, time, when I was dedicated to tearing away all false notions, all illusions, I would have been triumphant. By the time the revelation came I did not care, one way or the other. I had almost forgotten about Canterbury and Oxford and Cholmondeley, and that first England I had heard of from my mother, that ancient land of harmony and chivalry, of people on horseback, and good manners (though surely my grandfather's had broken, under the strain of a cruder life), of Simon de Montfort and Lorna Doone and hounds and castles and the New Forest, all fresh and rural, ceremonious, civilized, eternally desirable.

And I had already had my eyes opened to some other things, by the visit of Cousin Iris.

That happened when I was living in Vancouver. I was married to Richard then. I had two small children. On a Saturday evening Richard answered the phone and came to get me.

"Be careful," he said. "It sounds like Dalgleish."

Richard always said the name of my native town as if it were a clot of something unpleasant, which he had to get out of his mouth in a hurry.

I went to the phone and found to my relief that it was nobody from Dalgleish at all. It was Cousin Iris. There was a bit of the Ottawa Valley accent still in her speech, something rural—she would not have suspected that herself and would not have been pleased—and something loud and jolly, which had made Richard think of the voices of Dalgleish. She said that she was in Vancouver, she was retired now and she was taking a trip, and she was dying to see me. I asked her to come to dinner the next day.

"Now, by dinner, you mean the evening meal, don't you?"

"Yes."

"I just wanted to get it straight. Because when we visited at your place, remember, your folks always had dinner at noon. You called the noon meal dinner. I didn't think you still would but I wanted to get it straight."

I told Richard that a cousin of my mother's was coming to dinner. I said she was, or had been, a nurse, and that she lived in Philadelphia.

"She's all right," I said. I meant decently educated, well enough spoken, moderately well-bred. "She's travelled all over. She's really quite interesting. Being a nurse she's met all sorts of people—" I told about the millionaire's widow and the jewels in the carpetbag. And the more I talked, the more Richard discerned of my doubts and my need for reassurance, and the more noncommittal and unreassuring he became. He knew he had an advantage, and we had reached the point in our marriage where no advantage was given up easily.

I longed for the visit to go well. I wanted this for my own sake. My motives were not such as would do me credit. I wanted Cousin Iris to shine forth as a relative nobody need be ashamed of, and I wanted Richard and his money and our house to lift me forever, in Cousin Iris's eyes, out of the category of poor relation. I wanted all this accomplished with a decent subtlety and restraint and the result to be a pleasant recognition of my own value, from both sides.

I used to think that if I could produce one rich and well-behaved and important relative, Richard's attitude to me would change. A judge, a surgeon, would have done very well. I was not sure at all how Iris would serve, as a substitute. I was worried about the way Richard had said *Dalgleish*, and that vestige of the Ottawa Valley—Richard was stern about rural accents, having had so much trouble with mine—and something else in Iris's voice which I could not identify. Was she too eager? Did she assume some proprietary family claim I no longer believed was justified?

Never mind. I started thawing a leg of lamb and made a lemon meringue pie. Lemon meringue pie was what my mother made when the cousins were coming. She polished the dessert forks, she ironed the table napkins. For we owned dessert forks (I wanted to say to Richard); yes, and we had table napkins, even though the toilet was in the basement and there was no running water until after the war. I used to carry hot water to the front bedroom in the morning, so that the cousins could wash. I poured it into a jug like those I now see in antique stores, or on hall tables, full of ornamental grasses.

But surely none of this mattered to me, none of this nonsense about dessert forks? Was I, am I, the sort of person who thinks that to possess such objects is to have a civilized attitude to life? No, not at all; not exactly; yes and no. Yes and no. Background was Richard's word. *Your background.* A drop in his voice, a warning. Or was that what I heard, not what he meant? When he said Dalgleish, even when he wordlessly handed me a letter from home, I felt ashamed, as if there was something growing over me; mould, something nasty and dreary and inescapable. Poverty, to Richard's family, was like bad breath or running sores, an affliction for which the afflicted must bear one part of the blame. But it was not good manners to notice. If ever I said anything about my childhood or my family in their company there would be a slight drawing-back, as at a low-level obscenity. But it is possible that I was a bit strident and self-conscious, like the underbred character in Virginia Woolf who makes a point of not having been taken to the circus. Perhaps that was what embarrassed them. They were tactful with me. Richard could not afford to be so tactful, since he had put himself in a chancy position, marrying me. He wanted me amputated from that past which seemed to him such shabby baggage; he was on the lookout for signs that the amputation was not complete; and of course it wasn't.

My mother's cousins had never visited us again, en masse. Winifred died suddenly one winter, not more than three or four years after that memorable visit. Iris wrote to my mother that the circle was broken now and that she had suspected Winifred was diabetic, but Winifred did not want to find that out because of her love of food. My mother herself was not well. The remaining cousins visited her, but they did so separately, and of course not often, because of distances. Nearly every one of their letters referred to the grand time they had all had that summer, and near the end of her life my mother said, "Oh, Lord, do you know what I was thinking of? The water-pistol. Remember that concert? Winifred with the water-pistol! Everybody did their stunt. What did I do?"

"You stood on you head."

"Ah, yes, I did."

Cousin Iris was stouter than ever, and rosy under her powder. She was breathless from her climb up the street. I had not wanted to ask Richard to go to the hotel for her. I would not say I was afraid to ask him; I simply wanted to keep things from starting off on the wrong foot, by making him do what he hadn't offered to do. I had told myself that she would take a cab. But she had come on the bus.

"Richard was busy," I said to her, lying. "It's my fault. I don't drive."

"Never mind," said Iris staunchly. "I'm all out of puff just now but I'll be all right in a minute. It's carrying the lard that does it. Serves me right."

As soon as she said *all out of puff*, and *carrying the lard*, I knew how things were going to go, with Richard. It hadn't even taken that. I knew as soon as I saw her on my doorstep, her hair, which I remembered as gray-brown, now gilt and sprayed into a foamy pile, her sumptuous peacock-blue dress decorated at one shoulder with a sort of fountain of gold spray. Now that I think of it, she looked splendid. I wish I had met her somewhere else. I wish I had appreciated her as she deserved. I wish that everything had gone differently.

"Well, now," she said jubilantly. "Haven't you done all right for yourself!" She looked at me, and the rock garden and the ornamental shrubs and the expanse of windows. Our house was in Capilano Heights on the side of Grouse Mountain. "I'll say. It's a grand place, dear."

I took her in and introduced her to Richard and she said, "Oh-ho, so you're the husband. Well, I won't ask you how's business because I can see it's good."

Richard was a lawyer. The men in his family were either lawyers or stockbrokers. They never referred to what they did at work as any kind of business. They never referred to what they did at work at all. Talking about what you did at work was slightly vulgar; talking about how you did was unforgivably so. If I had not been still so vulnerable to Richard it might have been a pleasure to see him met like this, head on.

I offered drinks at once, hoping to build up a bit of insulation in myself. I had got out a bottle of sherry, thinking that was what you offered older ladies, people who didn't usually drink. But Iris laughed and said, "Why, I'd love a gin and tonic, just like you folks."

"Remember that time we all went to visit you in Dalgleish?" she said. "It was so dry! Your mother was still a small-town girl, she wouldn't have liquor in the house. Though I always thought your father would take a drink, if you got him off. Flora was Temperance, too. But that Winifred was a devil. You know she had a bottle in her suitcase? We'd sneak into the bedroom and take a nip, then gargle with cologne. She called your place the

Sahara. Here we are crossing the Sahara. Not that we didn't get enough lemonade and iced tea to float a battleship. Float four battleships, eh?"

Perhaps she had seen something when I opened the door—some surprise, or failure of welcome. Perhaps she was daunted, though at the same time immensely pleased by the house and furnishings, which were elegant and dull and not all chosen by Richard, either. Whatever the reason, her tone when she spoke of Dalgleish and my parents was condescending. I don't think she wanted to remind me of home, and put me in my place; I think she wanted to establish herself, to let me know that she belonged here, more than there.

"Oh, this is a treat, sitting here and looking at your gorgeous view! Is that Vancouver Island?"

"Point Grey," said Richard unencouragingly.

"Oh, I should have known. We went out there on the bus yesterday. We saw the University. I'm with a tour, dear, did I tell you? Nine old maids and seven widows and three widowers. Not one married couple. But as I say, you never know, the trip's not over yet."

I smiled, and Richard said he had to move the sprinkler.

"We go to Vancouver Island tomorrow, then we're taking the boat to Alaska. Everybody said to me back home, what do you want to go Alaska for, and I said, because I've never been there, isn't that a good enough reason? No bachelors on the tour, and do you know why? They don't live to be this old! That's a medical fact. You tell your hubby. Tell him he did the right thing. But I'm not going to talk shop. Every time I go on a trip they find out I'm a nurse and they show me their spines and their tonsils and their whatnots. They want me to poke their livers. Free diagnosis. I say enough of that. I'm retired now and I mean to enjoy life. This beats the iced tea a mile, doesn't it? But she used to go to such a lot of trouble. The poor thing. She used to frost the glasses with egg white, remember?"

I tried to get her to talk about my mother's illness, new treatments, her hospital experiences, not only because that was interesting to me, but because I thought it might calm her down and make her sound more intelligent. I knew Richard hadn't gone out at all but was lurking in the kitchen.

But she said, no shop.

"Beaten egg white, then sugar. Oh, dear. You had to drink through straws. But the fun we had there. The john in the basement and all. We did have fun."

Iris's lipstick, her bright teased hair, her iridescent dress and oversized brooch, her voice and conversation, were all part of a policy which was not a bad one; she was in favour of movement, noise, change, flashiness, hilarity, and courage. Fun. She thought other people should be in favour of these things too, and told about her efforts on the tour.

"I'm the person to get the ball rolling. Some people get downhearted on a trip. They get indigestion. They talk about their constipation. I always get their minds off it. You can always joke. You can start a singsong. Every morning I can practically hear them thinking, what crazy thing is that Chaddeley going to come up with today?"

Nothing fazed her, she said. She told about other trips. Ireland. The other women had been afraid to get down and kiss the Blarney Stone, but she said, "I've come this far and I'm going to kiss the damn thing!" and did so, while a blasphemous Irishman hung on to her ankles.

We drank; we ate; the children came in and were praised. Richard came and went. Nothing fazed her; she was right. Nothing deflected her from her stories of herself; the amount of time she could spend not talking was limited. She told about the carpetbag and the millionaire's widow all over again. She told about the dissolute actor. How many conversations she must have ridden through like this—laughing, insisting, rambling, recollecting. I wondered if this evening was something she would describe as fun. She would describe it. The house, the rugs, the dishes, the signs of money. It might not matter to her that Richard snubbed her. Perhaps she would rather be snubbed by a rich relative than welcomed by a poor one. But had she always been like this, always brash and greedy and scared; decent, maybe even admirable, but still somebody you hope you will not have to sit too long beside, on a bus or at a party? I was dishonest when I said that I wished we had met elsewhere, that I wished I had appreciated her, when I implied that Richard's judgments were all that stood in the way. Perhaps I could have appreciated her more, but I couldn't have stayed with her long.

I had to wonder if this was all it amounted to, the gaiety I remembered; the gaiety and generosity, the worldliness. It would be better to think that time had soured and thinned and made commonplace a brew that used to sparkle, that difficulties had altered us both, and not for the better. Unsympathetic places and people might have made us harsh, in efforts and opinions. I used to love to look at magazine advertisements showing ladies in chiffon dresses with capes and floating panels, resting their elbows on a ship's rail, or drinking tea beside a potted palm. I used to apprehend a life of elegance and sensibility, through them. They were a window I had on the world, and the cousins were another. In fact the cousins' flowery dresses used to remind me of them though the cousins were so much stouter, and not pretty. Well, now that I think of it, what were those ladies talking about, in the balloons over their heads? They were discussing underarm odour, or thanking their lucky stars they were no longer chafed, because they used Kotex.

Iris collected herself, finally, and asked when the last bus ran. Richard had disappeared again, but I said that I would take her back to her hotel in a cab. She said no, she would enjoy the bus ride, truly she would, she always got into a conversation with somebody. I got out my schedule and walked her to the bus stop. She said she hoped she hadn't talked Richard's and my ears off and asked if Richard was shy. She said I had a lovely home, a lovely family, it made her feel grand to see that I had done so well in my life. Tears filled her eyes when she hugged me goodbye.

"What a pathetic old tart," said Richard, coming into the living room as I was gathering up the coffee cups. He followed me into the kitchen, recalling things she had said, pretentious things, bits of bragging. He pointed out grammatical mistakes she had made, of the would-be genteel variety. He pretended incredulity. Maybe he really felt it. Or maybe he thought it would be a good idea to start the attack immediately, before I took him to task for leaving the room, being rude, not offering a ride to the hotel.

He was still talking as I threw the Pyrex plate at his head. There was a piece of lemon meringue pie in it. The plate missed, and hit the refrigerator, but the pie flew out and caught him on the side of the face just as in the old movies or an *I Love Lucy* show. There was the same moment of amazement as there is on the screen, the sudden innocence, for him; his speech stopped, his mouth open. For me, too, amazement, that something people invariably thought funny in those instances should be so shocking a verdict in real life.

Row, row, row your boat
Gently down the stream.
Merrily, merrily, merrily, merrily,
Life is but a dream.

I lie in bed beside my little sister, listening to the singing in the yard. Life is transformed, by these voices, by these presences, by their high spirits and grand esteem, for themselves and each other. My parents, all of us, are on holiday. The mixture of voices and words is so complicated and varied it seems that such confusion, such jolly rivalry, will go on forever, and then to my surprise—for I am surprised, even though I know the pattern of rounds—the song is thinning out, you can hear the two voices striving.

Merrily, merrily, merrily, merrily,
Life is but a dream.

Then the one voice alone, one of them singing on, gamely, to the finish. One voice in which there is an unexpected note of entreaty, of warning, as it hangs the five separate words on the air. *Life is*. Wait. *But a*. Now, wait. *Dream*.

Troller

BY KEVIN ROBERTS

"O Lord your sea is so strong, and our boat is so frail."

The sea burst against the bow where Bill lay on the starboard bunk, and the boat timbers shivered and trembled the full ten-metre length of the *Pacific Maid*. Mel, the skipper, had been sick for three days now and so had his son, Bert, and the fishboat was barely under control. Bill lay there in his floater jacket, the rubber tailpiece drawn up between his thighs and hooked to the front. Bert had made a number of cracks about that, but as soon as the wind hit the boat, when they passed the moaning fog horn of Tofino harbour, Bill'd put the jacket on and left it on. This was his first trip as a deck-hand on the outside and the sheer size of the Pacific disturbed him deeply. Two bad seasons on the inside coast, no sockeye run, no pinks worth a damn, and his small fishboat had been claimed by the Royal Bank. He'd had no choice but to find a job, start again at the bottom, as a deck-hand on a large Pacific troller. And he was lucky to get on with Mel, he knew. But he didn't want to be here.

He had been stunned on that first day out when Mel had confessed that he was always seasick for the first couple of days, and sometimes for longer in bad weather. It seemed crazy, even dangerous, to put yourself into a job where you suffered so much, where control over your body was in such jeopardy. But, Mel had added, seasickness was a lot more common than most fishermen admitted. Greed and pride kept them at it; that, and the strange attraction the sea had for some men. That was the hardest to believe.

Above him, outside in the dark, the wind thrummed on the wires of the poles like a mad guitarist. Beside him on the other bunk, Bert moaned, and above and behind him, Mel lay suffering in the wheelhouse bunk. The gale rose and fell in wild bursts and he was glad he could not see the swells, topped with flying white lace, that rolled ominously and endlessly from the heart of the dark Pacific.

Four days ago, they'd smashed and rolled their way eighty kilometres out from Tofino, the weather channel voice predicting falling winds and sea. They'd fished that first morning, their thighs braced hard against the sides of the fish-well in the stern, slapping the gurdies in on only half the lines because the yawing, pitching boat could not be held straight, even on the Wagner autopilot. It was a monstrously unstable world, where the sky swung like a mad chandelier, and at the bottom of a swell, the boat seemed totally enveloped in the seething grey sea. He had not realized how totally enveloped in the pitching bowl of the Pacific they were, until they encountered another fish boat, the *Ocean Rambler*, about the same size, and its toy-like struggle to lift up from the weight of the sea, smashing endlessly on its bow, caused him to fear that this other frail cockle of wood, a half a kilometre away, could not, would not rise this time, or the next, out of the green mass that rolled again and again and again, pushing the whole boat down and down, until, when both boats were on the bottom of the swell, the *Ocean Rambler* would disappear completely from sight. It was then, too, that he realized that the *Pacific Maid*, his own boat, must also look a frail shell waiting for one great wave to take it under.

They had caught fish that first day, coho and a few medium springs, but the big fish broke the lines or ran amok with ease about the barely controllable boat. He had brought one big spring alongside, fifteen kilos, maybe more, and swung the gaff down and into its head, but, instantly, the boat yawed and the gaff and fish pulled beyond his strength and he let go before he too was tipped into the maelstrom. The skipper's curses were torn from his lips by the wind as he came aft in a running crouch. He shouldered Bill aside, and with huge hands, criss-crossed with the white scars from nylon fish line, manhandled the flapping spring with the gaff still in its head into the checkers, and expertly killed it with a single blow behind the head.

Though he could not hear Bert's jibes from the other side of the boat, he was embarrassed, but not for long. The skipper, with a sudden lurch, pushed by him again, green-faced, and vomited into the spume. Bert soon followed his father, and both of them leaned over the side and vomited time and time again.

It was then that he'd taken charge, scuttled to the wheelhouse to adjust the Wagner, crouched and run back to run the lines, pulled the salmon, ran out the lines again, cleaned the fish and stocked them in the checkers. But the wind and sea grew and the main line and the deep line of the starboard side crossed and tangled and for half an hour he struggled to bring both of them in and clear the gear. The skipper watched, red-eyed, and finally told him to pull all the lines in and lash them down.

Incredibly, though the skipper stopped regularly to retch overboard, Mel worked with him until all the gear was on board and the lines and lead cannon balls lashed down with cutty hunk. Together they pulled the prostrate Bert into the wheelhouse and down into the bunk. Bill went out again to the stern, staggered back with armful after armful of salmon, crawled deep down into the hold of the boat, stuffed handfuls of ice into the cleaned bellies of the fish, and stacked them into the waiting ice.

"Sea-anchor, Bill," mumbled Mel, pointing to the bow. "I'll run the boat up, you drop it." Bill looked through the window. The weighted parachute with the red Scotsman buoy was lashed to the foredeck. It had to be eased overboard so it sank and opened deep beneath the sea. A long rope, coiled now on the bow, then ran from the capstan on the bow down to the chute flowering under the sea. With this down, the boat rode easily, moving with the tide a kilometre or so in and out, on the ballooned tension of the underwater anchor. But it was dangerous to put out in a high wind. If the chute snapped open in the gale the rope would whip out like a snake striking. If the boat was not held tight against the smashing swell, the rope jerked about and the feet and body of the man, already threatened by the great wash of water pounding against it, could be washed overboard instantly. The very idea of walking out there, out to where the grey sea bounded onto the bow, was almost too much for him, except for the haggard look of the skipper, white-faced and red-eyed. He knew then that he had to do it, not just for them on the boat, but for himself, because the sea was building relentlessly and it was doubtful if they could turn and run safely before it back to Tofino. The danger of broaching, or of the stern going under in the massive rolling seas was such that he looked an instant at Mel, and saw in his watering eyes that there was only one choice.

And he had shuffled grimly out along the deck, gripping the handrail tightly with both hands, past the wheelhouse and out onto the bow. There, the first burst of swell knocked him soaking and breathless to his knees.

Worse, the suck of the sea off the deck rushed about him and loosened his footing. In the second or two before the next wave burst upon him, he worked with one hand on the lashed parachute. He timed his work so that in the brief dip of the bow, before the next swell deluged him, the parachute and its chain and rope were freed. He hooked one foot about a stanchion, braced the other, and in the same two-second dip, let the parachute and rope slip through his left hand over the side. Despite his effort the rope kicked and jumped and burnt his wrist and hand.

It was not classic seamanship. There were many men of the West Coast fishing fleet for whom this act was daily bread, but for him the final "tung" of the rope tight against the capstan, the red Scotsman floating before the boat now easing back, was a gong of triumph. He sat, hanging onto the rail, his knees braced against the stanchion, totally exhausted, wet through, and not at all jubilant. His hands were scored and torn by the rope. He though of the poached salmon steaks he'd seen once for an exorbitant price, served in silver chafers in a restaurant on Sloane Square in London, and the enormity of the callous economics of it made him burst out with laughter. Eventually, he crawled back on his knees, gripping the rail, and got into the wheelhouse.

He told himself through clenched teeth that this was it, that never again would he risk the plunge and certain death in that cold and bitter sea. It was over. He'd get a shore job, pumping gas, unloading fish, anything to avoid this pulse and roll and madness of the sea.

The skipper sat with his head down on the wheel, and Bill crawled past him and down into the bunk next to Bert. The boat now rode more easily, tossing like a massive child whose fever has broken and, even though the sea still smashed and burst against the hull, he fell quickly asleep. He dreamed he was in a strange moving bed with a beautiful green woman who undulated under and away from him every time he tried to possess her.

A rumbling sound growing nearer brought him to wakefulness. He got up unsteadily, his limbs rigid with cold, and stepped up into the wheelhouse. Mel lay asleep on the wheelhouse couch, his white face garish every second or two from the flash of the strobe light on the mast top. The sea was unabated. Green frills ran constantly up and down the wheelhouse window, obscuring the bow light. On the port bow one kilometre and closing, at the tops of the massive swells, he could see a row of lights in the whirling darkness. He fervently hoped the radar operator on the freighter out there was awake and that the many blips of the fishing fleet tossing at anchor were clear in the stormy night. The freighter passed quickly, unperturbed it seemed by the muscular walls of water in which it moved. He wished then, as many fishermen have, for a boat so big the sea could not threaten it. He thought, too, of the wreaths rotting on the Anglican Church wharf at Bamfield, and the inscription, "O Lord your sea is so strong, and our boat is so frail."

He looked about him at the unutterable darkness, the wild wind and crashing sea, and felt a great loneliness, until, in the distance, the quick flash of a tiny strobe appeared, another fishboat, anchored too in this hissing vortex, and another flash, and another; and suddenly all about, at the top of the swells, the flick, flick, sometimes kilometres away, sometimes closer, magical in the storm. Bill felt strangely and utterly comforted by the pattern their lights made, flickering, kilometres away from home and warmth and safety. Again he looked at his hands, throbbing now with the red lines of the chafe marks. He knew it was a mark, along with the lights, of a community; the boats of the West Coast fishing fleet, held by the flowers of their sea anchors, a pattern of faith one with the other in this arduous endeavour upon the encircling sea.

Strawberry Time

BY SUZANNE JACOB

TRANSLATED FROM THE FRENCH BY SUSANNA FINNELL

A young girl faces her mother's illness.

I was holding them in my hands and had to open the door in a complicated way with my elbows and knees, finally kicking it shut. I ran to the kitchen. Our kitchen has a swinging door without handles. I sent it slamming into the green chimney. I'm too loud, my mother always says, my movements are too sweeping, my mouth is too big, I talk too loud, I overflow and that wears her out.

"Mom!"

I looked to see if she was in the yard, sometimes she goes for a breath of air and to look at the trees in the yard. She stands on the porch, looks at the sky and rubs her forehead. She wasn't out there. The bathroom door was closed. I knocked with my elbow because my hands were full.

"Not so loud my God can't you wait a minute?"

Her voice is really something else these days. I'm never quite sure if she is talking or crying, you might say she swallows her words, you are never sure if the words are coming out or going in.

"What's the matter, are you sick?"

It's silly to ask, she is always sick, but then she is never sick. It's her specialty these days and it takes up all her time because she would have to decide once and for all whether or not she is sick and she hates decisions, decisions exhaust her.

"Of course not... my God... you're late. The others have already left again."

"Close your eyes before you come out of the bathroom."

It's obvious that I'm bothering her. If I disturbed her less, she would probably move even less, maybe she would get to the point of not moving at all. At least that's what I've been thinking lately. You could say that there is no movement coming from her any more, from deep inside. You could say that it's us who keep her alive, my brothers and I, because we need to eat and brush our teeth and go to bed. You could say that these are the only things she is holding onto, you could also say that they are what's holding her together.

I walked around tapping my feet to get on her nerves. I heard water running from the tap. At times she runs the water to wash her hands and then she just stands there listening to it or watching it run. You really have to push her to get her out of it.

"That's enough of it, come on out now!"

"All right... "

She turned off the water.

"Wait! Are your eyes closed? Don't open them until I say so."

My brothers don't notice anything. No one besides me notices because my sisters are in boarding school and besides my sisters there is no one who would really be interested except my father. He notices, but we don't have the same way of noticing. He prefers that those who notice don't talk about it or admit it to each other. That way reactions are freer and there's no need to start a discussion that might turn into an argument, and in any case, you don't know the nature of the virus and maybe there is no virus at all.

She was pale, even paler than before, and the brown spots on her forehead and temples stood out and she was rubbing the back of her hand. Her hair was dry and flat like after a bad case of the flu and fever and she doesn't like going to the hairdresser, it's too tiring, it takes all her energy for three days and then three more days to get over it. I wondered for a few seconds if I should go on worrying about her. When I see her like this, I wonder, I tell myself that it might be better to leave her alone. To be still is what she really wants, what she desires, not to eat, or take baths or to get up anymore, ever, at all.

She kept her eyes closed, just as I told her. Maybe she would rather keep them like this because the light hurts her eyes, especially when my father isn't around, when he's away. OK, she was leaning against the fridge.

"You're home late. Marc and Oliver went back to school a long time ago. It's one o'clock! You have ten minutes left to eat, your food is going to be cold, it's already cold."

That's all she could say. That was proof of her maternal presence and of the good care she gives me. Eating cold food or eating hot food makes no difference at all to her. Her ideal is to never be hungry again, to not need food in order to live. Ideally, life should be lived through sleep, and sleeping should be all that's needed.

I put my hands under her nose to see if the smell would wake her up even though I knew she wasn't really sleeping, but I feel better when she is really sleeping than when she is leaning against the fridge like this, rubbing the back of her hand, and you can see those brown spots grow bigger around her eyes and on her forehead.

"Don't you smell anything?"

She lifted her head and tried to take three little sniffs of air. It takes all her strength these days. I opened my hands for the smell to reach her switched-off face. That's it, her face is switched off, and you can't figure out any more how to switch it on, nobody can, nothing works, because she has seen lots of doctors and takes all sorts of medication but she is still not switching on.

But now her nostrils were moving, she swallowed and I saw saliva, just a bit of saliva wetting her lips and they opened a little more and then she opened her eyes and said "Oh."

It worked. It wasn't exactly the greatest "Oh" you could imagine, but for a person going through a difficult time like my mother, it was quite extraordinary.

Usually she has black eyes, for as long as I can remember she has had black eyes that shone. Then they stopped shining. It's been about a year. Now, you could say they're fading, but her hair is still very black without any grey strands. She looked at my hands with these faded eyes and I told her to open her mouth, that I was going to give her the solemn communion of the first strawberries of spring from the end of the world—we are far from everything here and the first strawberries come after everyone else has had them according to the paper.

"Don't joke around with these kinds of things my God."

She says this because I said "solemn communion" and she doesn't like it if people make fun of sacred things like communion, being part of religion it must remain sacred because if you can't tell the difference between what's sacred and what's not, what will become of you, you wouldn't know any longer who you owed what to, or who you owed nothing to because debts are sacred too, my father and my mother are in agreement on this, there is a commandment that says to honour them and there is nothing like people who honour their debts, you can trust them forever.

Anyway, I put three strawberries on her tongue, the three reddest, the three largest. Her jaws didn't move, I was watching closely, I was watching to see if her tongue would start moving, but nothing moved and she swallowed.

"You swallowed them whole! You could chew them!"

"My God oh no they melt between your tongue and the roof of your mouth."

That's the kind of surprise my mother can give you. You think she's in a coma and then she comes out with something like that, she'll say she likes butter as much as candy or she'll say "Did you notice the form of this apple, Julie?" It seems as if an electric current gets the better of her sleep in moments like that. It makes me sweat, I was sweating, this idea that without a single movement of her muscles, she could notice that the strawberries were melting in her mouth and that made me proud of myself. Then her eyes made a sort of inspection of my hands, blouse, jumper, and shoes, all without moving her head, nothing but her eyes, slowly, in one go, and she murmured "strawberries... "

There, she was off again. OK. I walked over to the sink, changed my mind and went over to the garbage can, slamming the lid against the wall.

"Not happy?... I'll throw them out."

She moved. She unstuck herself from the fridge and stopped rubbing the back of her hand and opened the cupboard and took out a bowl.

"Don't do that, good God, strawberries... "

"I haven't had any. See, and there isn't a single stem on them."

It was true. I had not eaten a single one. The patch isn't big. When I saw fat Bérubé coming towards me asking if I had found ripe ones, it made me so mad. Every year she thinks that the patch belongs to everybody because it's in a vacant lot and the edges of roads and ditches are public property. She thinks first-come first-served are just words, she says it every spring each time I find the patch of red berries and it's always me who first thinks of double-checking these kinds of things and just because she lives two steps from us, she thinks she has the same rights to what I see first. *It is my patch.* The Bérubé woman is perfectly useless in a strawberry patch. She doesn't know how to look, she only knows how to squash them with her fat feet, and she only knows how to complain that she can't find anything and how come you find everything and it isn't fair. She really gets on my nerves.

My mother squinted her eyes looking out the window over the sink into the yard. I put the strawberries into the bowl. I washed my hands and dried them on the dish towel. It stained the towel red. My mother saw it and sighed. That's the way it is. When she sighs it means she has enough air in her chest for another breath.

"Your lunch is on the table. I'm going to lie down for a while. I'll keep the strawberries for my snack. Thanks dear, they are splendid, splendid."

I repeated the word to myself. Splendid, splendid. It's the kind of word she uses for strawberries or pebbles she sometimes finds in the yard. It's a word for everything and nothing, a word to toss off for something you don't have, for something that really is missing, even if it might exist.

I wasn't hungry. I looked at my shoes. They are brown Savage shoes, the best for children and adolescents. Monsieur Turgeon who fits us with shoes told my mother that and my mother does not want to buy shoes that are not Savages because Savages are durable, too.

I like my shoes. They are scratched just the way I like and really fit my feet without making blisters.

I was late anyway. A little more or less wouldn't matter, I could take my time. It's like when I know there's a mistake in my dictation, I won't correct it. It's all or nothing with me. If I'm sure there won't be any mistakes, then good, I correct the text. But if I know I will make some mistake anyway because there's a word I can't spell, or a verb I'm not sure about, then, too bad, I won't correct it.

I could hear my mother turning over in her bed even though the door was closed. Before, she used to sing a lot. Now with my brothers at school, it's quiet in our house. Then I hear her crying.

Gerald says that women are made for crying. He says his mother cries about everything, but he and his dad never do. He says crying doesn't help anything.

Because our floor creaks, I was careful not to make any noise as I tiptoed up to the door of their room. It was like I said, I wasn't mistaken, she was crying. She cries funny, my mother. First of all, she is not like Gerald's mother, she doesn't cry for nothing, she doesn't ever cry even though you might think she did now because of her faded eyes and the brown circles around her eyes and on her forehead. She cried once when my sister stepped on a nail and she was the fourth one to step on a nail and that meant work and foot-baths and lotions. It takes a long time to heal feet, it shouldn't, after all you walk with them. But that's the way it is.

That was it all right, she was crying more and more with sobs and sighs. Standing on the other side of the door with one hand on the door-knob, I asked myself what to do. I was thinking that I should hurry back to school, after all I had no business here because I'm usually at school at this time and as far as my mother knew I really was at school.

I turned the knob very carefully so she wouldn't jump, scaring her is not what you want to do to someone who thinks she is alone in the house, especially since our house is rather big and she is crying, assuming that no one can hear her.

I quite like their room. It's the biggest one in the house. They have a big bed with a dark wooden headboard. On one of the walls, the one where the baby bed is, there is wallpaper with white birds on a royal blue background. I don't think my mother will have any more babies, I don't know, but she keeps the baby bed in their room just in case. There is a royal blue down cover on their bed. Now, the royal blue down cover, rising and falling, looked as if it was crying.

I don't know what's wrong with her. Something must be wrong. It can happen to anyone, something goes wrong and sometimes it lasts a long time, it's persistent. I know that. But she isn't like everybody. That's my opinion. But what could I do. They each have their dresser and drawers. She reached out towards her dresser and took the whole box of Kleenex with her under the covers. She didn't see me but she could have because of the mirror, she would have jumped, she wouldn't have believed it was me because she doesn't think that I can do anything without making lots of noise or without moving everything including the air.

I don't know, I left their room, I was too hot. I felt my head to see if I had a temperature because I get fevers for no reason at all and my temples were throbbing. If something could make her temples beat like this, I wonder if she would cry, I don't know.

I ran. I straightened my jumper and went to class. Of course Sister had to make some comment, I can't do anything without her making some comment. If I wanted her to stop making comments, I would have to be like everyone else here and even then she would find a way to prove to herself that I am like everyone else in order to be different. She says I always find a way to be noticed.

"You're late, Miss Chavarie."

That's just like her. That's the way she is, slipping in a comment even if there is no point in disturbing the *whole* class because *one* student comes in late, when it's obvious that everyone has already seen that anyway. But she always has to make a fuss over something or other.

"You're right, Sister, I'm late, excuse me for being late, Sister."

I must have said it in a certain tone. Everyone snickered except Sister and me. There was nothing funny about it but it's true that I said it in a certain way, I agree, she could hold that against me, I'm ready to admit my mistakes when I make them, I admit them most of the time and when I haven't any, I invent them, I invent them even for others if necessary, it doesn't bother me. I opened the top of my desk.

My books and notebooks are all covered with brown wrapping paper, the kind that has a dull side and a shiny side, from the Crépeault grocery store. I wrap my books shiny side out because I think that side is waterproof.

My books were stacked neatly because there had been a general clean-up of our desks since it was close to the Department of Public Instruction examination and that was a good excuse to clean up. An orderly desk is beautiful because the eyes are the mirror of the soul and what is well perceived comes across clearly. With my head in my desk and the lid on my head, I listened to the silence I had produced in the class. There are many qualities of silence, everybody knows that, I knew this particular silence was waiting for me to lower the top of my desk because the open top disturbed the whole class, upset the horizon line that Sister needed in order to concentrate because we were in the review period.

I don't know. It was like I was stuck behind this top. It was like I was paralyzed by this lid that I held up with my head while my hands went through my pencil bag for no reason at all. My desk is in the row by the blackboard because in the row by the windows I get too distracted and talk about what is going on outside and I tell the others what's happening in the school yard and who is going down or coming up Second Street and it drives Sister crazy to hear me talk about the nearby real world. You can only talk about the outside world the way it's told in the books, for and by the books. The School Board's policy is to use textbooks to teach us the colour of the Seine in Paris, its temperature and width and all, and to never talk about the Harricana that cuts right through town here, you cannot talk about that ever ever ever. In any case, this is a colonized country, and that is why you can't ever start out by knowing the names of the trees and bushes and everything and fire engines are red anyway like everywhere else, it's international and the world is bigger than before, when my mother was born the world was much smaller because the mass media had not, at that point, made the whole planet within reach the way it is now. Anyway, Sister had moved my desk to eliminate the distraction. I'm sure that the School Board agrees with this decision and I had no say in it.

"Come on Julie, when are you going to come out of your desk?"

Managing to come out of this desk is just what I wanted most in this internationalized world. She couldn't imagine, and I wasn't going to tell her at the very end of the school year that we could, she and I, share the same hope even if only for a few seconds. I couldn't do that to her because she would have been too upset at the thought of having been wrong about me for so long. It often happens that I don't correct other people's ideas about me because it's simpler and I figure that everyone else does the same, even to themselves, otherwise we'd be rushed and things would change too fast around us and rapid changes tire most people, causing nausea, migraines, and problems.

Well, I felt like crying. I no longer knew where to turn or how to hide. I said to myself that it was absolutely necessary to hold out until four o'clock, seeing as I was the toughest kid in the whole school and of all the students that Sister had ever taught since she started teaching in Nicolet, and from there in Yamachiche, from Yamachiche to La Tuque, from La Tuque to Macamic and from Macamic to Amos and maybe in other towns, I was the toughest, the biggest tomboy, the one with the least heart. I wasn't going to ruin my reputation in two seconds of physical and chemical weakness due to a sudden overproduction by my lachrymal glands. Whatever one says, reputations are made by how others see you. Like now, this could go all the way up to the principal of this school and it could be influential. So I clenched and unclenched my jaw, I bit my tongue, I tried to think of the last dirty joke Gerald had told me, I tried hard to find a crazy laugh, nothing.

So I lowered the top of my desk because she was coming closer, I just felt it and also I felt that given the tension in the room, there was going to be a cloudburst of words.

She was already next to my desk, I was looking up the holes of her flared-out nostrils, I sat and she stood, like a cop on the road looking down at a driver.

Our eyes met. I saw it in her eyes. The game was won because there was one thing she did not expect at all and she never ever would have imagined me doing such a thing because I really was the one with the least heart and the toughest. I knew that she would lower her eyes as soon as I did it and I did it. I cried right in her face, without letting her go with my eyes or anything, I cried and cried.

So Sister was severely punished by this move but I know that something is wrong with my mother and as far as my mother is concerned it doesn't get me anywhere to have someone punished.

Red Plaid Shirt

BY DIANE SCHOEMPERLEN

A young woman sifts through the past of her emotional life, as she looks through the clothes in her closet.

RED PLAID SHIRT

that your mother bought you one summer in Banff. It is 100% Pure Virgin Wool, itchy but flattering against your pale skin, your black hair. You got it in a store called Western Outfitters, of the sort indigenous to the region, which stocked only *real* (as opposed to designer) blue jeans, Stetson hats, and $300 hand-tooled cowboy boots with very pointy toes. There was a saddle and a stuffed deer-head in the window.

Outside, the majestic mountains were sitting all around, magnanimously letting their pictures be taken by ten thousand tourists wielding Japanese cameras and eating ice-cream cones. You had tricked your mother into leaving her camera in the car so she wouldn't embarrass you, who lived there and were supposed to be taking the scenery for granted by now.

You liked the red plaid shirt so much that she bought you two more just like it, one plain green, the other chocolate brown. But these two stayed shirts, never acquiring any particular significance, eventually getting left unceremoniously behind in a Salvation Army drop-box in a grocery-store parking lot somewhere along the way.

The red plaid shirt reminded you of your mother's gardening shirt, which was also plaid and which you rescued one winter when she was going to throw it away because the elbows were out. You picture her kneeling in the side garden where she grew only flowers—bleeding hearts, roses, peonies, poppies—and a small patch of strawberries. You picture her hair in a bright babushka, her hands in the black earth with her shirt-sleeves rolled up past the elbow. The honeysuckle hedge bloomed fragrantly behind her and the sweet peas curled interminably up the white trellis. You are sorry now for the way you always sulked and whined when she asked you to help, for the way you hated the dirt under your nails and the sweat running into your eyes, the sweat dripping down her shirt-front between her small breasts. You kept her old shirt in a bag in your closet for years, with a leather patch half-sewn onto the left sleeve, but now you can't find it.

You were wearing the red plaid shirt the night you met Daniel in the tavern where he was drinking beer with his buddies from the highway construction crew. You ended up living with him for the next five years. He was always calling it your "magic shirt," teasing you, saying how it was the shirt that made him fall in love with you in the first place. You would tease him back, saying how you'd better hang onto it then, in case you had to use it on somebody else. You've even worn it in that spirit a few times since, but the magic seems to have seeped out of it and you are hardly surprised.

You've gained a little weight since then or the shirt has shrunk, so you can't wear it any more, but you can't throw or give it away either.

> RED: crimson carmine cochineal cinnabar sanguine scarlet red ruby rouge my birthstone red and blood-red brick-red beet-red bleeding hearts Queen of fire god of war Mars the colour of magic my magic the colour of iron flowers and fruit the colour of meat dripping lobster cracking claws lips nipples blisters blood my blood and all power.

BLUE COTTON SWEATSHIRT

that says "Why Be Normal?" in a circle on the front. This is your comfort shirt, fleecy on the inside, soft from many washings, and three sizes too big so you can tuck your hands up inside the sleeves when they're shaking or cold. You like to sit on the couch with the curtains closed, wearing your comfort shirt, eating comfort food: vanilla ice cream, macaroni and cheese, white rice with butter and salt, white toast with Cheez Whiz and peanut butter. Sometimes you even sleep in it.

This is the shirt you wore when you had the abortion three days before Christmas. They told you to be there at nine in the morning and then you didn't get into the operating room until nearly twelve-thirty. So

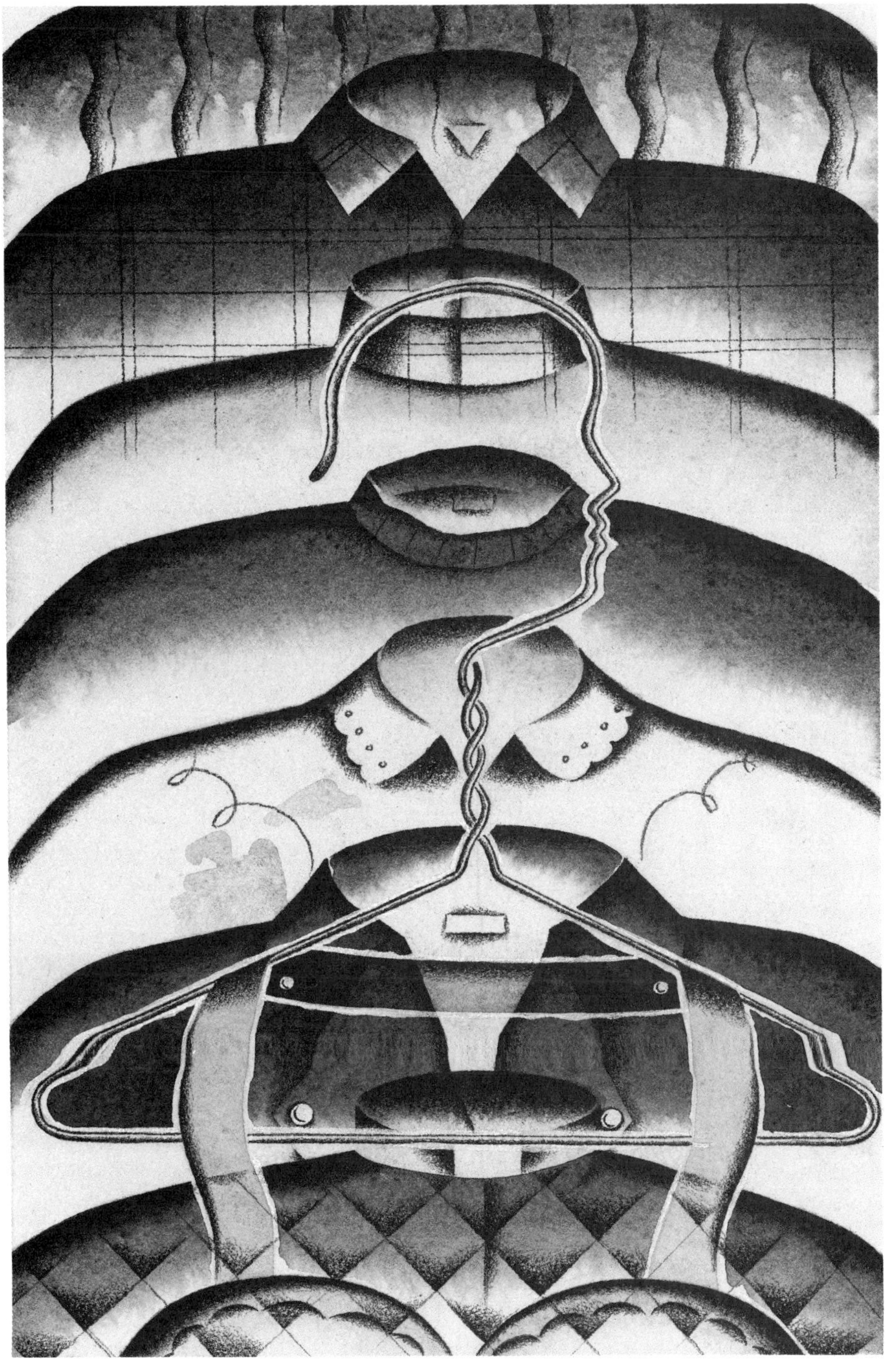

you wore it in the waiting room with the other women also waiting, and the weight you had already gained was hidden beneath it while you pretended to read *Better Homes and Gardens* and they wouldn't let you smoke. After you came to, you put the shirt back on and waited in another waiting room for your friend Alice to come and pick you up because they said you weren't capable yet of going home alone. One of the other women was waiting there too, for her boyfriend, who was always late, and when he finally got there, first she yelled at him briefly and then they decided to go to McDonald's for a hamburger. At home, Alice pours you tea from the porcelain pot into white china cups like precious opaque stones.

None of this has diminished, as you feared it might, the comfort this shirt can give you when you need it. Alice always puts her arms around you whenever she sees you wearing it now. She has one just like it, only pink.

> BLUE: azure aqua turquoise delft and navy-blue royal-blue cool cerulean peacock-blue indigo ultramarine cobalt-blue Prussian-blue cyan the sky and electric a space the colour of the firmament and sapphire sleeping silence the sea the blues my lover plays the saxophone cool blue he plays the blues.

PALE GREY TURTLENECK

that you bought when you were seeing Dwight, who said one night for no apparent reason that grey is a mystical colour. You took this judgment to heart because Dwight was more likely to talk about hockey or carburetors and you were pleasantly surprised to discover that he might also think about other things. You spotted the turtleneck the very next day on sale at Maggie's for $9.99.

You took to wearing it on Sundays because that was the day Dwight was mostly likely to wander in, unannounced, on his way to or from somewhere else. You wore it while you just happened to put a bottle of good white wine into the fridge to chill and a chicken, a roast, or a pan of spinach lasagna into the oven to cook slowly just in case he showed up hungry. You suppose now that this was pathetic, but at the time you were thinking of yourself as patient and him as worth waiting for.

Three Sundays in a row you ended up passed out on the couch, the wine bottle empty on the coffee table, the supper dried out, and a black-and-white movie with violin music flickering on the TV. In the coloured morning, the pattern of the upholstery was imprinted on your cheek and your whole head was hurting. When Dwight finally did show up, it was a Wednesday and you were wearing your orange flannelette nightie with all the buttons gone and a rip down the front, because it was three in the morning, he was drunk, and you had been in bed for hours. He just laughed and took you in his arms when you told him to get lost. Until you said you were seeing someone else, which was a lie, but one that you both wanted to believe because it was an easy answer that let both of you gingerly off the hook.

You keep meaning to wear that turtleneck again sometime because you know it's juvenile to think it's a jinx, but then you keep forgetting to iron it.

Finally you get tough and wear it, wrinkled, grocery-shopping one Saturday afternoon. You career through the aisles like a crazed hamster, dodging toddlers, old ladies, and other carts, scooping up vegetables with both hands, eating an apple you haven't paid for, leaving the core in the dairy section. But nothing happens and no one notices your turtleneck: the colour or the wrinkles.

Sure enough, Dwight calls the next day, Sunday, at five o'clock. You say you can't talk now, you're just cooking supper: prime rib, wild rice, broccoli with Hollandaise. You have no trouble at all hanging quietly up on him while pouring the wine into the crystal goblet before setting the table for one with the Royal Albert china your mother left you in her will.

> GREY: oyster pewter slate dull lead dove-grey pearl-grey brain my brains silver or simple gone into the mystic a cool grey day overcast with clouds ashes concrete the aftermath of airplanes gunmetal-grey granite and gossamer whales elephants cats in the country the colour of questions the best camouflage the opaque elegance an oyster.

WHITE EMBROIDERED BLOUSE

that you bought for $80 to wear with your red-flowered skirt to a Christmas party with Peter, who was working as a pizza cook until he could afford to play his sax full-time.You also bought a silken red belt with gold beads and tassels, a pair of red earrings with dragons on them, and ribbed red stockings which are too small but you wanted them anyway. This striking outfit involves you and Alice in a whole day of trudging around downtown in a snowstorm, holding accessories up in front of mirrors like talismans.

You spend an hour in the bathroom getting ready, drinking white wine, plucking your eyebrows, dancing like a dervish, and smiling seductively at yourself. Peter calls to say he has to work late but he'll meet you there at midnight.

By the time he arrives, you are having a complex anatomical conversation with an intern named Fernando who has spilled a glass of red wine down the front of your blouse. He is going to be a plastic surgeon. Your blouse is soaking in the bathtub and you are wearing only your white lace camisole. Fernando is feeding you green grapes and little squares of cheese, complimenting your cheekbones, and falling in love with your smooth forehead. You are having the time of your life and it's funny how you notice for the first time that Peter has an inferior bone structure.

> WHITE: ivory alabaster magnolia milk the moon is full and chalk-white pure-white snow-white moonstone limestone rime and clay marble many seashells and my bones are china bones precious porcelain lace white magic white feather the immaculate conception of white lies wax white wine as a virtue.

YELLOW EVENING GOWN

that you bought for your New Year's Eve date with Fernando. It has a plunging neckline and a dropped sash which flatteringly accentuates your hips. You wear it with black hoop earrings, black lace stockings with seams, and black high-heels that Alice forced you to buy even though they hurt your toes and you are so uncoordinated that you expect you will have to spend the entire evening sitting down with your legs crossed, calves nicely flexed.

You spend an hour in the bathroom getting ready, drinking pink champagne, applying blusher with a fat brush according to a diagram in a women's magazine that shows you how to make the most of your face. You practise holding your chin up so it doesn't sag and look double. Alice French-braids your hair and teaches you how to waltz like a lady. Fernando calls to say he has to work late but he'll meet you there before midnight.

You go to the club with Alice instead. They seat you at a tiny table for two so that when you sit down, your knees touch hers. You are in the middle of a room full of candles, fresh flowers, lounge music, and well-groomed couples staring feverishly into each other's eyes. The meal is sumptuous: green salad, a whole lobster, homemade pasta, fresh asparagus, and warm buns wrapped in white linen in a wicker basket. You eat everything and then you get the hell out of there, leaving a message for Fernando.

You go down the street to a bar you know where they will let you in without a ticket even though it's New Year's Eve. In the lobby you meet Fernando in a tuxedo with his arm around a short homely woman in black who, when you ask, "Who the hell are you?", says, "His wife." In your black high-heels you are taller than both of them and you know your gown is gorgeous. When the wife says, "And who the hell are *you*?," you point a long finger at Fernando's nose and say, "Ask him." You stomp away with your chin up and your dropped sash swinging.

Out of sight, you take off your high-heels and walk home through the park and the snow with them in your hands, dangling. Alice follows in a cab. By the time you get there, your black lace stockings are in shreds and your feet are cut and you are laughing and crying, mostly laughing.

> YELLOW: jonquil jasmine daffodil lemon and honey-coloured corn-coloured cornsilk canary crocus the egg yolk in the morning the colour of mustard bananas brass cadmium yellow is the colour of craving craven chicken cats' eyes I am faint-hearted weak-kneed lily-livered or the sun lucid luminous means caution or yield.

BLACK LEATHER JACKET

that you bought when you were seeing Ivan, who rode a red Harley-Davidson low-rider with a suicide shift, his black beard blowing in the wind. The jacket has rows of diagonal pleats at the yoke and a red leather collar and cuffs.

Ivan used to take you on weekend runs with his buddies and their old ladies to little bars in other towns where they were afraid of you: especially of Ivan's best friend, Spy, who had been hurt in a bike accident two years before and now his hands hung off his wrists at odd angles and he could not speak, could only make guttural growls, write obscene notes to the waitress on a serviette, and laugh at her like a madman, his eyes rolling back in his head, and you could see what was left of his tongue.

You would come riding up in a noisy pack with bugs in your teeth, dropping your black helmets like bowling balls on the floor, eating greasy burgers and pickled eggs, drinking draft beer by the jug, the foam running down your chin. Your legs, after the long ride, felt like a wishbone waiting to be sprung. If no one would rent you a room, you slept on picnic tables in the campground, the bikes pulled in around you like wagons, a case of beer and one sleeping bag between ten of you. In the early morning, there was dew on your jacket and your legs were numb with the weight of Ivan's head on them.

You never did get around to telling your mother you were dating a biker (she thought you said "baker"), which was just as well, since Ivan eventually got tired, sold his bike, and moved back to Manitoba to live with his mother, who was dying. He got a job in a hardware store and soon married his high school sweetheart, Betty, who was a dental hygienist. Spy was killed on the highway: drove his bike into the back of a tanker truck in broad daylight; there was nothing left of him.

You wear your leather jacket now when you need to feel tough. You wear it with your tight blue jeans and your cowboy boots. You strut slowly with your hands in your pockets. Your boots click on the concrete and you are a different person. You can handle anything and no one had better get in your way. You will take on the world if you have to. You will die young and in flames if you have to.

> BLACK: ebon sable charcoal jet lamp-black blue-black bruises in a night sky ink-black soot-black the colour of my hair and burning rubber dirt the colour of infinite space speeding blackball blacklist black sheep blackberries ravens eat crow black as the ace of spades and black is black I want my baby back before midnight yes of course midnight that old black dog behind me.

BROWN CASHMERE SWEATER

that you were wearing the night you told Daniel you were leaving him. It was that week between Christmas and New Year's which is always a wasteland. Everyone was digging up recipes called Turkey-Grape Salad, Turkey Soufflé, and Turkey-Almond-Noodle Bake. You kept vacuuming up tinsel and pine needles, putting away presents one at a time from under the tree. You and Daniel sat at the kitchen table all afternoon, drinking hot rum toddies, munching on crackers and garlic sausage, playing Trivial Pursuit, asking each other questions like:

What's the most mountainous country in Europe?

Which is more tender, the left or right leg of a chicken?

What race of warriors burned off their right breasts in Greek legend?

Daniel was a poor loser and he thought that Europe was a country, maybe somewhere near Spain.

This night you have just come from a party at his friend Harold's house. You are sitting on the new couch, a loveseat, blue with white flowers, which was Daniel's Christmas present to you, and you can't help thinking of the year your father got your mother a coffee percolator when all she wanted was something personal: earrings, a necklace, a scarf for God's sake. She spent most of the day locked in their bedroom, crying noisily, coming out every hour or so to baste the turkey, white-lipped, tucking more Kleenex up her sleeve. You were on her side this time and wondered how your father, whom you had always secretly loved the most, could be so insensitive. It was the changing of the guard, your allegiance shifting like sand from one to the other.

You are sitting on the new couch eating cold pizza and trying to figure out why you didn't have a good time at the party. Daniel is accusing you alternately of looking down on his friends or sleeping with them. He is wearing the black leather vest you bought him for Christmas and he says you are a cheapskate.

When you tell him you are leaving (which is a decision you made months ago but it took you this long to figure out how you were going to manage it and it has nothing to do with the party, the couch, or the season), Daniel grips you by the shoulders and bangs your head against the wall until the picture hung there falls off. It is a photograph of the mountains on a pink spring morning, the ridges like ribs, the run-off like incisions or veins. There is glass flying everywhere in slices into your face, into your hands pressed over your eyes and the front of your sweater is spotted and matted with blood.

On the way to the hospital, he says he will kill you if you tell them what he did to you. You promise him anything, you promise him that you will love him forever and that you will never leave.

The nurse takes you into the examining room. Daniel waits in the waiting room, reads magazines, buys a chocolate bar from the vending machine, then a Coke and a bag of ripple chips. You tell the nurse what happened and the police take him away in handcuffs with their guns drawn. In the car on the way to the station, he tells them he only did it because he loves you. The officer who takes down your report tells you this and he just keeps shaking his head and patting your arm. The police photographer takes pictures of your face, your broken fingers, your left breast which has purple bruises all over it where he grabbed it and twisted and twisted.

By the time you get to the women's shelter, it is morning and the blood on your sweater had dried, doesn't show. There is no way of knowing. There, the other women hold you, brush your hair, bring you coffee and cream-of-mushroom soup. The woman with the broken cheekbone has two canaries in a gold cage that she carries with her everywhere like a lamp. She shows you how the doors are steel, fifteen centimetres thick, and the windows are bullet-proof. She shows you where you will sleep, in a room on the third floor with six other women, some of them lying now fully dressed on their little iron cots with their hands behind their heads, staring at the ceiling as if it were full of stars or clouds that drift slowly westward in the shape of camels, horses, or bears. She shows you how the canaries will sit on your finger if you hold very still and pretend you are a tree or a roof or another bird.

> BROWN: ochre cinnamon coffee copper caramel the colour of my Christmas cake chocolate mocha walnut chestnuts raw sienna my suntan burnt umber burning toast fried fricasseed sautéed grilled I baste the turkey the colour of stupid cows smart horses brown bears brown shirt brown sugar apple brown betty brunette the colour of thought and sepia the colour of old photographs the old earth and wood.

GREEN SATIN QUILTED JACKET

in the Oriental style with mandarin collar and four red frogs down the front. This jacket is older than you are. It belonged to your mother, who bought it when she was the same age you are now. In the black-and-white photos from that time, the jacket is grey but shiny and your mother is pale but smooth-skinned, smiling with her hand on her hip or your father's thigh.

You were always pestering her to let you wear it to play dress-up, with her red high-heels and that white hat with the feathers and the little veil that covered your whole face. You wanted to wear it to a Halloween party at school where all the other girls would be witches, ghosts, or princesses, and you would be the only mandarin, with your eyes, you imagined, painted up slanty and two sticks through a bun in your hair. But she would never let you. She would just keep on cooking supper, bringing carrots, potatoes, cabbages up from the root cellar, taking peas, beans, broccoli out of the freezer in labelled dated parcels, humming, looking out through the slats of the Venetian blind at the black garden and the leafless rose bushes. Each year, at least one of them would be winter-killed no matter how hard she had tried to protect them. And she would dig it up in the spring by the dead roots and the thorns would get tangled in her hair, leave long bloody scratches all down her arms. And the green jacket stayed where it was, in the cedar chest with the hand-made lace doilies, her grey linen wedding suit, and the picture of your father as a small boy with blond ringlets.

After the funeral, you go through her clothes while your father is outside shovelling snow. You lay them out in piles on the bed: one for the Salvation Army, one for the second-hand store, one for yourself because your father wants you to take something home with you. You will take the green satin jacket, also a white mohair cardigan with multicoloured squares on the front, a black-and-white striped shirt you sent her for her birthday last year that she never wore, an imitation-pearl necklace for Alice, and a dozen unopened packages of pantyhose. There is a fourth pile for your father's friend Jack's new wife, Frances, whom your mother never liked, but your father says Jack and Frances have fallen on hard times on the farm since Jack got the emphysema, and Frances will be glad of some new clothes.

Jack and Frances drop by the next day with your Aunt Jeanne. You serve tea and the shortbread cookies Aunt Jeanne has brought. She makes them just the way your mother did, whipped, with a sliver of maraschino cherry on top. Jack, looking weather-beaten or embarrassed, sits on the edge of the couch with his baseball cap in his lap and marvels at how grownup you've got to be. Frances is genuinely grateful for the two green garbage bags of clothes, which you carry out to the truck for her.

After they leave, you reminisce fondly with your father and Aunt Jeanne about taking the toboggan out to Jack's farm when you were small, tying it to the back of the car, your father driving slowly down the country lane, towing you on your stomach, clutching the front of the toboggan which curled like a wooden wave. You tell him for the first time how frightened you were of the black tires spinning the snow into your face, and he says he had no idea, he thought you were having fun. This was when Jack's first wife, Winnifred, was still alive. Your Aunt Jeanne, who knows everything, tells you that when Winnifred was killed in that car accident, it was Jack, driving drunk, who caused it. And now when he gets drunk, he beats Frances up, locks her out of the house in her bare feet, and she has to sleep in the barn, in the hay with the horses.

You are leaving in the morning. Aunt Jeanne helps you pack. You are anxious to get home but worried about leaving your father alone. Aunt Jeanne says she'll watch out for him.

The green satin jacket hangs in your front hall closet now, between your black leather jacket and your raincoat. You can still smell the cedar from the chest and the satin is always cool on your cheek like clean sheets or glass.

One day you think you will wear it downtown, where you are meeting a new man for lunch. You study yourself in the full-length mirror on the back of the bathroom door and you decide it makes you look like a different person: someone unconventional, unusual, and unconcerned. This new man, whom you met recently at an outdoor jazz festival, is a free spirit who eats health food, plays the dulcimer, paints well, writes well, sings well, and has just completed an independent study of eastern religions. He doesn't smoke, drink, or do drugs. He is pure and peaceful, perfect. He is teaching you how to garden, how to turn the black soil, how to plant the seeds, how to water them, weed them, watch them turn into lettuce, carrots, peas, beans, radishes, and pumpkins, how to get the kinks out of your back by stretching your brown arms right up to the sun. You haven't even told Alice about him yet because he is too good to be true. He is bound to love this green jacket, and you in it too.

You get in your car, drive around the block, go back inside because you forgot your cigarettes, and you leave the green jacket on the back of a kitchen chair because who are you trying to kid? More than anything, you want to be transparent. More than anything, you want to hold his hands across the table and then you will tell him you love him and it will all come true.

> GREEN: viridian verdigris chlorophyll grass leafy jade mossy verdant apple-green pea-green lime-green sage-green sea-green bottle-green emeralds avocadoes olives all leaves the colour of Venus hope and jealousy the colour of mould mildew envy poison and pain and snakes the colour of everything that grows in my garden fertile nourishing sturdy sane and strong.

Stones

BY SANDRA BIRDSELL

"Mother played with the pegs in the pouch and made little squares in the dirt with her foot while Mrs. Hallman said how pleased she was to be living in the country instead of the city, so much nicer for the children, didn't she think?"

Mother made a new apron the day after she and Father quarrelled and he slammed the door and went walking. She didn't come away from the kitchen window for a long time, and I tiptoed around the house feeling nervous because she hadn't noticed that it was past my bedtime.

She was wearing the apron when she met the doctor's wife, Mrs. Hallman, out by the clothesline, only you couldn't see it for the pouch of clothespegs tied around her thick waist. Mrs. Hallman stood tall and slim, her red toenails sticking out the end of her white sandals, and she smelled like the sweet william that grew in a patch beside the back porch. I hung around like a sticky fly in August and listened while they talked. Mother played with the pegs in the pouch and made little squares in the dirt with her foot while Mrs. Hallman said how pleased she was to be living in the country instead of the city, so much nicer for the children, didn't she think? Then she asked which one I was and Mother told her, Lureen the second of five and one was coming.

Mrs. Hallman said, "Oh how nice," her Jane Russell lips forming a raspberry circle and I wished suddenly that Mother would take off the pouch so the ric rac on the apron would show. Mrs. Hallman patted her flat stomach and told Mother that it sure was good to be slim again and that was *it* for her. Then she laughed and her voice went high and tinkly like a wind chime. Mother laughed too, and her laughter was like rubbing two stones together.

At supper Mother said to Father that the kids were terrible. And how could she invite Mrs. Hallman in? He hadn't built the cage he'd promised now for a month and Rudy let Jeepers loose again in the kitchen and Sharon wouldn't come down from the kitchen table. She'd offered Mrs. Hallman some tomatoes, but they're allergic to tomatoes, and it was too bad, but she couldn't play bridge with Mrs. Hallman because she had better things to do with her time.

When Mrs. Hallman came for coffee, Mother would send me to the cellar for a jar of jelly and spread a clean tablecloth. Then she would sit drawing circles with her finger, smiling and nodding while Mrs. Hallman rattled her charm bracelet and talked about Toronto and Minneapolis and "my husband the doctor." I would sit listening to her wind chime laughter, unable to move when told to go out and play with the others.

When Mrs. Hallman left, Mother would bang pots and pans on the stove or put on Father's fishing hat and chop weeds in the garden, making chunks of earth fly up around her feet.

The oldest daughter, Emily, and I became friends. She played store with real groceries and let me watch. She had bubble gum and pop whenever she wanted and sometimes gave me sips. She had her own bicycle and she wouldn't let me ride it. I gave up my perch in the maple tree where I'd spent the summer building a tree house and began moping about the kitchen complaining of having nothing to do. When I asked Mother why we didn't have one measly bike, she slammed the oven door hard and said stoves were more important than bicycles and if we ever got anything new around this house it would be a stove that works right.

Then Rudy tried fly casting at the telephone wires and caught a fish hook in his finger. Mother sent me to the Hallmans' and the doctor said he'd come over and then stayed to have a slice of fresh bread, his eyes never leaving the cupboard where Mother had piled her batches of bread and buns. And when he asked if it was really true, did she really make that delicious bread, she smiled at him the way she smiles at Father when he pulls the little curl on the back of her neck and says she's keeping her girlish figure.

The doctor stood in the door with two loaves of our bread under his arm and asked if they could have the recipe. He said some more and

Mother laughed high and tinkly like the wind chimes and said she'd always wanted to play bridge, she'd just never had anyone offer to teach her and yes, she'd be glad to give him the recipe.

She sent me the next day with the recipe which I put under a stone for a moment while I helped Rudy untangle Father's fishing reel, which was tied to a kite. We couldn't fix it, so we buried the reel in the garden and when I got back, I stood and watched the wind flip the paper under the stone. Then I saw Emily's bicycle lying in her driveway and I lifted the stone and let the recipe blow away. I told Mother the doctor's wife said she didn't have time to bake bread.

When Father came home for supper, Mother was banging pots on the stove and said that she wouldn't bother with bridge after all, she had too much to do. Father said there was no rest for the wicked and Mother laughed, and her laughter was like rubbing two stones together.

What I Learned from Caesar

BY GUY VANDERHAEGHE

"I reasoned the way I had to, for my sake, for my father's. What was he but a man dishonoured by faceless foes?"

The oldest story is the story of flight, the search for greener pastures. But the pastures we flee, no matter how brown and blighted—these travel with us; they can't be escaped.

My father was an immigrant. You would think this no penalty in a nation of immigrants, but even his carefully nurtured, precisely colloquial English didn't spare him much pain. Nor did his marriage to a woman of British stock (as we called it then, before the vicious-sounding acronym WASP came into use). That marriage should have paid him a dividend of respectability, but it only served to make her suspect in marrying him.

My father was a lonely man, a stranger who made matters worse by pretending he wasn't. It's true that he was familiar enough with his adopted terrain, more familiar than most because he was a salesman. Yet he was never really *of* it, no matter how much he might wish otherwise. I only began to understand what had happened to him when I, in my turn, left for greener pastures, heading east. I didn't go so far, not nearly so far as he had. But I also learned that there is a price to be paid. Mine was a trivial one, a feeling of mild unease. At odd moments I betrayed myself and my beginnings; I knew that I lacked the genuine ring of a local. And I had never even left my own country.

Occasionally I return to the small Saskatchewan town near the Manitoba border where I grew up. To the unpractised eye of an easterner the countryside around that town might appear undifferentiated and monotonous, part and parcel of that great swath of prairie that vacationers drive through, pitying its inhabitants and deploring its restrooms, intent only on leaving it all behind as quickly as possible. But it is just here that the prairie verges on parkland, breaking into rolling swells of land, and here, too, that it becomes a little greener and easier on the eye. There is still more sky than any country is entitled to, and it teases the traveller into believing he can never escape it or find shelter under it. But if your attention wanders from that hypnotic expanse of blue and the high clouds drifting in it, the land becomes more comfortable as prospects shorten, and the mind rests easier on attenuated distances. There is cropland: fields of rye, oats, barley, and wheat; flat, glassy sloughs shining like mirrors in the sun; a solitary clump of trembling poplar; a bluff that gently climbs to nudge the sky.

When I was a boy it was a good deal bleaker. The topsoil had blown off the fields and into the ditches to form black dunes; the crops were withered and burnt; there were no sloughs because they had all dried up. The whole place had a thirsty look. That was during the thirties when we were dealt a doubly cruel hand of drought and economic depression. It was not a time or place that was kindly to my father. He had come out of the urban sprawl of industrial Belgium some twenty-odd years before, and it was only then, I think, that he was beginning to come to terms with a land that must have seemed forbidding after his own tiny country, so well tamed and marked by man. And then this land played him the trick of becoming something more than forbidding; it became fierce, and fierce in every way.

It was in the summer of 1931, the summer that I thought was merely marking time before I would pass into high school, that he lost his territory. For as long as I could remember I had been a salesman's son, and then it ended. The company he worked for began to feel the pinch of the depression and moved to merge its territories. He was let go. So one morning he unexpectedly pulled up at the front door and began to haul his sample cases out of the Ford.

"It's finished," he said to my mother as he flung the cases onto the lawn. "I got the boot. I offered to stay on—strictly commission. He wouldn't hear of it. Said he couldn't see fit to starve two men where there was only a living for one. I'd have starved that other sonofabitch out. He'd have had to hump his back and suck the hind tit when I was through with him." He paused, took off his fedora and nervously ran his index finger around the sweat-band. Clearing his throat, he said, "His parting words were, 'Good luck, Dutchie!' I should have spit in his eye. Jesus H. Christ himself wouldn't dare call me Dutchie. The bastard."

Offence compounded offence. He thought he was indistinguishable, that the accent wasn't there. Maybe his first successes as a salesman owed something to his naivety. Maybe in good times, when there was more than enough to go around, people applauded his performance by buying from him. He was a counterfeit North American who paid them the most obvious of compliments, imitation. Yet hard times make people less generous. Jobs were scarce, business was poor. In a climate like that, perceptions change, and perhaps he ceased to be merely amusing and became, instead, a dangerous parody. Maybe that district manager, faced with a choice, could only think of George Vander Elst as Dutchie. Then again, it might have been that my father just wasn't a good enough salesman. Who can judge at this distance?

But for the first time my father felt as if he had been exposed. He had never allowed himself to remember that he was a foreigner, or if he had, he persuaded himself he had been wanted. After all, he was a northern European, a Belgian. They had been on the preferred list.

He had left all that behind him. I don't even know the name of the town or the city where he was born or grew up. He always avoided my questions about his early life as if they dealt with a distasteful and criminal past that was best forgotten. Never, not even once, did I hear him speak Flemish. There were never any of the lapses you might expect. No pet names in his native language for my mother or myself; no words of endearment which would have had the comfort of childhood use. Not even when driven to one of his frequent rages did he curse in the mother tongue. If he ever prayed, I'm sure it was in English. If a man forgets the cradle language in the transports of prayer, love, and rage—well, it's forgotten.

The language he did speak was, in a sense, letter-perfect, fluent, glib. It was the language of wheeler-dealers, and of the heady twenties, of salesmen, high-rollers, and persuaders. He spoke of people as live-wires, go-getters, self-made men. Hyphenated words to describe the hyphenated life of the seller, a life of fits and starts, comings and goings. My father often proudly spoke of himself as a self-made man, but this description was not the most accurate. He was a remade man. The only two pictures of him which I have in my possession are proof of this.

The first is a sepia-toned photograph taken, as nearly as I can guess, just prior to his departure from Belgium. In this picture he is wearing an ill-fitting suit, round-toed, clumsy boots, and a cloth cap. The second was taken by a street photographer in Winnipeg. My father is walking down the street, a snap-brim fedora slanting rakishly over one eye. His suit is what must have been considered stylish then—a three-piece pin-stripe—and he is carrying an overcoat casually over one arm. He is exactly what he admired most, a "snappy dresser," or, since he always had trouble with his p's, a "snabby dresser." The clothes, though they mark a great change, aren't really that important. Something else tells the story.

In the first photograph my father stands rigidly with his arms folded across his chest, unsmiling. Yet I can see that he is a young man who is hesitant and afraid; not of the camera, but of what this picture-taking means. There is a reason why he is having his photograph taken. He must leave something of himself behind with his family so he will not be forgotten, and carry something away with him so that he can remember. That is what makes this picture touching; it is a portrait of a solitary, an exile.

In the second picture his face is blunter, fleshier: nothing surprising in that, he is older. But suddenly you realize he is posing for the camera—not in the formal, European manner of the first photograph but in a manner far more unnatural. You see, he is pretending to be entirely natural and unguarded; yet he betrays himself. The slight smile, the squared shoulder, the overcoat draped over the arm, all are calculated bits of a composition. He has seen the camera from a block away. My father wanted to be caught in exactly this negligent, unassuming pose, sure that it would capture for all time his prosperity, his success, his adaptability. Like most men, he wanted to leave a record. And this was it. And if he had coached himself in such small matters, what would he ever leave to chance?

That was why he was so ashamed when he came home that summer. There was the particular shame of having lost his job, a harder thing for a man then than it might be today. There was the shame of knowing that sooner or later we would have to go on relief, because being a lavish spender he had no savings. But there was also the shame of a man who suddenly discovers that all his lies were transparent, and everything he thought so safely hidden had always been in plain view. He had been living one of those dreams. The kind of dream in which you are walking down the street, meeting friends and neighbours, smiling and nodding, and when you arrive at home and pass a mirror you see for the first time you are stark naked. He was sure that behind his back he had always been Dutchie. For a man with so much pride a crueller epithet would have been kinder; to be hated gives a man some kind of status. It was the condescension implicit in that diminutive, its mock playfulness, that made him appear so undignified in his own eyes.

And for the first time in my life I was ashamed of him. He didn't have the grace to bear an injustice, imagined or otherwise, quietly. At first he merely brooded, and then like some man with a repulsive sore, he sought pity by showing it. I'm sure he knew that he could only offend, but he was under a compulsion to justify himself. He began with my mother by explaining, where there was no need for explanation, that he had had his job taken from him for no good reason. However, there proved to be little satisfaction in preaching to the converted, so he carried his tale to everyone he knew. At first his references to his plight were tentative and oblique. The responses were polite but equally tentative and equally oblique. This wasn't what he had hoped for. He believed that the sympathy didn't measure up to the occasion. So his story was told and retold, and each time it was enlarged and embellished until the injustice was magnified beyond comprehension. He made a damn fool of himself. This was the first sign, although my mother and I chose not to recognize it.

In time everyone learned my father had lost his job for no good reason. And it wasn't long before the kids of the fathers he had told his story to were following me down the street chanting, "No good reason. No good reason." That's how I learned my family was a topical joke that the town was enjoying with zest. I suppose my father found out too, because it was about that time he stopped going out of the house. He couldn't fight back and neither could I. You never can.

After a while I didn't leave the house unless I had to. I spent my days sitting in our screened verandah reading old copies of *Saturday Evening Post* and *Maclean's*. I was content to do anything that helped me forget the heat and the monotony, the shame and the fear, of that longest of summers. I was thirteen then and in a hurry to grow up, to press time into yielding the bounty I was sure it had in keeping for me. So I was killing time minute by minute with those magazines. I was to enter high school that fall and that seemed a prelude to adulthood and independence. My father's misfortunes couldn't fool me into believing that maturity didn't mean strength to plunder at will. So when I found an old Latin grammar of my mother's I began to read that too. After all, Latin was the arcane language of the professions, of lawyers and doctors, those divinities owed immediate and unquestioning respect. I decided I would become either one, because respect could never be stolen from them as it had been from by father.

That August was the hottest I can remember. The dry heat made my nose bleed at night, and I often woke to find my pillow stiff with blood. The leaves of the elm tree in the front yard hung straight down on their stems; flies buzzed heavily, their bodies tip-tapping lazily against the screens, and people passing the house moved so languidly they seemed to be walking in water. My father, who had always been careful about his appearance, began to come down for breakfast barefoot, wearing only a vest undershirt and an old pair of pants. He rarely spoke, but carefully picked his way through his meal as if it were a dangerous obstacle course, only pausing to rub his nose thoughtfully. I noticed that he had begun to smell.

One morning he looked up at me, laid his fork carefully down beside his plate and said, "I'll summons him."

"Who?"

"Who do you think?" he said scornfully. "The bastard who fired me. He had no business calling me Dutchie. That's slander."

"You can't summons him."

"I can," he said emphatically. "I'm a citizen. I've got rights. I'll go to law. He spoiled my good name."

"That's not slander."

"It is."

"No it isn't."

"I'll sue the bastard," he said vaguely, looking around to appeal to my mother, who had left the room. He got up from the table and went to the doorway. "Edith," he called, "tell your son I've got the right to summons that bastard."

Her voice came back faint and timid, "I don't know, George."

He looked back at me. "You're in the same boat, sonny. And taking sides with them don't save you. When we drown we all drown together."

"I'm not taking sides," I said indignantly. "Nobody's taking sides. It's facts. Can't you see...," but I didn't get a chance to finish. He left, walked out on me. I could hear his steps on the stairway, tired, heavy steps. There was so much I wanted to say. I wanted to make it plain that being on his side meant saving him from making a fool of himself again. I wanted him to know he could never win that way. I wanted him to win, not lose. He was my father. But he went up those steps, one at a time, and I heard his foot fall distinctly, every time. Beaten before he started, he crawled back into bed. My mother went up to him several times that day, to see if he was sick, to attempt to gouge him out of that room, but she couldn't. It was only later that afternoon, when I was reading on the verandah, that he suddenly appeared again, wearing only a pair of undershorts. His body shone dully with sweat, his skin looked grey and soiled.

"They're watching us," he said, staring past me at an empty car parked in the bright street.

Frightened, I closed my book and asked who was watching us.

"The relief people," he said tiredly. "They think I've got money hidden somewhere. They're watching me, trying to catch me with it. The joke's on them. I got no money." He made a quick, furtive gesture that drew attention to his almost naked body, as if it were proof of his poverty.

"Nobody is watching us. That car's empty."

"Don't take sides with them," he said, staring through the screen. I thought someone from one of the houses across the street might see him like that, practically naked.

"The neighbours'll see," I said, turning my head to avoid looking at him.

"See what?" he asked, surprised.

"You standing like that. Naked almost."

"There's nothing they can do. A man's home is his castle. That's what the English say, isn't it?"

And he went away laughing.

Going down the hallway, drawing close to his door that always stood ajar, what did I hope? To see him dressed, his trousers rolled up to mid-calf to avoid smudging his cuffs, whistling under his breath, shining his shoes? Everything as it was before? Yes, I hoped that. If I had been younger then and still believed that frogs were turned into princes with a kiss, I might even have believed it could happen. But I didn't believe. I only hoped. Every time I approached his door (and that was many times a day, too many), I felt the queasy excitement of hope.

It was always the same. I would look in and see him lying on the tufted pink bedspread, naked or nearly so, gasping for breath in the heat. And I always thought of a whale stranded on a beach because he was such a big man. He claimed he slept all day because of the heat, but he only pretended to. He could feel me watching him and his eyes would open. He would tell me to go away, or bring him a glass of water; or, because his paranoia was growing more marked, ask me to see if they were still in the street. I would go to the window and tell him, yes, they were. Nothing else satisfied him. If I said they weren't, his jaw would shift from side to side unsteadily and his eyes would prick with tears. Then he imagined more subtle and intricate conspiracies.

I would ask him how he felt.

"Hot," he'd say, "I'm always hot. Can't hardly breathe. Damn country," and turn on his side away from me.

My mother was worried about money. There was none left. She asked me what to do. She believed women shouldn't make decisions.

"You'll have to go to the town office and apply for relief," I told her.

"No, no," she'd say, shaking her head. "I couldn't go behind his back. I couldn't do that. He'll go himself when he feels better. He'll snap out of it. It takes a little time."

In the evening my father would finally dress and come downstairs and eat something. When it got dark he'd go out into the yard and sit on the swing he'd hung from a limb of our Manitoba maple years before, when I was a little boy. My mother and I would sit and watch him from the verandah. I felt obligated to sit with her. Every night as he settled himself onto the swing she would say the same thing. "He's too big. It'll never hold him. He'll break his back." But the swing held him up and the darkness hid him from the eyes of his enemies, and I like to think that made him happy, for a time.

He'd light a cigarette before he began to swing, and then we'd watch its glowing tip move back and forth in the darkness like a beacon. He'd flick it away when it was smoked, burning a red arc in the night, showering sparks briefly, like a comet. And then he'd light another and another, and we'd watch them glow and swing in the night.

My mother would lean over to me and say confidentially, "He's thinking it all out. It'll come to him, what to do."

I never knew whether she was trying to reassure me or herself. At last my mother would get to her feet and call to him, telling him she was going up to bed. He never answered. I waited a little longer, believing that watching him I kept him safe in the night. But I always gave up before he did and went to bed too.

The second week of September I returned to school. Small differences are keenly felt. For the first time there was no new sweater, or unsharpened pencils, or new fountain pen whose nib hadn't spread under my heavy writing hand. The school was the same school I had gone to for eight years, but that day I climbed the stairs to the second floor that housed the high school. Up there the wind moaned more persistently than I remembered it had below, and intermittently it threw handfuls of dirt and dust from the schoolyard against the windows with a gritty rattle.

Our teacher, Mrs. MacDonald, introduced herself to us, though she needed no introduction since everyone knew who she was—she had taught there for over ten years. We were given our texts and it cheered me a little to see I would have no trouble with Latin after my summer's work. Then we were given a form on which we wrote a lot of useless information. When I came to the space which asked for Racial Origin I paused, and then, out of loyalty to my father, numbly wrote in "Canadian."

After that we were told we could leave. I put my texts away in a locker for the first time—we had had none in public school—but somehow it felt strange going home from school empty-handed. So I stopped at the library door and went in. There was no school librarian and only a few shelves of books, seldom touched. The room smelled of dry paper and heat. I wandered around aimlessly, taking books down, opening them, and putting them back. That is, until I happened on Caesar's *The Gallic Wars*. It was a small, thick book that nestled comfortably in the hand. I opened it and saw that the left-hand pages were printed in Latin and the right-hand pages were a corresponding English translation. I carried it away with me, dreaming of more than proficiency in Latin.

When I got home my mother was standing on the front step, peering anxiously up and down the street.

"Have you seen your father?" she asked.

"No," I said. "Why?"

She began to cry. "I told him all the money was gone. I asked him if I could apply for relief. He said he'd go himself and have it out with them. Stand on his rights. He took everything with him. His citizenship papers, baptismal certificate, old passport, bank book, everything. I said, 'Everyone knows you. There's no need.' But he said he needed proof. Of what? He'll cause a scandal. He's been gone for an hour."

We went into the house and sat in the living room. "I'm a foolish woman," she said. She got up and hugged me awkwardly. "He'll be all right."

We sat a long time listening for his footsteps. At last we heard someone come up the walk. My mother got up and said, "There he is." But there was a knock at the door.

I heard them talking at the door. The man said, "Edith, you better come with me. George is in some trouble."

My mother asked what trouble.

"You just better come. He gave the town clerk a poke. The constable and doctor have him now. The doctor wants to talk to you about signing some papers."

"I'm not signing any papers," my mother said.

"You'd better come, Edith."

She came into the living room and said to me, "I'm going to get your father."

I didn't believe her for a minute. She put her coat on and went out.

She didn't bring him home. They took him to an asylum. It was a shameful word then, asylum. But I see it in a different light now. It seems the proper word now, suggesting as it does a refuge, a place to hide.

I'm not sure why all this happened to him. Perhaps there is no reason anyone can put their finger on, although I have my ideas.

But I needed a reason then. I needed a reason that would lend him a little dignity, or rather, lend me a little dignity; for I was ashamed of him out of my own weakness. I needed him to be strong, or at least tragic. I didn't know that most people are neither.

When you clutch at straws, anything will do. I read my answer out of Caesar's *The Gallic Wars*, the fat little book I had carried home. In the beginning of Book I he writes, "Of all people the Belgae are the most courageous...." I read on, sharing Caesar's admiration for a people who would not submit but chose to fight and see glory in their wounds. I misread it all, and bent it until I was satisfied. I reasoned the way I had to, for my sake, for my father's. What was he but a man dishonoured by faceless foes? His instincts could not help but prevail, and like his ancestors, in the end, on that one day, what could he do but make the shadows real, and fight to be free of them?

Now for the Dance

BY PATRICK O'FLAHERTY

"He just didn't want to make a fool of himself in front of thirty or forty experts in the nomenclature of the arts. There were words he'd make a mess of, for sure. He just knew it. How could he avoid 'mister,' for instance, among so many Ottawa bureaucrats? Anyway, the meeting would soon be over and he'd be on a plane to St. John's."

He still had trouble with certain words. Not with spelling them or understanding what they meant and how to use them, but just with saying them. In the middle of what could be quite a reasonable attempt at discourse, he would stumble. Maybe it was his distant bog Irish ancestry coming back to haunt him. He recalled that once as an undergraduate he had been close to winning a debate on the history of capitalism when he said the word "mer**cant**ilism," and it provoked such laughter in the audience that he had lost his edge and become flustered. Years later, in a postgraduate seminar at the University of London, the professor of medieval English literature had added: "Who here knows the name of the Icelandic scholar who rediscovered the manuscript of *Beowulf?*" Of course he had known; it was Grimur Thorkelin. Once he realized that no other student in the room had the answer, he blurted out "Thor**keel**in, Sir." "The accent, my dear boy, is on the first syllable. It is **Thork**elin, not, ah, whatever it was you said," said Professor Arthur Smith amiably. Tim O'Reilly knew that his *faux pas* would not be quickly forgotten. Stories would be still circulating about him in the Senior Common Room. "Had a chap here from the colonies a few years back, fellow named Reilly—or was it Keilly?—no matter—who said Thor**keel**in found the *Beowulf* manuscript," Smith would say. Loud snorts of laughter would follow. "Asshole," he had said to himself after the seminar, walking to the tube station.

Ten years later, now a professor of English and, for the past nine months, a member of the board of directors of the Canada Council, he was still wary of using certain words. For some reason words ending in *er* were starting to cause him grief: for "mister" he either said "mistah," slipping over the final syllable as if he were a cottonpicker from Mississippi, or else "mist**er**," emphasizing the syllable in such a way as to create a ludicrous effect of a different kind. When he did a piece for the CBC nowadays, he took out all the words ending in *er* before going on the air. Finding substitutes for such words could be damned tricky. And words ending in *air* were also giving him trouble, though for years he had them down pat: "fair," for example, he often inexplicably pronounced "fayer." Just a few days ago he noticed as well that "here" was coming out "hair." He felt as if he should consult a speech therapist. But he didn't.

He brooded on all this as the quarterly meeting of the Canada Council was drawing to a close. It was the third one he had attended, and so far he hadn't dared make an intervention. He just didn't want to make a fool of himself in front of thirty or forty experts in the nomenclature of the arts. There were words he'd make a mess of, for sure. He just knew it. How could he avoid "mister," for instance, among so many Ottawa bureaucrats? Anyway, the meeting would soon be over and he'd be on a plane to St. John's.

"Now for the dance," said the chairman of the Council, Harold Heath. Art, music, video, and literature had been dealt with in the morning session; it only remained to dish out money to the big ballet companies. All three wanted a ten percent increase in their operating budgets. In addition, towards the end of the blue book that contained the submissions from the "big three" were requests from two small dance troupes amounting to a mere $5000. Once this business was dealt with, Council members could head home.

"These are very carefully presented submissions, Mr. Chairman," said historian Jim Milbourn, the Council member from Toronto. "The three companies appear to have operated in 1982-83 with scrupulous attention to financial restraint, as we requested, and at the same time have kept a careful eye on quality. I heartily endorse their requests for a substantial increase in base funding, and I hope and pray that my colleagues sitting around the table will think as I do. But before I finish, may I say how grateful I am, we all are, if I can be so bold as to speak for everyone—and I don't see anyone objecting—how very grateful we all are to the Council's staff for providing such detailed supporting information to help us arrive at a decision, and for doing it in such a way as to make this difficult area of arts administration comprehensible, even to those not, as it were, in the know. It is a masterful job, and I repeat that the staff is to be commended. Even those who have come only recently to the Council"—Tim thought the venerable historian glanced in his direction—"can't help but be impressed. I think the minutes should record our appreciation." This was greeted by "hear, hear!" from two or three members seated at the semi-circular table at which final budgets for arts organizations were approved.

"Watch Milbourn, and learn," Heath told Tim when he took his place as the representative from Newfoundland. Tim had already seen old Milbourn operate in some tricky situations at Council meetings; he always got his way. An imposing figure, well connected in both the arts and politics, with white hair, thick glasses, and a voice that rang with authority, Milbourn spoke only at certain strategic times and with the consummate skill that came from decades of serving on important committees. He gave the appearance of being a busy man, much in demand. Messages would be slipped to him by Council secretaries who tiptoed into the chamber while discussions were underway, and he would rise, excuse himself, and go off to make phone calls in anterooms. Tim would see him in the distance on the phone, making passionate points no doubt to the prime minister or his publisher in London. On returning after lunch to begin the afternoon session, the sage would often doze off, but in such a way that if you weren't looking closely you might think he was deep in reflection on a thorny point of cultural policy.

Arnold Safeway spoke next. Boy, they've got the big guns out for the ballet companies, Tim thought. Arnold was one of the corporate executives appointed to the board by the feds to ensure that fiscal responsibility would prevail in the Council's operations. He owned a chain of supermarkets in Montreal and rumour had it that he was worth a cool $30 million. His speeches were full of phrases such as "bottom line," "corporate plan," and even "merchandise." He tended to be gruff and to the point: you heard from him the plain talk of a man with far more important matters on his mind than the state of the arts in Canada. He attended only every second

Council meeting. "Let's give the three companies the money they want," he said, "to preserve both their excellence and their international reputation. But frankly, Mr. Chairman, I don't see why the little folk groups from Nova Scotia and Saskatchewan listed in the back of the book need $5000. I think we could make savings there. It's not a lot, but we do have a bottom line, and a buck's a buck."

Next on the list of speakers was Sylvia Peso, a former ballerina who had had a hand in the founding of the National Ballet some decades ago. The trace of a cultivated English accent lingered in her voice, overriding what Tim thought was a hint of cockney. "I would like to add, Mr. Chairman," she said, "how much I too appreciate the efforts of our excellent staff, especially those in the Dance Section (she pronounced dance "dawnce"), but also how much I value the support shown by the previous speakers for the National Ballet and the other two companies. These are the country's national treasures, and no effort should be spared on our part (she said "pawt") as they continue to enhance ("enhawnce") their reputation overseas. Our ballet companies must continue to get international exposure; the world must get to know them, and travel costs a lot of money." She now paused briefly. "May I also add just a word about the submissions of the Maritime and Saskatchewan troupes. I support what Mr. Safeway has said on that matter. Regrettably, Mr. Chairman, and I say this with genuine sorrow"—Tim noticed a look of pain on her face—"these troupes are sadly lacking in artistic quality, and I can't see at this point that there is any justification for awarding them the $5000 they want. It would take much more than that to create good dance in places like Nova Scotia, Saskatchewan, and Newfoundland." She pronounced it New**found**land.

Norman Lighthead, the B.C. member who, at Tim's left, turned to him and whispered, "No ballet in the boonies, old cock." This was greeted with laughter by Tim's neighbour on the right, a wily but companionable woman from Manitoba named Mickey Hewlett. "Ballet in Newfie!" she said. "That's a joke. You can't dance in long rubbers!" "Not leaky ones, anyway," said Norman. Tim grinned. He took a lot of ribbing as a Newfoundlander. "Order, please," said the chairman.

The stage was now taken by the representative from Northern Ontario, Sherry Sampson, an English professor who made a practice of promoting the interests of Inuit and Native people. She had even been made an honorary Chief at a recent Ojibway ceremony. Tim thought she might well have defended the Maritimers, but she started on her usual spiel. "Plato,

Mr. Chairman," she said, "emphasized form as the essence of things, the spume of ideas; but I am an Aristotelian. To my way of thinking, form must be melded with matter to create truth, the true thing, the object we call art. I repeat, I am an Aristotelian; we must not have just the skeleton of form, but flesh on the skeleton, if I can say that. Only then do we have art. Let me put this another way...." Tim knew she would expand on this for five or ten minutes. Looking to his left and right, he saw eyes glaze over and members slip down in their seats, pretending to consult the blue book. One or two put on the headsets supplied for simultaneous translation. Arnold was looking at his watch.

No good dancing in Newfoundland! Tim slipped back forty years to a cold night just before Christmas in the old family house in Long Beach. The tree was up, there was cake on the table, and he could have all the syrup he wanted. Since the rest of the house was cold, all members of the family clustered around the woodstove in the kitchen. What excitement! He was playing snakes and ladders with his brothers when his uncles came in, unannounced, from up the shore, to visit their sister: Gus and Eddy Hogan, with two friends, one of them a girl from Smooth Cove whom Eddy was courting. Their faces were red from the cold, and their overshoes covered in snow. "Come on in, Eddy, give us a dance," his father said. Off came the overcoats, off the gaiters, and out came the accordion. Gus played and Uncle Eddy stepdanced, for their pleasure and to entrance the girl he loved. Oh, how he danced on the kitchen floor that dark, cold night, shaking the funnel of the stove, rattling the cups in the dresser, sweating profusely in his ecstasy! "Give it to 'er, Eddy b'y," someone would shout. Sometimes he winked at Tim, and sometimes (though Tim resented this) at his brothers. His shiny black shoes twinkled; Gus played on. Eddy swung each leg up and clapped his hands under; all the family clapped too, even their grandmother. Eddy turned his heels up and looked behind as if to see that his shoes were properly soled; he playfully slumped forward, letting his arms dangle close to the floor, laughing as the feet kept tapping behind. Tim's mother beamed. Out came the home brew from the keg behind the stove. All but the children had some. Eddy drank deeply, took off his jacket, and stepped out again. Off came his tie, his shirt sleeves were rolled up, his shirt tails were out. He danced and danced; and in his magic feet shadowy generations of downtrodden Irish men and women from the farmhouses of Youghal, the narrow streets of Kilkenny, and the banks of the River Suir danced also. And their descendants in the forgotten outharbours of Newfoundland? Yes, these too darkly came forward and stepped out in his beloved Uncle Eddy's dancing, within that warm room of a cold house.

Tim's uncle, Eddy Hogan, could dance. And if the uncle could dance, the nephew could talk.

Professor Sampson now finished her oration and the time had come to vote. "I take it," said Heath, "that the $4.3 million requested by the major ballet companies is approved, but that the $5000 for the troupes in Nova Scotia and Saskatchewan, which belong rather to folklore than to art proper, is not?" This was a question. Tim noticed widespread nodding around the table. Milbourn said loudly: "Come on. Let's do it." Even the Aristotelian chief nodded. No voice of protest was raised. "Can we then move on to a couple of items of other business?" Heath asked. "Our time is getting short. People have planes to catch." Again there was a lot of nodding. The gavel was about to fall to confirm official approval for the major dance funding when Tim put up his hand. "Mr. Reilly, you wish to say something?" asked Heath.

"Yes, I do," said Tim.

"On an item of new business, or on the dance?"

"On the dance, Mistah Chayerman," said Tim, "I'm afraid we're deadlocked."

Then he started.

Burn Sugar

BY MARLENE NOURBESE PHILIP

As a woman makes a Christmas cake, she thinks over many different things—her past, her relationship with her mother, and the history of her people.

This story is told in the speech patterns of Trinidad and Tobago because it takes place inside the mind of someone who is remembering her childhood there, who is listening to the voice of her memory.

It don't come, never arrive, had not—for the first time since she leave, had left home; is the first, for the first time in forty years the Mother not standing, had not stood over the aluminum bucket with her heavy belly whipping up the yellow eggs them and the green green lime-skin. "People does buy cake in New York," she say, the Mother had said, "not make them."

Every year it arrived, use to in time for Christmas or sometimes—a few time well—not till January, once it even come as late as March. Wherever she is, happen to be, it come wrap up and tie up in two or three layers of brown wrapping paper, an tape up in a Peak Freans tin—from last Christmas—oven-blacked black black from the oven. And it address on both sides—"just to make sure it get there," she could hear the Mother saying—in the Mother funny printing (she could never write cursive she used to say). Air mail or sea mail, she could figure out the Mother's finances—whether she have money or not. When she cut the string she use to, would tear off the Scotch tape—impatient she would rip, rip off, rip the brown paper, prise off the lid, pause… sit back on she haunches and laugh—laugh she head off—the lid never match, never matched the tin, but it there all the same—black and moist. The cake.

The weeks them use to, would pass, passed—she eating the cake, would eat it—sometimes alone by sheself; sometimes she sharing, does share a slice with a friend. And then again—sometimes when she alone, is alone, she would, does cry as she eating—each black mouthful bringing up all kind of memory—then she would, does choke—the lump of food and memory blocking up, stick up in she throat—big and hard like a rock stone.

She don't know—when she begin to notice it she doesn't know, but once she has it always, was always there when she open the tin—faint—but it there, undeniable—musty and old it rise up, an odour of mouldiness and something else from the open tin making she nose, her nostrils twitch. Is like it cast a pall over she pleasure, shadowing her delight; it spoil, clouded the rich fruity black-cake smell, and every time she take a bite it there—in she mouth—hanging about it hung about her every mouthful. The Mother's advice was to pour some more make-sure-is-good-Trinidad rum on it. Nothing help, it didn't—the smell just there lingering.

And then she know, she knew that something on its annual journey to wherever she happened to be, something inside the cake does change, changed within the cake, and whether is the change that cause the funny smell, or the journey, the travel that cause the change that cause the funny smell… she don't know….

It never use to, it didn't taste like this back home is what the first bite tell she—back back home where she hanging round, anxiously hanging about the kitchen getting in the Mother's way—underfoot—waiting for the baking to start—

"Wash the butter!" The Mother want to get her out of the way, and is like she feeling the feel of the earthenware bowl—cool, round, beige—the Mother push at her. Wash the butter, wash the butter, sit and wash the butter at the kitchen table, cover with a new piece of oilcloth for Christmas; wash the butter, and the sun coming through the breeze blocks, jumping all over the place dappling spots on she hand—it and the butter running competition for yellow. Wash the butter! Round and round… she pushing the lumps of butter round with a wooden spoon.

Every year she ask the same question—"Is why you have to do this?" and every year the Mother tell she is to get the salt out of the butter, and every year she washing the butter. The water don't look any different, it don't taste any different—if she could only see the salt leaving the butter. The Mother does catch she like this every year, and every year she washing the butter for hours, hours on end until is time to make the burn sugar.

Now! She stop. The Mother don't tell she this but she know, and the Mother know—it was understood between them. The coal-pot waiting with it red coals—the Mother never let she light it—and the iron pot waiting on the coal-pot, and the Mother waiting for the right time. She push her hand in the sugar bag—suddenly—one handful, two handful—and the white sugar rise up gentle gentle in the middle of the pot, two handfuls of white sugar rise gently… she had never, the Mother had never let she do it sheself, but to the last grain of sugar, the very last grain, she know how much does go into the pot.

She standing close close to the Mother, watching the white sugar; she know exactly when it going change—after she count to a hundred, she decide one year; another year she know for sure it wasn't going change while she holding her breath; and last year she close she eyes and know that when she open them, the sugar going change. It never once work. Every time she lose, was disappointed—the sugar never change when she expect it to, not once in all the years she watching, observing the Mother's rituals. Too quick, too slow, too late—it always catch she—by surprise—first the sugar turn sticky and brown at the edges, then a darker brown—by surprise—smoke stinging, stings her eyes, tears run running down she face, the smell sharp and strong of burning sugar—by surprise—she don't budge, she stand still watching, watches what happening in the pot—by surprise—the white sugar completely gone leaving behind a thick, black, sticky mass like molasses—by surprise. If the pot stay on long enough, she wonder, would the sugar change back, right back to cane juice, runny and white… catching she—by surprise.

The Mother grab up a kitchen towel, grabs the pot and put it in the sink—all one gesture clean and complete—and it sitting there hissing and sizzling in the sink. The Mother open the tap and steam for so rise up and *brip brap*—just so it all over—smoke gone, steam gone, smoke and steam gone leaving behind this thick thick, black liquid.

She look down at the liquid—she use to call it she magic liquid; is like it have a life of it own—its own life—and the cake need it to make it taste different. She glance over at the Mother—maybe like she need the Mother to taste different. She wonder if the Mother need her like she need the Mother—which of them was essential to the other—which of them was the burn sugar?

She stick a finger in the pot and touch the burn sugar; turning she finger this way and that, she looking at it in the sunlight turning this way and that, making sure, she make sure she don't drop any of the burn sugar on the floor; closing she eyes she closes them, and touching she touch she tongue with her finger... gently, and she taste the taste of the burn sugar strong and black in its bitterness—it bitter—and she skin-up she face then smile—it taste like it should—strong, black and bitter it going make the cake taste like no other cake.

She hanging round again, watching and waiting and watching the Mother crack the eggs into the bucket—the aluminum bucket—and she dying to crack some in sheself—if she begged she got to crack a few but most of the time she just hanging, hung around watching and waiting and watching the Mother beat the eggs. Is like the Mother thick brown arm grow an appendage—the silver egg whisk—and she hypnotizing sheself watching the big arm go up and down scraping the sides of the bucket—a blur of brown and silver lifting up, lifts the deep yellow eggs—their pale yellow frothy Sunday-best tulle skirts—higher and higher in the bucket. The Mother stop and sigh, wipe she brow—a pause a sigh, she wipes her brow—and she throw in a piece of curly, green lime-skin, add a dash of rum—"to cut the freshness"—a curl of green lime-skin and a dash of rum. She don't know if the Mother know she was going to ask why, to ask her why the lime-skin—anticipating her question—or if she was just answering she own question, she don't know, but the arm continued, keep on beating as if it have a life of it own with a life of its own, grounded by the Mother's bulk which harness the sound of she own beat—the scrape, swish and thump of her own beat.

She watching the Mother, watches her beat those eggs—how they rise up in the bucket, their heavy, yellow beauty driven by the beating arm; she remember the burn sugar and she wonder, wonders if change ever come gently... so much force or heat driving change before it. Her own change had come upon her gently... by surprise... in the night of blood... by surprise... over the months them as she watch her changes steal up on her... by surprise... the days of bloodcloth, the months that swell up her chest... by surprise... as she watched watching the swelling, budding breasts, fearful and frighten of what they mean, and don't mean. There wasn't no force there, or was there? Too old and ancient and gradual for she or her to notice as she watch the Mother and wait, waiting to grow up and change into, but not like—not like she, not like her, not like… she watching… the Mother face shiny with sweat shines, she lips tie up tight tight with the effort of the beating arm, lips held in tight and she wondering, wonders whether she, the Mother, have any answers… or questions. Did she have any—what were they?

Nobody tell she but she hand over the bowl, the bowl of washed butter she pass to the Mother who pour off the water and put in the white sugar—granulated and white she add it to the lumpy yellow mass, and without a word the Mother pass it back to her. She hand too little to do it for long—cream the butter and sugar—her arm always grows too tired too soon, and then she does have to pass it back to the Mother. But once more, one more time—just before the Mother add the eggs, she does pass it back to her again for she to witness the change—surprise sudden and sharp all the way from she fingers right up she arm along she shoulder to she eyes that open wide wide, and she suck in her breath—indrawn—how smooth the texture—all the roughness smooth right out and cream up into a pale, yellow swirl. When she taste it not a single grain of sugar leave behind, is left to mar the smooth sweetness.

She want it to be all over now—quick quick, all this mixing and beating and mixing, but she notice the sound change now that the eggs meet the butter—it heavier and thicker, reminding her it reminds her of the Mother—she and the Mother together sharing in the Mother's sound.

She leans leaning over the bucket watching how the eggs and butter never want to mix, each resisting the other and bucking up against the Mother force. Little specks and flecks of butter, pale yellow in defiance, stand up to fight the darker yellow of the eggs them, and little by little they disappear until the butter give up and give in, yields—or maybe is the other way around—the eggs them give in to the butter. Is the Mother hand that win, the Mother's arm the victor in this battle of the two yellows.

The Mother add the dry fruit that soaking in rum and cherry brandy for months now, then the white flour; the batter getting thick thickens, stiffens its resistance to the Mother's hand, the beating arm, and all the time the Mother's voice encouraging and urging—"Have/to keep/beating/all the/ time"—the words them heavy and rhythmical, keeping time with the strokes. The batter heavy and lumpy now, and it letting itself be pushed round and round the bucket—the Mother can only stir and turn now in spite of she own encouragement—but she refuse to let it alone, not giving it a minute's rest.

The Mother nod she head, and at last she know that *now* is the time—time for the burn sugar. She pick up the jar, holding it very carefully, and when the Mother nod again she begin to pour—she pouring the Mother stirring. The batter remain true to itself in how it willing to change—at first it turn from grey to brown—just like me she think, then it turn a dark brown like she sister, then an even darker brown—almost black—the colour of her brother, and all the time the Mother stirring. She empty the jar of burn sugar—her magic liquid—and the batter colour up now like she old grandmother—a seasoned black that still betray sometimes by whitish flecks of butter, egg and sugar, and the Mother arm don't stop beating and the batter turning in and on and over itself.

"How you know when it ready?"

"When the spoon can stand in it," and to show what she mean, the Mother stick the spoon the batter and it stand up stiff stiff.

Her spoon like the Mother's now stood at attention—stiff and alone in its turgid sea of black. It announced the cake's readiness for the final change of the oven. Was she ready? and was it the Mother's cake she now made? Or her own? Just an old family recipe—the cake had no other meaning—its preparation year after year only a part of painting the house, oiling the furniture, and making new curtains on the Singer machine that all together went to make up Christmas. She had never spoken to the Mother about it—about what, if anything, the cake and the burn sugar might mean....

It was its failure to arrive—the absence of the cake—even with its 'funny' smell that drove her to this understanding, this moment of epiphany as she now stood over her cheap, plastic bowl and watched the spoon. She looked down at her belly, flat and trim where the Mother's easily helped balance the aluminum bucket—not like, not like, not like her—she hadn't wanted to be like her, but she *was* trying to make the Mother's black cake, and all those buckets of batter she had witnessed being driven through their changes were now here before her—challenging her. And she *was* different—from the Mother—as different perhaps as the burn sugar was from the granulated sugar, but of the same source. Here, over this bucket—it was a plastic bowl—she met—they met and came together—to share in this old old ritual of transformation and metamorphosis.

The Mother would surely laugh at all this—all this fancy talk with words like "transformation and metamorphosis"—she who had warned of change, yet was both change and constancy. "Is only black cake child, is what you carrying on so for?" she could hear the voice. They didn't speak the same language—except in the cake, but now the Mother was sitting looking at her make the cake.

"Look Mammy—look, see how you do it—first, the most important thing is the burn sugar—the sweetness of the cake need that bitterness—you can't have black cake without it." Mammy was smiling now.

"You was always a strange one."

"Shut up Mammy and listen," (gently of course) "just listen—the burn sugar is something like we past, we history, and you know that smell I always tell you about?" Mammy nod her head, "I now know what it is—is the smell of loneliness and separation—exile from family and home and tribe—even from the land, and you know what else Mammy—is the same smell of—"

"Is only a cake child—"

"The first ones—the first ones who come here rancid and rank with the smell of fear and death. And you know what else Mammy? Is just like that funny smell of the cake when I get it—the smell never leave—it always there with us—"

"Is what foolishness you talking child—fear and death? Just make the cake and eat it."

"But Mammy that is why I remember you making the cake—that is what the memory mean—it have to mean something—everything have to have a meaning—"

"Let me tell you something girl," Mammy voice was rough, her face tight tight—"some things don't have no meaning—no meaning at all, and if you don't know that you in for a lot of trouble. Is what you trying to tell me, child—that it have a meaning for we to be here—in this part of the world—the way we was brought here? That have a meaning? No child"—the voice was gentler now—"no child, you wrong and don't go looking for no meaning—it just going break you—"

"Mammy—"

But Mammy wasn't there, at least not to talk to. She looked down at the batter. The burn sugar she used was some she the Mother had made earlier that year, accompanied by the high-pitched whine of the smoke alarm. She had made the batter by hand, as much of it as she could, even adding the green green corkscrew of lime-skin, although according to Mammy "these modern eggs never smell fresh like they suppose to—like those back home."

When they were done she almost threw the cakes out. She had left them too long in the oven and a thick crust had formed around them; the insides were moist and tasted like they should—the bitter, sweet taste perfectly balanced by the deep, rich, black colour. But the crust had ruined them. Obviously she wasn't ready, and only the expense of the ingredients had prevented her from throwing them out immediately.

It was the Mother's advice that saved them. Following her instructions by phone she cut all the crusts off the cakes, then poured rum over them to keep them moist. She had smaller cakes now—not particularly attractive ones either, but they tasted like black cake should, and without that funny smell.

Was that hard crust a sign of something more significant than her newness at making the cake? Was there indeed no meaning to the memory, or the cake, or the funny smell? She wanted to ask the Mother—she almost did—but she knew the Mother would only laugh and tell her—"Cake is for eating not thinking about—eat it and enjoy it—stop looking for meaning in everything."

She thanked the Mother, lowered the receiver slowly and said to herself—"You wrong Mammy, you wrong—there have to—there have to be a meaning."

To Every Thing There Is a Season

BY ALISTAIR MACLEOD

A man remembers how his family was when he was a boy.

I am speaking here of a time when I was eleven and lived with my family on our small farm on the west coast of Cape Breton. My family had been there for a long, long time and so it seemed had I. And much of that time seems like the proverbial yesterday. Yet when I speak on this Christmas 1977, I am not sure how much I speak with the voice of that time or how much in the voice of what I have since become. And I am not sure how many liberties I may be taking with the boy I think I was. For Christmas is a time of both past and present and often the two are imperfectly blended. As we step into its nowness we often look behind.

We have been waiting now, it seems, forever. Actually, it has been most intense since Halloween when the first snow fell upon us as we moved like muffled mummers upon darkened country roads. The large flakes were soft and new then and almost generous and the earth to which they fell was still warm and as yet unfrozen. They fell in silence into the puddles and into the sea where they disappeared at the moment of contact. They disappeared, too, upon touching the heated redness of our necks and hands or the faces of those who did not wear masks. We carried our pillowcases from house to house, knocking on doors to become silhouettes in the light thrown out from kitchens (white pillowcases held out by whitened forms). The snow fell between us and the doors and was transformed in shimmering golden beams. When we turned to leave, it fell upon our footprints and as the night wore on obliterated them and all the records of our movements. In the morning everything was soft and still and November had come upon us.

My brother Kenneth, who is two and a half, is unsure of his last Christmas. It is Halloween that looms largest in his memory as an exceptional time of being up late in magic darkness and falling snow. "Who are you going to dress up as at Christmas?" he asks. "I think I'll be a snowman." All of us laugh at that and tell him Santa Claus will find him if he is good and that he need not dress up at all. We go about our appointed tasks waiting for it to happen.

I am troubled myself about the nature of Santa Claus and I am trying to hang on to him in any way that I can. It is true that at my age I no longer *really* believe in him yet I have hoped in all his possibilities as fiercely as I can; much in the same way, I think, that the drowning man waves desperately to the lights of the passing ship on the high sea's darkness. For without him, as without the man's ship, it seems our fragile lives would be so much more desperate.

My mother has been fairly tolerant of my attempted perpetuation. Perhaps because she has encountered it before. Once I overheard her speaking about my sister Anne to one of her neighbours. "I thought Anne would *believe* forever," she said. "I practically had to tell her." I have somehow always wished I had not heard her say that as I seek sanctuary and reinforcement even in an ignorance I know I dare not trust.

Kenneth, however, believes with an unadulterated fervour, and so do Bruce and Barry who are six-year-old twins. Beyond me there is Anne who is thirteen and Mary who is fifteen, both of whom seem to be leaving childhood at an alarming rate. My mother has told us that she was already married when she was seventeen, which is only two years older than Mary is now. That too seems strange to contemplate and perhaps childhood is shorter for some than it is for others. I think of this sometimes in the evenings when we have finished our chores and the supper dishes have been cleared away and we are supposed to be doing our homework. I glance sideways at my mother, who is always knitting or mending, and at my father, who mostly sits by the stove coughing quietly with his handkerchief at his mouth. He has "not been well" for over two years and has difficulty breathing whenever he moves at more than the slowest pace. He is most sympathetic of all concerning my extended hopes and says we should hang on to the good things in our lives as long as we are able. As I look at him out of the corner of my eye, it does not seem that he has many of them left. He is old, we think, at forty-two.

Yet Christmas, in spite of all the doubts of our different ages, is a fine and splendid time, and now as we pass the mid-point of December our expectations are heightened by the increasing coldness that has settled down upon us. The ocean is flat and calm and along the coast, in the scooped-out coves, has turned to an icy slush. The brook that flows past our house is almost totally frozen and there is only a small channel of rushing water that flows openly at its very centre. When we let the cattle out to drink, we chop holes with the axe at the brook's edge so that they can drink without venturing onto the ice.

The sheep move in and out of their lean-to shelter restlessly stamping their feet or huddling together in tightly packed groups. A conspiracy of wool against the cold. The hens perch high on their roosts with their feathers fluffed out about them, hardly feeling it worthwhile to descend to the floor for their few scant kernels of grain. The pig, who has little time before his butchering, squeals his displeasure to the cold and with his snout tosses his wooden trough high in the icy air. The splendid young horse paws the planking of his stall and gnaws the wooden cribwork of his manger.

We have put a protective barricade of spruce boughs about our kitchen door and banked our house with additional boughs and billows of eel grass. Still, the pail of water we leave standing in the porch is solid in the morning and has to be broken with the hammer. The clothes my mother hangs on the line are frozen almost instantly and sway and creak from their suspending clothespins like sections of dismantled robots: the stiff-legged rasping trousers and the shirts and sweaters with unyielding arms outstretched. In the morning we race from our frigid upstairs bedrooms to finish dressing around the kitchen stove.

We would extend our coldness half a continent away to the Great Lakes of Ontario so that it might hasten the Christmas coming of my oldest brother, Neil. He is nineteen and employed on the "lake boats," the long flat carriers of grain and iron ore whose season ends any day after December 10, depending on the ice conditions. We wish it to be cold, cold on the Great Lakes of Ontario, so that he may come home to us as soon as possible. Already his cartons have arrived. They come from different places: Cobourg, Toronto, St. Catharines, Welland, Windsor, Sarnia, Sault Ste. Marie. Places that we, with the exception of my father, have never been. We locate them excitedly on the map, tracing their outlines with eager fingers. The cartons bear the lettering of Canada Steamship Lines, and are bound with rope knotted intricately in the fashion of sailors. My mother says they contain his "clothes" and we are not allowed to open them.

For us it is impossible to know the time or manner of his coming. If the lakes freeze early, he may come by train because it is cheaper. If the lakes stay open until December 20, he will have to fly because his time will be more precious than his money. He will hitchhike the last hundred or hundred and fifty kilometres from either station or airport. On our part, we can do nothing but listen with straining ears to radio reports of distant ice formations. His coming seems to depend on so many factors which are out there far beyond us and over which we lack control.

The days go by in fevered slowness until finally on the morning of December 23 the strange car rolls into our yard. My mother touches her hand to her lips and whispers "Thank God." My father gets up unsteadily from his chair to look through the window. Their longed-for son and our golden older brother is here at last. He is here with his reddish hair and beard and we can hear his hearty laugh. He will be happy and strong and confident for us all.

There are three other young men with him who look much the same as he. They too are from the boats and are trying to get home to Newfoundland. They must still drive a hundred and sixty kilometres to reach the ferry at North Sydney. The car seems very old. They purchased it in Thorold for two hundred dollars because they were too late to make any reservations, and they have driven steadily since they began. In northern New Brunswick their windshield wipers failed but instead of stopping they tied lengths of cord to the wipers' arms and passed them through the front window vents. Since that time, in whatever precipitation, one of them has pulled the cords back and forth to make the wipers function. This information falls tiredly but excitedly from their lips and we greedily gather it in. My father pours them drinks of rum and my mother takes out her mincemeat and the fruitcakes she has been carefully hoarding. We lean on the furniture or look from the safety of sheltered doorways. We would like to hug our brother but are too shy with strangers present. In the kitchen's warmth, the young men begin to nod and doze, their heads dropping suddenly to their chests. They nudge each other with their feet in an attempt to keep awake. They will not stay and rest because they have come so far and tomorrow is Christmas Eve and stretches of mountains and water still lie between them and those they love. After they leave we pounce upon our brother physically and verbally. He laughs and shouts and lifts us over his head and swings us in his muscular arms. Yet in spite of his happiness he seems surprised at the appearance of his father whom he has not seen since March. My father merely smiles at him while my mother bites her lip.

Now that he is here there is a great flurry of activity. We have left everything we could until the time he might be with us. Eagerly I show him the fir tree on the hill which I have been watching for months and marvel at how easily he fells it and carries it down the hill. We fall over one another in the excitement of decoration.

He promises that on Christmas Eve he will take us to church in the sleigh behind the splendid horse that until his coming we are all afraid to handle. And on the afternoon of Christmas Eve he shoes the horse, lifting each hoof and rasping it fine and hammering the cherry-red horseshoes into shape upon the anvil. Later he drops them hissingly into the steaming tub of water. My father sits beside him on an overturned pail and tells him what to do. Sometimes we argue with our father, but our brother does everything he says.

That night, bundled in hay and voluminous coats, and with heated stones at our feet, we start upon our journey. Our parents and Kenneth remain at home but all the rest of us go. Before we leave we feed the cattle and sheep and even the pig all that they can possibly eat so that they will be contented on Christmas Eve. Our parents wave to us from the doorway. We go six kilometres across the mountain road. It is a primitive logging trail and there will be no cars or other vehicles upon it. At first the horse is wild with excitement and lack of exercise and my brother has to stand at the front of the sleigh and lean backwards on the reins. Later he settles down to a trot and still later to a walk as the mountain rises before him. We sing all the Christmas songs we know and watch for rabbits and foxes scudding across the open patches of snow and listen to the drumming of partridge wings. We are never cold.

When we descend to the country church we tie the horse in a grove of trees where he will be sheltered and not frightened by the many cars. We put a blanket over him and give him oats. At the church door the neighbours shake hands with my brother. "Hello, Neil," they say. "How is your father?"

"Oh," he says, just "Oh."

The church is very beautiful at night with its festooned branches and glowing candles and the booming, joyous sounds that come from the choir loft. We go through the service as if we are mesmerized.

On the way home, although the stones have cooled, we remain happy and warm. We listen to the creak of the leather harness and the hiss of runners on the snow and begin to think of the potentiality of presents. When we are about a kilometre from home the horse senses his destination and breaks into a trot and then into a confident lope. My brother lets him go and we move across the winter landscape like figures freed from a Christmas card. The snow from the horse's hooves falls about our heads like the whiteness of the stars.

After we have stabled the horse we talk with our parents and eat the meal our mother has prepared. And then I am sleepy and it is time for the younger children to be in bed. But tonight my father says to me, "We would like you to stay up with us a while," and so I stay quietly with the older members of my family.

When all is silent upstairs Neil brings in the cartons that contain his "clothes" and begins to open them. He unties the intricate knots quickly, their whorls falling away before his agile fingers. The boxes are filled with gifts neatly wrapped and bearing tags. The ones for my younger brothers say "from Santa Claus" but mine are not among them anymore, as I know with certainty they will never be again. Yet I am not so much surprised as touched by a pang of loss at being here on the adult side of the world. It is as if I have suddenly moved into another room and heard a door click lastingly behind me. I am jabbed by my own small wound.

But then I look at those before me. I look at my parents drawn together before the Christmas tree. My mother has her hand upon my father's shoulder and he is holding his ever present handkerchief. I look at my sisters who have crossed this threshold ahead of me and now each day journey farther from the lives they knew as girls. I look at my magic older brother who has come to us this Christmas from half a continent away, bringing everything he has and is. All of them are captured in the tableau of their care.

"Every man moves on," says my father quietly, and I think he speaks of Santa Claus, "but there is no need to grieve. He leaves good things behind."

The Other Family

BY HIMANI BANNERJI

"'But you? Where are you in this picture?' demanded her mother, by now thoroughly aroused. 'Where are we? Is this the family you would like to have? Don't you want us any more?'"

When the little girl came home it was already getting dark. The winter twilight had transformed the sheer blue sky of the day into the colour of steel, on which were etched a few stars, the bare winter trees and the dark wedges of the house tops. A few lit windows cast a faint glow on the snow outside. The mother stood at her window and watched the little hooded figure walking toward the house. The child looked like a shadow, her blue coat blended into the shadows of the evening. This child, her own, how small and insubstantial she seemed, and how alone, walking home through a pavement covered with ice and snow! It felt unreal. So different was this childhood from her own, so far away from the sun, the trees and the peopled streets of her own country! What did I do, she thought, I took her away from her own people and her own language, and now here she comes walking alone, through an alien street in a country named Canada.

As she contemplated the solitary, moving figure, her own solitude rushed over her like a tide. She had drifted away from a world that she had lived in and understood, and now she stood here at the same distance from her home as from the homes which she glimpsed while walking past the sparkling clean windows of the sandblasted houses. And now the doorbell rang, and here was her daughter scraping the snow off her boots on the doormat.

Dinner time was a good time. A time of warmth, of putting hot, steaming food onto the table. A time to chat about the important things of the day, a time to show each other what they had acquired. Sometimes, however, her mother would be absent-minded, worried perhaps about work, unsettled perhaps by letters that had arrived from home, scraping her feelings into a state of rawness. This was such an evening. She had served herself and her child, started a conversation about their two cats and fallen into a silence after a few minutes.

"You aren't listening to me, Mother."

The complaining voice got through to her, and she looked at the indignant face demanding attention from the other side of the table. She gathered herself together.

"So what did he do, when you gave him dried food?"

"Oh, I don't quite remember, I think he scratched the ground near his bowl and left."

The child laughed.

"That was smart of him! So why don't we buy tinned food for them?"

"Maybe we should," she said, and tried to change the topic.

"So what did you do in your school today?"

"Oh, we drew pictures like we do every day. We never study anything—not like you said you did in your school. We drew a family—our family. Want to see it?"

"Sure, and let's go to the living room, OK? This is messy." Scraping of chairs and the lighting of the lamps in the other room. They both made a rush for the most comfortable chair, both reached it at the same time and made a compromise.

"How about you sit in my lap? No? OK, sit next to me then and we will squeeze in somehow."

There was a remarkable resemblance between the two faces, except that the face of the child had a greater intensity, given by the wide open eyes. She was fine boned, and had black hair framing her face. Right now she was struggling with the contents of her satchel, apparently trying to feel her way to the paintings.

"Here it is," she said, producing a piece of paper. "Here's the family!"

The mother looked at the picture for a long time. She was very still. Her face had set into an expression of anger and sadness. She was trying very hard not to cry. She didn't want to frighten the child, and yet what she saw made her feel distant from her daughter, as though she was looking at her through the reverse end of a telescope. She couldn't speak at all. The little girl too sat very still, a little recoiled from the body of her mother, as though expecting a blow. Her hands were clenched into fists, but finally it was she who broke the silence.

"What happened?" she said. "Don't you like it?"

"Listen," said the mother, "this is not your family. I, you, and your father are dark-skinned, dark-haired. I don't have a blond wig hidden in my closet, my eyes are black, not blue, and your father's beard is black, not red, and you, do you have a white skin, a button nose with freckles, blue eyes and blond hair tied into a pony tail? You said you drew our family. This is not it, is it?"

The child was now feeling distinctly cornered. At first she was startled and frightened by her mother's response, but now she was prepared to be defiant. She had the greatest authority behind her, and she now summoned it to her help.

"I drew it from a book," she said, "all our books have this same picture of the family. You can go and see it for yourself. And everyone else drew it too. You can ask our teacher tomorrow. She liked it, so there!"

The little girl was clutching at her last straw.

"But you? Where are you in this picture?" demanded her mother, by now thoroughly aroused. "Where are we? Is this the family you would like to have? Don't you want us anymore? You want to be a *mem-sahib*, a white girl?"

But even as she lashed out these questions the mother regretted them. She could see that she made no sense to the child. She could feel the unfairness of it all. She was sorry that she was putting such a heavy burden on such young shoulders.

"First I bring her here," she thought, "and then I try to make her feel guilty for wanting to be the same as the others." But something had taken hold of her this evening. Panic at the thought of losing her child, despair and guilt galvanized her into speech she regretted, and she looked with anger at her only child, who it seemed wanted to be white, who had rejected her dark mother. Someday this child would be ashamed of her, she thought, someday she would move out into the world of those others. Someday they would be enemies. Confusing thoughts ran through her head like images on an uncontrollable television screen, in the chaos of which she heard her ultimate justification flung at her by her daughter—they wanted me to draw the family, didn't they? "They" wanted "her" to draw "the family." The way her daughter pronounced the words "they" or "the family" indicated that she knew what she was talking about. The simple pronoun "they" definitely stood for authority, for that uncontrollable yet organized world immediately outside, of which the school was the ultimate expression. It surrounded their own private space. "They" had power, "they" could crush little people like her anytime "they" wanted to, and in "their" world that was the picture of the family. Whether her mother liked it or not, whether she looked like the girl in it or not, made not one jot of difference. That was, yes, that was the right picture. As these thoughts passed through her mind, her anger ebbed away. Abandoning her fury and distance, the mother bowed her head at the image of this family and burst into sobs.

"What will happen to you?" she said. "What did I do to you?"

She cried a great deal and said many incoherent things. The little girl was patient, quietly absorbing her mother's change of mood. She had a thoughtful look on her face, and bit her nails from time to time. She did not protest any more, nor did she cry. After a while her mother took her to bed and tucked her in, and sat in the kitchen with the fearful vision of her daughter always outside the window of the blond family, never the centre of her own life, always rejecting herself, and her life transformed into a gigantic peep show. She wept very bitterly because she had caused this destruction, and because she had hated her child in her own fear of rejection, and because she had sowed guilt into her mind.

When her mother went to bed and closed the door, the child, who had been waiting for long, left the bed. She crossed the corridor on her tiptoes, past the row of shoes, the silent gathering of the overcoats and the mirror with the wavy surface, and went into the washroom. Behind the door was another mirror, of full length, and clear. Deliberately and slowly the child took off the top of her pyjamas and surveyed herself with grave scrutiny. She saw the brownness of her skin, the wide, staring, dark eyes, the black hair now tousled from the pillows, the scar on her nose and the brownish pink of her mouth. She stood a while lost in this act of contemplation, until the sound of soft padded feet neared the door, and a whiskered face peeped in. She stooped and picked up the cat and walked back to her own room.

It was snowing again, and little elves with brightly coloured coats and snow in their boots had reappeared in the classroom. When finally the coats were hung under pegs with names, and boots were neatly stowed away, the little girl approached her teacher. She had her painting from the day before in her hand.

"I have brought it back," she said.

"Why?" asked her teacher, "don't you like it any more?"

The little girl was looking around very intently.

"It's not finished yet," she said. "The books I looked at didn't have something. Can I finish it now?"

"Go ahead," said the teacher, moving on to get the colours from the cupboard.

The little girl was looking at the classroom. It was full of children of all colours, of all kinds of shapes of noses and of different colours of hair. She sat on the floor, placed the incomplete picture on a big piece of newspaper and started to paint. She worked long at it—and with great concentration. Finally it was finished. She went back to her teacher.

"It's finished now," she said, "I drew the rest."

The teacher reached out for the picture and spread it neatly on a desk.

There they were, the blond family arranged in a semicircle with a dip in the middle, but next to them, arranged alike, stood another group—a man, a woman and a child; but they were dark-skinned, dark-haired, the woman wore clothes from her own country, and the little girl in the middle had a scar on her nose.

"Do you like it?"

"Who are they?" asked the teacher, though she should have known. But the little girl didn't mind answering this question one bit.

"It's the other family," she said.

Ascension

BY AUDREY THOMAS

"'Christina,' Mrs. Papoutsia said. 'Nice name. Means golden one. Friends in Greece—lady friends—say "chrysomou"—my golden one.'"

Christine hadn't prayed in fifteen years, but now she prayed in a steady monotone of pleading as she kneaded and turned the bread. Please don't let her die please don't let it happen—knead, knead, then a quarter turn just as Mrs. Papoutsia had taught her—please don't let her die. She tried to imagine God as Mrs. P. must see him, a bearded patriarch in black robes and black beard with a hat like a piece of stovepipe. Okay, please, for my sake. She hastily, guiltily, corrected herself—I mean for her sake. Knead, turn; knead, turn: for all our sakes, Amen.

When the siren went, Christine was lying on the bed, half asleep. She thought it was the end of the world, shoved her feet into her slippers, ran downstairs and outside onto the wet grass. One of the volunteers from the south end of the island was just closing the doors of the ambulance. Christine ran across her yard and into the road shouting, "Stop, stop, what's happened?" He waved at her and slapped at his chest, then hurried around the passenger side. The vehicle sped away down the access road and onto the main road south. Wa Wa Wa Wa Wa Wa Wa. She could hear the dreadful sound as the ambulance raced towards the water-taxi.

It couldn't be too serious, Christine thought, or they would have got the helicopter or the Hovercraft. The government wharf was just down below and from time to time, even in the few months she had been on the island, a resident or weekender was taken off white-faced and, even if conscious, *vacant* somehow, as though the easiest way to deal with pain and fear and being in a horizontal and helpless position in full public view (not much public really, only those who lived close by and had heard the helicopter or Hovercraft coming in) was to absent oneself from the body which was causing all the trouble. Christine had seen the weekender who had chopped his finger off taken away like that, the finger in a plastic bag full of ice beside him. The injured man had seemed braver than the people around him, but of course he was in shock. He was a popular man and he put an ad in the local newspaper later on, thanking people for calls and cards and flowers: "Finger and hand reunited and doing fine." She had seen them take away Mr. Jenks, the plumber, who had been up on his roof replacing shingles when his foot slipped and he fell off the roof and broke his back.

The faces of the sick or injured were as grey as wasp nests, grey as ashes. And the awful noise. Surely the noise would make one sicker, more frightened? Wa Wa Wa Wa Wa. She could still hear it. The ambulance must be at Smugglers' Cove by now. All along the route people would stop what they were doing, turn to one another or pick up the telephone. Who was it that just went by? "Hello, Muriel, did you hear the ambulance just now?" Christine remembered a poem she had read in second-year university: "The Hound of Heaven." A powerful religious poem by a man half-crazy from despair and opium. But, said her teacher, a man who never lost his faith.

> I fled Him, down the nights and down the days;
> I fled Him, down the arches of the years; …

A shocking poem because she had been brought up, like everybody else she knew, to think of Heaven and Christ in gentler terms. Excess in anything, but especially religious fervour, was frowned upon. "Gentle Jesus meek and mild" was the Christ she knew.

The ambulance sounded like Thompson's Hound of Heaven. But perhaps it wasn't so bad that it made that noise after all—all human terror gathered into the single scream of the ambulance siren. Faint now, but she could still hear it. And Mrs. Papoutsia inside.

"Christina," Mrs. Papoutsia said. "Nice name. Means golden one. Friends in Greece—lady friends—say, '*chrysomou*'—my golden one."

"It's Christine, not Christina."

"Same thing."

Christine stood in the wet, winter-logged grass, uncertain what to do. She wanted to go down to the store and find out more but was afraid to seem nosy. "Bread," she thought now, "it's Thursday. She must already have started the bread." Still in her wet slippers she went into Mrs. Papoutsia's yard and up the back steps, searched for the key which she knew was hanging on a cup hook under the bathroom window, and let herself in. The big black woodstove was still throwing off heat, and two large earthenware bowls, covered with clean tea towels, sat on the warming shelf. The room had the slightly sour smell of yeast and rising bread plus the licorice smell of oil of anise.

Mrs. P.'s two cats glared at her from the tops of cupboards. They were still shaken by the invasion of strangers and the awful sound.

"It's okay guys," she said, "you can come down." The cats continued to glare.

("What are their names?"

"Perché."

"Both of them?"

"Sure. Perché in Greek mean 'why' and also 'because.' One cat 'why' and the other 'because.'" The old lady grinned, showing her gold-capped teeth. "Is joke.")

Christine lifted the heavy bowls down from the top of the stove and set them on the counter. She pulled off the towels and the waxpaper underneath. The dough had risen right up to the top and almost over the edge. She was just in time. She punched the dough down, hard, and it let out a little whoosh of air and a slick-slick sound when the bubbles burst. Christine knew enough about Greek bread by now to know, from the anise, that this was probably Easter bread. Next week Mrs. P. was going to show her how to make it. But what came after it rose again? Naturally there were no recipe books lying around. It would be a fancy bread, today of all days. It had to be braided and have hard-boiled eggs baked in the centre of it, or were those put in after the bread had baked? Christine looked in the fridge; there was a bowl of six bright red eggs already boiled and dyed. One problem solved at any rate. But did they go in before, or after?

Mrs. P. could not believe her new neighbour didn't know how to make bread.

"You never?"

"Never ever. I like good bread, but I guess I've always lived where I could get it from a bakery."

"Your mama, no?"

"No. Never. She made good baking-powder biscuits and wonderful pancakes, but we bought our bread. I even remember the name of the bakery because it sponsored a music show on the radio." Christine began to sing, to the "Tales from the Vienna Woods":

The famous Spalding Bakery
A name that stands for quality
We invite you to buy
We invite you to try
Delicious and pure Spalding Bread.

She laughed. "The songs they played were golden oldies—Frank Sinatra, Perry Como, stuff like that. My grandmother must've baked bread though. I remember long cylindrical hinged pans in the back of the kitchen cupboard." Her mother had given the pans to a church sale.

"Your grandmama good woman."

"My mother good woman too. She just didn't bake bread." Sometimes, when she talked with Mrs. P. she found herself leaving out parts of speech and wondered if the old woman thought she was mocking her.

"Staff of life—bread."

"Is that a Greek saying too? I mean, I've heard it all my life but do people in Greece say it as well?"

"In Bible! Isaiah! You no go to church?"

"I used to. I don't go any more."

"You don't believe?"

"Not any more."

Mrs. P. snorted. "Belief also staff of life."

"Maybe." The old woman gave her a hard look.

"You have nice voice. Why not join choir here? Not church choir, other one. Thursday night at Activity Centre. Meet people. Lovely to sing."

"I'm not staying long enough," Christine said. "There's no point."

When Christine came to the island in the New Year she had already made up her mind not to be overly friendly with her neighbours, whomever they turned out to be. After all, she was only renting for six months. She'd be gone by Canada Day. Besides, she was there to puzzle out certain things and the fewer complications the better. She had seen the ad in the *Times-Colonist* and answered it on a whim. She made all the arrangements before she told her friends. She also told them not to come and visit. Yeah, sure, they said. You'll get cabin fever in three weeks. You'll be on the phone begging us to come over or you'll be back here every weekend. But they were wrong. It was now the middle of April. She plugged the phone in only once a week, on Sunday mornings, to call her mother in southern Ontario. She did not answer letters, although she might have answered the one letter that never came.

"Where husband?" Mrs. Papoutsia said. "Where childrens?"

"No children," Christine replied. "No husband. Not any more. Husband gone." Mrs. Papoutsia dipped her cookie in her tea.

"You like nice Greek husband? My son arrange. He knows all Greek mens in Vancouver. He knows Greek mens in Greece."

"No thanks, I'm happy right now the way I am."

"What you do to husband that he leave?"

"What did *I* do! I didn't do anything."

"Hmnph."

Mrs. P. had a calendar from Greece above the kitchen sink. White stone houses that looked as though they had been dipped in the same powdered sugar she used for her raisin cake, her *kourabiethes*, her sesame turnovers. There were bright geraniums in pots and impossibly blue skies. "April" showed an old-fashioned windmill and two smiling men with a donkey. The simple life. But Christine knew that calendars could lie. She had lived in a city famous for its hanging baskets and old-world charm. Pictures of the teenage prostitutes never graced the dozens of calendars produced each year.

Michael had been gone for nearly a year and still she couldn't fall asleep right away, no matter how tired she was and still she dreamt of him, strange, disturbing erotic dreams. The first day she got here, after she had unpacked her things, she took her wedding ring out of its velvet-lined box, walked to the end of the government wharf and threw it in. She hoped no fish would swallow it, no fisherman appear at the door one day, wondering if she'd lost something. Their initials were on the inside.

"Listen," Michael said, "there's no nice way of saying this. I'm sorry." At least there were no children, her friends said, it's far worse if there's kids involved.

Christine gave the dough another big *thump*, turned it over to keep it oiled, replaced the paper and towels and put the bowls back on the shelf. Then she went down the steps and under the house for more wood. She felt she had to finish the bread, keep the fire going, if Mrs. Papoutsia was going to have any chance at all, that Mrs. P. would count on her doing this. The bread was for Greek Easter, only two weeks away. Mrs. P. was having a big feast for everybody at the North End Hall. Her son was coming over to roast the lamb. When Mrs. Papoutsia told her this it sounded like "Roast Lamp."

Had anyone called her son? Emergency numbers plus the son's telephone number and a few other numbers were posted neatly by the telephone. Everything in the small house was neat and tidy. On the window-sill by the back door there were clam shells, oyster shells, even walnut shells full of flower seeds to be planted as soon as the ground dried out a bit more. The little slips of paper identifying them were written in Greek but Christine could recognize a few of them by their shape: marigolds, cornflowers, nasturtiums. Glass jars held bean seeds and tomato seedlings were already sprouting on the front window sill.

Paper bags were neatly folded in a corner of the cupboard underneath the sink, rubber bands and twist-ties saved in the kitchen drawer. Everything that could be used again was used again; very little was thrown out. Christine thought of her own untidy life. If something happened to her, her friends and her mother would have a terrible time sorting things out. "I must get a divorce as soon as possible," she thought now, opening the fridge and taking out the cat food. The two cats, both huge grey blue-eyed Persians, were Mrs. Papoutsia's big indulgence. That and making breads and cakes. "I must give my life some order." She had taken a leave from teaching, on the grounds of illness. She had been experiencing dizzy spells at work and strange headaches. It was like being hit in the head with a snowball, she told the doctor, a sudden pain and then a dull ache. It scared her. The doctor sent her for tests but they all came back negative. She wept and he offered her a choice of Librium or Valium, "just until you pull yourself together." She declined and answered an ad.

There was quite a crowd at the store, discussing Mrs. Papoutsia. She'd had a bad pain in her chest and called the doctor. It was lucky she did, because by the time he arrived with the ambulance she was lying on her bed in great distress.

"Did she call you?" the storekeeper said, noticing Christine.

"My phone was unplugged," she said, and felt her face go red. Had she called? Christine imagined the doctor and the paramedics trying to get Mrs.

Papoutsia's heart to go, thumping it hard the way she had thumped the bread. Thump. Thump. "Where did they take her?" Christine asked. In spite of her shame and embarrassment she had to know. She bought some milk she didn't need and a Kit-Kat bar to give her visit some validity.

"Probably to the Royal Jubilee—if it's a heart attack. The doctor will know."

Christine went back up her path, called the doctor and got his wife. He was with Mrs. Papoutsia and they were on their way to Victoria, perhaps even there by now. "She has a son in Vancouver," Christine said, "do you know if he's been called? He runs a delicatessen on Broadway."

"I don't know. Shall I have Jim call you? He'll phone in for messages pretty soon."

Christine left the son's number, which she'd copied down, and also her own. It wasn't time to punch the dough again and then attempt to braid it. She didn't even know what temperature to use. The dough had eggs in it—did that mean a higher or lower temperature? Christine had so far attempted nothing more difficult than round white loaves and something Mrs. Papoutsia called "*starénio*," or "peasant bread," which was dark and dense and wonderful spread with Greek honey brought over by the son, who wore the nails of his little fingers very long—to show that he did not work with his hands. He called himself Mr. Pappas. Mrs. P. loved him fiercely but was impatient.

"Father fisherman, grandfather fisherman, good job, *honourable*. Now he wants make sure everybody know he don't work rough work. And change name! Easier for peoples, Mama. No trouble. Papoutsia *easy* name! Pa—poots—see—a." She grinned at Christine. "Husband Dmitri, English 'Jimmy.' His name in English Jimmy Shoes. I, Fotula, Mrs. Jimmy Shoes."

Fotula and Dmitri had come to the island every year when the herring were running. Their son, with scuba equipment, dove for octopus. Fotula and Dmitri decided to buy a small lot and build. Now that Dmitri was dead, the son and his wife wanted Fotula to come and live with them but she refused. There were no grandchildren. On the island Mrs. P. was "Yia yia," "Grandmother" to a couple of dozen little ones. She fed them sweetcakes oozing honey and nuts, wiped their sticky faces, kissed them, rocked them in her rocking chair. They saw her coming and ran to her with their arms outstretched.

"His doorbell play four tunes including Greek anthem. So what? Jimmy good boy but modern. Electric this, electric that. I no like."

Christine had very pointedly kept herself to herself and after a few weeks the neighbours accepted that she really meant it when she said no to morning coffee or afternoon tea, no to darts, no to the garden club, the women's auxiliary, to the firehall, no to Scottish country dancing. (Mrs. Papoutsia did Scottish country dancing every Tuesday night.) When Christine talked to people she felt that any second now she would crack and fall to pieces right before their eyes. She said she was writing a book and couldn't be disturbed. She was then invited to join the writers' group but declined. It was a book for teaching English as a Second Language, she said, not a creative book at all.

On the third Thursday someone knocked hard on the front door. An old woman stood on the porch, black skirt, black cardigan, black stockings and boots. She smelled of fresh bread and, faintly, of oranges. "Fotula Papoutsia," she said. "Your neighbour. I tell landlord I keep eye. Also clean on Fridays."

"Thank you very much," said Christine, who had been brought up never to be rude to elderly people, "that won't be necessary. I'm fine." The old lady walked right in and put something wrapped in a towel on the kitchen table. Delicious smells came up from under the towel. "Look," said Christine, trying not to sound annoyed. "It's awfully kind of you but—" The red kettle was being filled, the tea cannister taken down from the left-hand cupboard.

"Mr. Beldon and me—tea or *kaffes* together Thursdays, bread day. He keep eye on me, my eye on him. You have jam?" She opened the fridge and peered in. "Next time I bring."

Christine took a deep breath. "Mrs. Papoutsia, I don't know what your arrangement was with Mr. Beldon, but I'm here to be very quiet—no visitors."

"Crazy talk," said the old woman, pouring hot water into the teapot and swirling it around. "Me, I *prefer kaffes*—cof-fee—but Joe he like tea. Come, sit."

A warm loaf, butter, teapot, teacups and saucers. "Sit, eat." When Christine began to cry, Mrs. Papoutsia ignored her for a long while, sipped her tea, and buttered slices of bread, looked around the untidy room and muttered foreign words to herself. Finally, "*Andaxi*. Okay. You and me, we talk."

Now Christine felt the old panic returning—Mrs. P., her one friend, her support, had been taken away. She was learning to make bread, to understand the mysteries of yeast, of how the milk had to be scalded, the water just the right temperature. When she kneaded and turned, kneaded and turned, kneaded and turned, she felt the anger and hurt leaving her, even if, as yet, it only left for a while, one day a week.

"You can even," said Mrs. P., "get yeast out from air. I show you."

On bread-lesson days it was usually dark by the time Christine walked back to her own house, her basket full of Greek food she had sampled during the afternoon. When Mrs. Papoutsia told her about the Easter Feast at the North End Hall and had asked—demanded—Christine's help, she had felt strong enough to agree.

"Easy food. Greece not a *fancy* place. Cheese. Olive. *Dolmades*, little pies of spinach, son do the lamp outside. Easter bread—I show you."

Christine dialled the hospital in Victoria. Yes, they had a Mrs. Papoutsia in Intensive Care. Her son had just arrived. No, they could tell her nothing if she wasn't kin.

Was she conscious?

"I'm afraid I can't—"

Christine was shouting into the phone. "Well if she *is* conscious could you tell her, could somebody get word to her that Christina—yes, *Christina*, I'm her next-door neighbour—has seen to the bread. The *bread*. That's right. Tell her Christina has seen to the bread."

The son called just as Christina was taking the loaves out of the oven. The braids weren't even but they didn't look half-bad and she had been right to set the coloured eggs in before baking. She carefully put the hot pans on the racks she had already set out. The cats had come down and were watching her with a kind of angry interest. Where was their mistress—what had Christine done with her?

"Hello," Christine said, her own heart bumping loudly against her chest.

"Christina? Jimmy Pappas here. I tried your house then figured you'd be at my mother's."

"How is she?"

"She just slipped away. We lost her about fifteen minutes ago."

"Did she get my message about the bread?"

"She never regained consciousness." She could hear him struggling to keep his voice manly, in charge. "I'll come over tomorrow. Do you think you could feed the cats and keep an eye on things?"

"We'll have to have the Easter Feast," Christine said. "She'd want us to have the Easter Feast."

"Thank you for being such a good friend to her Christina—she often talked about you."

Christine hung up the phone. While the bread cooled she rinsed the pans and bowls and tidied the kitchen. Then she walked around looking at all the framed photographs on the walls: Fotula as a young girl; Fotula in her wedding dress with the six petticoats underneath; Fotula and Dmitri on their fish boat, *The Ariadne*; Fotula with young Dmitri in her arms. In none of the pictures was she smiling but there was a kind of fierce smile implied in the eyes, the mouth, the way she carried herself. A proud woman. Fulfilled.

And then, the most amazing photograph of all—Fotula shaking hands with an astronaut. She was all in black, as usual; he was wearing white. It was the only photograph in which she smiled. The astronaut was smiling too.

"Is that your son?" Christine asked when she first noticed it.

"No. No. Mr. Somebody—I forget name but I have clipping somewhere. I win big prize, go to Ottawa, meet astronauts."

"You won a big prize? Was it a lottery?"

Mrs. Papoutsia gave her a look of contempt. "What you mean *lottery?* I enter contest—think up good project to try out in space, project to benefit mankind."

"And?"

"And I win! Make bread in space," I say. "If go to new worlds need staff of life—try make bread in space." Mrs. Papoutsia and four others with the same idea had won the contest and been given the royal treatment. That wasn't all—they were to go to Cape Canaveral when the experiment actually went up. Mrs. P. had been looking forward to it enormously. If it hadn't been for the Challenger she would have gone already.

Christine sat in the rocking chair with one cat on her lap, the other at her feet. She had banked the fire in the stove and shut down the damper. The house smelled wonderful and in spite of her grief and shock Christine couldn't help smiling as she imagined the soul of her friend, fragrant, spicy, lighter than air, gradually rising up through the April skies towards a bright blue heaven.

Suburbs of the Arctic Circle

BY MARY BURNS

In a Yukon village, an old man freezes to death one winter night. Some people say racism killed him, and the national media swoops in.

How would you feel if it was your town or neighbourhood that was under the microscope? As the story opens up level after level in our understanding of the village of Raven's Roost—a village that is almost a symbol of Canada—we learn that things are never simple, and that individual people react in individual ways to every human situation.

"A town like this one demands all a person has. Those who cannot cope with the demands either leave or are diminished in mind by the truth they have discovered about themselves."

I have to laugh at people who think it's different up north, cleaner and freer. Oh, it's freer, I suppose. You don't find yourself running into barbed wire when you're out for a stroll and the Mounties are generally willing to ignore minor infractions of the law. There is only one Mountie in our town anyway, Frank McCloud, and Frank is new and doesn't yet know where to look for trouble. Andy Hanson was transferred to Labrador after Raven's Roost hit the national news last year. Andy knew where to look for trouble, but he also knew that if he didn't look he wouldn't see and for official purposes there would be no trouble.

I don't believe it is cleaner up here, but then I haven't been Outside for close to ten years. Still, most places have their undersides and R.R. is no different in that respect. Undersides are where you find the dust devils, the dirty socks and underwear shoved there in the heat of some moment you had forgotten until everything was turned upside down. The death of Esau Issac had that effect on Raven's Roost, but to understand why you'd have to know the place.

First of all, no one who lives here calls the town by its full name. It is embarrassing even to write it on the mail orders we send to Simpson-Sears. I picture the catalogue girls in Edmonton or Vancouver opening our letters and wondering who would ever live in a place called Raven's Roost? The trader who christened the settlement could have named it after himself, as so many have done, but no, he supplied his own interpretation of the words the Indians used.

R.R. lies south of the junction of the Yukon and White Fish rivers. At the north end of town, just past Peter Groenen's Esso station, is the big silver bridge you see pictured on postcards. The highway and the river form the main boundaries of R.R. The Catholics built their church on the east side of the highway, thinking they would encourage settlement there, but the Commissioner of the Territory, an Anglican, put a development freeze on the land surrounding the church and now it sits alone, directly beneath the cemetery and about half a mile south of the dump. Churchgoers load their pickups with the week's garbage on Sundays to save themselves a trip.

The town proper stretches along the river banks on the west side of the highway. The main town road cuts through the centre of it, leaving the Indians on one side, on the river flats, and the white people, the nursing station, the RCMP, the school, the teacherage, the stores and the Anglican church on the higher ground. We get tourists coming through who say we ought to do something about the appearance of the town. They say it's a shame to have such a ramshackle collection of buildings in the middle of this stunning natural setting. I imagine they would sooner see us living in neat little log cabins, or maybe Swiss chalets hung with flower-filled window boxes. Well we don't pay much attention to the tourists; they're gone as soon as the blackflies hatch.

They do have a point about the scenery, though. I felt the same way when I first saw it, before I got distracted by the business of daily life here. We have pines and spruces marching up the hill behind the Catholic church, halfway up Blue Mountain, and on the river banks we have the leafy trees, aspen, some birch, low willow, and alder. For a week or so in early June the new leaves are that cool popsicle-green colour that makes you wish you could open your eyes wider, to take more of it in. And right around that time, as well as for weeks after, we have the lupines; dark blue thickets of them surprising you, even though you know they were there last year. Later comes the fireweed, its colour explaining its name. The river changes with the seasons: in summer it is green as the trees on its banks; in fall and winter, before it freezes, it turns a colder and colder blue and reflects the low sun in coppery patches. In spring the river runs brown as the mud outside the RRX tavern at that time of year.

The RRX, which stands for Raven's Roost Crossroads, is located on the east side of the highway, too, but south of the main town road, whereas the Catholic church is north of it. You have to pass the RRX to get to town from anywhere south, and south is where people usually come from. South is the airport, the fastest link to the Outside; south is the only real city in the Territory. My husband Jack was one of the few who made regular trips north, but that is because it was his job to do so.

The setting is particularly important to this story because if the RRX had been anywhere else the incident would never have grown as it did. Think of the river as the bar of a T, and the main town road as the stem. The teacherage sits about a quarter mile down the stem, towards the river. You'll see that anyone coming into town from the RRX has to pass the teacherage on the way in.

Nat and Bonnie Hemple told the reporters from the CBC that six cars passed the teacherage the night Esau Issac died. That means at least six people had driven past the spot where Esau was sitting, at the junction of the highway and the main town road. We all heard Nat's voice on the radio, towards the end of *The World at Six*: "I can't believe it, but it's true. That road is the only way into town. We were sitting up late, grading papers and we could hear the cars clearly because engine sounds are brittle in that kind of cold. It was fifty below, I know because I checked the thermometer right before we went to bed. If only we'd known that poor Esau...."

Poor Esau! Nat didn't say that he and his wife were unlikely to know about Esau or anyone else in the town. They had applied for a transfer at Christmas, the whole town knew, and it didn't make them any more popular than when they'd arrived in September, all bright-eyed and itching to change things. The Department of Education did not accept their request for transfer, they were being forced to stay until the school year was finished. But they didn't have any friends by then so they kept to themselves, except when they were at the school. I don't think they ever drank at the RRX. I doubt they drank at all.

Say what you like about us, no one was happy to hear about Esau's death. He was a harmless old drunk who had been a fine trapper in his day. He was over seventy when he died and had been living alone in a cabin near the south end of the Indian village. The cabin had run down some since May, his wife, had drowned two summers earlier as they were coming downriver with their moose. But Esau kept his traps in good condition, they say, and spoke of going out on his line again one day. Esau might have wanted to die. Some said he sat out there on purpose, like the old Eskimo people who plant themselves on an ice floe and wait to freeze to death because they know they are no longer useful. But the Hemples would have none of this theory or any other the townspeople cooked up.

They told the news reporters that R.R. was "a hotbed of racial injustice." Those were their exact words. They said the north was not the friendly place Outsiders believed it to be, a place where people could depend on one another, but was just like that New York suburb where thirty-seven people watched a woman being stabbed to death without once attempting to help her. It was just the sort of shock story they use to finish the national news. We've all heard similar and I, for one, have felt satisfied that I didn't live in a place where people casually murdered each other and abandoned their babies. I have never written in, but I have felt smug.

I guess the story was printed in papers all over the country, because our post office was clogged with letters from righteous citizens for weeks afterwards. It was Judgement Day in Raven's Roost and we were all sentenced to shame on account of six people, five of whom probably hadn't even seen Esau. Knowing us to be isolated there on the highway, and to consist of only three hundred souls, more or less, depending on the season, you will understand that Esau's death, or Nat Hemple's story of it, hit our town harder than a fuel shortage in January. We had to depend on ourselves and this is how I learned something about what is generally called human nature. As I already said, I don't think our sins were any more original than those you would find in Vancouver or Toronto. It's just that cold contracts and you get in the habit of looking at things extra closely, as if through a magnifying glass.

Take Esau's funeral. Under ordinary circumstances there would not have been much of a turnout. The Indians would have held their potlatch and shared their grief; a few whites would have attended, the RCMP, and the priests. The mixed bloods, like my neighbour Jo Bouchard, might have gone depending on which way they were leaning at the time. But it would not have amounted to a town affair. The reporters were responsible for that. Despite the weather being almost as bad as the night Esau died, people flocked to the graveyard like fruit flies to browning bananas. There were TV cameras and a lot of indignant-looking young people from the Indian organization in Whitehorse. Predictably, the Indians stood on one side of the grave and the whites on the other. I stood with Jo Bouchard—Jack was out driving that day—close to the exact middle of those two groups, between the currents that passed from one to the other, and when it was finished I wanted a stiff drink. You had to suspect those who were crying hardest, it seemed they only were doing it to show they were better than the ones who stood there dry-eyed. Jo, for instance, was related to Esau; Esau had been her mother's half brother, but Jo didn't cry. Her brown cheeks stayed smooth as the bronze on Esau's casket. And that's another thing. The townspeople contributed money to the Band for Esau's funeral, something that never would have happened if it hadn't been for the publicity. Then, on the way down the road from the Indian graveyard to the community hall, where coffee was to be served, everyone told Esau stories: about the snowshoes he had made for them, or the time they went hunting with him, or brought him and May a hamper at Christmas. It was as if people wanted to connect with the dead Esau in a way they hadn't when he was alive.

We should have been stronger. We should not have let the accusations of Hemple and the Outsiders chafe us as they did. But fame has a momentum that can carry you away. I think of movie stars who complain about their privacy being invaded, but keep giving interviews all the same. Fame is a teaser and we fell for it.

Travellers who drive through R.R. no doubt wonder why there is a town here at all. While the filling stations serve a useful purpose, there is no need for an entire community around them. Well, the community began on the flats, which were the site of one of the largest Indian fishing camps on the river. You can find the old drying racks cartwheeled in the weeds behind the Indian village and dogs will dig up years-old fish skeletons. Two or three of the Indian families still set out nets in late summer, when the salmon are running upriver, but most rely on the stores for food and on government cheques to pay for it. Art Neary keeps an outfitters camp at the back of Blue Mountain, and some of the younger Native boys who haven't left R.R., or who have returned, guide for Art in the fall. Then there are those like Jo Bouchard, who fit themselves into the regular white life of the town. Jo was born in the village just after the highway was built, in '43. Her father, one of the army men who constructed it, didn't stick around for long and her mother died of smallpox before Jo was six, so Jo was sent to live with a foster family, the Bouchards, in Whitehorse. When the Bouchards moved south a few years later, Jo went right along with them. She was educated to grade thirteen in Vancouver, and eventually came back to R.R. with a welder, Noel Rien, and they set up a trailer on the lot next to ours.

Jo and I could see the Indian village clearly from the cliffside where our trailers sat, and aside from visiting relatives down there now and then, that seemed to be enough of a connection for Jo.

Sometimes I could hear the guitar-accompanied hymns from their gospel services, and the barks of their husky dogs, but usually the villagers were quiet and the flats appeared a sleepy gathering—much different from the time when everyone must have been astir, catching and drying fish. That's the Indian side of town.

The white side is like Noah's Ark; we have two of practically everything. Bill Luksic started it all with the service station he opened when the highway was smooth enough for regular vehicles to travel over. He soon saw he ought to have a café and a few rooms for overnighters, and once these were finished he applied for a licence to serve liquor. Edna Farrone, who runs the General Store with her husband Ted, says it was Bill who gave them the idea of moving down from the triangle of mining towns north of here and opening a store. Then the government got into the act, putting in a highway maintenance camp and a post office. The highway crews set up trailers and built houses and the population began to grow, which meant the government had to supply a nursing station and an RCMP post. We have two cafés now, Bill's and the diner the Groenens operate near the bridge, two stores, two churches, and two graveyards.

Bill Luksic was the unofficial mayor of R.R., the man who pressured the Territorial government into grading our streets in the spring and thawing our pipes in the winter. The summer before Esau died Bill had circulated a petition asking the Commissioner to grant us local government status. He didn't need to try too hard to convince us we should have some kind of say over our affairs, and since all of us ended up signing, we figured we would be declared a local government district before the year was up. We also figured Bill would be appointed chairman, which would make his unofficial position official. Bill had the confidence of a born leader and he knew how to settle an argument. He didn't look like the politicians you see pictured in magazines and newspapers. He was not a glad-hander, and he dressed the way the other men do here, in work greens and quilted down vests. If Bill had stayed in Edmonton his natural qualities might never have surfaced, but a town like this one demands all a person has. Those who cannot cope with the demands either leave or are diminished in mind by the truth they have discovered about themselves. Naturally there were some who, out of jealousy, resented Bill, but even they had to admit that if it hadn't been for Bill there would be no R.R. as we knew it.

Bill's wife Naomi was chairman of the school committee and had been for years. There was talk of replacing her long before Esau's death, because her own daughter was grown and gone and Naomi was out of touch with the times, but she was always re-elected, probably because most of us thought so much of Bill.

When there was an accident on the highway or a drowning in the river, Bill was the man the newspapers contacted for details, so of course it was him they called to get the other side of Nat Hemple's story. Bill wasn't very cooperative this time, though, and that was because it was Bill who knew, if anyone did, the six people who left Esau to freeze to death on the road. The six would have been coming from Bill's tavern, or most of them would have. You won't find many pleasure drivers out on a night like that. My husband Jack was out, but that was business. Bill told the reporters that he had not kept track of the time people left his place that night. And when they asked him if he agreed that there was racial tension in our town, Bill just said that the young teacher didn't know what he was talking about. He was uncharacteristically quiet on the subject and that didn't make life any easier in R.R.

Bill was over fifty-five, but he never looked his age until things started going bad. He was bald since before I met him, but wiry and always on the move and we never thought of him as one of the oldest men in town, apart from some of the Indians. The night he stopped by our trailer to talk to Jack was the first time I noticed the depth of his forehead creases and how his spotted hands were never still, but fiddled with the salt and pepper shakers on the table or spun the can of milk. His voice was weary, it had the rasp a person with a cold gets, only Bill did not have a cold. As far as I knew he had never been sick a day in his life.

"We've got a hell of a mess on our hands," he said.

Jack was at the fridge, opening beers for us. "I don't see why, Bill. This thing has got out of hand, is all, just because of that radio report. You know yourself that every town in the Territory has had something like it happen. Look at Whitehorse, wasn't it just last year a bartender threw an old drunk out of his place, just as he's supposed to do? But the bloody fellow up and and died on him. Nobody planned it that way."

Bill didn't answer immediately, but took a long drink of his beer, set the bottle down and then snapped and unsnapped the bottom of his vest several times.

"I had a visit from Groenen today."

"Oh?"

"He came by to remind me, as if he had to, about our petition sitting down in Whitehorse. Then he got around to what happened in White Fish Crossing last year, how the Indians wouldn't sign the petition so the government wouldn't give the rest of the community their local government. 'Mind you, Bill,' he said, 'we've always had a tighter town than they got up at White Fish. I'm not saying the same thing will happen here. But after all that publicity we got, we have to watch ourselves.'"

"What was he getting at?"

"Same thing Andy Hanson was getting at the day after he found Esau. Same thing the whole town thinks, that I know damn well who was in the tavern that night and that I ought to be the one who nails them so the rest of us can clear our names."

Bill looked at me and then at Jack and he raised his eyebrows as if to say, what do you make of that. He wasn't asking what we thought of Peter Groenen because he already knew. Groenen is a sour man, a Dutchman who feels that World War II was a plot directly aimed at his family. The war ruined them and this has given Groenen a grudge against life in general, and against Bill Luksic in particular because Bill had settled here first and in the best location. No, it wasn't Groenen Bill was worried about, it was the burden circumstance had laid on him, and it wasn't me he wanted to hear from so much as Jack. Bill trusted him more than any man in town, for he knew Jack's worth.

Bill had taken a chance on us when we were first married and arrived in R.R. with a nearly broken-down truck and all we owned in it. He put us up at the RRX and loaned Jack the money to repair the truck and start his hauling business. Another man might have run off with Bill's money or forgotten him when he wasn't needed anymore, but not Jack. Jack still trucked Bill's liquor up from Whitehorse once a month, for only the cost of the gas. Now Bill needed something more from Jack, but I wasn't sure exactly what.

"You know, Bill, there could have been ten cars pass the teacherage that night, or two. I don't care if those Hemples are schoolteachers, I don't think they can count. I drove past that corner myself that night, coming in from the triangle, didn't I, Shirl? I didn't see Esau. Hell, I've given him and the other old buggers plenty of free rides. Nobody's gonna make me feel like Judas just because I drove into town that night."

"Well you got home early anyway, Jack," I reminded him. The coroner had put Esau's death at approximately 11:30, which meant he might have been sitting out on the road from 10:30 or so. Jack had arrived home at ten, I was sure of it because the radio was on. I had to ask this next question because like everyone else in town I was curious. I couldn't help it.

"Do you know and are you just not saying, Bill?"

Jack looked mad enough to slap me. "It's his business. Either you're a friend or you're not. Now give it up, Shirl."

Bill didn't want to give it up, though. He had to tell someone and he probably thought Naomi would blab it all over town if he told her. That's what I thought then. Her change of life was hard on her is how Bill explained it. Ever since she hadn't been too sure of herself, but needed to prop herself up with positions, such as being chairman of the school committee and R.R. representative on the Territorial tourism board. She liked to flaunt the Hawaii vacations she and Bill could afford to take every year, to be on top of a pile of people she considered inferior. She didn't fool anyone though, especially not Bill.

"It's all right, Jack. Shirley doesn't mean anything. Fact is I probably could say. The place was slow that night. You know how it is when it gets that cold."

He was aching to tell us. His hand was white from gripping his bottle so hard and his foot was tapping a nervous beat on the lino floor. But Jack didn't want him to say, and that had me worried.

"Give it a miss, Bill. It won't do anyone any good to know those people now. Esau isn't going to rise from the dead. Besides, who's to say any of them actually saw the old guy? You know how exhaust freezes up in this weather. Each one of those cars was probably hid in its own cloud."

"Would you say that at the inquest?"

"I didn't know there was going to be one."

"There is. Hanson told me today. The coroner's coming up a week from Friday, and they're going to hold it at the school."

So that's why Bill had been acting so squirmy. It was one thing to have to answer reporters who were going to write what they wanted no matter what you said; another to have to testify before an official inquiry.

"I'll sleep on it, Bill," Jack said.

"Yeah, me too. If I can, eh?"

"Just remember who your friends are," Jack called as Bill stepped over the snow to his truck. We stood at the door and watched him drive away and I noticed that Jo Bouchard's lights were on and that she, or someone, had just slid the curtains shut.

Jo was not only my neighbour, she was my best friend aside from Jack. She had more formal schooling than me and she'd seen more of the world. It was Jo who persuaded me to join the library and to send for correspondence courses. Noel and Jack laughed at us for pursuing something as useless in R.R. as education, but I knew that in his heart Jack was happy to see me doing it. Besides keeping me busy while he was out on the road, the schoolwork was making me more my own person. Jo and I planned to study until we earned enough credits for our teaching certificates. We wanted to teach at the R.R. school. Before the Hemples came we had both worked as aides, but the Hemples didn't like having amateurs around and they got Naomi Luksic to support their point of view. Noel was glad. I think he understood that Jo was smarter than he was anyway, and that it would be hard not to face that if she actually became a certified teacher. He got her pregnant every year until they had five kids and she finally put her foot down and got some birth control.

The morning after Bill's visit I stopped by Jo's to get her to walk to the post office with me so I could tell her about the inquest.

"Bill was over last night and told us," I said, to give her a chance to say she knew because she had seen him leaving. But she didn't admit she'd been watching. She acted surprised to hear he was there.

"I thought old Luksic was lying low. I haven't seen him since the funeral and a good thing, too."

"What do you mean by that?"

"Come on, Shirley. You know damn well he's just trying to protect himself and some of his buddies. I bet I could name the guys who left Esau to die that night and one of them would be the same who turned in Billy Jim last summer for peddling whitefish to tourists. You know I don't have any love for Nat Hemple, but he wasn't all wrong about the prejudice part. It was pretty clear why Naomi didn't want me in that school and it wasn't because of a tight budget, like she said. I would have worked for nothing, they knew that."

"That doesn't make sense, Jo. She didn't want me either, and my mother wasn't an Indian."

Jo's face was getting redder as we walked and not just from the cold. Her eyes were burning and her lips were turned down so that the lower one squeezed the mole at the corner of her mouth.

"Think what you want, Shirley."

"I'll tell you what I think. I think a few of us ought to try and keep some sense in our heads. Don't you know that getting us riled and setting us against each other was just what the Hemples wanted? Why should we play right into their hands?"

Jo didn't answer me. She was into what I called her Indian princess snit, the silent treatment, which is how she got whenever she was pushed too far. She had responded like this when we got the notice from the school committee that we'd no longer be allowed to work as aides. She'd argued about it just so long, then let it drop completely and kept to herself for the better part of a month, which is a long time to go without visiting your next-door neighbour and your closest friend.

I have to think now of the timetable. Esau was found on a Tuesday. The radio and the newspaper reports filled in the days before the funeral, which was Saturday. Bill paid his visit to us on the Tuesday after and told us the inquest would be a week from that Friday. The government didn't know what it was doing, letting us all simmer that long. They shouldn't have stretched it out for another week. Anyway, the Hemples left on the Sunday after the funeral. They simply packed their car and drove off. So there was no school for ten days, until the Department of Education could find replacements.

Meantime, life had to go on. We couldn't just stop cold and wait until we were cleared or condemned. We had to go on eating and sleeping and working and filling in the evenings just as though nothing had happened, but it was hard because people were even jumpier than they usually are in February, and the kids being home just made it worse. The wives were getting irritable because of having to deal all day with bored and noisy kids, and were taking it out on their husbands when they got home at night. Ted Farrone, who managed the curling rink at the community hall, decided to close for a week and that was another bad decision. Curling was the only thing we had to do in winter besides snowmobiling. But Ted said nobody had been out for several days and he wasn't going to waste heat and electricity just to keep the place open.

I could see why nobody was interested in curling. Curling brought people together and forced them to look at one another and it was getting so none of us could bear to do that. Even though I knew everything was going to turn out all right, that in a year or so we'd probably laugh at ourselves, I got caught up too.

Instead of going to the store on Wednesday, when the fresh produce was delivered, I waited until Thursday and found that half the other women in town had decided to do the same thing. We were all a little embarrassed, too, and though we said hello and how's Johnny's cold, because we had to say something to each other, we didn't linger in the hardware section to see if there were any new kitchen goods there and nobody invited anyone home for coffee.

Edna Farrone was one of the few who dared to look people straight in the eye.

"That'll be $37.24, want it on your tab?" she asked. And through her dusty spectacles I saw her peering at me so intensely she must have thought she could read my mind. She probably wanted to come right out and ask me if I knew, but so far nobody had had the guts to do that. I tried to pretend it was an ordinary shopping day. "No, I'll pay, and say, Edna, did you ever get that arrowroot starch I ordered last month?"

"I asked for it. Don't blame me if it never got here." She was unnecessarily sharp about it.

Another thing that happened was that everyone started to group off. As I've said, there were two stores in town, Farrone's General, where just about every family did their big shopping, and the R.R. Market, which was run by a Danish man and his Indian wife. The Market carried much of what Farrone's had, but in smaller amounts, and didn't get a shipment of fresh meat and vegetables once a week but sold only frozen meat. The Market was closer to the Indian village than Farrone's and so did a big business in canned milk, sugar, and tea, things like that, and sold chips and pop to the Indian kids. Well through the week following Esau's funeral I noticed a gradual slackening of activity at Farrone's and an increase in the Market's business and the difference in clientele was the difference in skin colour and eye shape.

What surprised me most, though, was seeing Jo Bouchard pulling a

sled up the hill on Friday morning. Two bags of groceries sat on the sled and they had obviously come from the R.R. Market. I slipped on my parka and ran out to meet her.

"Just thought you should know that little Noel and Chrissie are playing at my place. Sure will be a relief when we get the new teachers, eh?"

"Sure will."

It was cold enough that our breaths made a fog between us as we stood there. "Well I better get this stuff inside," Jo said.

"Come for coffee when you're finished."

She said she would but she didn't. She called at five to say she'd got held up by some tax forms she was working on and asked me to send the kids home.

Peter Groenen's business picked up and he put up a help wanted sign in the window of the café. I think this was going too far. He couldn't have needed more help in the winter. The sign was just his way of thumbing his nose at Bill Luksic, for business at the RRX had fallen off drastically. Instead of stopping at Bill's place for their morning coffee, the highway crews switched to Groenen's. And as though the presence of graders outside Groenen's was a signal, the truckers started stopping there, too. Not all of them, of course, but enough to make a difference. Some people are like sheep, they will follow the tail they see directly in front of them. Bill kept the tavern open as usual, but business was down there, too. This is not to say that drinking came to a stop. People took their boxes of beer home to drink and Jack and me were no exception.

Of course when Jack had goods to haul up to the mining triangle, he'd be gone the whole day and a good part of the evening. By the time he got home it was usually too late to invite friends over, so we were used to spending our evenings alone. That was nothing new. We could have a few beers or tea, and I would read a book or catch up on mending while Jack sat nearby filing his tools or sharpening his knives or simply looking through the *Geographic*. When you've been married to someone for over ten years, there isn't much need to talk and Jack was never much for it anyway. But during that hard time in town I needed to talk. My skin felt itchy, as if I'd rubbed it with that angel hair the kids drag home from school after decorating for Christmas. My stomach felt jittery, too. I was only feeling the same as everyone else in town, but it was no comfort to know that. An itch is an individual thing with an individual cause and can only be relieved by an individual scratch. Jack seemed calm enough, but I thought I saw a private, worried look in his eye.

What I had told Bill Luksic about Jack coming home at ten the night Esau died was not exactly true. I thought he came in about then because it seemed to me I had just heard the ten o'clock news and dozed off for a minute when I heard his truck outside. But I didn't get up to look at the clock in the kitchen. So part of my reason for feeling itchy was not knowing for sure about Jack.

You see the feelings in town had got so bad that even we who knew we had nothing to do with Esau's death had developed guilt about one aspect or another of the case. Jo had said, right after hearing of it, that she'd planned on driving up to the RRX that night but didn't because it was too cold. So Jo felt guilty for *not* going out. Somebody else said he wished he hadn't given Esau any money for the hunting knife he wanted to sell because if Esau hadn't had any money he couldn't have gone to the RRX. I believe some person might have taken responsibility for the weather if he honestly could have.

"You know," I said to Jack when I could no longer stop myself, "we haven't had Noel and Jo over for cards in a long time."

Jack was flipping through the newest *Geographic* and he just grunted a reply.

"It's still early, I could ask them, but I bet they wouldn't come."

Jack did not look up or ask me why I thought that, so I kept going while my nerve was up. "Jo has been acting peculiar lately. I think she's avoiding me. I know that's been happening with some other people in town, but Jo and I have been friends for so long.... You know, Jack," I said, "I bet you there are plenty of couples sitting together like we are here tonight, feeling a little uneasy but not knowing what to do about it. If you think about it, if there were six, then six wives or husbands have something to feel ashamed about. I'm surprised nobody has told on anybody else, yet."

"It's not so surprising," he said after a while. "The only way a person would know who was out that night is if he was out, too, or if he was married to someone who came home about that time. Wives wouldn't tell and you can be sure a guilty person wouldn't tell on a guilty person. I'll be glad when this damn thing is over. It isn't the same town any more."

I took out another sock and dropped the darning egg into it. "I have an idea why Jo is acting so cold. She must have heard you come in that night. She probably thinks you were one of those who passed Esau."

Jack slapped his magazine down hard on the coffee table. "Damn it, Shirley. Do you suspect your own husband?"

"It isn't that I suspect you, honey, it's just that I want to be absolutely sure so I can say so without thinking someone might trip me up. I was asleep, remember?"

"All I can say is, it's bloody lucky those Hemples left when they did. Otherwise there might have been a couple more cases for the coroner."

"Well?"

"Well what?"

"Are you pretty sure you got in just after ten?"

"You just won't give it up, will you? Well I don't know what the hell the time was. I was more worried about keeping on the road than looking at my watch. If Esau Issac was sitting out on the highway when I came by, I sure as hell didn't see him. He didn't try to flag me down, that's for sure. Is that good enough? Do you think you can clear me with your half-breed buddy on the basis of that?"

His blue eyes were glinting like the bridge steel in the brightest winter sun. I was about to tell him it wasn't Jo I was concerned about so much as myself, but Jack wasn't finished having his say.

"You think knowing is going to solve everything? Jesus, Shirley, you're a smart woman, you ought to know better. Just how do you think you'd feel about testifying at some neighbour's trial, about buying groceries or curling with somebody half the country had accused of manslaughter? Eh? Did you ever think of that?"

He got up and headed for the bedroom then, without even saying goodnight. I couldn't blame him, really. It is terrible to think that the person who is closest to you in the world doesn't trust you, and it wasn't much easier being the one who doubted. I waited until Jack was asleep before I turned in, and I lay awake a long time wondering about how the town would survive the inquest. For what Jack had said was true. Once we knew who had been purposely neglectful our attitudes towards them would change. Friends could be set against each other, marriages could be affected. Some marriages already had been affected. I knew for a fact that Jo and Noel had been fighting more than ever since Esau died. Jo hadn't said as much, but when you live next door to someone for that long you get to noticing certain things about their habits, and when the habits change you can tell something is up. I'd heard them yelling at each other more, too: sounds carry sharply through the cold nights and reverberate on the metal of our trailer. I didn't hear anything from there the night Jack and I had our set-to, but that's because Noel had stamped out of their place that morning and gone to Whitehorse. The kids told me.

When I knocked on her door the next morning she was still in her bathrobe, the shocking pink velour I had helped her pick out of the catalogue. The kids were at the kitchen table playing with cereal, but Jo had been working at her desk. The desk lamp was on and there was a cigarette burning in the ashtray beside a pile of papers.

"Morning Josephine, busy?" I asked, as brightly as I could, to break the ice.

"Matter of fact I am, Shirl. There's these books...."

"I thought you did those last week. Noel couldn't be doing that much business, specially not from Whitehorse."

She didn't say anything to this, but scraped a pile of sugar off the table, into her hand.

"Is the coffee still hot?"

She couldn't refuse me. She poured two cups, handed me one, and we carried them into the sitting room, out of earshot of the kids.

"I was thinking we might get together and set up a little tutoring program for the kids, while we're waiting for the new teachers. But if you'd rather tell me about Noel, instead...."

"There's not much to say. He may be gone for good this time and I can't say I care. It was bound to happen someday."

"Anything to do with Esau?"

"Aw...." She leaned her head back against the chesterfield and closed her eyes.

"Look, Jo. I don't mean to pry. It's just that it was never considered prying before. You've been keeping your distance lately and I can't figure out why."

"You can't? Oh, come on, Shirley. The whole town's dividing up. You're either with me or against me, eh? You saw me walking up from the Market the other day, so I guess you can figure which way I'm gonna go. Noel saw it too. That's why he left."

"Because of the Market? But that's silly."

"Not only the Market. I've been doing the Band's bookkeeping. So far I've been doing it at home, but Charlie wants me to work at the Band office down in the village. I told Noel and he blew his stack and walked out. That was part of it, anyway."

"But you can't really work down there, Jo. You've got the kids to consider. Noel was probably just thinking of them."

"Yeah, them and the fact that his woman might be going back to where she came from, where she really belongs. Aunt Lizzie said she'd look after the little ones. Her cabin is just down the road from the Band office, you know. It would work. We could even move down there."

"What about me, though? You can't think it's come to me being against you, not after all these years. I haven't had a better friend, Jo."

"I didn't say I thought that. We can still be friends. I'll only be down the hill. You talk like it's the other side of the moon. And Shirley, I don't want you to think I've come to this decision just because of Esau. I've been thinking about it a long time. Maybe it's why I came back here in the first place. It was me more than Noel who wanted to come, you know. I've had advantages most of my people haven't had, Shirl. I have something to offer and they can use it. Esau's death and that radio report just pointed up what a lot of people have known for a long time. In a crunch you can't count on white people to come through."

"Oh, Jo. You can't believe that stuff Hemple said."

"You look around, Shirley Grant. Just open your eyes and see what there is to see. How many Indians do you see working on the highway crew, eh? It's the only decent work in town and it goes to outsiders, people who weren't born here. As for Luksic, did you ever see him throw a white out of his tavern?"

"Bill said Esau left on his own."

"Sure, Bill *said* that."

"Well I believe him. He's a good man."

"Uh, huh. Just like those six who left Esau to die. It could have been Aunt Lizzie or me or anyone, as long as they had brown skin."

I didn't believe it. Things just weren't that way in R.R. Jo was overreacting and I think the fact that she was related to Esau had more to do with it than she wanted to admit. But I wasn't going to argue with her. I could only hope she would change her mind when things cooled off. Of course there was something I didn't know at that point.

Bill Luksic paid us one more visit before the inquest. He called first, to see if Jack had got home. I said he had and Bill said he'd be right over. When the pink from the cold had left his face, Bill looked unnaturally white. We offered him a beer, but he said he'd rather have some of the brandy he'd given us at Christmas, if we had any left.

"Maybe I ought to turn in," I said, seeing how shaken he was. I knew it was Jack he wanted to talk to more than me.

"No, you stay, Shirley. You'll find out eventually anyway. Wives always do. I'd just as soon you hear it from me."

He drained the glass of brandy in one swallow, and when Jack reached for the bottle to give him a refill, he shook his head no. "Thanks anyway. I just wanted a little. My insides feel like I've been leaning on a riveter all day." He took a deep breath. "Last time I was here I asked you if you'd tell the coroner what you thought about the Hemples, about them not being able to tell how many cars there were, I mean. I just said it, then. Now I'm asking you seriously if you'll say that."

"Sure I will. It's what I honestly think. But it's not going to prove anything."

Bill dropped his head onto his arms and for a moment I thought he was crying. Except for the low murmur of the oil heater and the drip from the kitchen tap, there wasn't a sound in the trailer. Bill raised his head after a few long minutes, and his eyes were wet, sparkling anyway, with a combination of anger and shame.

"I know who passed Esau that night and left him to die. I don't know if every one of them saw him, but I know who drove past and it wasn't six people, it was five. I'm going to tell you who they are because...."

He paused for another long breath and I felt so scared my heart was beating like crazy. Jack was right: when it came right down to it I didn't want to know.

"Two of them were Indians. They were sitting with Esau earlier in the night and he had asked them to drive him home. But they were drunk and kept telling Esau how soft he was getting. How they heard he used to walk clear into Whitehorse in the old days. I don't know why Esau felt he had to leave just then. They would have taken him if he waited. Anyway, those two were the Jim boys, Rufus and Billy, and they were driving Billy's old car, so you were right when you said the Hemples couldn't count. There were only four cars.

"One of the others was Ted Farrone's. Ted hadn't been in long, only about a half-hour or so. He came to ask me about arrangements for the bonspiel, had one beer and left. Now Ted doesn't have much love to spare for Indians, but I can't think he would knowingly have left old Esau out there in the cold. Maybe he would have. Anyway, the third vehicle was Noel

Bouchard's. He was pretty drunk that night. He'd been fighting with Jo and just sat there all night, drinking steadily and not talking to anyone. I hear he's left town. Maybe that's why. I think I will take another shot of that Jack, if you don't mind."

"Jo! Well she said she almost went up there, maybe she was going to try and make it up with him. And for sure that's why she's been acting so funny. My God! Esau was her mother's half brother."

"Yeah, well he might not have seen Esau either. We'll never know I guess."

"So who was driving the fourth car, Bill?" Jack asked.

Bill drank his brandy down before he spoke, and kept his eyes on the table all the while. "That's really what I came to see you about. You see the fourth car was Naomi's. You now how it's been. She gets these notions into her head. Well, the school is one of them notions. I'm not saying she shouldn't have been re-elected chairman, it's been good for her in a way and I'm real thankful because I know, and you don't have to spare my feelings, that you would have preferred to have someone else.

"Well Naomi talks about the school in a real possessive way. She says things like, I have to go down and check my building today, and such, as though she owns it or something, and she talks of calling up the Minister about every little thing that goes wrong. That night she was worried that the file cabinet doesn't have a lock. I tried to get her not to go, but she insisted. So she drove past the teacherage twice, see, and I know she saw Esau because she told me she did. She pulled out shortly after he left. She said he was standing at the crossroads, trying to flag her down, but she didn't want him smelling up the car with vomit and she didn't want to drive into the village at night."

"And she saw him on the way back, too?"

"Yep, and that's the worst of it, because she could tell he was freezing. She said she'd been right not to stop the first time because he obviously had vomited and she could see in the car lights that it had frozen to his mouth and the front of his parka. He was sitting then, but he was still conscious because he raised an arm to hail her. She drove right by."

"Did she tell you right then?"

"She told me the next day, after Andy had found him. I knew she would have had to pass him. She admitted it right away, but she said a cruel thing. She said it served him right. I made her promise not to tell anyone, but it wasn't easy. She was proud of herself. And that was only the start. She won't come to bed at night, hardly sleeps at all. She sits in the bar writing letters to the government, the Commissioner, the Education Minister. Anybody. She says she knows people are stealing from the school and she knows it's the Indians who are doing it. She wants Indian kids barred from the school and a few of them put in jail. She was raving so bad this morning I had to take her into Whitehorse. They put her in hospital right away."

"Aw, Bill...."

It's funny how a man and woman go along with daily life, the colds, the money troubles, the sick kids, the bad feelings you wake up with some days and can't put a name to, shuffling the burden of those things back and forth between each other, so, looking back, none of them seem to have amounted to much. Then, suddenly you're hit with something that reminds you you're two separate people after all.

Jack was too good a man to rub it in. After we had done our best to comfort Bill and he'd gone home, surely colder and lonelier than he'd ever been, Jack didn't say, "Well, are you happy now, Shirl?" He sat on the chesterfield quietly, his long legs stretched out and his arms crossed on his chest, thinking, while I tidied the kitchen. When I was finished I sat down at the other end of the chesterfield, for I had some thinking to do, too.

Oh, I pitied Bill and I pitied Jo, but at the same time I was relieved that the trouble hadn't come any closer to me; as close as Jack, say. I was about to tell him this when Jack stood and stretched and headed for the bedroom. I followed him right in and we lay down on our favourite sides, and we stayed that way, not touching, for the rest of the night. I wondered what Jack was turning over in his mind, but was reluctant to ask him. As for me, I guess I mainly pondered how it was that two people—Noel and Jo, or Bill and Naomi, for two good examples—could live with each other as long as they did and still not know what each other had in them.

The next day I learned how that was true of me, too, for to my surprise, Jack decided to take charge of the town. He went so far as to cancel his route for that day, dress in his second best clothes, and go from house to house, on the flats and on the hill, talking to every R.R. citizen he could.

My eight-year-old, Tommy, is a lot like his dad. He can spend hours quietly entertaining himself with a game or a book. One thing he especially likes is building tall houses out of playing cards. He'll get one almost finished, a marvel of a delicate thing four cards high or so, when his little sister or me or Jack will come into the room, stirring the air just enough to throw the whole thing off balance and down it will come. Tommy might yell at us to watch what we're doing, but I can see he isn't really mad because he'll clear the table and just start all over again.

Well a card house is a lot like what we had going in R.R. and you can imagine how nervous everyone felt at the prospect that the inquest would collapse it, same as the radio report had done. The day before it, the Thursday, I practically tiptoed everywhere and by night it felt as if I'd been holding my breath all day. Anything *could* have happened. Charlie Benjamin, the Band Chief, could have used the inquest as a platform from which to state all his complaints about being Indian. And since Jo had got so chummy with him, she might have chimed in. Peter Groenen could have accused Bill and Naomi because he surely knew what had happened to Naomi by then, and it would have been a good opportunity for him to get rid of the Luksics. But then Bill could have said in public that Groenen had a policy against hiring Indians at his place. That's how it is in R.R. The corner of one life touches the corner of another, so that if we had been really determined to do it, we could have found ways to embarrass or destroy just about everyone.

What did happen was this. Nearly the whole town showed up at the school first thing Friday morning. The Coroner from Whitehorse, a court recorder, and a bunch of reporters were already there. The Coroner called Andy Hanson first, and Andy described when and where he had found Esau. Then the nurse testified as to how he had looked when Andy carried him into the nursing station. Then Bill was called. He said Esau had been drinking at the RRX since about seven that night and had left after ten by himself.

Did Bill know Esau didn't have a car? He did. Did Bill know what the temperature was that night? He did. Wasn't Bill concerned about the old man's ability to make it home in that weather? Bill hesitated here, knowing he should have been concerned. But he couldn't explain that he was more concerned with Naomi at the time and had actually been in his private quarters, arguing with her, at the time Esau left.

"I wouldn't have let him go if I didn't think he could make it."

A couple of reporters sniggered at this.

The Coroner then tried to get Bill to say who else had been in the bar that night. Bill said he couldn't remember, that people had come and gone as usual and he had not taken much notice of who had come in and who had left. The Coroner didn't go for the story, but he couldn't get Bill to change it.

I pitied him having to sit there and lie in public, but wouldn't it have been worse for him to incriminate his poor sick wife?

The Coroner asked if anyone else wanted to testify. Jack stood up and asked to be sworn in, and once he was he told the inquest about how he'd driven into town that night about ten and didn't see Esau or notice whose cars were parked at the RRX. He also said he believed the Hemples must have been mistaken, and that even if they had heard that many cars it was likely that none of the drivers saw Esau because the ice-fog would have hidden him from them, particularly if he were lying down in the snow.

"Thank you, Mr. Grant," the Coroner said. I could tell he wasn't impressed. "Anyone else wish to testify?" he asked.

The room was perfectly quiet. None of the townspeople even so much as shifted in their seats. After a few minutes I heard one of the reporters say, "Oh my God," and I was mad at the disgust I heard in his voice because he had no idea what was going on in that room. Esau was dead, there was nothing we could do about that. But we could spare each other and save our town: that was *all* we could do and it was something *only* we could do. It did not concern any of the Outsiders. I was so proud of my Jack, for he was the one who had convinced everyone to stick together.

As it ended up, Bill took the blame, for the Coroner wrote in his report that Bill should never have let Esau leave the tavern alone in his condition in that severe cold. One of the newspaper articles said there was some talk of charging Bill with criminal negligence, but that never happened.

It has been over a year since the death of Esau Issac turned R.R. upside down. We've got ourselves back to normal, but there have been the changes you'd expect, and for some of us, definitely me, life is different here now. I don't call Jo Bouchard my best friend any more. You see, I discovered that Jo had been keeping a lot from me, mainly that she had more going with Charlie Benjamin than bookkeeping.

The thing that caused Noel to leave, and who could blame him, was Jo telling him she'd been having an affair with Charlie. She was pregnant, in fact, during that whole mess. She has her baby now and she says she has her pride back, too: she says she's not ashamed she's Indian any more. Well, who would have thought she ever was?

Jo and Charlie came in the other night after the big bonspiel. Since the tavern was extra busy, I was helping Jack serve. Jo was in her cups, or had her nerve up for some other reason. She followed me to the bar and started telling me all this while I was pouring drinks, never thinking I might not want to hear it.

I didn't want to hear it because it seemed that when Jack took over the RRX and we moved up here, and Jo married Charlie and moved down there, we were forced into acting more like representatives of the two sides than pure people. So now there is that between us, a kind of fence in a place where no one even has a proper yard.

Margaret ATWOOD (1939–) is, along with Alice Munro, perhaps Canada's best-known writer. Born in Ottawa, she spent much of her childhood in the north and now lives in Toronto. She is acclaimed as a poet, novelist, short story writer, and essayist. Atwood is also active as a spokesperson on behalf of human rights and the environment.
Novels: *The Edible Woman* (1969), *Surfacing* (1972), *Lady Oracle* (1976), *Life Before Man* (1979), *Bodily Harm* (1981), *The Handmaid's Tale* (1985), *Cat's Eye* (1988).
Short fiction: *Dancing Girls* (1977), *Murder in the Dark* (1983), *Bluebeard's Egg* (1983), *Wilderness Tips* (1991), *Good Bones* (1992).
Non-fiction: *Survival* (1972), *Second Words* (1982).
Also much poetry; for example, *Selected Poems.*

Himani BANNERJI (1942–) was born in Bangladesh and came to Canada in 1969. She teaches sociology at York University in Toronto.
Essay collection: *The Writing on the Wall* (1993).

François BARCELO (1941–) studied French literature at the University of Montréal and has worked as an advertising writer. He lives in Montreal and, like Gonzague Gagnon in "The Man Who Stopped Trains," runs about 3000 km a year. He has written a runner's guide to Montreal.
Novels: *Agénor, Agénor, Agénor et Agénor* (1981), *La Tribu* (1981), *Ville Dieu* (1982).

Sandra BIRDSELL (1942–) was born in Morris, Manitoba to a French Catholic father and a Russian Mennonite mother, a family situation made familiar through her stories. After dropping out of school at 15 and marrying at 17, she was able to begin writing when her children became older. She lives in Winnipeg.
Novels: *The Missing Child* (1989), *The Chrome Suite* (1992).
Story collections: *Night Travellers* (1982), *Ladies of the House* (1984); collected in one volume as *Agassiz Stories* (1987).
Also a stage play and film scripts.

Neil BISSOONDATH (1955–) was born in Trinidad and came to Canada in 1973 to study French at university. He comes from a literary family: his grandfather Seepersad Naipaul was a journalist in Trinidad and his uncles include the world-famous writer V.S. Naipaul and Shiva Naipaul, whose equally promising career was cut short by an early death.
Novels: *A Casual Brutality* (1988), *The Innocence of Age* (1992).
Story collections: *Digging Up the Mountains* (1985), *On the Eve of Uncertain Tomorrows* (1990).

Mary BURNS (1944–) was born near Chicago and immigrated to Canada in 1970. Her stories have been published and broadcast in Canada, the U.S., and the U.K., and she has dramatized a number of them for radio.
Story collections: *Suburbs of the Arctic Circle* (1986), *Shinny's Girls* (1989), and *Centre/Center*, a trilogy of novellas (1992).

Garry ENGKENT came to Canada in the 1950s, from Guangdong province in China. He has a Ph.D. in English literature and has taught at a number of Canadian universities. He is currently writing a novel.

Brian FAWCETT (1944–) grew up in Prince George, B.C. At first a poet, he has turned to other kinds of writing and is known as an original and creative essayist and critic of Canada and modern culture. Although a long-time resident of B.C., Fawcett now lives in Toronto.
Story collections: *My Career with the Leafs* (1982), *Capital Tales* (1984), *The Secret Journal of Alexander Mackenzie* (1985).
Non-fiction: *Cambodia: A Book for People Who Find Television Too Slow* (1986), *Public Eye: An Investigation into the Disappearance of the World* (1990), *Unusual Circumstances, Interesting Times* (collected occasional pieces; 1991).
Also poetry.

Suzanne JACOB (1943–) was born in the Abitibi region of Québec. She was a singer/songwriter, with three albums to her credit, before she took to writing books. In 1978, Jacob founded the publishing house *le biocreux* with the writer Paul Paré.
Novels: *Flore Cocon* (1978), *Laura Laur* (1983), *La Passion selon Galatée* (1986), *Maude* (1988).
Story collections: *La Survie* (1979), translated as *Life, After All* (1989); *Les Aventures de Pomme Douly* (1988).

Paulette JILES (1943–) was born in Missouri, in the Ozarks. She came to Canada in 1969, and for ten years she worked in the north, mostly with Cree and Inuit communications organizations. Both a poet and a writer of different prose forms, Jiles teaches creative writing in Nelson, B.C.
Fiction: *The Late Great Human Road Show* (1986), *Cousins* (1992).
Non-fiction: *Sitting in the Club Car Drinking Rum and Karma Cola* (1986).
Also poetry; for example *Celestial Navigation* (1986).

Thomas KING (1943–) is Cherokee through his father, with Greek and German ancestry through his mother. Formerly a professor of Native Studies at the University of Lethbridge where he encouraged many Native writers, he is now chair of Native American studies at the University of Minnesota.
Novels: *Medicine River* (1990), *Green Grass, Running Water* (1993).
A number of short stories, not yet collected; also poems and a children's book, *A Coyote Columbus Story.*
King has also edited a collection of Native literature, *All My Relations*.

Gwendolyn MACEWEN (1941-1987) left school at 18 to become a writer, and over her life she became a unique force in Canadian literature. She is best known as a poet, but her work also includes translations, short stories, a novel, travel books, essays, and children's stories. She lived in Toronto.

Alistair MACLEOD (1936–) was born in Saskatchewan. When he was ten, his parents returned to the family farm in Cape Breton's Inverness County, where Scots Gaelic was a living language. He has worked in the woods and the mines, been a teacher, and now teaches English and creative writing at the University of Windsor.
Story collections: *The Lost Salt Gift of Blood* (1976), *As Birds Bring Forth the Sun and Other Stories* (1986). Selected stories plus one new novella re-released as *The Lost Salt Gift of Blood and Other Stories* (1992).

Lee MARACLE (1950–) is a Native orator, poet, and writer who learned to write in the middle of raising her own and other people's children. She is part-time writer-in-residence at the En'owkin International School of Writing for Native People in Penticton, B.C.
Books: *Bobbi Lee: Indian Rebel* (1975), *I Am Woman* (1990), *Sojourner's Truth and Other Stories* (1990).

Alice MUNRO (1931–) is world famous for her remarkable stories. She left university to get married and was able to begin writing only when her children became older. In recent years, she has moved back to Ontario's Huron County where she grew up and where most of her stories are set.
Story collections: *Dance of the Happy Shades* (1968), *The Lives of Girls and Women* (1971), *Something I've Been Meaning to Tell You* (1974), *Who Do You Think You Are?* (1978), *The Moons of Jupiter* (1982), *The Progress of Love* (1986), *Friend of My Youth* (1990).

Patrick O'FLAHERTY (1939–) was born in Conception Bay, Newfoundland. Since 1965, he has taught in the English department at Memorial University in St. John's.
Non-fiction (co-authored): *Part of the Main: An Illustrated History of Newfoundland and Labrador* (1983).
Novel: *Priest of God* (1989).
Story collections: *The Summer of the Greater Yellowlegs* (1987), *A Small Place in the Sun* (1989).

Marlene Nourbese PHILIP (1947–) was born in Trinidad and Tobago and moved to Canada in 1968. She worked for some time as a lawyer, while writing poetry, essays, and fiction. Nourbese Philip is known for her strong public writings against racism in Canada.
Novel: *Harriet's Daughter* (1988).
Non-fiction: *Frontiers* (1992).
Also poetry.

Kevin ROBERTS (1940–) was born in Australia and came to Canada in 1966. He has taught high school and has run his own salmon troller. He now teaches English at Malaspina College near Victoria, B.C.
Novel: *Tears in a Glass Eye* (1989).
Story collections: *Flash Harry* (1980), *Picking the Morning Colour* (1984).
Also poetry.

Diane SCHOEMPERLEN (1954–) was born in Thunder Bay, Ontario. After attending Lakehead University, she moved to Canmore, Alberta, where she lived for ten years and did a variety of jobs to support her writing, including bank teller and avalanche researcher. She lives with her husband and son in Kingston Ontario and teaches creative writing there.
Story collections: *Double Exposures* (1984), *Frogs and Other Stories* (1986), *Hockey Night in Canada* (1987), *The Man of My Dreams* (1990).

Audrey THOMAS (1935–) was born in New York State and moved to Canada in 1959. She has also lived in Australia, Scotland, and Ghana. Thomas teaches writing at both the University of Victoria and Concordia University, and lives on Gabriola Island in the Georgia Strait.
Novels: *Mrs. Blood* (1970), *Songs My Mother Taught Me* (1973), *Blown Figures* (1974), *Intertidal Life* (1984), *Graven Images* (1993).
Story collections: *Ten Green Bottles* (1967), *Ladies and Escorts* (1977), *Real Mothers* (1981), *Goodbye Harold, Good Luck* (1986), *The Wild Blue Yonder* (1990).

W. D. VALGARDSON (1939–) was born in Gimli, Manitoba, of Icelandic heritage. He now teaches creative writing at the University of Victoria.
Novel: *Gentle Sinners* (1980).
Story collections: *Bloodflowers* (1973), *God Is not a Fish Inspector* (1975), *Red Dust* (1978), *What Can't Be Changed Shouldn't Be Mourned* (1990).
Also poetry.

Guy VANDERHAEGHE (1951–) was born in Esterhazy, Saskatchewan, a small mining town. After working as a teacher, among other things, he won the Governor General's Award in 1982 for his first published story collection and was able to turn to full-time writing. His work has been extensively translated. He lives in Saskatoon.
Novels: *My Present Age* (1984), *Homesick* (1989).
Story collections: *Man Descending* (1982), *The Trouble with Heroes* (1982), *Things As They Are?* (1992).
Also a play.

Budge WILSON (1927–) was born in Halifax and has worked as a teacher and a librarian. Well-known as an author of books for young adults, Wilson lives in Peterborough, Ontario, in the winter and Hubbards, Nova Scotia, in the summer.
Juvenile novels: *Lorinda's Diary, Thirteen Never Changes.*
Story collections: *The Leaving* (1990).

Caroline WOODWARD (1952–) was raised on a rural homestead in the Peace River country of northern British Columbia. She currently lives in Nelson, B.C., where she works as an editor and writer.
Story collection: *Disturbing the Peace* (1990).

ACKNOWLEDGEMENTS

Permission to reprint copyrighted material is gratefully acknowledged. Every reasonable effort to trace the copyright holders of materials appearing in this book has been made. Information that will enable the publishers to rectify any error or omission will be welcomed.

Languages from *Afterworlds* by Gwendolyn MacEwen. Used by permission of the Canadian Publishers, McClelland & Stewart, Toronto.

Why My Mother Can't Speak English by Garry Engkent, *Calgary Magazine*, June 1985.

The Leaving by Budge Wilson from *The Leaving*. Reprinted by permission of Stoddart Publishing Co. Ltd., Don Mills, Ontario.

Saturday Climbing from *What Can't Be Changed Shouldn't Be Mourned*, copyright © 1990 by W.D. Valgardson, published by Douglas & McIntyre. Reprinted by permission.

My Career with the Leafs by Brian Fawcett from *My Career with the Leafs and Other Stories* © 1982 Brian Fawcett; Talon Books Ltd., Vancouver, Canada.

My Life as a Bat by Margaret Atwood. Copyright © 1992 O.W. Toad Ltd. Reprinted from *Good Bones* by permission of Coach House Press.

The Man Who Stopped Trains by François Barcelo, from *Intimate Strangers: New Stories from Québec* edited by Matt Cohen & Wayne Grady. English translation copyright © Matt Cohen, 1986. Reprinted by permission of Penguin Books Canada Limited and by permission of Le Groupe Ville-Marie Littérature.

Charlie by Lee Maracle, from *Sojourner's Truth and Other Stories* (Vancouver: Press Gang Publishers, 1990).

On the Eve of Uncertain Tomorrows by Neil Bissoondath. Reprinted with permission from *On the Eve of Uncertain Tomorrows* by Neil Bissoondath, published by Lester & Orpen Dennys Limited c/o Key Porter Books Limited, Toronto, Ontario. Copyright © 1990 Neil Bissoondath.

Night Flight to Attiwapiskat by Paulette Jiles, originally published in *Northward Journal*.

Traplines by Thomas King, copyright © 1991 by Thomas King. Used by permission.

Summer Wages by Caroline Woodward reprinted from *Disturbing the Peace* by Caroline Woodward, Polestar Press Ltd., Winlaw, B.C. Copyright © 1990 by Caroline Woodward.

Chaddeleys and Flemings: Connection by Alice Munro from *The Moons of Jupiter* by Alice Munro © 1982. Reprinted by permission of Macmillan Canada.

Troller by Kevin Roberts reprinted from *Picking the Morning Colour* by permission of the publisher, Oolichan Books.

Strawberry Time by Suzanne Jacob, translated by Susanna Finnell, from *Life, After All*, copyright © 1989 (Press Gang Publishers, Vancouver).

Red Plaid Shirt by Diane Schoemperlen from *The Man of My Dreams* by Diane Schoemperlen © 1990. Reprinted by permission of Macmillan Canada.

Stones by Sandra Birdsell from *Night Travellers* by Sandra Birdsell. Used by permission of Stoddart Publishing Co. Ltd., Don Mills, Ontario.

What I Learned from Caesar by Guy Vanderhaeghe from *Man Descending* by Guy Vanderhaeghe © 1982. Reprinted by permission of Macmillan Canada.

Now for the Dance by Patrick O'Flaherty, copyright © 1987 Patrick O'Flaherty. Published by Breakwater Books Limited, St. John's, NF. Used by permission of the author.

Burn Sugar by Marlene Nourbese Philip, first published in Canada by Women's Press (1988) in *Imagining Women*, Ed. Rhea Tregebov.

To Every Thing There Is a Season by Alistair MacLeod from *As Birds Bring Forth the Sun* by Alistair MacLeod. Used by permission of the Canadian Publishers, McClelland & Stewart, Toronto.

The Other Family by Himani Bannerji. Reprinted by permission of the author.

Ascension by Audrey Thomas from *The Wild Blue Yonder* by Audrey Thomas. Copyright © Audrey Thomas, 1990. Reprinted by permission of Penguin Books Canada Limited.

Suburbs of the Arctic Circle by Mary Burns. Published by permission of Penumbra Press, from *Suburbs of the Arctic Circle* ISBN 0 920806 791.

ILLUSTRATIONS

p. 27 Scott Cameron

p. 65 Chris Van Es

p. 105 Stuart Knox

p. 134 Kathryn Adams

p. 163 Thom Sevalrud

p. 209 Sue Gauthier

p. 235 Stuart Knox